THE LITTLE OLD LADY
BEHAVING BADLY

Catharina Ingelman-Sundberg, is the Swedish author of
the internationally bestselling *The Little Old Lady Who Broke
All the Rules* and *The Little Old Lady Who Struck Lucky Again!*
After pursuing a career in journalism and a stint as a marine
archaeologist, Catharina turned her hand to writing fiction.
Her books have been translated into thirty languages and
have sold over two million copies internationally. Catharina
lives outside Stockholm, in Sweden, and writes from a
log cabin in her garden.

To find about more, visit her website,
www.catharinaingelman-sundberg.com

Also by Catharina Ingelman-Sundberg

The Little Old Lady Who Broke All the Rules
The Little Old Lady Who Struck Lucky Again!

THE LITTLE OLD LADY BEHAVING BADLY

CATHARINA INGELMAN-SUNDBERG

Translated from the Swedish by Rod Bradbury

PAN BOOKS

First published in 2016 under the title
Rån och inga visor by Bokförlaget Forum, Sweden

This edition published 2016 by Pan Books
an imprint of Pan Macmillan
20 New Wharf Road, London N1 9RR
Associated companies throughout the world
www.panmacmillan.com

ISBN 978-1-4472-8167-2

A CIP catalogue record for this book is available from the British Library.

Typeset by Ellipsis Digital Limited, Glasgow
Printed and bound by CPI Group (UK) Ltd, Croydon, CR0 4YY

To my readers in English, all over the world.
Thank you for your enduring support.

Prologue

The little old lady put the bottle of champagne into the fridge. After a bank robbery it is always nice to celebrate, but of course you have to ensure that the bubbly is properly chilled.

Martha Andersson hummed a little to herself while she put out a tray, five tall champagne glasses and some light snacks on the kitchen table. Then she went into the bedroom to prepare herself for the coming night's adventures. While she got dressed, she went through the plan in her head one last time. In exactly two hours, the League of Pensioners would strike again, and this would be their most advanced crime yet. She picked up the keys from the hall table and went out into the dark.

1

When the refuse-collection lorry stopped outside the bank, nobody reacted. Not even when the suction tube mouthpiece was manoeuvred out and connected to the building's waste-disposal system. It was 4.30 in the morning and none of the people out on the streets of Stockholm at that time of day were interested in rubbish. With the exception of the League of Pensioners. A flash of lightning lit up the sky and the five pensioners looked contentedly at one another. Thunder was just what they were waiting for.

'Right you are!' said Martha and she glanced up at the large bank palace. 'Banks don't like it when you withdraw money. But now this will really be an eye-opener for them!'

She felt the buttons on the control panel for the pneumatic collector and looked out through the windscreen. The collection lorry could manage ten tons. And what was in the bank vault would easily fit. Now all they had to do was suck it all into the tank.

'OK, here are your face masks,' said Martha, handing out a bearded Pavarotti to Brains, a grinning Elton John to Rake and a clean-shaven Brad Pitt mask to Christina's son Anders. 'Out you get, and good luck!'

'What about me?' Anna-Greta objected, stretching out for the smiling Margaret Thatcher latex mask.

'Oh yes, of course,' mumbled Martha and she handed her the mask.

The presumptive criminals put on their masks, got out of the lorry and took up position on the street, while Martha and Christina remained sitting inside. This was it!

Down on the pavement, Brains contentedly patted the pipe leading to the waste-disposal system, adjusted his working overalls with the logo WE'LL CLEAN YOU OUT across his chest and walked towards the entrance. The considerably younger Anders from the same firm walked after him with two wheelie bins, and the others waited a while before they too followed. Rake had his bandanna neatly tied around his neck, and his colleague Anna-Greta, wearing a wide-rimmed felt hat, supported herself with her walking stick, for the sake of appearances. (It was, for that matter, still a little bent from when she had taken it with her to the sauna steam room at the Grand Hotel. But it was her favourite walking stick.) The friends looked up at the sky: heavy dark clouds, flashes of lightning and the first few drops of rain. It looked most promising.

A grey rain became all the more noticeable and the buildings turned into dark shapes in the gloomy light. You could hardly see the figures moving on the street, let alone identify them. That was just what they wanted. Brains punched in the door code and then held open the door for the others in a gentlemanly fashion.

'Don't forget to keep quiet. A few floors up, there are people asleep in their beds,' he admonished them.

'Absolutely, we won't make a sound!' said Anna-Greta with her bellowing voice. As usual, she wasn't wearing her hearing-aid.

The League of Pensioners quickly slipped in through the door, while Anders, who was wheeling the specially manu-factured bins in reinforced, extremely lightweight styrofoam, followed behind them. Martha had insisted on lightweight wheelie bins because the rest of the equipment – the folding ladders, tools and other paraphernalia – was rather heavy. If you were a crook in your eighties, you had to take care not to strain yourself.

They didn't care about the bank premises on the ground floor, but took the lift to the bank's staff entrance up on the first floor. The gang had studied a plan of the building and knew that if you were going to get into the vault the usual way, you would have to force doors that were two feet thick. Even the cotter pins were thicker than the biggest telephone poles. So it was better to concentrate on the floor above which was of pinewood and insulated with plasterboard and chipboard.

'That sort of jerry-built construction can be broken up by sneezing!' Martha had said when they planned the coup. 'Chip-board and plasterboard, goodness me, that's junk material!'

As part of their preparations, she had been inside the bank and discussed some investments, and on those occasions she had made a point of complementing the bank officer for the elegant flooring. And then, of course, she had asked how it was constructed and where could she get a similar floor because she wanted one just as fancy for her own flat. Indeed, as with every crime, good planning was of the essence.

Brains felt a drop of sweat on his chin. The work overalls were too warm and wearing a Pavarotti latex mask was admittedly a good way of fooling the police, but it was stickier than the worst toffee. Rake's Elton John disguise didn't seem nearly as uncomfortable, and Anna-Greta actually looked perfectly happy as Margaret Thatcher. Even though a former prime minister would hardly have gone around in work clothes with the logo WE'LL CLEAN YOU OUT written on them.

'Here it is!'

Brains looked around him, took a deep breath and quickly picked the lock to the staff entrance. Then he carefully opened the door, advanced a few quick steps to the alarm panel and short-circuited it. The others followed after him, and once inside the door they turned on their little diode lamps and let the beams sweep over the room. Dark brick walls, newly laid floor, some bookcases, chairs and a meeting table in the middle. It looked just like any other work place does – but this one was right on top of a bank vault with at least ten million kronor in it.

Brains pulled one of the wheelie bins towards him and fished out a compass saw, a drill, a hammer and some little blue and pink pigs he had got from Swedbank. They were piggy banks which preferably should not be shaken because, on this occasion, they were filled with explosives and not with coins. Brains, with his many years' experience as an engineer and inventor, had thought that twelve-inch firework bombs with black powder ought to make the work a bit easier and so, without Martha knowing about it, he had added some extra. In particular, the pink piggy bank had a very potent charge.

'And now the ladders,' said Brains, scratching himself under the Pavarotti beard. Anders lifted them out of bin number two, fumbled a bit in the semi-dark, but finally managed to put the pieces together, after which Brains took a deep breath and said:

'Right, my friends, now all we have to do is make some holes in the floor.'

The drill and compass saw were handed out and Brains, Rake and Anders set to work. Incidentally, Anders had chosen a Brad Pitt mask because he didn't want to look as old as the others, and now he regretted it. The mask was so tight that he could hardly breathe.

In the pale blue beam of the diodes, the men succeeded in drilling several holes and then enlarging them, with the compass saw, after which it was time for the piggy banks. Brains was perspiring so much that for a brief moment he worried that he would faint from dehydration, because he hadn't brought a water bottle with him. Dehydration in a bank? Who could have thought of that?

Martha looked up at the gable building that her disguised friends had entered. Only she and Christina were left in the lorry. Brains was going to give a signal when they had reached the vault and broken open a hole in the wall containing the shaft to the pneumatic refuse-collection system. So Martha and Christina had to be ready to start up the suction pump, and then it was full speed ahead . . . Martha tried to remember the blueprint of the building. It would take Brains and the others quite a while to make a hole in the floor and then perhaps another half-hour to break through the wall between the vault and the refuse shaft. If they didn't come across any unexpected difficulties, that is. They had chosen one of Stockholm's very biggest banks with the most cash. Because nowadays they had to think in terms of giant robberies, if they were to raise the necessary money for their charity work. And there ought to be lots of money in this bank vault. In the computer files at the central archive they hadn't been able to access the drawings of the floors above the bank office since they had been removed for reasons of security. But then Martha had shed lots of tears and, sobbing, told them about her important research work on historic buildings. She was writing a book about this palace-like building, and this was her life's work. The head of the archive gave in and she was given access to some old microfilms of the building.

She giggled to herself and ran her fingers over the joystick. What she now didn't know about the storerooms, the stairwell, the refuse shafts and the electrical wiring wasn't worth knowing. She even knew how thick the walls and floor were . . . She glanced up at the bank again. Why on earth was it taking such a long time? Nothing could have gone wrong . . . could it?

'Just look at that! Fifty centimetres thick, just like Martha said.' Rake nodded towards the drilled holes in the floor.

Brains put the compass saw to one side. 'OK, give me the piggy banks!'

'Here are our savings,' said Anna-Greta and she handed them over.

'A good job we didn't make a hole in the refuse shaft first. Then there would have been such a stench here,' said Rake.

Issued

Branch:Kingston Library
Date: 26/01/2024   Time: 10:30 AM
ID: 05700010468

ITEM(S)	DUE DATE
	24 Feb
The little old lady be...	2024
797574157	

Your current loan(s): 1
Your current reservation(s): 0

To renew your items please login
to your account at
https://miltonkeynes.spydus.co.uk

Thank you for using your local
library.

Brains pushed the piggy banks into the holes and with-drew.

'Quiet. Put your earplugs in and take cover!' he called out, and he signalled to the others to follow him into the bank director's room a bit further away. He didn't have a fuse and a firing device, but was going to set everything off electronic-ally.

'Ear plugs?! Have you ever tried putting ear plugs in a latex Elton John mask?' Rake muttered.

'Another miss,' mumbled Brains, and he shut his eyes and pressed the button.

Martha threw an anxious glance at the windows one floor above the bank. Sometimes she could discern a weak strip of light, that was all. Something must have gone wrong.

'Christina, wait here. I'll soon be back,' she said as she slid down from the seat.

'No, stop!' protested her friend, who was wearing male working clothes and a peaked cap pulled down over her brow. 'I can't work the suction pump on my own.'

'But I'll be back in a jiffy, I'll just make sure everything is in order.' Martha stroked her calmingly on the back of her hand. 'I need you here for the time being.'

Christina gave her an anxious look, and Martha patted her on her cheek too for good measure. She hoped she would remain calm. Her friend was always worrying unnecessarily.

'Back soon,' Martha told her again, and she opened the door and nipped out into the street. She looked around her, couldn't see anybody, walked up to the entrance and punched in the code. Then she went up the stairs and stopped in front of the staff entrance. There was silence. You couldn't even hear Anna-Greta's voice from inside. Martha felt the door handle, pressed it down and went in. Oh my God, what is Pavarotti doing here? Isn't he dead? went through her mind before she remembered that it was Brains's latex mask.

'I didn't dare use too much powder. It only went "plutt",' Brains mumbled. 'You said the charge shouldn't be more powerful than a firework,' he added in excuse and pointed at the floor where you could see that there were burns around the edges of a large hole.

'I meant a *large* firework,' said Martha.

'OK, then,' retorted Brains, and he fetched some more piggy banks from the bin. 'Now you'll see something. Take cover!'

If the Pavarotti mask hadn't been so stiff, then you would have been able to see Brains smile, but the rubber had the same latex smile as before and nobody noticed Brains's satisfied grin. The seniors withdrew and crouched down behind heavy oak tables and partitions. A few seconds passed, and then there was a huge bang.

'Bloody hell!' coughed a dust-covered Elton John in a Gothenburg accent when mortar, planks, floor tiles and plaster collapsed in a cloud of dust.

'Nice one!' could be heard from Anders in his Brad Pitt mask, as he shook some mortar out of his rubber hair and tried to smother a sneeze.

'Oh yes, ho, ho, ho. That did the job!' Anna-Greta neighed so loudly that her Margaret Thatcher mask was about to fall off.

Martha didn't say anything. Her heart was thumping away

so hard that she could hardly breathe. Brains had promised that he wouldn't use too powerful a charge, but this must have been heard throughout the building.

'We must hurry,' she managed to say, and she crept up to the edge of the hole. The force of the explosion had been merciless and had ripped open the floor so that now you could see right down into the vault below. And not only that. The security boxes had been damaged too, and the doors were hanging on loose hinges. Paper, jewellery, and even bars of gold were scattered among the remains of the plaster and mortar in the vault.

'Bring the ladders,' Brains urged, waving to Anders to come to him. Christina's son was their private home help and he usually carried out the heaviest tasks when the League of Pensioners struck. Now he put the ladders into place so that the gang could descend into the bank vault. They climbed down and looked about them. Everything was OK, except one vital feature. The brick wall in front of the refuse shaft was still there.

'Then I'll detonate another charge,' suggested Brains.

'No, wait!' said Martha, going up to the wall and feeling with her thumb along the wallpaper. 'Just as I thought. The building was renovated in the 1960s and then the builders didn't know anything. As if it wasn't enough that roofs, floors and walls became mouldy. Just look at this!' She peeled away a bit of the wallpaper and some plaster fell out. 'The joints are dissolving. They look all right at first sight, but inside they are like sugar. In those days they often mixed cement in brackish water. So we won't be needing any dynamite here. It—'

'You can hold your lecture until later. Just now we're robbing a bank,' muttered Rake.

'Yes, but so that you'll understand,' insisted Martha, 'you only need to hack away at the joints and lift the bricks out, and then we'll reach the refuse shaft directly. Back to work now. I must return to the lorry.' And with those words she hurried up the ladder, stepped into the bank director's room and sneaked out through the entrance.

Down in the bank vault, the rest of the gang kept at it. With the pointed geological hammer Anna-Greta hacked away at the mortar joints while humming a little tune to herself, a tune that the stone masons in Bohuslän on the west coast used to sing in by-gone days. Although a former bank officer herself, she was now remarkably laid back. The time since they had left the old people's home had undeniably done her good.

'I have a little more powder in reserve,' Brains called out, soaked in sweat under the Pavarotti mask and feeling around deep in the bin. Then, in triumph, he held up another two piggy banks, light-blue this time. 'You won't believe what a boost this will be!'

When Martha came out of the entrance, the street seemed to be just as quiet and deserted as earlier. A solitary nocturnal pedestrian came walking round the corner and, further away, she glimpsed a car. She screwed her eyes up a little and took a step back. Dearie me, a police car! It was going down Fleminggatan. It didn't stop, however, but turned in to Saint Eriksgatan and disappeared. Martha took a deep breath and then slowly exhaled. They had better look snappy before anyone suspected anything, she thought. The refuse-collection lorry might not have passed its MOT, or there might be some new legal requirement that the police had to check.

She looked down at her bright green work clothes with their reflex strips; she would have liked to have been wearing something more elegant than a bin-collector's uniform. Why hadn't she chosen something more discreet? She regretted that now, and when she got back into the cabin and sat next to Christina, she was very dissatisfied with herself. Her friend saw Martha's expression and, to console her, she held up a bag of Jungle Pastilles. Christina knew that Martha loved sweets even though she did her best to keep them for special occasions. But under extraordinary circumstances, such as a bank robbery, she liked to indulge herself with that little extra.

'Thank you,' said Martha and she took a handful. And then, rapidly, yet another handful. Christina looked at her out of the corner of her eye.

'Problems?'

'It takes a bit longer to rob a bank when you are old,' Martha answered. 'They hadn't even got through the brick wall.'

'You don't say . . . but Martha— oh, goodness gracious!' Christina's voice rose to a falsetto.

There was a sort of flash up on the first floor above the bank and a cloud of dust appeared behind the windows.

'Oh no! Brains has detonated yet another piggy bank!' said Martha. 'Now we must hurry!'

She pressed the joystick and the suction pump started up.

'Right, that's that,' said Brains, and he dropped the last brick down onto the pile of rubble. 'It just needed one more piggy bank to do the job.'

He swept away some light-blue bits of plastic and leaned towards the open refuse shaft. A heavy stench of rotting rubbish crept in under his mask and out into the room. 'Time to get the shovels and buckets. We must collect the goodies and do it quick!'

'But what a revolting smell.'

'Well, money doesn't come from heaven. It must be earned here on earth. Get to work now,' urged Anna-Greta from under her Margaret Thatcher mask.

'OK, OK, don't nag,' could be heard from the others and then Pavarotti and Elton John started to shovel the riches into the refuse shaft, assisted and cheered on by Brad Pitt. Jewels, gold and banknotes were swallowed by the modern pneumatic refuse shaft. Swoosh and they were gone, and everyone realized that Martha had the suction pump at full throttle.

Three golden necklaces, five bars of gold and three hundred thousand kronor in large banknotes were counted by Anna-Greta before she realized that she actually was counting. She didn't have to do that, she wasn't working in a bank any longer!

They worked hard and all the members of the League of Pensioners were panting ominously. It was particularly heavy going when you had to exert yourself behind a latex mask, but none of them dared take them off. There was CCTV after all.

'Just a little bit left,' Brains urged them on and worked even faster. Thankfully, the heaps of riches were getting smaller and smaller, and now they could hear a pleasant gurgling sound from down the refuse shaft. Brains saw how banknotes, certificates and jewels were sucked down the shaft and, after a really loud gurgle, he found himself wondering how many millions they had shovelled in. Just as long as the people living higher up in the building didn't wake up and throw their kitchen rubbish into the system, because that would really mess things up, he found himself thinking. Suddenly a large plastic bag with banknotes was sucked into the shaft but got stuck and blocked the opening.

'I'll sort that,' said Anna-Greta briskly and, before anyone could stop her, she prodded the bag with her walking stick. But she prodded so hard that not only the bag but also the walking stick were sucked into the shaft.

'Oh dearie me,' she exclaimed in horror while the stick rattled down the shaft making a hell of a din. That will probably wake the residents, she realized, and cheerily chirped, 'It's time for us to say goodbye . . .'

'This is not a time to joke! We're risking a prison sentence here, you do know that?' hissed Rake behind his stiff latex grin. He'd hardly finished speaking before he was interrupted by the sound of newly awakened voices followed by shouts and screams.

In the big, fancy refuse lorry Martha noticed how the suction pump started to cough worryingly while at the same time lights were turned on higher up in the building above the bank.

'Oops! We had best be moving. We've already got lots of millions,' she said with her mouth full of Jungle Pastilles. She reached out to get some more, but the movement was so sudden that the bag fell to the floor.

'I'll pick it up,' said Christina, eager to help. She threw herself forward, but ended up with her tummy on top of the control panel. A roaring sound could be heard from the suction pump.

'What was that? A heavy sack of valuables?' Martha wondered out loud.

'I think that I might have . . .' mumbled Christina.

'I had better increase the suction force,' said Martha, pulling the control panel towards her and pushing the joystick to maximum.

'No, no,' shouted Christina in panic because she had pressed the button that said: REVERSE. The newly stolen riches were now being pumped back into the refuse shaft!

Inside the bank vault, the League of Pensioners were on their way up the ladders when they suddenly heard a sound like when water has been turned off in a building and then turned on again. A coughing, knocking and rattling noise was coming from the refuse shaft which soon expelled an enormous burst of old rubbish, followed by plaster, bits of board and mortar. After that came banknotes, brochures, wills and golden bracelets like projectiles into the bank vault and, last of all, a golden necklace wrapped round Anna-Greta's bent walking stick.

'But Martha, dear! Turn it off, turn it off!' moaned Brains as he and Anders tried to push the big oak table against the opening to stop the flow.

'Well, well, my walking stick,' sighed Anna-Greta and sadly

felt the handle which hadn't fared well. A piece of it had splintered off.

Then they heard a new, strange roar, followed by a long whooshing sound. Then silence. Martha had evidently turned the pump off. But then it started up again, the sound increased and everything, including Anna-Greta's stick, was sucked back down the shaft again. But now they could hear other sounds too. Police sirens. And they were very close.

Down on the street they were getting nervous inside the refuse-collection lorry.

'It would seem that the neighbours have phoned the police,' Christina commented.

'Oh my God, yes, we'd best be moving,' said Martha nervously, finding it hard waiting for the last of the loot to be sucked up. Then she hurriedly pressed the clutch and put the lorry into reverse gear.

'But Martha! Don't forget the suction pump,' protested Christina, quickly jabbing her foot hard on the brake.

'Oh dearie me, there is so much to bear in mind nowadays,' muttered Martha blushing slightly. 'I mean, it is so easy to forget.'

'Help, now I can see a police car,' Christina broke in.

'If they come, then I'll say that we've got a problem with food waste in the suction pump,' said Martha unfolding an old, sticky pizza carton. 'This sort of thing always causes a blockage in the pump.'

'Oh, you think of everything!'

'Yes, when I don't forget it . . .'

'But, usch, what a horrible smell,' said Christina.

'My dear, this isn't a taxi, it is a refuse-collection lorry,' answered Martha.

The League of Pensioners down in the bank vault heard the police sirens, checked that they hadn't forgotten anything and then hurried back up to the meeting room. There they quickly brushed the worst of the dust and dirt off one another and then, as calmly and coolly as possible, went out to the stairwell and down into the street with the refuse bins between them. A drunkard who walked past the bank gave a start when he saw Brad Pitt, Elton John and Pavarotti with two wheelie bins, closely followed by Margaret Thatcher. He rubbed his eyes. It was never a good idea to drink liqueur. Liqueur drinks could contain just about anything.

The police car was approaching the corner of Saint Eriksgatan and Fleminggatan and it slowed down outside the bank just as the rain started to become more intense. The side window was lowered.

'Hey, you!'

Elton John and Brad Pitt heard the policeman's voice behind them but pretended they hadn't, and quickly disconnected the suction pipe as nonchalantly as they could. For the sake of appearances they even picked up a beer can and some messy paper serviettes from McDonald's and threw them into one of the bins. Meanwhile, Martha pressed the buttons on the control panel so that the suction pipe was retracted and turned off completely, after which the hydraulic arm lifted the wheelie bins into place. Her hands fumbled to find the plastic bag with the emergency solution and then – that very moment – the rain turned into a cloudburst. The policemen, who were just getting out of their car, stopped mid-movement, shut the doors and quickly raised the side window.

Anders, with his back turned to them, quickly removed his Brad Pitt mask and headed towards the nearest underground station, waving goodbye to the pensioners. Brains and Rake went up to the lorry and took their places on the spare seats behind Martha and Christina. It was a bit of a squeeze and had meant a lot of welding work and lots of prior planning. But instead of two lorries, they only wanted one. Making your escape in two vehicles was always more of a risk than just having one vehicle.

'We seem to have sucked up some really nasty-smelling rubbish.' Rake sniffed in dissatisfaction and pressed the nose of the Elton John mask as tightly as he could.

'Yes, indeed,' said Martha. 'If you drive a refuse-collection lorry, you need to play the part convincingly, so I brought this along with us in case the police should get too close for comfort.' She opened the plastic bag which contained fermented herring – a Swedish delicacy, but one which smelled so horrible that even the gourmands who like to eat it usually put a clothes peg over their nostrils while they do – the odour of which now filled the cabin even though she lowered the side windows.

'Hold your noses! Now we're off!'

With a heavy turn of the steering wheel she swung out into the middle of the street, pressed the accelerator and set off past the police car before driving down Saint Eriksgatan in a calm and dignified manner. The policemen, who had just lowered their side windows once more, rapidly raised them again to prevent the stench from coming in, and it took them a while to collect their thoughts to such a degree that they were then able to rush into the bank with their pistols at the ready.

'Do you know why Norwegian refuse-collection lorries drive so fast?' began Martha, with her hands firmly gripping the steering wheel, in an attempt to lighten the atmosphere in the cab.

'Because they are afraid they will be robbed!' came the reply in unison from the back seat. And then they all giggled while they continued their drive by turning off towards Roslagstull and continuing on towards their new hometown of Djursholm. In the lorry's refuse container they now had at least ten, if not fifteen, million for the poor who needed a brighter existence. But in actual fact, the League of Pensioners needed to haul in several hundred million more to realize Martha's great dream: a place where ancient seniors could meet together, amuse themselves and enjoy life; yes, a place with lots of lovely things. A bit like an old-fashioned village where everybody managed nicely but with a more modern name – a Vintage Village or a Pleasure Village perhaps? Or why not a Panther Nest, she had thought, remembering how she had heard about a group of American oldies who had called themselves the Grey Panthers.

2

It is the mistakes that are made *after* a crime that lead to many crooks being caught, Martha thought as she steered the refuse-collection lorry out of the city. How many robbers have relaxed after carrying out their crimes, done something silly and then got caught? No, that was *not* going to happen to the League of Pensioners. Everyone in the gang must retain their concentration and not relax for a moment, she thought as she veered away at the last moment from a solitary pedestrian on the street, after which she skidded into a curve with screaming tyres before she understood that she must drive a bit slower. She took a hold of herself and gripped the steering wheel hard with both hands.

She thought about how stupid those young men had been, years ago it was, when they stole paintings from the National Museum. The culprits had fled in a boat from the quay outside the museum in the middle of December, but then they had been so noisy once they were out in the bay that a skipper had become suspicious. After that, it didn't take long for the police to find them. Not to mention the notorious helicopter robbery. On that occasion, the crooks left their GPS on a passenger seat in the helicopter, so the police could easily ascertain that they had been at the crime scene! That sort of farce was not going to happen with the League of Pensioners – they already had their plan ready. They weren't going to leave any tracks at all . . . So, in good time before the robbery, they had fitted up their new villa in Djursholm with its own pneumatic refuse system so that all they had to do was connect the lorry's suction pipe to the system. With the press of a button they would then do everything in *reverse* so that the entire haul would end up in their own cellar before they drove the lorry back to the depot. Simple and brilliant. Nobody would think of looking for the loot from a big robbery in the house of some old pensioners in Djursholm. No, in reality oldies just sat at home and solved crossword puzzles.

Martha turned off from Norrtäljevägen in the direction of Djursholm square. By the shop she took the steep hill up to the right, passed the top and slowed down when they reached their new permanent home in life, Auroravägen 3. The picturesque old villa from around 1900 had a lovely position on a slope with bushes and oak trees and it was one of the many large old houses in the area. It had three storeys and was clad in dark-stained wood; it even had a tower with a glazed veranda. She loved the villa and if it hadn't been for the grumpy multi-millionaire Bielke who lived next door, the place would have been absolutely idyllic. There had once been a lovely Jugend villa on his plot, but grizzle-guts had had it demolished and instead built a rectangular, fortress-like box construction. And in front of the grey concrete bunker he now had a luxurious swimming pool with steps and railings and around that were large concrete pots with neglected plants that were slowly suffocating from all the goutweed and dandelions.

But worst of all were the tasteless garden sculptures in stone and plastic. A large granite lion with its front paw on a globe and a Father Christmas in jolly red colours with a split plastic hood and a sack on his back. If it hadn't been for the lilac bushes and rows of apple trees which hid most of the abomination, Martha would never have gone along with buying the house next door. She wanted to be surrounded by beauty and lovely nature.

Martha missed the lovely old house in the country outside Vetlanda down in the south of the country that they had been forced to leave. But the local council had decided to build a motorway right outside and they had no choice but to move back to Stockholm. They hadn't dared return to Värmdö where they had lived earlier, but had chosen to settle in Anna-Greta's old home district of Djursholm, a very posh northern suburb of the city. It felt safer there. Not so much motorbike gang and bandits, but more financial dribblers in fancy suits. And they didn't tend to knock down pensioners. Besides, Djursholm was a calm and peaceful place with a well brought-up population who liked culture. This, for example, is where the storyteller Elsa Beskow had once lived. Martha could imagine how she would have sat there in her large 1940s villa, played the piano, drawn pictures and thought up stories. Perhaps it was this that had made Martha herself dream of creating a wonderful existence for older people. Yes, a Vintage Village, a real Panther Nest with a cinema, theatre, spa, garden, Internet cafe, hairdresser, swimming bath and bar; yes, a wonderful retreat for seniors where you could enjoy the last years of your life. She wanted to get the League of Pensioners to realize this dream, but if she was going to succeed in convincing them, she would have to proceed with caution. Because as soon as her friends understood how much money would be needed, they would also understand that they must carry out new crimes. Millions in a bank were all very well, but a Panther Nest or a Pleasure Village, if you could call it that, would demand thousands of millions of kronor.

Martha changed to a lower gear, had a look in the wing mirror to make sure there was nobody behind them, and drove in towards the carport next to the cellar. It was rather hard to manoeuvre the heavy vehicle so unfortunately the lorry ended up at a bit of an angle, but even real refuse collectors can park their lorries a bit carelessly sometimes. Now the most important thing was to quickly unload their booty!

'Time to connect the suction pipe,' she said, nodding to the others. A sleepy Pavarotti (Brains) and a just-as-sleepy Elton John (Rake) climbed out of the cab of the lorry while Martha got hold of the control panel and lowered the pipe. The men dragged it across to the cellar wall and were just about to connect it when they both felt an urgent call of nature . . . the early hours of the morning have a strange effect on elderly men and both Pavarotti and Elton John had to pee.

'Hang on a moment!' Brains signalled to Martha as he nipped round the corner with Rake right after him. But Martha didn't grasp the signal and she went ahead and pressed the joystick. A stench of rotten herring erupted from the lorry together with some wills, bars of gold and banknotes, before the men – clutching their belts – rushed back in horror and connected the pipe as they should have done straight away. Martha heard all sorts of sounds and imagined how banknotes, coin collections, gold bars and lots of other things were landing in the cellar. But then there was a sudden blockage and the pump stopped with a crack as if somebody had fired a rifle.

'Oh no, Anna-Greta's walking stick!' squeaked Christina as there was another crack and the remains of the stick were ejected into the cellar.

'Poor Anna-Greta, what shall we do now?' mumbled Martha while the noise slowly diminished before finally stopping completely.

'We'll buy her a nice new stick if Brains can't repair the old one,' said Christina, and Martha nodded in agreement. Then she signalled to the men to disconnect the pipe. But nothing happened. Enraged, Martha got out of the cab.

'What's going on?' she demanded.

'Some stuff fell by the wayside,' said Brains pathetically and pointed at a few banknotes and a gold bar on the ground. 'I think there's even a bit under the lorry too.'

'I'll fix that. I'll park the lorry on the slope,' said Rake, ever ready to show his skills. 'We men know about such things and we're used to heavy vehicles.'

'Well, fine, then, but I'd better get rid of that rotten herring first,' said Martha, opening the door and lifting out the bag with the stinking fish.

'Oh bloody hell, we'll never get rid of that stench!' mumbled Rake. He squeezed his nose but only got a piece of latex in his hand. Muttering to himself, he climbed up into the driver's seat, looked about him, and had just started to back the vehicle when Martha knocked on the windscreen.

'The pipe, Rake, retract it first.'

'Was just about to do that,' he said with his face growing red, then he did as she said and drove up the slope where he parked on their neighbour's private parking space. The stinking-rich neighbour was on a round-the-world trip, so they didn't have to worry about him. Nor his garden either. He had contracted the garden upkeep to a company that had since gone bankrupt, but the League of Pensioners had kept quiet about that. They enjoyed not having to hear the sound of the lawnmowers, trimmers and other machines that were so common in Djursholm. As far as they were concerned, they would be happy to see the garden turn into a jungle!

Rake got out and when he came back to the house he picked up a gold bar and the remains of a stamp album from the ground, but he couldn't find anything more. He went in to join the others.

They had hardly got inside the refuse room in the cellar before they all broke out in wild cheering. On the floor lay gold bars and bundles of banknotes all higgledy-piggledy, and Anna-Greta rushed forward in a state of ecstasy. She beamed with delight as she waved one of the bundles as if she was fanning herself with a fan of feathers.

'Aaah,' she sighed, and closed her eyes.

'But there is such a mess here,' said Martha, horrified. 'What if somebody comes. We'd better hide everything right away.'

'Nonsense, there aren't any police in Djursholm, just swindlers and big finance crooks,' Anna-Greta giggled, virtually drunk with delight, and she threw some bundles into the air. 'Aaah,' she joyfully exclaimed yet again, bending down and sniffing the money. 'Mind you, they don't exactly smell like money, more like rotten fish.'

'No, that's right. Cleaning stained notes after a bank robbery is one thing, I can do that, but getting rid of the stench of rotten fish? God knows if I can manage that!' muttered Brains who had finally taken off his Pavarotti mask.

'Now listen to me! We must get serious; we can't make the same mistake as other robbers. We must cover our tracks. And do it properly!' urged Martha.

'Yes, right. But we'll never get rid of the smell,' said Anna-Greta, holding a bundle of banknotes at arm's length. 'I know, we can send a press release to the papers and call this the Stink Robbery,' she went on, before breaking out into such a neighing that Christina had to give her a kick on her shins.

'Pull yourself together, Anna-Greta, we mustn't make a fool of ourselves.'

And just as she uttered those words, a strange sound could be heard from somewhere above. There was a bit of squeaking, thumping and a banging on the ground, and the noise was getting all the louder. Indeed, it sounded as if something was coming down the slope. And it wasn't a car or a motorbike, but something much heavier. And the closer it came, the stronger the stench of rotten herring.

'Oh no, my God, I do believe . . .' Martha managed to utter before they all rushed to the door. They got out just in time to see the refuse-collection lorry smash through the bushes, bump down the steps and start sinking in the neighbour's pool. Big bubbles came up to the surface and there was a plopping and slurping sound while the lorry settled slowly on the bottom. Then all was silent.

'Goodness gracious me!' said Christina, pressing her hands over her face in shock.

'A refuse-collection lorry in a swimming pool, that's something I've never seen before,' Brains announced.

'Well, at least it will be clean now,' mumbled Martha.

'And it won't smell either,' Anna-Greta added.

Rake didn't say anything, he just stared. He had pulled up the handbrake, of course he had done that, but perhaps he'd forgotten to put the lorry in gear . . .? Or something like that.

'What were you saying, Rake, about you men being accustomed to heavy vehicles?' Martha wondered.

'Yes, perhaps you also know how to drive them out of a swimming pool?' Christina chipped in with a little giggle. Then everyone turned silent and they all looked glumly at the lorry that had crushed the bushes, smashed the security fence and filled the entire swimming pool. Up on the roof of the lorry you could see a branch from a lilac bush and a dandelion leaf.

'Lucky for us that our neighbour had such a deep pool,' said Martha in an attempt to be positive.

'I won't contradict you on that,' said Rake, trying to straighten up the remains of a gooseberry bush. 'He tested diving apparatus there for his adventure trips.'

'And have you thought of something? We really have been rather lucky. Nobody will go looking for a refuse-collection lorry in a swimming pool,' Martha went on.

'Nope, I'll grant you that,' said Rake, immediately feeling in somewhat better spirits. 'But it is clearly visible there in the water.'

'That's true, but there ought to be a remedy for that, there always is,' said Brains. 'I bet you that our neighbour has a powered pool cover.'

Brains looked around and caught sight of the little shed next to the pool. He picked the lock and disappeared inside. Shortly afterwards, the sound of a little motor starting up could be heard. Slowly the pool cover extended across the surface and soon it had covered the entire pool. There was no sign of the lorry!

'Neat, isn't it?' Brains turned off the motor, unscrewed a few screws and pulled out one of the cables in the control panel. 'Now nobody will be able to remove the pool cover in a hurry. That gives us a little time to contemplate the situation.'

'Yes, we're going to need that,' said Martha.

3

A bank robbery is like being high on cocaine, Martha thought
– but with only a very vague grasp of what being high on
cocaine really involved. She was sticky with sweat, must have
tossed and turned in her bed at least a hundred times, and the
sheets were twisted like the stripes on a piece of sticky rock.
Her brain was spinning at top speed and time after time she
went over the bank robbery hunting for any mistakes they
might have made. She didn't think they had left any tracks, or
had they? And then there was that incident with the refuse-
collection lorry. She had let Brains park it so that he would
feel like a real man, and then it had all gone wrong – if you
were a bank robber, you shouldn't get soft and sentimental
and think of others, no, a robbery was a robber's job, and as
such a job that had to be done in a professional manner; it
was as simple as that! Mind you, it had all turned out OK in
the end. If the police made a connection between the refuse-
collection lorry and the bank robbery, it wouldn't help them
very much. They could check however many lorry depots
they wanted and not find anything. But a refuse-collection
lorry in a swimming pool! She couldn't have thought up anything better herself . . .

Martha and her friends hadn't had the energy to go through all the booty straight away, but had first taken a power nap. A little snooze simply helped clear your brain before you started counting money. And then they had to celebrate. No robbery without champagne – or, at the very least, some exciting liqueur. Martha yawned, got up and pulled out a pen and paper. As soon as they had sorted and hidden the loot, they would have to decide how they were going to give away their Robin Hood money. Martha drew up a things-to-do list and then slowly got dressed. Then she took the pen and notepad and went down the stairs and into the kitchen. It was high time for a meeting.

Before long, Martha and her friends were sitting, each with a cup of coffee, around the big oak table in the cellar. The little gable window was covered with black cloth and the lights were turned on. A heavy stench of rotten herring seemed to have settled in the room and now and then deep yawns could be heard. They were all tired and would have liked to have snoozed a bit longer, but the stolen millions had to be dealt with as soon as possible. Besides which they must solve the problem of the lorry in the swimming pool. To their great fortune, not only was their grumpy neighbour not in residence, but all the other neighbours were away too. And nobody seemed to have noticed what had happened. The lilac bushes and the rest of the overgrown garden hid most of the tracks, and when the League of Pensioners had tidied up a bit, it didn't really look much different to any other neglected garden. But still. It only needed one person to become curious and want to peep under the pool cover. And besides, there was a stench of rotten herring in the whole house. As

Brains put it: the smell of fermented herring is like bills. Not something you can get rid of just like that.

'Five gold bars, tons of bundles of banknotes, three collections of coins and a collection of stamps. Not bad, not bad at all.' Anna-Greta's slightly bureaucratic tone of voice echoed around the downstairs hide-away. She sounded unusually bright and joyful.

'But those banknotes. The authorities will have the numbers, won't they? They are so dreadfully strict at the currency exchanges nowadays,' said Christina rather timidly. Her religious upbringing in Jönköping, the heart of the Swedish bible belt, still made itself felt and she found it hard to get used to bank robberies. And when they had to deal with the booty, well, that caused her even more angst. She felt ashamed, like a crook, and she was always worried that they would get caught.

'We can buy caravans, luxury cruisers and other stuff on the Internet,' Rake proposed and put a calming arm around her shoulder.

'But what if they're stolen, then it would be a criminal offence: receiving stolen goods.' Christina shook her head.

'No, of course, we should steer clear of anything illegal like that,' Martha announced and gave the others a strict look.

'Then I reckon you're in the wrong line of business,' said Rake.

'But the whole point of our crimes is to spread joy,' she insisted.

'Not so sure that *everyone* would agree.'

The League of Pensioners clinked their coffee cups together, helped themselves to the wafer biscuits and contemplated the heap of valuables on the floor. Now and then, they shifted the bundles of banknotes as if weighing up what they could be used for. Anna-Greta thumbed through the banknotes and looked thoughtful. Then she suddenly stopped and a broad smile stretched across her face.

'You know what? I've had a brilliant idea,' she exclaimed, and you could hear a merry clucking gradually transforming into a jolly horse-like neigh before she managed to stop herself at the last moment. 'We start a company, buy an old people's home or a school with the money from the bank robbery, then quickly sell the company and transfer the profit to the West Indies.'

'Not like those greedy venture capitalists, surely!' Christina shouted.

'Stop and explain yourself! We are not going to make a profit on the elderly and schools. We're going to *give away* the money, don't forget that,' Martha protested.

'Yes, but that's precisely what we would be doing. *Give away!*' Anna-Greta insisted, as she nonchalantly pushed her long grey hair behind her ears and sat up straight. Smiling, she looked at her friends. 'Profit-making companies within schools, health care and other social fields transfer enormous amounts of money out of Sweden without paying tax, and the government has no control of this at all!' Her cheeks glowed red with excitement. 'And we don't even have to plunder a company first, we already have the money! We just send it to the Caribbean, start a company there and then transfer the money back home again without paying tax. That way the money will grow!'

'But who the hell pays tax on money they have robbed?' asked Rake, perplexed.

This was followed by silence for a remarkably long period and they all looked at each other, a little embarrassed – until Anna-Greta sat up straight, looked around at them and cracked her neck.

'Don't you get it? We launder the money over there in the Caribbean and then we can hand out *even more* money to the poor.'

This was a bit difficult for the members of the League of Pensioners to follow, and Anna-Greta had to go on to explain how they, with the help of a lawyer, could arrange the whole thing.

'And the more companies we start, the harder it will be for the authorities to work out what we're up to,' she said.

'I think it ought to suffice with one company; wouldn't that be enough?' said Brains, who didn't want to complicate life unnecessarily. He wanted to work on his lathe, do his carpentry and busy himself with his inventions. Not play fancy tricks with money.

'We must have two companies, one in the West Indies and one in Sweden. Then we get a Visa card for the Swedish company and we can get at the money right away.' Anna-Greta's eyes glimmered with delight.

'In one of those hole-in-the-wall machines, you mean?' asked Rake, wide-eyed.

'Yes, yes, that's right. Then the company in the West Indies can lend money to our company in Sweden, and charge an extortionate interest rate so that we make an enormous loss.

There wouldn't be any tax at all to pay, and we would get *even* richer. Just like the multi-millionaires.'

'But Lord above, why should we bother with all that? Can't we just do some good instead?' Brains broke in.

'Absolutely. That financial circus is not for us. We shall pay tax in Sweden, otherwise we aren't the slightest bit better than the usual crooked businessmen,' said Martha.

'That's quite right. Tax is necessary for society to function,' Christina added, pulling out her nail file and starting to carefully file her nails. She hadn't varnished them for two days and it was high time to take care of them. 'And if you are rich, that is – you'll have to excuse me if I haven't really understood this, but if you have lots of money, then you can afford to pay tax, can't you? So why don't people do so?' she asked.

Sucks and ums and ers could be heard from all while they reflected on the powerful world of finance. Evidently loads of billions were swirling around in cyberspace and they never seemed to reach the people who really needed them, while at the same time the banks lent fictive money they didn't have. No wonder it was hard to understand. In the end, Martha held up her hands in a decisive gesture.

'Anna-Greta, instead of dribbling hither and thither with our capital, I want to know how we can share our bank robbery money as quickly as possible.'

'As soon as I can get hold of a good lawyer, I'll ask him to make monthly payments to the City Mission for their charity work. We can do that, because in the Caribbean our account will be kept secret and nobody will know where the money comes from.'

They all thought that was a good idea and nodded in agreement, but sighed at the same time over the fact that they had so little money to share out. Nowadays so many people needed help to manage. The low-paid working in health care, people with only the lowest state pension, schools, old people's homes, cultural organizations . . . the League of Pensioners would really have to set to work to manage all this. Besides, there was something else to think of. Martha pulled out her knitting. It was all very well giving money to those in need, but an unfortunate characteristic of money was that it disappeared, she thought. While the members of the League of Pensioners were still able and active, they ought to create something that would last. Something that would bring joy even after they themselves were dead: the Pleasure Village, the dream of a place for the elderly.

She shut her eyes and saw a gang of happy seniors in front of a swimming pool. Some others sat in the bar cosseted in comfortable armchairs with umbrella drinks in their hands, while others again were busying themselves with gardening in one of the senior centre's many greenhouses. A theatre group performed *Arsenic and Old Lace* up on the stage and from the boules pitch you could hear chatter and joyful laughter. What a marvellous vision . . .

'Your knitting!' Brains exclaimed, saving it just as the whole lot was about to fall to the floor.

'Thank you,' mumbled Martha fumbling with the stitches. The problem was that the Pleasure Village or the Panther Nest would certainly cost lots and lots, much more than one of those huge sport arenas that the politicians built to keep on good terms with the building industry. But of course they wouldn't have to build the whole village all at once; rather, they could start with a spa or a restaurant. A few hundred million kronor, that was all. Martha fingered the half-finished scarf, raised her eyebrows and tried to concentrate her thoughts. If lots of puppy-like twenty-five-year-olds from the Business School could get rich, then surely five adventurous seniors could also succeed?

'You know what? We have lots to do. If we are going to give away eighteen million, or however much we managed to haul in, then we must get to work.'

'Pah, that's easy. Give them to the state and then they'll disappear without trace before you know it!' said Rake.

'Regardless, we're going to need to hide everything we've stolen,' Brains commented, and the others agreed with him. They quickly made a joint effort to stuff the booty into dirty pillowcases and duvet covers which they then pushed into three laundry baskets together with the rest of the dirty laundry. On top they put Rake's and Brains's unwashed underpants, after which they threw the Pavarotti, Thatcher and Elton John masks into the oil-fired burner. When they were done, Rake fetched the champagne and five glasses.

'And now we shall celebrate too, right?'

'Yes, indeed,' said Martha and she nodded to Rake. He handed out the champagne glasses and with a slight bow filled them. 'Cheers and thanks to everyone!' said Martha, raising her glass.

'Cheers!' responded her friends. They clinked the champagne glasses against each other and drank in a solemn mood.

'To think that we've been successful again,' said Anna-Greta, throwing out her hands in a gesture of happiness.

'Anna-Greta, robbing a bank is the simple part,' said Christina. 'Laundering the money and giving it to those who are in need – that seems to be ten times harder!'

All the members of the League of Pensioners realized that they had a lot of work before them and they knew that they needed their midday siesta. The meeting was adjourned and they went up to their respective rooms. Martha was halfway up the stairs when she felt a hand on her shoulder.

'Martha, I want to talk to you!' Brains's voice sounded serious and his hand felt warm and pleasant. Nevertheless, she felt a little worried. He had sounded so decisive.

'Now?'

'Yes, this minute. Let's go into the library.'

Sleepy and with a feeling that he had something important to say, she obeyed. If there was a problem, then it was best to solve it directly. He waited until she had come into the room, then he looked around and closed the door. He straightened his jacket, followed by the old 1950s trousers, after which he slowly and cautiously went down on his knees. She looked at him in astonishment. Heavens, he looked so embarrassed and lost!

'Martha, I want to marry you.'

'But my dear, you don't have to go down onto your knees to propose, you only have to say so,' said Martha, horrified as she saw Brains end up in a heap on the floor.

'I am fed up of being secretly engaged. I want us to get married now,' he mumbled and got back up onto his knees somewhat breathlessly. He took hold of the door frame and stood up in as dignified a manner as he was capable of. Then he fished out a gold ring from his pocket and held it up to Martha.

'Thank you my friend,' she mumbled, blushing as she received it. 'So kind of you,' she went on, but, in her eagerness, she bumped into him so that the ring rolled off across the floor. Brains went down onto the floor tiles again.

'Now you understand why I want you all to do gymnastics every day, right?' said Martha far too quickly, before she realized that it wasn't perhaps the most tactful comment at that very moment.

'Hmmf!' came the response from Brains.

'Sorry, but it is a good idea to keep fit and healthy,' she went on and again, almost as she said the words, she realized that this, too, was not exactly what she should be saying. Brains managed to get up on his feet again, this time without needing to support himself against the wall. And now he was looking decidedly rebellious.

'Gymnastics? Yes, sure, my dear, but I get my litheness from yoga. The yoga sessions with Christina have taught me a lot,' he said, and his voice sounded unusually defiant.

Martha stared at him. He had contradicted her! Ever since the day they had got engaged, he had started getting cheeky. Now, he could be really stubborn and regularly tried to defy her. A woman should never get married, it was better that the menfolk had to make a bit of an effort and not take you for granted, Martha thought. And to be proposing now! They had hardly recovered from the bank robbery! Or was he afraid that she would propose a new crime straight away? She sneaked a look at the ring that Brains held firmly between his thumb and first finger.

'You'll get the other one when we get married. Then we'll have a party!' said Brains and he slipped the glimmering gold onto her finger. She stroked the ring with her index finger and looked at him. She *did* want to live with him, but . . .

'Get married? Yes, my friend. That sounds nice, but as I said, we must hand out the money from the bank robbery now, yes, you know—'

Brains pushed her aside.

'So the money from the bank robbery is more important?'

'Oh no. Not at all. Only just now. We can't disappoint the elderly and the poor. The money must be distributed now.'

'Giving money away *is* more important, then?' Brains's voice sounded shrill.

'No, no, my dear, you know perfectly well that you and me, we belong together!' said Martha, and she leaned forward and hugged him tightly until she felt that he had calmed down. 'We'll just postpone the wedding a while.'

'A while? OK, then we'll get married fairly soon, you mean?' mumbled Brains, relieved. He could feel himself blushing as he was sucked into her field of force again. He had hoped that they would get married straight after the big bank robbery. But, of course, the money must be handed out too. So he couldn't risk everything with his romantic marriage plans. The wedding would have to be later. Martha was right. As always. He just had to accept that.

'OK. We distribute the money first, but then get ma—'

'Wonderful, Brains, you are so flexible,' Martha cut him off and again wrapped her arms around him. 'There is no one like you! Oh, how I love you!'

And then Brains blushed again and was completely lost for

words. Hand in hand they went upstairs and now everything felt so good between them. It was OK that Martha got to decide now, but later, when they were married, then he would show her who was boss, he would indeed – that was, if they didn't end up in prison.

By now it was late afternoon and they were all still a little tipsy from the champagne – except Martha who, though chirpy and happy, remained sober. After all, it was not every day that somebody proposed to her. But neither she nor Brains had been able to relax, so they had followed all the news bulletins. The robbery had been the top item on the TV and radio news and the police were out in force. Everything the League of Pensioners did over the next few hours could be decisive for whether they would get caught or not. They must lie low, act wisely and not – under any circumstances – make any mistakes.

The police were hunting the perpetrators of the great Nordea robbery and Martha asked herself how the constables reasoned. One of them might start thinking about the League of Pensioners since the robbers had not used a machine gun, had not thrown caltrops onto the street, had not burned cars or taken hostages. That meant there weren't so many robber gangs to choose from. On the other hand, they *had* used explosives, and that had a definite criminal ring to it. Rake had actually suggested that they shoot a volley (at the ceiling, of course) with a machine gun to appear professional, but Martha had firmly opposed that idea. To start with, they never used weapons as a matter of principle, and second, just because others behaved badly it was no reason for them to do the same. Besides, the League of Pensioners had 'disappeared' some time ago and nobody could know that they were back in the field again.

Martha wheeled the dining trolley up in the tower and started to lay the table with herbal tea, wholemeal biscuits and other organic foods (Christina was in a health phase). To get everyone into a good mood, she had also put out some really yummy chocolate wafers and their old favourite, cloudberry liqueur. It was important that everybody enjoyed themselves and felt good.

When she had laid the table, she rang the little bell to call the others. The veranda at the top of the tower was a delight, and the rattling indoor lift took them up there without difficulty. It was a cosy place to sit. Here, too, they could look out across the road and the next-door plot and keep track of what happened should any undesired person turn up. Meanwhile, they could hold their meeting.

'Welcome, and help yourself to coffee,' said Martha when they had all gathered there. 'I mean healthy herbal tea.'

Anna-Greta stepped in and settled in her favourite armchair, Christina turned back in the doorway to fetch her handbag with her cosmetics, and Brains and Rake wandered in, both very sleepy. A midday siesta was all very well, but they could have slept a lot longer.

When Christina came back and all had been served, the atmosphere became calm. There was a clinking of cups and the occasional discreet cough. They were not entirely sober, but Martha considered that they didn't have time to relax properly. She looked around her, smothered the impulse to ring the bell yet again, and cleared her throat discreetly.

'We have talked about how we can best use the capital in the robbery fund. This time I vote for putting it into health care and schools. And, of course, care for the elderly and culture,' Martha started. 'Then we can create a project of our own, a Vintage—'

'Don't forget our seamen. They ought to get some money too,' Rake said. 'Flagging out and all that.'

'And inventors,' Brains added. 'In Sweden there are innumerable brilliant inventors, but they don't get any support from the state. Fantastic ideas are bought up by foreign companies or are simply stolen. We ought to support them.'

'Of course, seamen and inventors should be on the list,' Martha agreed and made a note on her pad. 'But at the same time we ought to think in the long term and invest in something that will last. I've an idea for a lovely place for the elderly, a Vintage—'

'What about librarians?' Christina chipped in. 'They support our entire culture. And remember all the nurses, teachers and—'

'Now listen, we're not sitting on Sweden's national budget here, we have only carried out a small bank robbery,' Martha reminded them.

'Small? Did you say small? There was a great big bang when the floor gave way,' Rake said, grinning.

'Order in the ranks!' Martha commanded in a loud voice and put her hands together in front of her so that she almost looked like a priest. 'I vote that we first of all give money to those who work in home care and home health care, as well as in health care in general. Then we move on and there I'd like to suggest a new fancy project, a Vintage Village, a real Panther Nest, yes, a village for the elderly.'

'A Jurassic Park for oldies, you mean?' Rake grinned.

'You what? A vintage village? That sounds like old clothes, no, I think that all the money should go to those who are underpaid. They ought to get a bonus just like the directors,' Brains contributed.

'A bonus to the underpaid? What a great idea!' Rake added.

'Yes, indeed, but then I've got a plan,' said Martha.

'We don't doubt that for one second,' said Brains, and took her hand. 'But one thing at a time. We can't do everything at once.'

One thing at a time? Martha leaned back in the chair. They were right, she ought to calm down. There was no point robbing banks if you didn't hand out the money to the people who needed it before you started with the next project. But after that . . . well! Brains could say what he liked, but she wasn't going to drop the idea of that Vintage Village, or whatever it was to be called.

4

Chief Inspector Per Jöback at the City Police had had a hectic night. First, an elderly lady had phoned in and said that she had seen Pavarotti and Elton John outside the Nordea bank branch on Kungsholmen. The lady in question, who must have been seventy plus, had been out with her dog when she had seen them and now she was philosophizing as to whether they could have been crooks in disguise. Jöback had been friendly and had politely said that he too adored Elton John and Pavarotti, but that he didn't really think they would rob a bank. Then the lady added that she had also noticed a lady who looked like Margaret Thatcher and that she too could have been involved. Then he said that he had noted the tip and that he would check it out, but that regrettably he must leave the station to answer an emergency alarm call. Then he had yawned widely and put his feet up on the table.

Two hours later, he was woken up by a call from Djursholm that made him really furious. Mrs Astrid von Bahr, the wife of a diplomat, suffered from insomnia and she had gone out onto her balcony to read and to get a bit of fresh air. Out there she had thought about her unfaithful husband – who, after forty years of marriage, had left her for a younger woman – when she suddenly heard a weird noise. It had sounded like a lorry and when she'd looked up from her e-reader she had glimpsed a refuse-collection lorry which was rolling backwards down a steep slope. Then she had heard a terrific crash and then everything went silent. She had listened for a long time but hadn't heard the lorry drive away again and nor had she heard any voices, and she thought that was strange.

'A refuse-collection lorry can hardly go up in smoke, Constable.'

Jöback agreed about that and he talked with her for a long time until he tired of all her theories about terrorist deeds and the mafia. Indeed, he was beginning to be too old to be on night duty since he had far too little patience. People were so incredibly stupid.

'Well, thank you for phoning,' he attempted to end the conversation, emptying his lungs in a long exhalation.

'But the refuse-collection lorry might have ended up in the ditch,' said the lady.

'Yes, that is, of course, a possibility,' said Jöback.

'Or what if somebody had hijacked it?'

The refuse-collection lorry? No, there aren't any Norwegians in Djursholm, he intended to reply, but he swallowed the words.

'Then a black hole? Are there sinkholes in Djursholm?'

'Sinkholes? Oh how unpleasant!' said Chief Inspector Jöback with pretended empathy in his voice.

'Yes, isn't it!'

'But are you sure it was a refuse-collection lorry, and not an ambulance or a fire engine?' asked Jöback.

Then the lady had accused him of teasing, but he had reassured her that he took her interest in public order most seriously. After which he thanked her for the tip, quickly brought the conversation to an end and told his police dog, Cleo, that elderly ladies should not live alone too long. At the very least, they ought to have a dog as company, just like he had. Otherwise they got too many strange ideas.

Brains got up, went across to the tower window and looked out across the garden. A few weeks had passed since the big robbery and the police had not interrogated them. The detectives did not believe the coup against the Nordea bank had been the work of Swedish robbers, but rather everything pointed to an international gang. Swedes would not have worn a Margaret Thatcher mask, said the police, nor would Pavarotti or Brad Pitt have featured. The likelihood would have been greater if they had worn an Abba mask or a mask of Björn Borg or the Swedish king. Thus the League of Pensioners had not even been named in the speculations in the media.

'One shouldn't commit oneself to a single theory but have all one's candles burning,' Jöback declared straight into the TV cameras, presumably inspired by a former police commissioner who used to say the same. 'We are working on a broad front,' he added and looked very important.

The articles about the big bank robbery grew less and the columns all the smaller, and now the robbery hadn't been mentioned at all for several days. The members of the League of Pensioners started to relax and Brains thought it was high time to hold a wedding. Yes, he ought to make a new attempt to talk with Martha. But it wasn't easy. He paced around in the tower room, stopped in front of the window and looked out across the garden while he tried to collect his thoughts. A great tit flew past and settled on one of the branches outside. There were a lot of trees in the garden and, my God, they did look a mess. They grumbled about the neighbour, but their own garden was not much better. The black iron gates needed repainting and the gravel paths had patches of weeds and moss. On the slope from the house to the fence there were several oaks that should have been trimmed long ago and what had once been a fine lawn was now just high grass. Brains sighed and thought that their house with its tower looked just like one of those classic old mansions with their fancy woodwork, more or less dilapidated, typical of Djursholm. Usually inhabited by elderly ladies who played the piano and read books but who didn't have the energy to look after the house or the garden any longer.

Both he and Rake suffered, because they couldn't manage a garden of this size either and they didn't dare employ a gardener as long as they busied themselves with their illegal activities. Brains stole a look at Martha. It was actually her fault because she could never relax, and was always committing them to new projects all the time, so both the house and the garden suffered as a result. And even though he had proposed, she hadn't planned the wedding. When he paced back and forth in front of the window, he suddenly grew angry. There she sat with a book in her hand not caring about what the garden looked like. And she didn't care about their wedding either. He went up to her.

'Martha, have you thought any more about when we can

get married?' he asked, in what was an unusually sharp voice for him.

'Get married, did you say?' Martha wondered, sitting in her favourite flowery armchair and reading. She thumbed the pages a little nervously and felt the pressure from her fiancé. She was reading *The Mystery of Ageing: How to Live Longer*, written by one of those health journalists in one of the major dailies. Brains, for his part, had brought up an old computer that he had started to take apart; he was going to learn how it worked. But evidently he hadn't had much success because he had abandoned the semi-demolished computer and stood by the window a long while.

'Yes, get-mar-ried,' he said, emphasizing every syllable, before returning to the computer's innards.

Martha put her book aside and stroked Brains gently on his head in a gesture midway between a pat and a caress. There were too many things going on around her. Not only did she have to plan crimes and share out the proceeds, but she also had to eat properly, do gymnastics and keep her brain in good trim. And now Brains wanted to get married. Yes, it could be nice, and after all she did feel very fond of him, but first and foremost they must share out their newly stolen money with the people who needed it. Besides, being married wasn't all easy-going, she had heard. Suddenly men could become so *demanding*. After taking you out to dinner and courting you, they suddenly wanted to *own* you. Before she knew it, she would be standing there baking cakes and serving him. She had heard of how a forty-year-long relationship had worked as smoothly as can be, but when the couple had moved in together in their old age, the man in question suddenly expected her to wash his socks and underwear at 6.30 in the morning. No, no way! Never ever! The wedding would have to wait a little longer. At any rate, a few months . . . but what could she blame that on now?

'Yes, Brains, darling! You know that you are the man in my life. But if we don't hand out our bank robbery money now, then whole hospital wards will have to close. Nurses and other health-care staff must get paid more. It is high time to fix a bonus for them.'

'So nurses are more important than our wedding?' Brains sniffled.

'No, not at all, my dear,' said Martha somewhat absently thinking about how they could administer a bonus and at the same time realize a Vintage Village. Besides, they must soon retrieve the millions they had hidden in a drainpipe at the Grand Hotel after a previous robbery. There was simply no time for a wedding! She didn't dare look Brains in the eye and for a long time she fidgeted with the hem of her skirt before she met his gaze. 'There is so much going on now. And it would of course be really annoying if our millions in that drainpipe start rotting away before we can get at them.'

'So a *drainpipe* is more important than our relationship?'

'But goodness me, my love. I didn't mean that at all. Just that we ought to retrieve that money. The banknotes are stuffed inside Anna-Greta's tights and they won't last forever,' said Martha, leaning forward to give him a hug.

'So old *tights* are more important than – well, that's just—!' He got up quickly, gave the computer a kick and left the room slamming the door behind him.

5

Anna-Greta swept along in her Ferrari with a cigarillo in her hand. The wind caught up her grey hair which swirled around like streamers behind her neck. *'Here comes Pippi Longstocking, ladida, ladida,'* she sang out loud while the shops on Kungsgatan swished by. She tried to puff on her cigarillo but the smoke irritated her throat and she started coughing. Usch, it wasn't easy to smoke when you had the roof down. She stubbed out the cigarillo in the ashtray and concentrated on driving instead.

Martha had said that you must lie low after a crime, but you could still indulge in a Ferrari, Anna-Greta thought. Her whole life she had nourished a dream of owning a luxury car like this, and now finally she had achieved it. To be on the safe side, she had bought it second-hand on the Internet and not bothered to send in the papers to the vehicle registry so for a few months she could drive around incognito on the country's roads. After that she would have to get rid of it, but at least she would have had a bit of fun. At her age it was high time to realize her dreams, and besides, she needed the vehicle for her image. She was on her way to see a shady lawyer with a bad reputation who had recently been expelled from the Swedish Bar Association. She had googled and discreetly asked around about Nils Hovberg, and came to the conclusion that he would suit them just right. He had his legal office in the posh city district of Östermalm and among all the camel-hair ulster coats and minks in this part of Stockholm, there were shady characters (like her), semi-fishy individuals, who wanted to get money out of the country. She glanced at the sports bag on the passenger seat. Bribes, a hell of a lot of bribes. It ought to suffice. This time at any rate . . .

She had discovered that Hovberg specialized in Panama and the West Indies, and he had been recommended by obscure sources on shady websites like Flash Net. Besides, he had the best homepage. She had chosen his legal office since the description seemed to be exactly what they were looking for. Above all, she had been enthused by reading:

> We are Sweden's most client-friendly legal bureau for international affairs. We want to invest time and resources in your company so that you will achieve your most ambitious goals. Our legal staff specialize in money transfers to foreign destinations and our advisory service has a global reach suited to your organization.

Anna-Greta pushed the ashtray with her cigarillo in under the dashboard, and hummed. There was one particular detail on the homepage that had made her decide. It was:

We have local knowledge of criminal regimes and business practices in the parts of the world you choose to do your business. We can thus ensure that your investments are safe.

Oh, how she loved the Internet! That really did sound most promising. She parked her car on Grev Turegatan and reached out for her new walking stick, one that Martha had bought for her. You could attach a water bottle to it and it even had a little bell which was useful if you wanted people to get out of your way. She was already very fond of this walking stick even though she still missed the old one – which Brains was trying to repair. Then she climbed arduously out of the car (which was dreadfully low) and lifted out her newly purchased sports bag on wheels. She stood on the pavement for a few moments and recovered her breath; after filling her lungs with some deep inhalations she felt ready to go to the office on Grev Turegatan 93. It was important that she presented her business as seriously as possible.

After she was shown in by a secretary, she found herself sitting in a posh designer armchair in front of a large oak table. Behind the desk sat a little man with a round face and small hands. He stood up when she entered, and greeted her with a little bow and a firm handshake.

'Well now, madam, how can I help you?' he asked as he glanced at the sports bag.

'My husband,' said Anna-Greta as she pulled out her lace handkerchief. 'He has just passed away and now I want to do something charitable with the money he has left.'

'Ah, I see, that is a kind thought . . . do you have the papers?'

Anna-Greta pulled out a forged identity card, her fictive husband's death certificate and a gold ring with the names Oskar and Anna-Greta engraved on it. It looked very fancy. Brains had aged the ring with ash and toothpaste and darkened it with hydrogen sulphide or whatever the chemical he used was called. The ring looked at least fifty years old. 'Though I don't know whether you need the ring too. I would like to retain that as a keepsake,' said Anna-Greta, sniffling a little for the sake of appearances and then loudly blowing her nose on the handkerchief.

'No, no. I won't need that. Well, then, so what help do you want from me?'

And then Anna-Greta started to tell him about her dear departed husband whose great dream in life had been to open a care home for the old and needy. But to avoid all the money disappearing in inheritance tax, he had wanted her to start a health-care company in the Caribbean with a daughter company in Stockholm. By doing that, he had worked out that they would pay less tax and then she could use more money for the good cause. The lawyer looked up and ran his fingers over his bushy eyebrows.

'And how much money are we talking about here?'

'Well, Oskar saved money all his life. And besides, he was very stingy and didn't indulge in any extravagances for himself – or for me, unfortunately. And we didn't have any children either, so the treasure chest got quite full. Then he inherited from his mother and he never spent that money because he didn't trust banks. When he lay on his deathbed, he told me to sell his shares and antiquities, everything in the house and a farm in Vetlanda. So you can imagine that I've got a whole lot of cash.'

'And are we talking about millions here?'

'Fifteen.' Anna-Greta thought that was a suitable sum, because she didn't want to name the exact amount that was missing from Nordea bank.

'Fifteen million,' said the lawyer. 'But the tax authorities won't let you transfer that abroad.'

'No, but I have been led to understand that you are especially skilled at arranging such matters,' said Anna-Greta and winked.

'Yes, indeed, I do realize that is why you are here.'

The lawyer smiled, pressed a few keys on his computer keyboard and swung the screen towards her so that she could see. Then he talked a long time, pointed at various diagrams and suggested one ingenious solution after the other. When they had discussed this for a while, Anna-Greta lifted up the sports bag and put it on the desk.

'This is a small advance for your services. I'm sure we can come to an agreement. Now I need your help to register a company. Why not start a health-care company like my husband said?' She leaned her head to one side and licked her lips seductively like she had seen sensual ladies do in films.

'Well, now, that's um . . .' said the lawyer and he felt the weight of the sports bag.

'Just a little sum for your petty cash.' Anna-Greta smiled. 'Please help me; my husband would have been so happy.' She again pulled out her lace handkerchief and started to cry. The tears ran now, and only with considerable effort did she manage to say: 'You don't know what it is like to lose a life partner. We were inseparable for fifty-three years. Oskar was such a good man and I would like to fulfil his last wishes. A health-care company in the West Indies and then a little daughter company here in Stockholm, that's all.'

'Yes, yes, I understand,' said Mr Hovberg, obviously embarrassed by Anna-Greta's tears. 'I assure you, we can arrange all this, just you see.'

'And then a final request, perhaps the most important of all. Half of the money shall be donated to the City Mission. I want them to get a dollop every month.'

'Yes, I understand.'

'Half of fifteen million is seven and a half, and you can divide that up into monthly instalments of a suitable amount. Well, then, thank you very much,' she concluded, tucking her lace handkerchief back into her bag and getting up. Then she left without taking the sports bag with her. It contained one million kronor in used notes. They had been new, but Brains had given them a special antique treatment.

6

The League of Pensioners sat in the kitchen in their old mansion drinking herbal tea. Christina had insisted that they should drink tea instead of coffee because she had made her very own blend. It sharpened one's senses and was otherwise beneficial for health. The others nodded amicably and put up with it.

The kitchen was fairly large. They hadn't yet had time to decorate it according to their own taste, but it would have to do for the time being. The walls were painted in a warm white colour with light-blue panelling around the decoratively panelled doors and the two mullioned windows. The cupboards were narrow and high with new light fittings and on the kitchen bench next to the sink was a coffee-brewing machine and a centrifugal juicer. In pride of place in the middle of the room was a heavy mahogany table with white armchairs and on the floor a worn, patterned carpet which didn't fit in with all the rest. But since it had come from Brains's home in Sundbyberg, nobody said anything but just let it stay.

Martha and her friends had laid the table with hot scones and marmalade and they were sipping the tea from delicate cups in light-blue Gustavsberg china while they waited to hear Anna-Greta's report from the visit to the lawyer. She had implied that she had a lot to tell them. She finished her scones, brushed the crumbs from her lace blouse and looked around her with a smile. Without thinking about it, she picked up a cigarillo and put it in her mouth.

'Now we're rolling, and soon we'll be able to use the money from Nordea,' she proudly announced. The cigarillo hung from the corner of her mouth and jolly wrinkles of laughter were clearly visible across all of her face. 'You should have seen Hovberg's expression when I gave him the sports bag with all the banknotes. Now I've got him truly hooked.'

'Rolling? What do you mean?' asked Christina.

'A whole bag of money to bribe him?' Brains looked surprised.

'Yes, Mr Hovberg is our investment in the future.' Anna-Greta fumbled in her bag to find her cigarette lighter and was just about to use it when she remembered that her friends had prohibited her from smoking. 'Sorry, I wasn't thinking.' She coughed and the others gave her worrying looks.

'You haven't started smoking again, have you? Smoking kills!' said Martha.

'Not at all, it was just for my image at the lawyer's. How else can an elderly lady gain respect?'

'Exactly.' Rake nodded.

'Hovberg is helping us to start a company. Soon fifteen million will land in the West Indies and when we get our Visa card then we can withdraw cash here in Stockholm. He knows exactly how to take advantage of laws and regulations between different countries. And a bribe of a million kronor isn't very much in that context.'

'A million? When you can buy a company on the Internet for twenty thousand kronor,' said Rake.

'But I have contracted the services of a lawyer who will help us in the *long term*,' Anna-Greta retorted, blushing slightly. 'He will take care of all our business here in Sweden and the Caribbean, and he is bound by professional secrecy.'

'What if we lose all our money?' exclaimed Christina, feeling extremely confused.

'Don't worry,' said Martha nodding encouragingly towards her friend. 'I believe in Anna-Greta, she knows what she is doing.'

'Heavens above, I really hope so. Soon fifteen million will shoot off into cyberspace just like that!' sighed Brains with a resigned gesture towards the ceiling. 'I simply don't get it. How can money we sucked out of a bank vault in Kungsholmen end up in the West Indies?'

'Mr Hovberg is an expert. Over there in the Caribbean they don't care how the money has been earned. They are just happy to have real money in their bank accounts,' Anna-Greta went on. 'He's going to start a fictive health-care company on the Cayman Islands.'

'Yes, that's the trick. Watertight. Nobody can poke their noses in there,' said Rake.

'We'll pay out money from that company to home care and health care, without anybody suspecting anything. And besides, he promised to look after the monthly payments to the City Mission. And if he doesn't behave himself, I shall report him immediately. I've got evidence!' Anna-Greta fished out her mobile and held it up. Then she clicked until the pictures appeared. On her way out of the lawyer's office she had managed to take photos of him as he picked some notes out of the sports bag and stuffed them in his pockets.

'Now listen to me, that wasn't a nice thing to do, Anna-Greta,' Brains pointed out.

'You find the biggest fish in the calmest waters,' said Anna-Greta in delight and reached out for a champagne glass. Her hand fumbled in thin air until she saw the teacup. 'Oh, of course, we're drinking herbal tea, aren't we!' She poured a cup and looked at the yellowish liquid for a long time. 'If we drink a whole cup of this, can we then have a glass of champagne as a reward?' she added, and then erupted into such a neighing that the others had to calm her down.

Martha had been sitting quietly a long time listening to Anna-Greta. The business of transferring money from one account to another in the far-off Caribbean sounded dull. They ought to have something to do so that they didn't get restless and totally bored – all of them. It would be best, of course, if they could combine the charity work with opening a restaurant. As a first step in the project to realizing the Vintage Village. Yes, it was high time they got their teeth into something. Before they all relaxed and became apathetic.

7

The water glimmered in the Sveaviken bay and Djursholm residents were taking a peaceful Sunday walk along Strandvägen. But not the League of Pensioners. Martha had taken her friends on a power walk with poles and they were proceeding at quite a pace. On account of Christina's yoga sessions, she didn't arrange so many gymnastics lessons but instead forced the gang out on even more Nordic walking outings.

'How are you getting on?' she called out to the others who had lagged behind a little. 'Speed up a bit! This is good for the heart and lungs. And besides, it uses almost twice as much energy.'

'But weren't we supposed to *get* more energy?' said a panting Rake, who found it hard to keep up. 'And anyway it's Sunday. You should respect the day of rest.'

'My dear, you can do that later,' Martha retorted and raised her voice. 'And remember that Nordic walking is much gentler on your knees and back than running.'

'Martha, I've never had the slightest intention of jogging, not me,' snorted Rake.

'Another thing is that you use more muscles. Above all it's

the muscles in your legs, stomach, back, arms and chest that get to work.'

'If only you could restrict yourself to just one group of muscles. Now we'll get muscle soreness in every part of our bodies,' Rake groaned.

'That's only because you are not fit.'

'Me, not fit!!' he exploded.

Anna-Greta got up closer to Martha and put a hand on her shoulder. 'Martha dear, you really ought to ease up a bit. Men don't like being ordered about.'

Martha bit her lip. 'No, that's true, perhaps you're right,' she mumbled and continued in a lower voice. 'The words just slip out. I ought to think first, before I say anything.'

'Well, that applies to us all.' Anna-Greta smiled.

'Now listen, I think we've had enough exercise now. What about a bite to eat?' Christina butted in, and leaned on her poles. 'You have to eat properly too. I wonder whether they have health foods at Djursholm Inn?'

'Oh yes, it's time to eat,' Brains called out. 'Why not roast pork and potatoes and some bread with a thick layer of butter and bacon. Then we can add something with yummy mayonnaise oozing with oil. And top it all with a plate of cream cakes, don't you think, Christina? Then we can have a lie-down on the sofa and digest the food.' He looked at Martha out of the corner of his eye to see how she reacted. But his beloved hadn't heard, or perhaps was pretending not to have heard. She didn't react at all.

'But talking of restaurants,' said Martha, 'I'm glad you brought that up. I'm thinking of that Vintage Village where there would be nice things for the elderly to do. My dream is of a complete Pleasure Village with a spa, theatres, hair-dresser's, greenhouses, boules pitches and places to eat for us seniors.'

'Pleasure Village? That sounds great! How many houses of pleasure must there be to make up a whole Pleasure Village?' Rake wondered, and winked at Brains. Martha lost the thread and they all burst out laughing.

'Well, then, Dream Village,' she went on. 'We could start with a restaurant. That would be stage one, and we'd do all the rest later.'

'Restaurant? That's a good idea,' Christina chipped in and looked happy. 'It could be called the Penshy Restaurant, "Penshy" as in "pensioners", and be especially adapted for the elderly. Lots of fruit, organic ingredients and all that.'

'Yes, real Grey Panthers food,' Martha added.

'A beef casserole would be nice,' said Rake. 'And the restaurant should be called The Texan Ranger.'

'Or why not the Easy-to-Chew Restaurant?' Brains suggested, and gave Rake a little prod. The men grinned.

'That's enough, Brains!' protested Martha. 'Now we can sit down and talk this through.' She pointed at a green-painted bench not too far away.

'I can go along with sitting on a bench,' said Brains.

The League of Pensioners sat down on the bench and got their breath back. From here, they had a view of Germania Bay and the luxury villas along Strandvägen. By the waterside you could see one or two embassies and some tall old houses of several storeys. When Anna-Greta was a child here, and had been a pupil in the local school, teachers, librarians and florists could afford to live in the old idyllic villa district. Now the town was a reserve for the rich.

'Do you remember those horrible microwave meals they served at the Diamond House retirement home?' Christina asked.

'Oh yes, what an insult to us elderly!' replied Anna-Greta.

'Now we ought to arrange something that is top quality instead!' Christina took out her powder compact, flipped up the mirror and improved her lipstick. She thought best when she was doing her make-up, and she used to always claim that to be so when the others complained because she was forever fussing with her appearance. But it had been quite a while since she had had a facelift, so it was really important to get it right with her lipstick and powder. 'We shall serve excellent gourmet food in a restaurant where you feel at home. Just imagine if we could find suitable premises close to the water and with a nice view too.'

'That's smart, Christina, smart indeed,' said Anna-Greta. 'I know, Hornsberg Strand on Kungsholmen. There was once an asphalt works and a brewery there, but now the area has been cleared and sanitized. They probably still have sites for sale. From there, you can look out across the water.'

'Hornsberg Strand, what a good idea,' exclaimed Martha.

'Yes, and there are empty premises that still haven't been rented out,' Anna-Greta went on. 'We could try to get a contract for one of those buildings.'

Martha took a pen and a notepad out of her waist bag.

'If we're going to open a restaurant, then we must make sure we get lots of guests. Have you an idea for a good theme?'

They all thought it was fun to develop the idea, and while

they looked at the gulls flying over the water, they discussed various themes and Martha made notes. When they had finished, the notepad was full of her jottings. She looked up.

'Well, do you want to hear what our dream restaurant should look like?'

They all nodded, and even Rake looked expectant. Martha thumbed through her notes and read out loud:

'All the staff should have a decent wage and employment conditions and the premises should be easily accessible for wheeled walkers and wheelchairs—'

'And even for those using walking sticks,' Anna-Greta chipped in.

They all nodded.

'It should be a quiet restaurant without background music. But to please everybody, there should be earphones at every table just like in an airplane so that those who wanted to could listen to their favourite artiste,' Martha went on.

'Good. Then those who are hard of hearing have the volume as high as they want,' Anna-Greta added.

'There should be a mixer at every table so that if something is too hard to chew, you only need to drop the bits of meat in and press a button,' Brains contributed.

There was sudden silence and they all looked at Brains to see if he was joking. But since he looked so serious, they all smiled and nodded.

'And quite all right if there isn't too much noise,' put in Anna-Greta, who had difficulty hearing in noisy environments. 'And the food shouldn't swim in sauce any old way.'

'Great,' said Martha turning the page in her notepad.

'Incidentally, Christina, I like your suggestion here. The idea that the restaurant should have a dating table for singles.'

'Exactly, a dating table for people on their own. They could be widows or widowers, and, of course, elderly bachelors and spinsters,' she said and looked pleased. 'They should have comfortable chairs and spicy, erotic food. And on the table there should be only one salt shaker and only one pepper shaker so that the guests will have to ask each other to pass them across. A neat idea, right?'

'Perfect, Christina.' Martha nodded.

'What a good idea,' Anna-Greta agreed, now being single again. 'And we could have speed dating on certain evenings in the week. Every dinner guest gets a number on a card that we put into a glass bowl. Then we draw two numbers now and then, and the numbers that come up get to date each other,' she brainstormed, with a dreamy look crossing her face. Anna-Greta had tired of her boyfriend Gunnar since he only talked computers and work all the time but knew nothing when it came to general knowledge. Life wasn't just mathematics and information technology. There was something called art, music and literature too. Culture. But all he knew besides figures were the names of the players in his favourite football team, AIK, and when Brynäs had won in ice hockey. She snorted to herself. No, she would have to get a new man in her life and why not start by dating at their own Penshy Restaurant?'

'And the restaurant shall have Sweden's best chefs and waiters, of course, but we shall only employ the elderly,' Martha went on.

'We ought to have some younger waitresses though,' Rake

66

interjected and Brains nodded in agreement. A brief discussion ensued, but they settled on a compromise where the employees should preferably be sixty plus. But they wouldn't write that down on paper because it might not comply with equality legislation and would thus risk being labelled age discrimination. And there could be exceptions to their rule, so younger people could be accepted in certain cases, said Martha with emphasis to mollify the men.

'What about the food?' Martha asked, happy that they all seemed to be committed to the idea.

'I want traditional Swedish dishes like oven-baked pancakes with pieces of sliced pork and with cranberry jelly,' said Rake, glancing at the inn close by. He was starting to feel hungry.

'No, we ought to be modern with vegetarian, health food and organic,' Christina announced.

'I won't go into a restaurant that doesn't have meatballs, stuffed cabbage rolls, falun sausage and root mash,' Brains protested.

'Of course we shall have the best food,' Anna-Greta agreed. 'And we can call the restaurant Gourmet Serenity.'

'But if we're going to open a restaurant, then we'll have to work. And it is high time to start!' Christina concluded.

8

The dining hall's grey walls, the long shabby tables and the bleached, greyish-green curtains in the windows felt very 1950s and weren't a bit homely. But in the high-security prison, interior decoration wasn't a priority; what counted here was incarceration. Some of Sweden's most dangerous prisoners were locked up here and money was spent on alarms and barbed wire rather than comfort.

It was time for today's lunch and some of the internees went up to the counter and helped themselves to fried herring and mashed potato. Others chose venison steak and cranberry sauce, while most of them took pizza. The fluorescent lamps flashed and the sound of cutlery and scraping chairs mixed with expletives and laughter. There was more noise than usual. Sweden had just won a qualifying match in football and they all tried to talk above the din.

Kenta Udd glanced at the TV and looked around at the others in the hall. Jeans, tattoos and grim countenances. They had long criminal records, every one of them. He himself had been in and out of prison many times and was beginning to tire of life behind bars. He always thought like that when he was inside, but unfortunately he had a tendency to end up in bad company when he was released, and soon he was back in again. Because he was a large and muscular man, he was popular in criminal circles. He was good at fighting and he made people pay their debts. The problem was that he sometimes hit too hard and then he would be sentenced for grievous bodily harm. But now he had got to know a girl on the Internet. She seemed really decent and they had met a few times when he had been out on day leave. If only he could break free of the criminal world and lead an ordinary everyday life instead. Open a workshop to repair cars, or a pizzeria or something like that. The girl knew her way around a kitchen and the idea of a pizzeria was attractive. Perhaps they could open one together. A roar could be heard from the TV and Kenta looked up.

'Fucking hell, what a goal! Zlatan's overhead kick, wow!' was heard from one of the gang.

'Not bad, but he's getting bloody lousy passes,' ventured a guy Kenta didn't recognize. A newcomer.

'Well, what of it, he can't just stand there waiting for the ball. He's got to make a bit of an effort too!' Kenta chipped in, burping loudly as he got up. He liked nosh, and waddled across to the counter for a second helping. He glanced at the trays and even though he knew it would be better to scoff some meat or fish, he took the pizza. Two large calzones to round off his lunch, nice one. He was just about to sit down again when he felt an elbow dig into his ribs.

'Hey, mate, Zlatan's great, don't groan about him!' The newcomer, a weasel-like guy in his thirties, gave him a penetrating look. The inmate, who had only been there a few days, had a muscular body and was tattooed so far up on his throat that you could see it above his T-shirt.

'But he's fucking lazy, right?'

'Nope, he's one of the best footballers in the world. OK?'

'OK, OK. All right he is,' muttered Kenta and sat down again. The weasel followed and sat down next to him. The guy had a sharp, inquisitive gaze. Short hair, blond and sticking out, and he had a ring in his ear.

'I'm Johan. Johan Tanto,' he said and held out his hand. 'But most folk call me Weasel. I used to play football.'

'Oh, fuck. I'm Kenta, Kenta Udd,' Kenta responded and looked at the newcomer. Yes, the guy had a very suitable nickname, that was for sure. Weasel was so thin and wiry that he could have slithered through any concrete pipe. But he had plenty of muscles too.

'Been here long?' he asked.

'A few years, demob in a month.'

'Why did the screws lock you up?'

'Fucking bad luck.'

'Ah, come off it. What did they get you for?'

'Coke and drugs, well, you know,' Kenta answered evasively.

'The usual, then. We get the cola for the upper classes, but we are the ones who get done for it.' Weasel wiped his mouth on the back of his hand.

'And you?'

'Roughed up a bloke a bit too much. He didn't pay, the bastard – a restaurant thing . . .'

'Ah, extortion and protection racket?'

'If you don't fork out, you've only got yourself to blame.

But the bloke refused and I lost it.' Weasel gobbled up his food and went on talking with his mouth full. 'The bloke started getting stroppy so in the end I gave him a free facelift. Didn't notice the CCTV.'

'Shit happens.'

'You should've seen him. I thought the fucking bastard had died.' Weasel suddenly looked serious. 'I'll fucking have to cool it a bit.'

Kenta gave him an inquisitive look, sliced up a large wedge of a calzone and opened wide. But the piece was too big and he started coughing. 'How many years did you get, then?'

'Four, but no way am I fucking sitting here that long.'

'Hard to get out of the place.' Kenta Udd tried again with the pizza and took a smaller bite this time.

'There's day leave, isn't there? Not a cat in hell's chance that I'm going to rot away inside. But you'll be out soon, right? Got anything lined up?'

'Thought I'd open a pizzeria. Launder money. But difficult getting the permits and all that.'

'Pizzeria?' Silence reigned for a few moments while Weasel observed him. 'So, restaurant and protection?' He got up to fetch some more nosh but stopped with the plate in his hand. 'Tell you what, if you can get me out of here, then I'll help you. There won't be any incendiaries or any of that shit. I promise. Think about it.'

Kenta eyed him a long time. Weasel seemed to be a man of action who knew what he wanted, a guy who got things to happen. Perhaps he was a mate you ought to keep on good terms with. If he helped him get out of the bunker, he himself might be able to return to a normal life at last. Because as an ex-con it wasn't easy to return to a life among ordinary folk; certainly not if you wanted to go into the restaurant business. If he kept on the right side of Weasel, then he might get protection.

9

Chief Inspector Per Jöback sat leaning over his computer playing Candy Crush. Occasionally amusing himself with video games was his way of clearing his brain. It allowed his grey cells to work in peace, and then he would find new ways to approach difficult cases. By now he had become quite advanced and he played at least an hour a day. It was amazing that he had become so fascinated by a video game! His friends said that he had become a Candy Crush abuser, but he categorically dismissed all such insinuations. In his most manic periods, he did, however, wonder if it was the same sort of kick you got from heroin, but he didn't dare express that thought out loud. No, he had total control; that much was certain! Suddenly he heard steps out in the corridor followed by a firm knocking on the door. Reluctantly, he looked up.

'Come in!'

'You've got a visitor,' announced his colleague, Jungstedt. 'It's him again.'

'Not Blomberg, surely?'

'Yes, the very same, and he has some pastries with him.'

'Say that I'm not in!'

'Too late. Enjoy yourself!' Jungstedt grinned and a few

moments later Blomberg stood in the door with a broad smile on his face. Chief Inspector Ernst Blomberg had been one of the police IT experts but had recently retired. There were many stories about him. It was said that he had admittedly been a skilled hacker but unfortunately less competent as a boss. When he became a pensioner, he received the usual leaving presents, but nobody had missed him since he left. Some officers did, however, feel sorry for the old guy since he had lost a large fortune with bad investments and now lived in a small bedsit in Sundbyberg with a small pension. He tried to improve his lot with freelance work, visiting the country's police stations and offering them his services. He could hardly survive on his pension.

'How nice to see you, Jöback,' Blomberg began, fishing out a coffee Thermos from his shoulder bag (always when he came visiting, Jöback said that the coffee machine was broken, so this time he had brought coffee with him). 'I'm not disturbing you, am I? I've got some proper old-fashioned coffee with me today, so we can enjoy that!' He patted the Thermos and laughed heartily. 'Well, how are things with you today?'

'Fine thank you, although we have too much to do,' complained Jöback, but he regretted it the very same moment.

'Then you might need some extra help? I've got a lot of experience and I still keep up with developments in the IT sector. Just let me know. Perhaps I can hack some computers for you?'

'Thank you, good for us to know, but for the time being our budget won't allow it.'

'But what about the Nordea bank robbery? You could do with some extra help there. How's it going, got any leads?'

'That's a tricky case, an international gang, but we're coop-erating with Interpol. Nasty business when the mafia comes to Sweden.'

'The mafia? I don't think so. That lot are ordinary bank rob-bers. Why would international gangs come to little Sweden? No, they can get much bigger hauls abroad.'

'You're wrong there, Blomberg. Remember the Military League? They robbed small banks out in country towns. What we've got here is a gang that concentrates on small countries instead.'

'Well, who knows! But help yourself to some pastries. Straight from the oven. It's surprising what one can get up to as a pensioner. I have even planted flowers and started to grow vegetables.' Blomberg gave a wide smile, opened the bag of pastries and put it on the table. Jöback had a sweet tooth and Blomberg knew that.

The chief inspector hesitated. If he indulged in the pas-tries, then Blomberg would certainly come back even more often. He must unfortunately abstain.

'Regrettably, I must think of my figure!' was his excuse.

'Oh, go on! Be daring! Don't say that I have baked in vain. I was really looking forward to coffee and cakes with you, and to discussing the latest cases. Perhaps I could give you a fresh new angle which might be the lead you need. Yes, help you, quite simply. I've quite a lot of experience to draw upon. It is so nice to sit here again and chat to old colleagues.' With a big smile, Blomberg took a first bite of one of the larger cakes.

It will take him at least fifteen minutes to finish that cake, and I can hardly shoo him out with a half-eaten cake in his hand, Jöback thought. Meanwhile, his mouth was watering.

He had worked without a break, he needed a cup of coffee and the smell of Blomberg's cakes was really getting to him. Perhaps he could take a little bit, after all. Just a titbit, a few crumbs.

'Well, have a cup of coffee at the very least,' Blomberg insisted, setting out two plastic mugs he had brought with him, and unscrewing the top of the Thermos. Then he poured out the coffee and gave Jöback a cup. 'Classic strong coffee and hot as can be!'

The smell of newly baked cakes mixed with the aroma from the coffee. The cakes were baked with lots of butter and eggs, and looked deliciously sweet. Blomberg saw Jöback's expression.

'Go on, just a taste! You can't just eat health foods all the time.'

The smell of the cakes pushed past the hairs in his nostrils, and Jöback had been up late last night. Besides, he had to write a lot of important emails. He needed a cup of coffee now and then, and, really, what was wrong with a few bites of cake? Then he could say that he was going away for a month, or tell them in reception never to let Blomberg in again. The retired chief inspector ought to stay at home and not visit his former work place several times a month! Jöback reached out for a cake.

'Difficult cases. So easy to get stuck in a rut,' said Blomberg while he sipped the hot coffee. 'When I worked with—'

'No, we haven't got stuck. We've got lots of ideas. Goodness, that was very tasty!' Jöback took a second cake.

'But that talk of an international gang. Are you sure about that? What if they are Swedish?'

'Oh no, not a chance.' Jöback finished the second cake, spilling some crumbs on the table.

'Even though you think you've got lots of ideas, you can still get stuck in a rut. I remember a case when everybody was convinced—'

'You don't need to worry. Like I said, we haven't committed ourselves to just one line of inquiry, but are going ahead on a broad front.'

'What about the League of Pensioners? Have you looked at them?'

'Those seventy-year-old guys who robbed a bank down in the south? That gang of old blokes? No, we're thinking of something more international.'

'No, not those old guys, I'm thinking of the oldies who spirited away the paintings from the National Museum last year.'

'Blomberg, that's history. The paintings came back, too. But these cakes were really tasty.' Jöback took a last mouthful and put his hands on the arms of his chair, ready to stand up.

'They were crafty, those pensioners, especially that woman called Martha. You can't exclude her and her friends. They might—'

'Oldies like that couldn't carry off a bank robbery. It's not on the map. No, we know what we're doing, you can rest assured. Now take the rest of the cakes and treat the girls in reception. They will certainly be pleased. I've got my hands full and regrettably we'll have to chat another time.' Jöback drank the rest of his coffee and turned on the computer.

'Nice bit of hardware you've got there. In my day the computers were much bigger and slower.'

'Yes, indeed, that's very likely, but—'

'If you run into problems accessing your computer or some awkward sites, I'll be happy to help out. Just let me know!' Blomberg leaned back in his armchair and showed no sign of moving. He slowly chewed his cake. 'And how are the indoor bandy games going on? Any goals?'

'As I say, work calls!' Jöback got up and held out his hand.

'Jöback, there's some coffee left. Won't you have some more?' Blomberg held up the Thermos. 'That League of Pensioners who kidnapped the paintings, you know. I can tell you about when—'

Chief Inspector Jöback showed Blomberg to the door and sighed with relief when finally his old colleague had left the room. There ought to be a law against pensioners visiting their former place of work, so that they couldn't come in three or four times a month. He went back to his desk and settled in front of the computer. He was going to show that Blomberg how a pro worked. Soon he would catch the robbers who had raided the Nordea bank. It would be a lesson for that smartarse. The perpetrators of the Pavarotti robbery would soon be behind bars!

10

Riddarfjärden, the bay of Lake Mälaren on the north side of the Old Town, lay black and shiny and you could hear the sound of the city not so very far away. The silhouette of the City Hall rose up dark and majestic on one side, and boats rocked in their moorings along the Norr Mälarstrand quay. In the background the traffic from the Slussen roundabout could be heard. Two darkly dressed men turned off from the street and into Rålambshov Park. Weasel stopped and waited for Kenta.

'We'll cut across the park and then take Smedsuddsvägen towards Marieberg,' he said, nodding towards the footpath. It was cold and damp, an August night without a full moon.

'OK,' said Kenta Udd, keeping his eye on Weasel's back and following close after him. Weasel had done what he had said, absconded on his first day leave and come to see him in his bedsit in Fredhäll. His mate needed a place to kip down and, in exchange for help with his new pizzeria, Kenta had gone along with helping him. After that, as a former prisoner and now new owner of a pizzeria, he would be able to sleep soundly at night. Weasel was fair. He had kept his promise and prevented several extortion attempts against the pizzeria.

79

But of course Kenta had also kept him hidden and provided food and a place to stay. Harbouring a prisoner on the run was tricky, and he could get into trouble himself. But that was life; you had to give and take all the time. He looked up. They had almost reached the abutment of the bridge.

'There! Can you see it?'

The shadow of a vessel could be made out under Västerbron Bridge. It was an old steam boat which had had an extra deck added on top with large windows. The Galaxy restaurant. Kenta inhaled the damp air through his nose and shivered. This restaurant had been given four stars in the local paper, but the owner hadn't had the sense to pay. The bastard had refused to fork out protection money and had employed people he chose himself, despite the fact that Weasel and his mates had put the pressure on. So he only had himself to blame. A bloke like that spoiled things for others in the business. He was a pariah, a fucking weed in the flower bed, and the restaurant must be got rid of.

Kenta and Weasel exchanged glances and approached cautiously. They each had a backpack and Kenta's was cutting into his shoulder, but Weasel walked so fast that Kenta didn't dare stop to adjust it. He was panting. Fuck, those extra kilos he had put on in prison, they could be felt now. He speeded up, looked around uneasily but couldn't see anything suspicious. It was 4.15 a.m. and most people were asleep. They had come across one or two people having a late night and those who were going to or from their night work. But here on Smedsuddsvägen it was silent and deserted. Not many people dared go out alone in the dark at this time of the day.

'Shush!' Weasel made a sign, adjusted his backpack and

went on. They continued in silence and when they went under the bridge they got a good view of the steamship. It lay there in the half-dark, the deck was empty and curtains were visible in the large windows. Inside you could see the outline of tables and chairs. Nobody seemed to be on board, but to be on the safe side Kenta and Weasel waited a while under the bridge arches and kept watch. It was dark and the boat rocked slightly in its moorings. There were no lights and no red flashing light from any burglar alarm. The owner must be a thicko, Kenta thought as his gaze swept over the deck and up towards the funnel where 'GALAXY' was written in large letters. Or perhaps he had a hidden alarm somewhere. It was a weird name for a restaurant anyway, but it was easy to remember. And a lot of people came to eat here. The place was well known for its cosy atmosphere and the excellent Dover sole and salmon with their home-made sauces. Over the last two years the place had been always full and had taken customers from other restaurants in the area. That was punishable. Weasel took off his backpack and pulled out the fenders, which he had slit up the sides.

'Jerry can!'

Kenta opened his backpack and Weasel pulled out the jerry can. He quickly looked in every direction, filled the fenders with rags soaked in petrol and made sure he had a long wick at the top. Once again he looked all around before giving the jerry can back to Kenta, who quickly put it back in his backpack again. There was a dreadful stink of petrol; he'd have to make sure he got rid of it as quickly as possible. Weasel put the fenders in a plastic bag and climbed on board. Once he was up on the deck he hung up the fenders and tied a tarred string between the wicks. Then he pulled out his cigarette lighter, pressed it and held the flame against the string. When it started burning, he nipped back to the stern and jumped back onto the quay. He waved to Kenta and together they ran from the place, crouching as low as possible. They were well into the trees before the flames shot up. The owner of the *Galaxy* hadn't wanted to employ the restaurant mafia's cleaners and had refused to buy meat and alcohol from the correct suppliers. He only had himself to blame.

11

The members of the League of Pensioners were sitting up in the tower relaxing when they heard the lorry. The got up unusually fast and went across to the window. The sound of the engine grew all the louder, the vehicle slowed down and after a while you could see the big concrete mixer lorry by the gate. The driver stopped and then started to back the lorry in through the gateposts.

'Is this really a good idea, Martha dear? You don't think we decided this too fast?' Brains gave his fiancée a worried look. He leaned forward to get an even better view. The big, heavy vehicle by the gate was on its way into the neighbour's garden. Charley Concrete had come an hour late and they had been waiting nervously. But now he was there with his concrete and there was no going back. Rake stood in the neighbour's garden in his overalls next to the swimming pool and guided the reversing concrete mixer lorry so that it could park by the side of the pool. Christina, who was acting as his wife, waved a little too, and now and then looked anxiously around her as if their neighbour might suddenly decide to come home just today from his round-the-world sailing trip.

'That pool cover would have fallen apart sooner or later,

and then we would have been exposed. We had no choice,' said Martha. 'We were forced to do something.'

'But Charley Concrete of all firms! Can we really trust him?' Anna-Greta couldn't keep her hands still.

'Oh yes, he's good, he only has foreign workers. His Polish drivers go home again after a month or so and they won't tell tales. Then he'll bring in a new gang,' Martha consoled them.

'But what if our neighbour suddenly returns,' Brains sighed. 'It's turned into such a nervous business, being a crook. So many things happen that we haven't counted on.'

'Yes, all right, but we have to take some risks and the refuse-collection lorry can't just stay there and rust away. Besides, there must have been some rubbish left inside. I mean, that stench . . .

'It was perhaps a little too ambitious with that fermented herring, but now things are as they are.' Martha folded her hands over her stomach and looked out through the window. 'The stupid thing about crimes is that the police always come after you and you have to cover all your tracks.'

'With concrete?'

'Yes, now that they have intensified their investigation.'

And that is what they had done. Martha was worried. The League of Pensioners had observed police cars in the area and every time a Volvo with 'POLIS' written on its side drove past, they had become all the more nervous. They drank herbal tea by the bucketful to calm their nerves, but instead were forever getting up in the middle of the night to go to the loo. In the end, Martha had concluded that they had had enough of all the worry, and that it was better that they did something radical about it. But what? Then Rake had given her an idea.

'I remember when we transported cement from Portland when I was young,' he had told them one evening out on the veranda. 'I had signed on as a deckhand on a ship, one of those cement freighters that went between Portland and New York. You can't imagine how scary it was. We were always afraid of colliding with other ships. Then we would have sunk straight away. Just like all the other ships that disappear in the Bermuda Triangle.'

'Usch, how horrible,' said Christina. 'To think that you've been involved in such dangerous things.'

'Yes, I have actually thought about writing my memoirs,' Rake went on and looked important. 'At my age it's a matter of urgency that you tell what you've been through before you forget it all. And like I said, I have been through quite a lot.'

'Did you say cement?' Martha suddenly asked. 'How many tons can a freighter hold?'

'Let me think, we had loads of a hundred tons and more . . .'

'Well, we would only need a few tons to fill the swimming pool. Do you get it? We can cover the lorry with cement!'

'Everything turns up sooner or later. But if it is buried in concrete it will never turn up!' Christina chortled.

'Exactly. We just fill the whole pool and will never need to worry again!' Martha went on.

And then she had got up and put lots of goodies on the dining trolley. Besides the cups of steaming hot tea, there was cloudberry liqueur and wafer biscuits, and the League of Pensioners sat out on the veranda until midnight. Martha's notepad filled with jottings and Brains busied himself with his pocket calculator to work out some figures. To be on the safe side, the whole gang had then gone out and measured the swimming pool to make sure they had it right. And when they lifted part of the covering they saw how the water had become coloured with rubbish, mould and rust.

'Yes, just look at this. It really is high time we did something,' said Martha.

But even so, a whole week passed before they plucked up the courage to go into action. The project was risky, to put it mildly. But only fifty metres away from their house there was a weighty piece of evidence – several tons of refuse-collection lorry. That was evidence that must be eliminated.

12

Charley Concrete backed the concrete mixer lorry the last bit up to the edge of the pool, stopped and pulled up the handbrake. He turned off the engine, climbed out of the driver's cabin and stood there with his arms folded and stared. At the edge of the black pool cover you could see several black pipes sticking up.

'What the hell is this?' He pointed at the protruding pipes.

'The concrete is going down there.'

'But what the fuck do you need the concrete for?!'

'That's secret, a high-security shelter, you know,' said Rake. 'National security and all that.'

'So you want me to pump the concrete down into the pipes you mean?'

'Exactly, you see the joints there? Just connect your pipe and start pumping. My men will do the rest,' said Rake pointing at the connecting pipes that Brains had laid next to the edge of the pool. Under the pool cover several manifolds then distributed the concrete so that it would flow evenly into all parts of the pool. 'The shelter will accommodate at least ten people, so my men will have lots of work.'

'Yeah, yeah, typical fancy Djursholm ideas! You can't be

satisfied with what's good enough for everybody else, you have to have your own fucking shelter too,' mumbled Charley Concrete shaking his head. Muttering to himself, he climbed up into the cab again, started the engine, got the pipe into position and tried to connect it to the others by the pool. But the joints didn't fit. He tried two others and then a smaller pipe, and finally that worked. Thank God for that, because now the concrete mixer was in full operation.

'You're not going to change your mind? So you want me to pump the concrete down your pipes?' Charley Concrete asked again and looked at Rake with some scepticism.

'Yep, sure as hell. And the quicker the better. I've got men waiting to start after we've got the concrete in.'

'All right, then,' said Charley Concrete. He called to his workers, checked the pipe connection one last time, got hold of the joystick on the control panel and started the pump. Soon after that, concrete started to move through the lorry's pipe, and you could hear a slurping and sloshing sound as it ran into the pipes protruding from the pool cover. After half an hour, Charley and his men had emptied the mixer lorry.

'Great, then just two loads to go,' said Rake, offering him a portion of Scandinavian snus. 'We've got two mixers going at maximum in the cellar now, and we need the rest of the concrete as quickly as possible. The men who are going to do the bricklaying will arrive soon.'

Charley Concrete nodded. This was about delivering concrete and not about asking questions. Just as long as he got paid in cash. His Polish workers did a good job. They worked hard and didn't ask about holiday pay or employer contributions or tax and other such nonsense. As long as they got their money, that was all that mattered. However, a few who had now settled in Sweden were more difficult. They had long lunch breaks and coffee breaks, and stopped working at five o'clock. But his men kept working until the job was finished. No messing. He got out his mobile phone, made a quick call and turned to Rake.

'The rest of the concrete will soon be here.'

Brains, Martha and Anna-Greta, who had stood at the window upstairs and watched, had become so absorbed that they had completely forgotten lunch. That's how nervous they were. Watching and knowing what was under the covering was pure torture. Several times, Martha had wanted to go down and give orders, but Brains had stopped her.

'CC is Rake's thing,' he had said.

'CC? But we haven't got TV cameras down there, have we?'

'CC – Charley Concrete – is Rake's project and you ought to stay in the background.'

When another two lorries had emptied their loads, the concrete in the pool started to rise.

'Oh goodness me!' said Anna-Greta.

'OK, it's all there. Now we have to wait for it to harden,' said Brains.

'Right, so in the meantime we can go across to Rake and help him get everything in order,' said Martha.

With quick steps they went over to their neighbour's garden. When they reached the swimming pool, Rake and Christina stood there staring down into the former pool.

'A good job you've come,' said Rake with some snus under

his upper lip. 'As soon as Charley and his gang have left, we can remove the pool cover.'

'No, no, for fuck's sake don't do that. The concrete is wet. Are you planning a mafia graveyard?' Brains joked.

'No, but we must keep an eye on it as it sets,' said Rake, drying his brow with his bandanna. He was looking rather glassy-eyed and he didn't calm down until he had paid Charley Concrete and they had driven off with their lorries.

'Uff, now it's over. Those guys made me nervous,' he said, wiping his forehead and then standing there with his bandanna in his hand. Much of the day had passed and there was a pleasantly cooling afternoon breeze.

'Are you sure they swallowed that talk about the fallout shelter?' Martha asked.

'It seems so. I said something about Russia and that we live in troubled times. And then I rambled on about the atom bombs they tested in the 1950s and that you never knew what could happen in the future.'

'Well, I can agree with you as far as the future is concerned,' said Anna-Greta.

'I'm glad the Polish workers have left.' Rake smiled and held his bandanna up in the wind so that it fluttered. 'Man the rigs! Full sail!'

The very next moment, the wind caught his bandanna, and it whirled around before vanishing in the direction of a pipe.

'Oh no! not my favourite bandanna!' Rake called out, rushing after it. But in his haste he ran straight into a garden gnome, tripped and fell head first against the knee-high concrete lion next to the steps. His forehead hit a front paw and the hard blow made him see stars. He collapsed in a heap while his bandanna was sucked into the pipe and ended up in the concrete.

'Rake!' howled Christina.

But Rake didn't move. He'd been knocked out.

When he came to his senses again, he was very embarrassed and acted as if nothing had happened. And he categorically refused to go to see a doctor. Not until he started feeling nauseous and to vomit did he agree to go to A & E. He was never sick, and tripping over a garden gnome wasn't reason enough to require the intervention of the health service which was overworked as it was. In the end, Christina managed to get him into a taxi and take him to Danderyd Hospital. It was Friday evening and the start of the weekend rush, and Christina had heard that you should never be admitted to hospital at such a time, but now they had no choice. Rake was looking very poorly and she didn't dare wait until Monday when the ordinary doctors would be on duty again. She hated hospitals and she got the creeps as soon as they set foot in the A & E reception area. People were coughing, looked pale and dejected, and a child with a runny nose was walking around sneezing, so she was worried about catching something.

'We've got an emergency case here,' said Christina, grabbing hold of the first white coat that passed her. It was worn by a young woman with dark, beautiful eyes and long black hair. She had a name label which said 'Camilla, Nursing Assistant'.

'I'll be with you soon, just have to—', she excused herself, rushing past so quickly that Christina didn't have time to catch her explanation. She took a queue number and sat

91

down with Rake in the waiting room. Christina looked around her while she fidgeted with the queue-number ticket. The room was barren with light-grey walls, brown sagging armchairs and some low tables with magazines. There was a faint smell of disinfectant.

Rake had stopped vomiting but still seemed rather groggy, more or less as if he had been up in a boxing ring and had suffered quite a beating. When the nurse appeared again, Christina jumped up from her chair and stood in the way.

'I phoned in advance and you said that we should hurry. He is very poorly.'

'No, no, there's nothing wrong with me,' said Rake glancing with interest at the young nurse.

'Sssh!' Christina prodded him in the ribs and turned to the nurse again.

'He had a blow to his forehead and I've heard that can be dangerous.'

'*A seaman loves the waves . . .*' sang Rake.

'Yes, we shall admit him, but unfortunately I'm on my own just now. We are slightly understaffed, so – Yes, the doctor will have a look at him—' That very same moment, the entrance door banged open and three drunken youths stepped into reception. They shouted and roared and two of them had to support each other so as not to fall over. The youths were bleeding from cuts on their faces and on their hands, and their clothes were torn. One had had his nose pushed in and blood was dropping everywhere, the other was bleeding from his upper lip.

'We need a doctor. Now!' slurred the youth with the swollen lip.

'He's busy, I'm afraid.'

'Where the fuck is the doctor?' roared his mate.

'Pah, we'll go in here,' said the swollen lip and wobbled towards the door which said 'DOCTOR'. He took a few unsteady steps and almost fell over an elderly lady who lay on a stretcher trolley in the corridor waiting to have some stitches. She had hurt her hand.

'A bedpan, I need a bedpan,' the old lady moaned.

'Yes, of course, I'll come at once,' replied the nurse while trying to fend the youths away from the door. Then the one with the swollen lip vomited.

'Oh fucking hell!' said his mate and he held his nose. 'Sister, come here and wipe up this fucking mess!'

'Sit down for the time being and we'll take care of that,' said the nurse in as friendly a tone as she could, laying a calming hand on the youth's shoulder. 'The doctor will be here soon.'

The stressed nurse managed to get the youths to sit on some chairs, then returned to Christina.

'A blow to the head, right. I'll phone X-ray and warn them. The doctor will be here any second. You can sit down and wait.'

'I stumbled over a garden gnome,' Rake informed her.

'He is very poorly,' said Christina. 'What if there is an internal haemorrhage?'

'Then I fell onto a lion's paw,' Rake went on, and pointed at his forehead.

'It was a stone sculpture, a stone sculpture of a lion, that is,' Christina explained. 'Rake needs attention, he has vomited.'

'*A seaman loves the waves . . .*' Rake went on humming, but then stopped himself and started to sing a classic drinking song: '*Cheers to Santa, fill our glasses and have fun . . .*'

Now the nurse reacted.

'A head wound, yes, right. I'm sorry, this will have to be attended to at once,' she said, and stumbled in the direction of the doctor's room. Then the door opened and the duty surgeon could be seen.

'How long must I wait, nurse? The patient in here needs stitches, and I need assistance. I said that half an hour ago.'

'Yes, yes, I'm coming, I'm on my own this evening, it isn't so easy—'

'I must do the suture now!' said the doctor. 'Not yesterday and not tomorrow, but now!'

'We must take him first!' protested the nurse. 'Head injury.'

The doctor looked confused, went back into his room and closed the door. Then Rake lost his patience.

'Suture this and suture that. What the hell are we doing here? They haven't got time to deal with us,' he muttered. With a dissatisfied snorting, he got up, causing the magazines to fall off the table. 'We're going home now. A man can look after himself.' He pulled out his steel comb from his trouser pocket and looked around for a mirror. A bit giddy, he made his way to the toilet and had just turned on the light when Christina caught up with him.

'You must take it easy, Rake. Head injuries are not child's play,' she said and she put her arm under his. 'Now please come with me.'

'Pah, there's nothing wrong with me,' Rake calmed her

and lifted the comb to his hair to straighten his parting. Then he caught sight of the enormous bruise on his forehead, the swelling that had formed a soft hill and the dried blood that had seeped out of the wound.

'Oh my God, help!' he gasped and then a heavy thud could be heard. He had passed out again.

Christina sat there and kept an eye on him all night between blood tests and X-rays. Towards the morning he finally got to see a specialist who had reassuring news. Nothing could be seen on the X-ray, he had concussion and must keep still the next twenty-four hours.

'I haven't time for that,' Rake answered and adjusted the bandage around his head.

'Rake, please,' said Christina. 'Take it easy!'

'Well, it would be for your sake, then,' he muttered, taking her hand and patting her on the cheek. She had been by his side the whole night and had supported him, a real friend. And to be honest, he wasn't feeling too good and he thought it was nice to have her nearby. He looked at her with a thoughtful expression and felt warm inside. Yes, Christina was a good sort and he could rely on her. If he hadn't felt so poorly he would have liked to cuddle a bit.

'If it feels worse, you must phone,' said the doctor.

'It won't,' said Rake and he headed in the direction of the exit. In the doorway he almost collided with the nurse. She smelled nicely of almond and violet and was less stressed now.

'The bandage suits you,' she said with a friendly smile. And then Rake almost fainted a third time. Nurses, he thought, how they slaved away! The next time they handed out their bank robbery money they must be certain to include nursing staff and lowly paid home-care workers too.

The next morning Rake slept a long time and didn't hear when Christina's son Anders came with a load of gravel and two tons of earth which were arduously shovelled over the concrete. (At any rate, he pretended he didn't hear anything.) Finally, all except Rake rolled out the turf they had bought at the garden centre. It was a bit tricky but with Anders' help they managed in the end. They took a few steps back and looked at what they had achieved. Then they walked right round the former swimming pool, looked at each other and nodded. Now no visitor could have any idea what was hidden under the soil, and a sense of calm returned to them all. All except Christina, who felt that she must still keep an eye on Rake. When they were back in the house, she took a book and went and sat in an armchair in Rake's room to be close if anything happened. When he was finally on his feet again, a few hours later, she found it difficult to help him because he wanted to walk unaided. He managed to make his way down to the others in the kitchen, but then they all said that he looked unusually pale and something of a sorry figure – not the Rake they knew.

'Pah, I'm all right,' he assured them and sat down slowly and deliberately. And there he sat and kept quiet for a long time, while now and then looking out of the window towards the neighbour's. After drinking a cup of coffee and eating a bun, he put his hands on his hips and announced in a decisive voice:

'You know what? We must write to our neighbour. The changed appearance of the garden must be explained in some way.'

13

Martha had been sitting in the library phrasing and rephrasing the letter they would send to Bielke. What did you write to a neighbour you didn't know when you had just filled his beloved swimming pool with concrete? Sorry, the load of concrete was dumped in the wrong place? Or, I promise not to do it again? This wasn't easy, but suddenly Martha realized how they should do this. Nothing could beat true bureaucracy.

She giggled to herself, fetched a chocolate wafer biscuit and a cup of coffee, turned her computer on and started typing. Half an hour later, she was finished.

'That's it,' she said in an exhilarated mood, pressing the 'print' button. The printer clicked and in a few seconds the sheet of paper landed in the basket. That same moment, Brains came into the room. She picked up the sheet of paper and handed it to him. 'Have a look at this. I've tried a few different versions. What do you think of this one?'

Brains looked at her expectantly, lowered his spectacles onto his nose and started to read.

Message to the owner of property 1:374, Auroravägen 4, Djursholm, Danderyd.

On the plot comprising property 1:374 Djursholm, severe sanitary problems have arisen, for which reason the municipality has been obliged to take action.

Your swimming pool has for a considerable time been invaded by the pathogenic bacteria planktus mytos truxis which has affected the entire pool. Since this bacteria and even other organisms in your pool are known to spread diseases, the municipality's environment department was forced to take action.

We have repeatedly written to you about this, but since you have not answered these letters and nobody has opened the door when we have visited, we have finally been forced to deal with the acute problem ourselves. As the decay in the pool had reached such an advanced stage, we regrettably have had to take extraordinary measures. As a consequence, the pool has been sanitized, filled with concrete and a lawn has been laid on top. The cost for this amounts to 280,000 kronor.

As soon as you have arranged this with your insurance company, we request that you pay this sum to the municipality's bank account number 0537-8896929, Djursholm Street and Property Department. The payment slip should be marked with the reference 1:374 Djursholm.

Yours sincerely,
Elizabeth Olsson
Environment Department
Danderyd Municipality

Brains pushed his glasses up onto his forehead and laughed out loud. He tenderly stroked Martha on her cheek.

'You've got quite a nerve! That is our bank account. First you wreck our neighbour's pool, then you want him to pay for it!'

'Yes, you're right, but that's how things are done nowadays. Municipalities upgrade a road going past your property, a road that you don't want, and have never asked for, and then you – as the property-owner with frontage – have to pay for it regardless. We are in keeping with the times, Brains.'

'Ah, that's how it is,' he mumbled and glanced out through the window. It looked nice out there now. A green lawn lay where the swimming pool had been and Christina had followed Rake's instructions and put some large flower pots filled with showy plants along the former rim of the pool. In the middle of the lawn stood a table, a parasol and elegant garden furniture from Mornington. It looked as if the garden had always been like that.

'Pah, I was just joking. We can't put our account number there so that they can trace us,' Martha giggled. 'And it does look nice now with that lawn, but there will be chaos when our neighbour comes home. Seriously speaking. Do you think it might be a good idea to go away somewhere for a while so that nobody will connect us with this? At least till things have calmed down.'

'But we were going to get married, weren't we?' Brains's smile withered away.

'Yes, of course, but if we end up in jail, then we would be separated for several years. No, we should be together, shouldn't we?' said Martha, and she hugged him. She waved the letter in front of his face. 'We'll post this and then go off travelling. We ought to lie low a while. We can regard it as a honeymoon trip,' she ventured.

'Do you believe that yourself? What about the drainpipe money? Weren't you going to fetch that?'

'Yes, that's right,' said Martha. 'Perhaps we ought to do that. It'll take a bit of time before all our bank accounts in the Caribbean are working, and, like I said, health care is in crisis. We do have five million up there in the drainpipe, and we ought to give that away.'

'What was it I said? A drainpipe is more important than what we have together.' Brains sighed.

'But Brains, dear. It was you who suggested we should fetch that money, and you were quite right. God knows how long banknotes will survive stuck inside a drainpipe. Let's fetch the money now and then we can leave after that. We can go somewhere nice where nobody would look for us, and there we can really look after each other.'

But when she looked up, Brains wasn't there. He had already gone off.

That evening, he kept away and didn't come down to dinner. The man in her life who always used to be warm and comforting and who had her best interests at heart was, quite simply, grumpy. Martha felt deeply worried and realized that she must take better care of him and do something drastic to get him in a good mood again. She thought it over. Why not let him be in charge of Operation Drainpipe so that he would have something exciting to occupy himself with? People had to feel responsibility and have something meaningful to do, if they were going to feel comfortable.

★

Martha raised the issue the next day when they drank their evening tea. It was eight o'clock when they sat down with a cup of tea out on the veranda. A cosy glow came from the old chandelier hanging from the ceiling, and they had three pillar candles on the table. The League of Pensioners had just finished dinner and even though Brains hadn't said very much, he had at least joined them. Outside the tower room you could hear the wind in the trees and a tile was rattling up on the roof. It sounded as if it might soon fall off. Just like the other big villas from around 1900, their old house needed maintenance. But they didn't have time for that now.

'Listen, everybody, we must get that money out of the drainpipe before it rots away,' Martha began and she put her teacup down. 'Nobody knows how long a pair of tights will last.'

'Oh yes, mine were of the best quality and they had re-inforced heels and toes,' said Anna-Greta, looking almost offended.

'And I wrapped the whole bundle very carefully in those black bin bags. It ought to last. And the drain pipe is right next to the balcony in the Princess Lilian suite. We can go out there and fish it out. Believe me, that five million is, so to speak, already ours,' was Rake's opinion.

'But only presidents and super celebrities stay there. Don't forget we're talking about the Grand Hotel. I don't think they would let us in again.'

'Putin or Obama will have to fish out that pair of tights next time they are in Stockholm,' Rake said, grinning.

They all seemed interested except Brains, who hadn't said

anything at all yet. Martha stirred her tea and looked at him out of the corner of her eye. He wasn't his usual self.

'Brains, what do you say? The staff at the Grand Hotel are not likely to let us in to that suite again, but we must get at that money.'

'Hmm,' said Brains.

'But I'm sure you've got an idea.'

He was silent a long time and managed to guzzle three oat cakes before he finally opened up.

'I know,' he suddenly said and immediately looked a little happier. 'We don't need to stay at the Grand Hotel for eighty thousand kronor a night. We can rent an aerial work platform, a skylift.'

'A skylift!' they all shouted and looked much brighter.

'Yes, absolutely. We'll rent a really high skylift, pretend that the drainpipe needs repairing and take it home with us. Then the loot is ours.'

'Fantastic, Brains. To think that you can come up with such things! But do you really believe it will be as easy as you say?' Martha wondered.

'Yes, of course. There are lots of different skylifts and you can get a driving licence for them in one day.'

'All right, then,' said Martha pulling out her notepad and a pen. 'You know what, I think it would be best if you men take care of this. And then we others can be on stand-by down on the ground as best we can.'

Brains and Rake exchanged some quick glances, nodded and got up. They went up to the bar cupboard. Brains found it hard to choose among the cognac bottles, but eventually took out the most expensive.

'A drop of this, then we'll certainly work out how to do it.'

And that's what they did. Operation Drainpipe was now the boys' own project.

The countdown to Operation Drainpipe was finished, and Brains and Rake had gone about the task with great seriousness. Since Rake was still troubled by headaches after his concussion, Brains had to do the lion's share. In a very decisive and bellowing voice, which sounded most authoritative, he had announced to the rental company in Solna that he needed to rent a skylift for a delicate renovation job at the Grand Hotel. The hotel with its fine old traditions was going to get a very important but secret visit from the other side of the Atlantic, so it was urgent. Then there had been no problem about renting a skylift, and Martha couldn't praise him enough for his energetic efforts. But since neither of the elderly gentlemen considered that they could carry out the mission, Christina's son Anders had been sent on a course in Oskarshamn and been given a driving licence. A one-day course at the company called Motivera had left him thinking that he had now mastered virtually every skylift in the whole world and the driving licence had given him an impressive degree of self-confidence. In fact, so much so that Christina was a little worried.

'But, my boy, do you really think you can disconnect that drainpipe from the skylift platform and then bring it down without anything going wrong?' she asked.

'No problem. I know exactly how to do it,' answered Anders.

'It's one thing to drive the skylift, but you must carry out a tricky job too,' said Martha.

'Pah, it's actually quite simple. You've just got to use your common sense,' said Anders. He was going to get a fancy sum for the task when the millions had been recovered and he was very keen. As usual, he was unemployed and he needed all the contributions he could get.

'But aren't you going to practise first?' Christina wondered.

'No, no, Mum, it's a piece of cake!'

Anders sounded very cocky and this made Christina nervous. Self-confident men who 'can do everything' are *always* a great source of worry.

It was an early Sunday morning, with almost no traffic and only a few people outside the hotel. Shortly after midnight, the League of Pensioners had cordoned off the area outside the Cadier bar with orange plastic cones and hung up a sign: WORK IN PROGRESS. And that was true, after all, even though it wasn't an ordinary job. The idea was that Anders would dismantle the part of the drainpipe with the money in it, replace it with a similar metal pipe and then descend to ground level again. Once on firm land, it was simply a question of loading the money into the minibus and driving back to Djursholm, while Anders, for his part, returned the skylift to the rental company. Since the owner of the skylift had only advertised his services on a popular site on the Internet he would probably not be a serious entrepreneur and there would be no invoices and receipts. No, the plan seemed to be watertight. Besides, Anders had checked the diameter, joints and lengths of the drainpipe. Everything was well prepared.

The sun was shining and it was one of those early late-summer mornings when the air was clear and the colours vivid. Inside the minibus, the League of Pensioners sang an Evert Taube ballad. This gave them strength and self-confidence, which they really needed now. They all felt ready for action. On a morning like this, it was simply impossible not to be in a good mood and be very optimistic. Brains laid his hand over Martha's.

'Now we'll sort this out and then we'll have one problem less, just you wait and see, Martha dear.'

'I'm really glad about that, I can assure you. It feels so good that you are here, it makes me calm.'

Brains gave her hand an extra squeeze and Martha felt most warm all over. It was really lovely to have a life comrade like she had when they ran into problems. The task was difficult and in the worst scenario they could get caught.

'That's nice, Anders is already here,' said Brains pointing to a large lorry with a skylift next to the Cadier bar. 'Now everything is ready to go!'

Anders, who had been in Solna and had fetched the lorry, had driven up to the Grand Hotel and parked next to the Cadier bar. When he caught sight of the familiar minibus he got out and made a thumbs-up sign to the others. The cones were still in place even though the warning sign hung at a bit of an angle. Besides the minibus with Christina and her friends, there was nobody to be seen in the vicinity. The Waxholm archipelago local ferry boats rocked in their moorings and on the other side of the bay the royal castle was reflected in the shiny water surface. Anders seemed pleased as he looked at the Rothman 270, a skylift that he had heard a great deal of good about on his training course. The skylift was mounted on a lorry and looked solid and stable.

'How's it going?' Christina wondered when she arduously climbed out of the minibus with the others and went across to Anders. 'You will be careful, won't you, so that you won't get stuck or fall down?' she said, looking anxiously at the transport basket at the end of the long hydraulic arm.

'No problem, Mother. This is a top-notch skylift. It can be steered up and down and sideways, and the basket can rotate so you can get at everything. It couldn't be better,' he answered, humming while he fastened the belt with the control panel around his waist.

'Nice belt you've got there,' said Brains, prodding his waist. The skylift started buzzing.

'No, no, don't touch!' Anders exclaimed, horrified.

'Just joking. You will work discreetly, right?'

'Yes, of course! With a skylift more than twenty metres high I shall be as invisible as I can!'

'I meant noise. If you accelerate slowly it won't be so loud.'

'Yes, I shall select silent mode,' Anders muttered and climbed into the basket. He took a few steps inside it, but by mistake bumped into the basket railing so that the control panel was squeezed. The joystick was pushed right up, the engine accelerated and he disappeared up into the air.

'Oh good God!' exclaimed Anna-Greta, clasping her hands together. Christina didn't dare look.

Anders was sweating up there in the basket. Accompanied by a strong buzzing noise, he was going higher and higher and not until the skylift had almost reached its maximum height did he regain control of the beast. Somewhat shaken, he looked out over the edge of the basket railing and quickly drew back when he saw how high up he was. He suddenly felt dizzy. Vertigo, oh heavens above, he suffered from acrophobia and he hadn't even thought about that!

He avoided looking down and tried to concentrate. Anna-Greta's tights were stuffed deep down inside the drainpipe's second section, counting from the balcony gutter, so he needed to steer the basket so that he was right next to the pipe. With trembling fingers he gripped the control panel's joystick and steered it so that the basket ended up in the right place. Uff, he heaved a sigh of relief, he had managed it. As long as he took things slowly and didn't look down, it would be OK. But the drainpipe looked rustier, now that he was up close, than it had done when he had reconnoitred earlier with binoculars. To start with, he was worried about how Anna-Greta's tights had fared in the damp mess inside the pipe, but he consoled himself when he remembered that they in turn were wrapped inside black bin bags and secured with Rake's seaman's knots. It should be OK.

He carefully manoeuvred the basket so that he came close up to the pipe joint. He stopped there and leaned forward to twist the pipe loose. His hands took a firm grip of the metal and he tried to turn the pipe. But however hard he struggled, he couldn't budge that section. He tried again but nothing moved. The pipe had rusted and the joint was no more. Anders felt a growing panic. He couldn't take the entire drainpipe, could he? But what if he tried to unscrew two sections at once, would that work? But then he must go almost up to the balcony of the Princess Lilian suite. Anders tried to think what was best. What had he learned at the skylift course? Well, the best strategy was to use very small movements and take it nice and easy, as the course instructor had explained.

Nice and easy, yes, and – most particularly – nice and slow! He steered the basket towards the first roof ridge, round the sharp copper edging and in towards the sloping roof. This was going very nicely indeed, and if the Princess Lilian suite was empty this weekend, it should all work out very well. Slowly, oh so slowly, he steered the basket so that it stopped right under the upper opening of the drainpipe. Once again, he breathed deeply, flexed his muscles and tried to twist the pipe. He twisted, pulled, shook – he did everything he could to loosen the damned pipe but nothing moved. Not even if he had the best anti-rust liquid in the world, could he manage this. The old metal drainpipe ought to have been replaced years ago.

But luckily he had a plan B. He had taken Brains's invention with him, a long fishing rod with a fishing line with several barred special hooks. 'If something goes wrong, you can always resort to the fishing trick,' Brains had said, and patted him on the back. Anders had wanted to avoid this. Dangling a fishing line down a drainpipe was not exactly his thing . . .

He moved the joystick downwards and the skylift went a bit higher. If there were guests in the suite, it was to be hoped that they wouldn't wake up. He looked down to the street below and could see the faces of the others looking up at him. Oops, he got all dizzy again. He felt a strange hollow sensation in his stomach, his legs seemed to lose their strength and he sank down against the basket's railing. The skylift on the course hadn't been anywhere near as high as this. But if he could just get hold of the drainpipe and hold on to it. No, he must pull himself together. He breathed deeply a few times until he felt that he had control again. Then he steered the basket towards the uppermost part of the drainpipe. When he was about one and a half metres above the top opening, he stopped, extended the fishing rod, held it over the opening and lowered the hooks. He moved the rod a little sideways until he felt that something was stopping the line. It didn't seem to be hard and it was slightly uneven. Besides, it was on one side of the pipe without blocking it completely, just like the sack of money would be. It must be the package with the tights. Lovely! He started to jig the line so that the barbs on the hooks would catch, and he felt rather silly. Not only was he standing there with a fishing line down a drainpipe, but he was also jigging too. At that very moment, he heard a sound and when he looked up he saw a girl wearing only panties standing on the balcony of the Princess Lilian suite. She called out into the suite.

'Darling, somebody is standing there fishing in the drainpipe.'

'Yes, right, sweetie, but come back inside now. Don't stand out there and ruin your good reputation.'

'Don't be silly. It's true, I promise. There's a bloke out there fishing in the drainpipe. With a real fishing rod.'

'Has he caught any fish?' A loud laugh could be heard from inside the suite. 'Come on now, come in. You've drunk too much again.'

'But look yourself, then!'

'Ha, ha! I hope he gets a good catch. What about something nice for breakfast? Can you get us a mackerel?'

'Now you're being stupid!'

'What about pike?'

'Idiot!'

Anders heard angry steps and realized that the woman had gone inside to the man. Or perhaps, quite simply, gone to fetch him? Anders quickly pulled up the line and put the fishing rod back in the basket. He had better get out of there, and quick. He pushed the joystick right down but happened to nudge the rotation control too. He found himself whirling round and round at high speed in the basket while the skylift went back and forth under the balcony like a windscreen wiper. Then the man came out.

'What the hell?'

'I told you there was a bloke out here fishing.'

'Fishing? But this is a fucking monster!'

Anders pulled the control panel closer, there was a roaring sound and the next second the basket started to descend rapidly down to the lorry. With a final effort, Anders managed to stop the descent just in time and land softly. Trembling, he stepped down onto the street.

'What happened?' Martha asked.

'Er, the machinery got jammed.' Anders shrugged his shoulders as if it wasn't a big deal.

'So it wasn't human error, then?' she wondered.

Then Anders started swearing, stumbled into the lorry and started the engine. He lowered the side window.

'We must get out of here straight away!'

'And you were so self-assured. What happened, my boy?' Christina asked. But Anders had already raised the window again.

'Well, that's several thousand kronor in skylift rent down the drain. Not to mention all the millions still in the drain-pipe,' Anna-Greta sighed.

'Usch, these machines are always a bit awkward. We'll go home now and have a cup of tea with scones. Into the bus everybody!' Martha called out. She opened the minibus door and got into the driving seat.

'Well, I vote for coffee with something strong,' Rake muttered as he got into the back seat, while Brains sat quietly. He and Rake had been in charge of this mission and he himself had intended showing Martha that he was in control of everything. And then it had turned into a fiasco. Martha glanced in the rear-view mirror and saw his glum countenance. She made a U-turn and drove quickly out of the parking area in the direction of the NK department store and Sveavägen. Then she said:

'That wasn't us. It was youth that faltered. Now we're going home and we can plan a new attempt. It always works out in the end. If at first you don't succeed . . .' she said.

Brains hummed a while and said nothing, but his heart was full. He realized why he was so fond of Martha. One of the reasons was that she always had something encouraging to say. Even if Doomsday was near, she would still retain her good mood. Isn't it interesting, she would say, this is bound to be an exciting experience. He gathered his thoughts and clasped his hands over his stomach.

'Sometimes a failure is a good thing. You learn something and that can always give you new ideas.'

'Just what I think,' Martha answered and her voice sounded nice and warm. 'And you know what? Next time you and Rake will think up the ultimate solution.'

'Maybe. But first we must take it easy, a change of scenery perhaps? There has been so much going on for quite a while now,' Brains said.

'Yes, why not visit Gothenburg?' Rake suggested.

Martha glanced at them in the rear-view mirror. A change of scenery and lying low for a while didn't entail delaying their plans. On the contrary, they could well come up with fresh ideas. And if it made Rake happy, then why not?

14

Martha and her friends played cards while the train rolled along through the Swedish countryside. Considering that they were on the wanted list, they were far too noisy and high-spirited and really ought to calm down a little, but they were all pleased to finally be going somewhere. They had been nervous right up until they had started their journey. When they had left the Grand Hotel, Martha had almost collided with a police car, and if Brains hadn't called out to warn her things could have been very nasty. On the news that evening, they heard that the police had called in extra staff and intensified their investigation. That had felt most worrying. In her eagerness to get hold of more money, Martha had forgotten that they were already actually on the wanted list. She didn't see herself as a criminal; it was more a case of the League of Pensioners having taken on the task of re-establishing the good old society that had started to decay in the 1980s. But then, of course, they must be careful so that the police didn't catch them. Because if they ended up in prison, who would help the weak and marginalized?

Brains had been a bit in the dumps since the failed attempt to retrieve the booty from the drainpipe, but Martha had done everything to console him. She bought wigs for them all so that they could go out and around town in a light disguise. She had gone with him twice to Clas Ohlson so that he could study the latest technical apparatuses and then they had gone to flea markets and the City Mission's charity shop to find some solid old tools. They had also been to visit a car and motorcycle fair and she had stood by his side and waited while he studied the various exhibits. She knew that if only Brains could potter around among technical objects he liked, then he would soon be his old nice and happy self. She even went so far as to take a taxi to the Delselius coffee shop in Gustavsberg and buy his favourite cakes. She did what she deemed necessary to put him in good spirits. When the atmosphere among the friends was nice and cosy, and they were all feeling happy like they used to, that was when Martha had proposed that they should now take the chance and make the trip to Gothenburg. Above all, it would do Rake good. The concussion had taken its toll and even though he pretended that everything was back to normal again, he still went to bed unusually early in the evening. On the train towards his old home city, however, he had become a lot more lively.

He had already started cheating when they played Bullshit. Cards disappeared all the time and it didn't get any better when they changed to bridge and canasta. Now and then, a card would turn up in the aisle, a card that nobody could explain where it had come from, but since Rake was winning all the time they did, of course, have their suspicions. However, nobody said anything since they were all pleased that their comrade was in a buoyant mood and had evidently survived the concussion better than expected. And of course he was soon going to meet his son, Nils. The forty-year-old lived in Gothenburg and was Rake's only child. Rake and Nils had the same way of thinking, understood each other well and didn't need to bicker unnecessarily. His son was a captain on container ships and oil tankers and spent most of his life at sea so they couldn't meet very often, but for the time being he was at home and Rake was looking forward to seeing him. Rake had neglected him when he was a child as he had been at sea himself, but now he wanted to make up for what he had missed. And very soon they were going to meet again. Nils still lived in his beloved Majorna district in old Gothen-burg and had promised to lend his summer cottage to his father. And who would think of looking for a pensioner-gang of bank robbers there? The League of Pensioners intended to stay at least two weeks on the west coast, so that Rake could spend plenty of time with Nils.

'Of course I'll fix somewhere to stay, Dad. And you'll have a garden too. You'll love it!' Nils had said.

Martha had mumbled something about it being difficult to switch from a three-storey Djursholm villa to a cottage, but Rake had assured them that the west coast was fantastic and so the house didn't really matter. Besides, they didn't have any option. On the radio they had heard that the police were fol-lowing a new lead. Shortly, said a Chief Inspector Jöback, they would be issuing descriptions of wanted criminals. It had sounded decidedly threatening.

'We are close to solving the case now,' the constable had declared and then said something about a new gang being active in the country that hadn't figured in the investigation earlier. Now the police were closing in. Had somebody who had seen them with the skylift outside the Grand Hotel raised the alarm, or what if Charlie Concrete had snitched? Martha recalled how she, Brains and Anna-Greta had rather carelessly gone across to the neighbour's garden to look at the pool that had just been filled with concrete. Then all five of them would have been visible. They had admittedly got rid of the evidence, but perhaps there were things they hadn't thought about? And if truth be told, you could still smell rotten herring in the cellar.

No, it would be a relief to get away for a while and the west coast wasn't at all bad. Suddenly the train came to a halt and the lights went out.

'What's going on now? Problem with the signals, fallen overhead power lines or reversing trains?' Martha wondered, peering out through the window.

'No, a sun kink in the rail track,' Anna-Greta ventured.

'Or leaves covering the tracks,' Christina suggested.

'Unless it's a snowstorm or the points have iced up, of course,' muttered Rake.

'Don't be so negative,' said Brains. 'Now they've privatized the entire railway system we ought to be pleased to even arrive at all.'

'Don't confuse SJ and the Transport Administration,' Martha corrected him. 'SJ is the state-owned company that runs most of the trains, while the Transport Administration—'

'Next time I'll bloody well go by boat. Then at least you can be certain of reaching your destination,' Rake cut in, very grumpy on account of the delay.

This was followed by a discussion in which they all regretted that they had taken the train instead of flying, until

Martha opened her big flowery handbag and laid out plastic tumblers, nuts, crisps, carrots and different sorts of dipping sauces. Then, with a knowing look, she paused for effect before pulling out a bottle of Ronar champagne.

'One can always find an opportunity to celebrate. Now we are celebrating that the train has travelled many miles without derailing.'

'If we're going to celebrate every mile we manage, then we're going to be totally sloshed when we disembark in Gothenburg,' said Rake.

'Pah, you only live once,' Martha declared, poured the bubbly into the tumblers and proposed a toast.

Eight hours later the pensioners, somewhat the worse for wear, arrived at Central Station in Gothenburg where Rake's son Nils met them. He was tall and lanky, with a leather jacket and a tattoo on one wrist. His movements were quick and his eyes never relaxed. Slightly horrified, he met the happily babbling oldies who could barely keep their balance and switched from singing drinking songs to cursing the Transport Administration. He quickly realized that Rake and his friends had evidently not had anything to eat (the electricity hadn't worked properly on board the train) so he rapidly escorted them all to a restaurant by Slottsskogen Park in the Majorna district.

Martha and her friends, who were extremely hungry, settled in a corner of the restaurant at a solid wooden table with a tablecloth and a vase of flowers. It smelled good and homemade and Martha grabbed the menu before they had even sat down. They all ordered fish, except Christina, who wanted a

Greek salad, and they chose soda water to go with it. While they ate, they were all silent, but as soon as their feelings of hunger had been satisfied and they had cleaned their plates, they started talking about where they would stay. Rake wanted to hear a little more about the cottage and how they would share the rooms between them.

'Well, it's just a shed, Dad. You're not all thinking of staying there, are you? I mean I sold the old cottage and have recently bought a new one, you see; it's very small . . . 'No matter, we aren't so fussy. We can all squeeze in!' Rake happily announced, still decidedly tipsy.

'Well, it would indeed be a squeeze,' said Nils. 'I mean, it really isn't a large place, so I think it would be best to—'

'No problem, we aren't your average oldies. We can put up with most things. And in comparison with care homes, your place must be pure luxury. And, you know, it can never be like in the sailing ships. When I sailed the Atlantic, there were eight of us in one cabin of just a few square metres. Like sardines in tiny bunks with straw mattresses! You should have seen it when a storm was blowing, so—'

'I can book hotel rooms,' Nils suggested.

'Oh no, now we want to see where we're going to stay,' Rake exclaimed and waved his hand dismissively. He was proud of Gothenburg and his old Majorna district and wanted to show his friends. Of course they would stay at Nils's place, he would hear of nothing else. And if they were going to be hiding from the police, then they would have to rough it a bit . . .

15

There was a smell of early autumn and harvest time in the allotment gardens by Slottsskogen Park. Many allotments also had a shed or a tiny cabin-like cottage. The trees were magnificent with a maze of colours and on the gravel paths you could already see the first autumn leaves. The berry bushes no longer had any berries, and here and there you could still see some apples and pears in the trees. Some of the gardens were rather overgrown, others a miracle of well-tended lawns, fruit trees and flower borders. There were lots of very small picturesque cabins, some just glorified sheds, with white edgings and mullioned windows. The atmosphere was one of peace and quiet. Nils stopped in front of a neatly painted gate and pointed.

'An allotment cottage in the Majorna is nothing to be ashamed of. You can't imagine how desirable they are. There's water and sewerage and lots of owners live here during the summer. Welcome to my cabin!' he said and he opened the gate. A newly raked gravel path led up to a little red-painted wooden cabin with a flag pole in the garden. The cabin had a saddle pitch roof, the construction was framed in white and there was a little glazed terrace with a table and chairs and small sofa. Outside was a hammock and a largish tool shed. The garden had an apple tree, some plum trees and a few berry bushes. Some neat borders ran along the side of the fence.

'So this is all that is left of the summer cottage?' Rake asked, disappointment in his voice.

'But Dad, I told you, right? I said that I'd sold the old cottage and that the new one was very, very small.'

'Small yes, but we aren't bloody pygmies!' Rake groaned, tugging at his chinstrap beard. But he said this very quietly, because he didn't want to admit that he hadn't really listened.

'Yes, I don't really understand what you were thinking, Rake. Surely you aren't planning on our staying here?' Martha wondered.

'Don't worry. This is the sort of cabin that looks little from outside, but is much bigger inside,' he ventured.

'Uh huh, and I suppose you believe in fairies too?' said Martha.

Nils unlocked the door, opened it and let them step inside. Just on the immediate left was a minimal kitchen with a fridge, a little stove, a shelf and a sink. In the cabin's living room the furniture consisted of a dining table, a few chairs, a sofa-cum-bed and an armchair. You could glimpse a sort of loft at the back. Some rag rugs covered the floor and there was an old-fashioned wall clock on the long wall behind the sofa.

'Yes, it's so spacious here that there's an echo,' said Brains as he veered to avoid bumping into the dining table. He hadn't understood at all why they had to travel to Gothenburg. Only rarely had he been outside his home town Sundbyberg just north of Stockholm, and if they were going to have to lie low a while, they could have done so there. But most of all he was thinking about the wedding. Martha seemed to have everything but the wedding on her mind. Good God, how long would he have to wait?

'No, there isn't exactly much room to sleep,' Christina said, looking around.

'But I can sling a hammock up,' Rake offered. 'We often had those on board. You roll them up in the daytime and then there's room for everyone.'

'Yeah, why not. And there are two mattresses in the tool shed and a bed up in the loft. If you use the one up there, then there would be room for three to sleep in here,' said Nils.

'The loft?' Martha stared at the opening near the ceiling. 'So you had planned on catapulting me up there, or what?'

'But don't you worry, Martha dear. I'll take the loft berth,' said Brains. 'You won't have to use those steep steps.' But then he looked a little closer. In fact, he probably couldn't climb up either, and besides, there was his prostate to think about. He couldn't manage any number of nocturnal wanderings. It would have to be the tool shed for him.

Anyhow, it didn't take very long (for obvious reasons) to look around the house, and once they had done that the oldies sat down on the sofa. Nils started up the coffee machine and soon a delightful aroma of brewed coffee spread through the room.

'This reminds me of the scouts. Lots of people in the same tent,' said Brains pulling his legs in when Nils stretched out to reach the coffee pot.

'Just as long as it isn't put up with tent pegs and then blows away,' Martha added. Everything inside her was swaying. What on earth had they embarked upon? They were going to give money to health care and open a restaurant, but here they were sitting in an allotment cabin in Gothenburg. Something had sort of not really ended up as they had intended. But when it came to it, perhaps they could, after all, learn something about gardens here. The Vintage Village would have a greenhouse as well, so it would be a good idea to study some plants and horticulture too. That was the only positive aspect she could think of just now, so she would stick to it. There wasn't exactly a great deal otherwise to be pleased with now that they had to squeeze together, all five of them, in just a few square metres.

When the coffee was ready, Nils handed out plastic mugs to all, but the mood was somewhat depressed since there was a marked difference between a Djursholm villa and a cabin – and between an ordinary cottage and an allotment cabin. But after the coffee, Anna-Greta perked up a little.

'I've been thinking about something,' she said, putting her plastic mug down. 'We are here to lie low and keep away from the police. But don't you think we will be rather conspicuous, five oldies cooped up like this? It might lead to the opposite, and our being discovered.'

This was followed by the sort of silence that reigns when people are mulling over something. There was something in what Anna-Greta said, and Martha felt the tension in the air.

'My dear friends. There aren't any police in these allotments,' she tried to distract them, and then she opened her flowery handbag and pulled out a bag of Jungle Pastilles that were left over from the train journey. 'Let's sleep here tonight and then tomorrow morning we can discuss what we should do.'

They all thought this was a good idea and after guzzling the Jungle Pastilles and drinking up the coffee their mood improved. Nils fetched sheets and sleeping bags and when he left Rake and the others, it was nearly midnight and happy voices and singing could be heard from inside the cabin. This was accompanied by motley clinks and clonks when Brains and Martha played with spoons on empty cake tins. But they were too tired to go on for long, and the sound soon turned into a weak humming before everything went quiet. Nils smiled to himself. It would all sort itself out in the end.

16

In the middle of the night Anna-Greta woke when there was an enormous crash and the ground shook under the terrace. Mysterious sounds could be heard and even though the head torch lay next to her on the pillow, she didn't dare turn it on. What if it was burglars, or the police . . . With her hands clutching the pillow she listened to the noises and tried to identify them. No, it couldn't be the forces of law and order, it sounded more like someone digging a tunnel under the cabin. She thought about all the adventure films she had seen and she knew that you could dig a tunnel from somewhere far away and surface somewhere completely different. But why would anybody dig a tunnel that led to an allotment? The noise got louder and was accompanied by huffing and puffing and scraping. Anna-Greta started trembling and now regretted that she had volunteered to sleep on her own on the glazed terrace. What if it was a burglar!

Stiff and a bit unsteady on her legs, she got up from the sofa, went up to the window and peered out into the dark. She couldn't see anything. She carefully reached out to get hold of the head torch and tried to feel where the on/off switch was. No, it was best to find some sort of weapon first.

The grill accessories! She got hold of a skewer and pressed the torch switch. Then she saw something dark running across the lawn and disappear behind a fence. A badger!

Oh for goodness' sake! Relief mixed with horror. What if there were rats too? Perhaps she would have been calmer if she had a man to protect her. She remembered Gunnar, her computer hacker friend, and how she had sat in front of a computer with him for almost a whole year. For a while she had been totally enthralled, but then . . . He never wanted to go to the cinema or the theatre, or join her at an opera or an art exhibition. And she never saw him with a book in his hands. He was quite simply boring. At first, Gunnar had taught her a lot and they had had a good time together, but she had been far too quick to learn for his taste. And then he had done what he could to hold her back. Indeed, to stop her, in fact. There were all the fewer hugs and all the more excuses. In the end, she hadn't even wanted him to hug her. How could it have ended up like that? If only he had re-invented himself, but he had just plodded along in his own footsteps. Silence had settled between them. After a while he had begun to blame his absence on his having to go home to his nephew; those occasions became all the more common and he stayed away for longer and longer periods. When finally he didn't come back, she almost felt relief – but her life wasn't more fun because of it. She had discovered the happiness of sharing your life with somebody else and now she missed the company. Brains and Martha, Christina and Rake, they were paired off, but she was completely alone. Experiencing things and not being able to tell anyone – no, she must really do something about her life. Otherwise she would end up a grumpy old hag and she definitely didn't want that to happen.

She took her slippers off and lay down again. She needed a few hours' sleep before the morning because she had quite a lot to do. She had discovered that her mobile broadband worked here and so she must make sure that the lawyers had done their job and that the money transfers to the West Indies were working properly. Of course, it would have been nice to have somebody to talk to about all this. The responsibility for the money weighed so heavily on her, even though the others encouraged and tried to support her. And she could never be really free because cyberspace reached you everywhere – even if you were lying low in a little allotment cabin. Lawyer Hovberg's assistant had been of pensionable age. Could he be married, she wondered? And there was net-dating, of course. Perhaps she should try that? Deep in thought, she pulled up the covers to her chin, practised licking her lips sensually (a trick she had recently learned) and fell into a deep sleep. Soon she was snoring loudly while meeting – in her dreams – a young, stylish pensioner who liked her just as she was: tall as a drainpipe, not especially attractively dressed, well on in years, and far too intelligent. But the handsome pensioner wasn't afraid of her at all, and despite her laughing like a horse he kissed her a long time and passionately. That night she smiled in her sleep from midnight right up until the morning.

When the League of Pensioners, somewhat stiff and bruised, woke up the next day, the sun was shining. It was one of those madly beautiful autumn days of which there were only a few each year. Martha and her friends sat down with their coffee cups on the terrace and looked around at the small, well-tended cabins on every side. It was nice and cosy, just a bit bothersome in that you had to go to the communal building in the centre of the allotments to have a shower and freshen up. But as a pensioner you could take it easy and they didn't even have any new crimes coming up. Not just yet, at any rate. Martha finished her coffee and hummed a little before she started to speak.

'You know what, I think we can stay here a week or two,' she said. 'We need to get our strength back and to potter a bit in the garden like real pensioners are meant to do. That would be most excellent, surely? I think we can do nicely here.'

'Why not? I slept really well up there in the loft,' said Christina.

'And the sofa bed was comfortable. Besides, I can deal with my bank errands from here,' said Anna-Greta waving the modem for her mobile broadband.

'And I can look after the garden,' said Rake. 'There's lots to do, salad, radishes and all that.'

'In that case, we can prepare something vegetarian,' said Christina who had bought a book called *The Older You Are, the Healthier You Are*. 'With a lot of greens in our diet, we will all feel fit and live longer,' she went on and threw a glance at Rake. She tried to have projects together with him so that he wouldn't flirt with others and here on the allotment they could busy themselves in the garden together. 'For dinner I can make beetroot, chèvre cheese with honey and walnuts. Yummy!'

'But what about me?' Brains mumbled pathetically, feeling a bit left out. If they were going to say here two weeks, the wedding would be delayed even longer. And what would he do in this teeny weeny cottage in the meanwhile? Crochet? Not exactly his thing. And another thing was that here he couldn't sleep in the same room as Martha. He and Rake had their sleeping places in the shed so that the ladies could have the cottage for themselves. But Rake snored like a threshing machine and talked in his sleep as well. No, Brains was not particularly enthusiastic.

'Two weeks – there's a definite risk that we'll get on each other's nerves,' he started tentatively.

'We'll soon settle in. And anyway, this is better than prison,' Martha determined. 'We can make it cosy. Read a good book, Brains. And we can play Monopoly—'

'When there are computer games . . .' he muttered, and he got up and went out to the shed.

Rake watched him leave. Brains wasn't in good form, he never used to be so grumpy. It was high time to do something about it. He must get Brains to work on an invention, indeed, anything as long as his good old friend got into a better mood. He pulled on his chinstrap beard for quite a while before he came up with something. Brains would be given a real challenge. An invention that would be of use to them all.

17

Brains kept out of the way for several days. He ate his dinner but then went back into his quarters as quickly as he could. In the end, Martha became worried, put on her cardigan and headed out to the shed.

She knocked on the door, but nobody opened. She sniffed the air. A strange smell seeped through the crack in the door, a smell she didn't recognize. Still nobody opened. She impatiently pressed the door handle a couple of times. Then Brains opened the door a fraction and looked like a boy who had been caught doing something naughty.

'Oh, so you're coming to visit? I wasn't expecting – er, it's a bit of a mess here,' he said and looked troubled. 'I'm rather busy, perhaps we can meet later.' He tried to pull the door to, but Martha was quicker and put her foot in the way.

'But what on earth?' she exclaimed when she had stepped inside the cramped shed. Clothes and shoes were bunched together on the floor with a computer game and Rake's cravats. Under the bed lay a heap of empty juice bottles and a bucket, some flexible pipes and a toolbox. Above all, there was a dreadful stench. It really wasn't a good idea at all that two elderly gentlemen should share such a tiny space, she thought. And everything looked so very different! Instead of the bed where Rake had slept before, there was now a temporary bench with a sink and a garden hosepipe with a tap. On the bench was a little hotplate, a saucepan with a lid that had been taped shut and a plastic bucket. Between the plastic bucket and the saucepan ran a transparent pipe, and at the bottom of the bucket there was a drainage hose with one of those clamps that you use with a steam juicer.

'But my dearest friend, whatever are you up to?'

Brains backed into the shed and looked very guilty. He had never tried his hand at home distillation before. When he made his first batch he didn't have the activated carbon so he had tried to filter the liquid through two of Christina's organic wholemeal loaves of bread, but that hadn't worked either. Fusel alcohol smelled and despite his having put the loaves – drenched in spirits – in thick plastic bags and sealing them, the odour still hung heavily. He had heard that experienced drunkards often used loaves of bread to purify the spirits and he thought it would take away the smell. But now Martha was sniffing this way and that inside the shed, and had become very suspicious.

'Brains, you surely haven't started a home distillery?'

'Well, you see, all you others have something nice to occupy yourselves with, and then it occurred to me that I could make some apple liqueur. There is so much fruit in these allotment gardens so, well, I just constructed a little apparatus.' He bent down and pulled out a glass bowl which had been hidden under the bed. It was an old mixer that Christina had been using to make smoothies, but that Brains had now adapted. At the bottom of the bowl there was a valve and from there several tubes stuck out like the arms of an octopus. The tubes ended in a tap. 'Look at this!' Brains went on, and he pulled out several schnapps glasses which he placed under the pipes. Then he poured water into the bowl and opened the valve, upon which the liquid ran into the tubes and was distributed equally to all the glasses. 'There, you see. A good way to save time.'

Martha picked up one of the glasses and sniffed at the contents. A schnapps glass full of water. So that was the invention he had been busy with when he had refused to help with the dishes and blamed a headache. She couldn't help but smile. Brains looked so proud that it was impossible to be angry with him, and instead she felt a warm feeling spread inside her. However angry and down in the dumps he might be, he never gave up but always found something positive to do. You couldn't help but love a man like Brains.

'You haven't got any moral objections to this, Martha dear?' he wondered. 'I mean, this is a fine old Swedish tradition. And of course it would be a shame if the apples were just left to rot on the ground.' He pointed to the mixer. 'You see, I wanted to find out if I could invent an apparatus that was suited to allotment cabins. Here, people drop in on each other and with this you can make sure you can serve a bit of something strong with the coffee.'

'So where are the spirits, then?' Martha wondered.

'Well, at first it didn't go too well, but now we have made a new batch.' He pointed at three plastic containers. 'Now I'll dilute the spirits with water so that it'll be forty per cent. After that we can make a really tasty liqueur. Just say what sort you want.'

'Oh that's nice! Beetroot liqueur, perhaps, or why not mango and banana? Anyway, what does Rake think?' Martha asked, suddenly realizing that both Rake and his bed were gone. 'But for goodness' sake, where does Rake sleep?'

'Up there,' said Brains, pointing to the rolled-up hammock hanging from the ceiling. 'He pretends he is at sea and now his snoring doesn't sound so loud.'

'Well, I don't know what to say, but the main thing is that you're both doing all right,' Martha said.

Brains felt encouraged and leaned forward and gave her a hug.

'Come and sit down here so we can talk a little.' He cleared a space for her on the bed. 'How are you, my friend?'

'I'm fine, yes, even though I miss you now you're living out here in the shed.'

'Oh, so you do, then?' A hopeful glimmer lit up in Brains's eyes. 'You know what? I miss you too. Something awful. And I've been thinking about the future. What about a wedding here in Gothenburg? We could even arrange the marriage ceremony here in the Slottsskogen allotment gardens.'

'Perhaps, yes,' said Martha. 'But not until we've shared out the bank robbery money, of course . . .'

'Yes, and then there's the drainpipe,' Brains filled in.

'Oh that's right, I forgot.'

'Bank-robbery money and drainpipe. You can hear what that sounds like.'

'What?' said Martha, a little confused, regretting her insensitivity and leaning forward to give him a hug. But then Brains had turned angry. He got up and was already halfway out through the door. He needed a while on his own so he could think about his relationship with Martha. As things stood now, it didn't feel good at all.

Rake and Brains couldn't think of what they should do with the unsuccessful first batch of spirits. The stench of fusel got worse and worse, so in the end they decided to stuff the loaves into decomposable paper bags and bury them. According to their own calculations the bags would hold the damp wholemeal bread and rot in an environmentally acceptable manner in the soil. And thus nobody would find out about their illegal distillery and not even Nils would notice anything. No sooner said than done. The elderly gentlemen went out into the garden, dug a hole for the loaves and poured the rest of the fusel in, after which they covered it all over with soil and leaves. Then they put the spades back in the tool shed and returned to the storage shed again. Back inside, they made sure the door was properly closed before they opened the trapdoor in the floor – this was their new hiding place. Twenty or so large PET mineral-water bottles were lined up with their 40 per cent alcohol content. Brains picked up one of the bottles, unscrewed the cork and poured the liquid into the mixer. When that was done, he shut off all the tubes except two, opened the valve and let the spirits drip down into two glasses.

'Of course it might be quicker to pour it out directly, but if there are a lot of you, then this gains time,' said Brains handing one of the schnapps glasses across to his comrade.

'But you know what? Next time we can let it drop from all the tubes. Then we can drink one schnapps glass after the other without having to fill them again. Just a few more glasses to wash.' Rake grinned and sipped the transparent drink. 'And of course we must flavour this in some way. It's hardly got any taste at the moment.'

'We can do that tomorrow. It's potent stuff regardless. *Skål!* Here's to us!' said Brains, and he put his head back and emptied his glass.

With a satisfied 'Aaaah', the men sank comfortably down on Brains's unmade bed, lifted up the folding table top and put down the glasses. Rake opened a packet of crisps that he had kept hidden from Christina – and handed it over to Brains.

'Spirits and crisps, to think that it can be such a treat!' he said. He spat out his tobacco and took a fistful. The men toasted each other again and spent the rest of the evening drinking their home brew and eating crisps while they took turns to tell stories to each other about ships, motorbikes and their adventures with women. When the clock showed well after midnight they became quite sentimental, and with tears in their eyes swore each other friendship. They must stick together, they agreed, because since they'd left the old people's home, the women, for some strange reason, had ended up deciding far too much.

'Nothing can beat a conversation man to man,' said Rake and he put his arm round Brains's shoulders.

'That's true,' his comrade concurred. 'But women are all right as well,' he said as he had suddenly found himself thinking about Martha.

'In the right dose,' Rake added.

'Yes, of course, in the right dose,' Brains slurred and thought about Martha again.

*

The next day Martha woke up early and when she walked across to the shower rooms she discovered that there was now a large white tent in the gravel yard between the club hall and the outdoor dance floor. Yes, now she remembered, it was today that the allotment association's harvest festival was to take place, the first Sunday in September. Today they couldn't just sit inside the cabin and lie low, that would look suspicious. No, they must go out and socialize with all the neighbours. But that also had its risks, of course. It would be best if they too had something to display and sell, she considered, so that they could blend in among the allotment gardeners in a natural way. They could take a few apples, tomatoes and some beetroot from Nils's allotment, but that wasn't enough. They ought to have something more.

When Martha had finished her shower, she woke the others and while her comrades went to the shower rooms for their morning toilet, she quickly raided the cabin and sheds. She didn't find very much, but there were the pillowcases that Anna-Greta had embroidered with a flower pattern, the vinyl records that they had doubles of, four loaves of Christina's home-baked wholemeal bread and the concentrated lingonberry juice that she had bought from a neighbouring allotment and had tarted up a bit with some ginger and oriental spices that she didn't know the name of. The idea had been to have the spicy fruit juice themselves, but now she had found several bottles of mineral water under the trapdoor in the storage shed. Why not mix a home-made fruit cordial and sell that at the festival? The sun was shining, there would be lots of visitors who would be thirsty and something to drink would be popular. Admittedly, Martha did have a bit of a cold and perhaps shouldn't be handling food and drink, but she could use plastic gloves so that she wouldn't infect anybody. It was best she did it quickly so that it would all be ready before the others came back. She fetched her specially concocted lingonberry extract and the mineral water as well as some empty bottles she had found under Brains's bed. Then she set to work in the kitchen and mixed her home-made fruit drink. There were some packets of lemon wafer biscuits on the shelf too, so she would take those with her as well. In the end, she had gathered together everything in four bags and put them on the terrace. As soon as her friends returned, she would ask Brains to take it all to the sales stall.

'Harvest festival?' muttered Brains an hour later when he came back from the sales stall with the wheelbarrow. 'Nope, I'd rather take a trip to the harbour.'

'Did you say harbour?' Rake looked longingly towards the gate that led out from the Slottsskogen garden area. He was still a bit unsteady on his feet since the bump on his head (and the night's escapade) but a trip to the harbour would suit him nicely.

'It's only a short tram ride. Yes, brilliant, I'll join you! We can look at the East India clipper.'

The previous evening Rake had talked a lot about the East Indiaman *Götheborg*, and the conditions for seamen in times gone by. Brains thought it would be exciting to see the copy of the eighteenth-century clipper. In the old days artisans were extremely skilful and perhaps he could learn something new.

Besides, he had nothing against fleeing from the battlefield for a while. He didn't like large crowds. He went in to see Martha.

'Everything is set up. Your table is next to the lady who's selling waffles. I put the bags there. But you'll have to run the stall yourself. Me and Rake, we're going down to the harbour.'

He hadn't asked her, hadn't wondered if she had anything against it, but had simply told her what he was going to do. And Martha would just have to settle for that. He immediately felt proud, as if he had done something good and was taking control of his own life. Perhaps it was a good thing to be a little tougher?

'But aren't you . . . and me, um . . .' she began, but then turned silent. She looked a bit disappointed but soon composed herself. 'Oh right, yes dear, that sounds nice. So you're going down to the harbour? Well, have a good time and promise not to climb the rigging.'

Then she rang for a taxi because she didn't want the men to walk too far and get tired. They could fall down and break their hips. They had neglected their gymnastic exercises recently.

When she had waved Rake and Brains off and was on her way back to the cabin, she turned down the Carrot Lane path and thought about what Brains had said. He seemed to care less and less for her. She had thought that he would appreciate sitting with her for a while at the stall, looking at the other stalls and pottering around the allotment gardens. But no, it was as if he thought it was a relief to go off with Rake. Perhaps she ought to be careful and not take him for granted.

It was so easy to be blind to what you had, and to forget to look after those who are near and dear. And Brains was unique, there was nobody like him in the whole world.

18

The big harvest festival started at eleven o'clock and suddenly the entire allotment garden area was packed with visitors. Old and young, they filled the paths and were on the hunt for local produce at the various stalls. They filled their bags with several sorts of apples, plums and pears which were sold together with blueberries and lingonberries. There were even tomatoes for sale, as well as cucumbers and onions; indeed there seemed to be no end to what was on offer. Lots of flowers and plants too at this time of year, but Martha – who didn't have green fingers – had no idea what they were all called. (She was, however, clever when it came to knowing which plastic flowers lasted a long time, and which were very shoddy and fell to bits at the merest touch.) No, gardening, picking mushrooms in the woods and all that, it wasn't her cup of tea. But bearing in mind the idea of the Vintage Village she ought to learn something about them. Anyhow, that would have to be another time. Instead she looked at the jumble-sale stalls. Here too there were lots to choose from: books, kitchen equipment, porcelain, jigsaw puzzles and cartoon comics. And some stalls sold old VHS videos, as well as DVDs and CDs. She could have pottered for hours, but she had her own fruit cordial to sell. Best to get to work straight away.

She said hello to the lady in the adjacent stall, breathed in the lovely aroma of freshly made waffles and strawberry jam, and lined up her bottles. Lucky for her to have the waffle stand so close, as it would increase demand for her fruit drink. She had hardly finished putting out all her bottles before people thronged in front of the table and she didn't have a chance to have a taste of her own drink. Early in the morning, Brains had set up a sign proclaiming ORGANIC DRINKS by the stall and as soon as she opened there was a stream of customers. Nothing is as good as home-made cordial, she thought, and if this was a food programme on TV, they would say delicious, good old-fashioned lingonberry cordial, with a trace of ginger and a touch of the exotic . . .

The first customer was the allotment association's very own Mrs Grumpy. Her real name was Amanda Skogh and she was notorious for snooping around the allotments finding fault. Nils had said that she was rather bothersome and that they must be nice to her. Martha had done her best, and now Amanda bought a whole bottle. After her came a group from a local choir, from the nearby church, together with the vicar. Martha, who loved choral singing, started chatting and after selling them an old vinyl record and a couple of Anna-Greta's embroidered pillowcases, she suggested that they should have a little sing-along, for example an Evert Taube ballad. This got all of them in a jolly mood, and it ended up with the choir members all buying a bottle of Martha's drink. Some had a taste first, and asked how the drink could be so strong, but then she told them that it was her granny's recipe, and it contained many special spices and that this wasn't just your everyday fruit drink you found in the supermarkets.

'You see, I've used real organic ingredients,' she boasted.

After a while, four novices from the medieval nunnery in Vadstena came to Martha's table. They were visiting the allotments to see if they could find any medieval plants that had been imported by monks way back in the fifteenth century. Martha said she was sorry she couldn't help them, but instead she sold three pillowcases, two vinyl records with Salvation Army music and eventually persuaded them to buy some bottles too. Some of the choir members returned to buy a few more bottles, further reducing her stock. Business was thriving and a couple of hours later Martha had almost nothing left. That was when she caught sight of Amanda Skogh, who was rather unsteadily making her way along the Salad Lane path, a waffle in her hand. She sang joyfully and greeted everybody she met, asking them if they wanted to taste her waffle. She waved her arms, took dance steps and sang so loudly that everybody stared at her in dismay. She had only just gone when the church choir came staggering in from the left. The vicar was rambling on and touching the breasts of the sopranos, while the tenors and the stylish basses were competing to see who could sing the loudest. And right behind them came the four novices with their habits somewhat askew. They were, of course, respectfully attired, but they were chasing the lovely sounding basses, giggling as they lifted their skirts, sidestepping all the while. Commerce came to a halt and the visitors stared. Had the church folk eaten too many fermented berries, like elk in the forest, or were they genuinely under the influence?

'And what are you doing this evening, vicar?' wondered the pretty little novice Yvonne when she caught sight of the cleric, and she winked seductively, but then, luckily, the other novices intervened. Because if they hadn't stopped her, she would certainly have pinched him on the bottom. Martha was quite shocked and wondered if it was always like this at harvest festival time. And when there was so much chaos that she didn't think it could get any worse, she suddenly heard a weird gobbling sound. A badger came stumbling out onto Salad Lane with bits of bread hanging out of its mouth. It wobbled to one side and then to the other and finally fell into the ditch with its paws in the air. Martha watched this in astonishment, shook her head and thought it was now high time she returned home. With only one solitary vinyl record (a yodelling ballad singer) and one bottle left, she thought she had done her stint for the day.

'I saved this for us,' she said when she got home, and she pulled out a bottle of her fizzy drink and a picnic basket full of waffles. 'Now we're going to stuff ourselves!'

The gentlemen still hadn't come home, so the ladies settled on the terrace and ate and drank while conversing with jollity, with the hammock rocking and the evening passing. Soon you could hear verses of romantic songs when the merry, light female voices broke out in spontaneous vocal harmony.

When Brains and Rake came home later in the evening, they heard shrieks and laughter well before they reached the cabin. People were dancing and singing in the gravel yard and jolly voices could be heard from the allotment gardens. They had hardly opened the gate before they discovered the vicar behind a bush, cuddling a loudly giggling first soprano. Tipsy basses and tenors were wandering around and when Rake and Brains entered the little cafe, a new shock awaited them. There they saw a group of novices who seemed to have passed out sitting at the table with their heads resting on their arms. They were snoring.

'Oh my God!' said Rake.

'Yes, well,' said Brains, 'he doesn't seem to be here at any rate! We'd best be going home.'

Somewhat confounded they walked down Carrot Lane while tipsy allotment owners waved and wanted to treat them to a glass. But the men declined as graciously as they could and continued towards their own cabin. They stopped beside the gate. Somebody had been digging in the border where they had buried the fusel-soaked loaves.

'Oh my God!' exclaimed Rake again.

'There's a smell of fusel,' Brains declared and he hurried to fetch a spade and rake to sweep away the evidence. Just as he and Rake had finished, they caught sight of Martha, who was holding an empty pop bottle in her hand while the others were singing and supporting one another as best they could.

'Oh, so tasty, nothing beats a home-made lingonberry cordial,' Martha slurred after which Christina burst out in an uncontrollable giggling and Anna-Greta followed up with an explosion of machine-gun neighing.

'Why –' Martha began, looking at Brains with shiny eyes, 'why on earth didn't you say that the bottles contained spirits!'

'What?! What have you done?'

144

'Oh, nothing special. I just mixed lingonberry extract, spices and mineral water,' she giggled. 'The result was heavenly! I sold it all.'

'The spirits!' groaned Brains and Rake.

'No, lingonberry cordial,' said Martha. And then the ladies dissolved into such convulsions of laughter that it was simply impossible to talk to them. Rake and Brains had to help them into the cabin.

19

The following day everybody slept a long time in the Slottssko-gen allotment colony and nobody could remember that it had ever been so quiet on an ordinary morning in September. Apart from the chirping of birds and some snores that could be heard through open windows, it was remarkably silent. The church choir were sleeping off their intoxication in the congregation's guest flat, while the vicar, who had been caught with his first soprano, had been taken home by his angry wife. Deeply repentant, he tossed and turned on the hard, uncomfortable living-room sofa without being able to sleep, but what could he do when he had been banished from the bedroom? The novices for their part, who had never drunk so much cordial all their lives – they had never tasted a drink as good as this – were wondering why they were still there in the allotments since they had train tickets for their return journey to Vadstena the previous evening. Besides, they had a dreadful headache of a type they had never encountered before, a throbbing pain which didn't ease up despite their kneeling and many prayers. And those plants from the fifteenth century – they had forgotten to ask about them, and the carrots, beetroot and apples they had bought instead were actually the same ones they had brought with them and donated to the vegetable stall. In some weird way, everything had been sort of topsy-turvy, and the only thing that they could agree upon was that God was almighty and that the lingonberry cordial had been fantastically tasty.

The League of Pensioners themselves sat inside the allotment cabin and lay low. They didn't dare venture out. Since people had danced and sung instead of buying, the allotment owners had never sold so little as they had this year. And with unsold vegetables, burning headaches and empty cash tills, they were all a bit irritable. And inside Nils's allotment cabin too, there was a lively discussion.

'But Martha, dear, didn't you notice that the bottles were full of spirits?' Brains sighed and shook his head.

'But for heaven's sake, I've got a cold and didn't have time to taste. I've said I'm sorry!'

Martha was ashamed for having been so careless, but at the same time she found it hard to keep a straight face. Because it had been a hilarious evening and many a participant would surely remember this harvest festival for decades to come. But be that as it may, it would perhaps be for the best if she and her friends were to move on, because it was only a matter of time before the talk about the oldies in Nils's cabin would spread. Five elderly pensioners crammed together in an allotment cabin of only twenty-six square metres, yes, what on earth were they doing there? And the League of Pensioners were, after all, on the wanted list in Sweden and abroad. Martha looked at her friends round the dining table. It wasn't ideal here, of course it wasn't, but where else could they go? During the two weeks they had kept themselves hidden there they had listened to the news every day without hearing any more about the Nordea bank robbery, and that had made her uneasy. Were the police keeping a low profile, or had the crime now become a lower priority? Perhaps they could even go back to the villa in Djursholm? Here in the allotment colony it didn't feel as safe as it had before.

'Now listen,' she began, but she was cut off by Christina's loud laugh.

'Amazing! You should have seen how the novices were traipsing around with their skirts lifted. I have never seen the like!' she said, getting up to demonstrate.

'No, now hear me!' said Martha and she banged the salt shaker on the table. 'Order in the ranks! We must get into action. We can't hide here forever, and we must distribute the bank-robbery money. How are things going with the lawyer, Anna-Greta?'

'Mr Hovberg? He just sent me an email saying that he had managed to register a company on the Cayman Islands. Now he only has to link a Swedish company to it. Then we can share out the money.'

'Take the proceeds you got from selling the cordial too.' Rake grinned. 'No, seriously though, why not give the money to the poorly paid health-care staff? Nursing assistants must get better wages. Nursing sisters have a dreadfully stressful situation at the A & E.'

'Like that dark-haired girl who works at Danderyd Hospital, perhaps?' said Christina with a sharp glance at Rake.

'All those who are paid badly shall get higher wages,' Martha interjected. 'I am not going to end my life of crime until we have achieved a more just society where every person can live on their wage and their pension.'

'Oops, are you now going to change *all* of society again?' asked Brains. 'But the people who work harder must get a better wage than the others, right? I mean a wage according to ability and achievement. And doctors do have more responsibility and—'

'Ah, what do you actually mean?' Martha wondered and fixed her eyes on him.

'Well, I, er . . .' he began, and went quiet when he saw Rake's warning look.

'I've got an idea,' said Brains. 'We smuggle the money to those in need. At the Customs and Excise Museum I've seen how it can be done. If we buy lots of books, hollow out the innards and put some money in, then we can send them to all the nurses in the country.'

'Yes, exactly; we can put banknotes inside bibles. Wouldn't that be nice?' Christina said.

'A literary way of smuggling.' Rake grinned and patted her on the cheek. 'But, you know, there are seventy thousand nursing assistants in Sweden, so that would mean a lot of hard work.'

That said, the difficulty of arranging a nice way of sharing out the money became apparent to them all. How on earth could they achieve their aim?

20

There was a smell of apples and leaves, and the nights had become colder. In the old allotment garden cabin, the cold made itself felt at night-time. How much longer could they stay here and lie low? Anna-Greta glanced at her computer screen and read the latest email. Lawyer Hovberg had listed several transfers from the West Indies and the Swedish daughter company was now up and running. Very soon, the League of Pensioners would be in the field as the simplest of venture capitalists. No, it wouldn't feel right until they had given the money away. It was high time to return! She closed her computer, changed her mind and opened it again. Venture capitalists, yes. What if Carl Bielke, their unpleasant neighbour, had come home? They ought to find out about that. Perhaps he was on Facebook? Then she could keep track of him. Why hadn't she thought of that before?

She entered her password and immediately could see files, pictures and documents on the computer screen again. She had recently joined Facebook, but didn't dare use her own name, instead she called herself Eva von Adelsparre, which had a decidedly noble ring to it. While they had been staying in the allotment gardens, she had systematically made sure she became Facebook Friends with her childhood friends in Djursholm as well as neighbours old and new. Almost everybody had accepted her and with a name like von Adelsparre most of them probably assumed she was an old schoolmate from the local school, one of those pupils whose name they had forgotten. Then she had spent an hour every day checking what her newly made friends busied themselves with nowadays. It was exciting to scout out how people lived, who their neighbours were and what their summer houses and boats looked like. Many of the Djursholm locals had fancy summer houses out in the Stockholm archipelago, but their villas in Spain or on the Riviera were even more luxurious. To think what a life they lived, those old schoolmates; they moved in an entirely different world to ordinary people!

Anna-Greta took a lemon wafer biscuit and clicked her way into Facebook. Many new entries had come in. Humming, she scrolled down the start page. Somebody had been out picking mushrooms, others had posted humorous cuttings and – no, she must concentrate! She wrote 'Carl Bielke' in the search box and hoped for the best. There now, his page came up. Yes, that was their neighbour, the around-the-world sailor with a refuse-collection lorry in his swimming pool. She breathed faster. Could it really be true? Yes, a smiling Carl Bielke had posted a picture of himself standing on a fabulous motor yacht in the multi-million class. It was one of those huge motorboats that only royalty, sheikhs and billionaires were able to afford. And the water was not dark blue like in the Baltic, but rather a greener shade like in the Mediterranean.

Bielke had posted more pictures and soon she recognized

the harbour in Saint-Tropez where she had been on a language course when she was young. In those days the French fishing village was not so well known, but now it had developed into a popular hang-out for the jetsetters. But what in heaven's name was Bielke doing there? Their neighbour was meant to be sailing round the world. The boat he was standing on was evidently his, because he called it 'my motorboat'. She became curious and scrolled further. Bielke did seem to get about. The year before he had let himself be photographed on a sailing yacht in Cannes and even on a large motor yacht in Nice. One of those boats could be chartered and when she clicked on the link, she saw that it had a swimming pool and the most luxurious living room and bedroom. Ten thousand euro a week was the asking price! Good God!

On the deck you could see smiling young ladies and crew members in white uniforms. What if he had a blog too? Yes, indeed, after a few moments she found a blog where he boasted about his luxury boats and sailing tours. Anna-Greta became curious, wrote down what type of boat they were and googled their value. She gasped in astonishment. The motor yacht in Saint-Tropez was worth more than five hundred million kronor! How could he possibly afford that? She was so fascinated that she almost choked on the wafer biscuit, and not until she had recovered from the coughing could she gather her thoughts. Oh my God! She, Martha and the others in the gang were in actual fact the most amateurish of amateurs. The amount the League of Pensioners had got from the bank robbery was nothing in comparison with this.

Eagerly, she googled more motor yachts and luxury cruisers and discovered that some boats were for sale for more than seven hundred million kronor! And that was about seventy bank robberies at ten million a time! How could she and her friends have missed this? Now Anna-Greta's feeling for order and her past as a bank official led her to wonder whether Bielke had declared his assets. She quickly clicked her way into the Swedish tax authority's website, made a note of a telephone number she needed and then practised a few minutes to disguise her voice before she phoned.

'I am sorry to disturb you, but the matter concerns Mr Carl Bielke of Auroravägen four in Djursholm. I am intending to sell a house to him. Would you be so kind as to provide me with information about his income? It would be so dreadful to be cheated . . .'

Then she phoned the County Administration and the Enforcement Agency. While the telephone rang at the other end, she felt pleased with how well she was dealing with everything herself. Gunnar had taught her a lot and of course she missed his company sometimes. But everything was so quick and convenient now that she could handle the computer herself. In that way she could get at facts directly without having to ask nicely, to wheedle, to praise and put in a lot of effort generally! After just a few telephone calls she had found out what she wanted to know, and then she got up so quickly that she knocked over the coffee pot and the bowl of lemon wafer biscuits.

'My friends,' she called out into the cottage. 'You know Bielke? You won't believe what a tricky character he turns out to be!'

And then she went and fetched Brains and Rake and said to Martha and Christina that she had something important to

153

tell them. The friends gathered together in the cabin round the dining table, put their hands on their knees and listened. Proud and almost a little boastful, Anna-Greta told them what she had found on the Internet and then she described in detail tax-evader Carl Bielke's income and assets and yachts in the Mediterranean. The members of the League of Pensioners oohed and aahed and wondered how the man had managed to get so rich and avoid paying tax. Anna-Greta was in her element and gesticulated.

'He has assets by the billion but he has bypassed the Swedish state and most of it is formally owned on the Cayman Islands,' she explained.

'Disrespectful!' said Martha.

'Oh yes, I know some others who also—' mumbled Brains.

'Serves him right to get a refuse-collection lorry in his swimming pool,' Christina commented.

'If we can steal back those millions that the state never received in taxes, then we would be doing a good deed,' Rake pointed out. 'Then we'll have something to give to health care and all the rest. His assets are worth more than many bank robberies.'

'Yes, right, bank robberies are just pocket money,' said Anna-Greta.

'Bank robberies are for amateurs, hiding assets is for the professionals!' Christina added.

The League of Pensioners discussed this from various angles trying to work out what they should do, when they suddenly realized that they had missed the news on the radio. They were on the run and ought to keep themselves well informed. They all shook their heads at this carelessness, but when they turned on the wireless in time for the twelve o'clock news, they didn't know if they should be pleased or disappointed. There was nothing at all about the Nordea bank robbery.

Some days passed, and Martha and her friends wandered around in the cramped cabin without being able to decide whether they should travel home or not. Rake went on a few walks among the allotments and looked at the different gardens. He talked with the allotment owners and asked them about their plants and their borders. He had once again started to dream about a greenhouse of his own and wondered about erecting one in Djursholm in the spring. Besides, Martha had talked about that Vintage Village for the elderly. If they succeeded in creating one of those, perhaps he could get an active gardening club going with lots of members who could build their own greenhouses. That would be really lovely! Rake felt at home among these allotments and became all the keener, but Brains for his part became all the gloomier. He had nowhere to work on his inventions and he thought that he had become distanced from Martha. On the few occasions when they had argued or had differences of opinion they had always been able to talk things over before they went to bed, but now that he was living in the storage shed they didn't have that possibility. There hadn't been time for those heart-to-heart conversations and nor had there been any opportunities to cuddle her. He had recently asked her to marry him, and now here he was sitting on his own on a bed in a shed! No, he had had enough. The allotment cabin was too cramped for them, and staying on there would be utterly crazy.

The next day, Brains asked for a meeting. Martha felt a little uneasy when she saw his countenance and realized that this was serious.

Somewhat nervous, she put out the coffee pot and cups together with Christina's oatcakes and turned on the radio news. Just as she was about to pour out the coffee, there was a knocking on the door. They all looked at one another worriedly and didn't really know if they would dare to see who it was. Suddenly the door was swung open and Nils strode in. His leather jacket was not buttoned and his eyes gleamed.

'Now hold on tight!' he exclaimed and spread his arms wide. 'The police!'

21

The police? A murmur of horror could be heard, and Martha got up ready to flee. Brains got to his feet too, and was half-way out of the door before he quickly retraced his steps and put his arm around Martha.

'We'd better hide, my dear,' he said and quickly glanced out of the window. 'There must be good hiding places. I'll look after you.'

'No, no! Calm down, for God's sake! I've got good news,' said Nils and he plonked himself down on the sofa bed. 'The police have locked up three old blokes for the Nordea robbery. They are between fifty and seventy years old and are known as the Old Blokes Gang. Isn't that something!'

'Wonderful!' said Christina and she hugged Rake.

'Old Blokes Gang! Just because you're more than fifty you don't have to be called an old bloke,' snorted Rake.

'So the Old Blokes Gang have been arrested for the Nordea robbery.' Martha smiled with a glance at the men in her league. 'Could it be that the technology you used was a little old-fashioned?'

'What are you talking about? It worked just fine!' Brains objected.

'Sorry, sorry, I didn't mean it like that, I was mainly thinking that we didn't use weapons,' she tried to smooth things over.

'Hmm,' said Anna-Greta. 'As long as the Old Blokes Gang are behind bars we can continue at full speed. We could start up our Penshy Restaurant.'

'Yes, that would be wonderful indeed,' said Christina, all eyes. 'I can work out some menus and do some preliminary sketches for the interior. If we start work now, we could have it ready by Christmas! The first stage of the Vintage Village.'

'Pleasure Village,' Rake interjected.

'Well, whatever, but we should definitely travel back to Stockholm tomorrow.'

'I agree, because as soon as the police realize that they have arrested the wrong people, we'll be back in the danger zone,' said Martha. 'But we can manage to do a lot in the meantime.'

'An Old Village with a disco for Grey Panthers, for example,' said Rake.

'But first we must celebrate,' Brains chipped in.

'With tap water and lingonberry juice? Or what about mineral water?' Rake made a face. 'There isn't a drop left. Martha sold it all.'

'We can celebrate later, we must lie low,' Christina pointed out.

'When I grow up I'm going to be a dachshund. Then it would be easier to lie low,' said Rake.

'In Djursholm we've got lots and lots of bottles of champagne,' Martha tempted them and when she saw the smiles she knew that they were all on the same wavelength. It was high time to return to Stockholm. The capital awaited them.

The retired former police chief inspector Blomberg sat on his brown corduroy sofa from IKEA and swore out loud. He had drunk his beer and the bowl of crisps was empty. He felt in the bowl and swore again. On the TV news he had just heard that the Nordea bank robbery was solved and that the culprits had been apprehended.

'But what bumbling amateurs! The Old Blokes Gang? Not a chance that it could have been them. Those young beginners at the Kungsholmen station haven't a clue!' he burst out and hissed so loudly that the cat, Einstein, leapt up from the sofa and ran and hid in the wardrobe. Of all the criminal gangs, Chief Inspector Jöback and his team had gone and arrested the members of the Old Blokes Gang! How could they be so stupid? There was no way that those blokes could have robbed the bank. They had used weapons during their previous crimes and would never rob a bank without their pistols. And then the detectives went and arrested the old blokes even though they didn't find a single cartridge. No the culprits must be people like the oldies in the League of Pensioners. People who didn't resort to guns but managed to carry out their robberies nevertheless. Admittedly, nobody had seen those silver pensioners for quite a while, but they could have been deliberately keeping a low profile and were now back because they'd run out of dough. That was how it went for many criminals. And the Nordea bank robbery was unique. The explosive material and the way the fuse had been set up, all of that pointed to old-fashioned methods. They still hadn't stopped him from accessing the police archives on Kungsholmen, and he had scoured all the documents.

Blomberg contemplated visiting the police station to present his theories, but hesitated. He had begun to tire of Jöback and the team up there. They didn't seem to respect his knowledge and they never offered him coffee and cakes. No, he was always the one who had to take something with him. In fact, that was pretty galling. So why shouldn't he keep his theories to himself? Not until they offered a reward for information would he, perhaps, assist them with his tips. That Jöback did indeed try to be friendly, but he couldn't hide his pomposity and arrogance. But, of course, he was a beginner and only forty-eight years old, almost still a trainee. Blomberg mulled things over. What if he were to open a detective agency, a private detective agency of his very own . . . Yes, then he could carry out investigations, gather information and subsequently sell it to the police. Or perhaps, even better, catch the crooks himself. He had dreamed of having his own detective agency since he was ten years old when he read Astrid Lindgren's book *Blomkvist, the Master Detective*. Instead, he had become a policeman and had been satisfied with that, in the past. But now he wanted more. Why not fulfil his old dreams?

First and foremost he needed to track down the oldies in the League of Pensioners. Perhaps he could get them put on trial for earlier robberies in Stockholm. If he succeeded in doing that, then he would get lots of extra jobs to do for the police. And it would pay well too. Of course, there were other possible suspects who could have committed the crime, but not many gangs of pensioners had taken on banks before.

When he was still on active service, he had actually tipped off some colleagues at Interpol, but he had not actually followed up on those contacts before he retired. But now? Well, why not contact his mates at Interpol and get a little help to nail the League of Pensioners? Of course, he was a pensioner too, but at least he had been the one to first come up with this line of inquiry.

Blomberg immediately felt in a much better mood. He got up and went into the kitchen. He opened the fridge door and eyed the beer cans a long while before selecting a strong brew for himself and a packet of fresh herring for Einstein. From now on, the oldies would be his top priority. Everything else would have to wait.

22

Martha and her friends had been home a few days recuperating. It was Anna-Greta who had made the travel arrangements; she had had the tickets sent to her iPhone, and she was so proud of herself that you could hardly speak to her. But the journey and all the hullabaloo in the allotment gardens had taken their toll, and the whole gang had been obliged to take things a bit easy. At their age you weren't as energetic as you used to be, and there were limits to their capacity. Martha hadn't even managed to start up their gymnastics exercises again, so they all realized that she too was worn out. But after a weekend of computer games and reading up in the tower and some bracing walks around Djursholm, they got their energy back. On Monday morning Martha had announced that they would ensure that the bank robbery money ended up among those who needed it. The question was how they should go about it. The League of Pensioners had gathered together in the library and Martha spoke first.

'We decided to share out the bonus money to those in health care,' she said and rocked back and forth in the rocking chair with a wholemeal biscuit in her hand. There was a tray on the table with different-coloured tumblers and a jar of health drink which Christina had recommended, something with ginger in it. And in a deep dish next to that were wholemeal biscuits – or flake biscuits, as Rake called them.

'Righto, that idea of hiding money in bibles wasn't perhaps so brilliant,' Christina thought out loud. 'But think how nice it would be to hand out the bonuses personally. And we could take flowers with us too.'

'Yes, but we can't visit tens of thousands of people all over Sweden and give them flowers. We'd all be dead before we've finished,' Rake objected.

'Usch,' said Anna-Greta.

'I know. We can announce a lottery with cash prizes,' Martha suggested with a pleased look on her face.

'Lottery?' Brains interjected. 'That sounds plain daft.'

'Listen now. A lottery with cash prizes could be called "Bonus wages to those who were left without" and to take part you must send in your name, address and email address to us.'

'And once we get the addresses, we can check their annual earnings in the Tax Authority databases so that we can be sure that no high earners have sneaked in by mistake. Then we send the bonus money directly to the winners,' said Anna-Greta. 'Excellent!'

'But how will people find out about the lottery?' Brains wondered.

'We can put an advert in *Medicine Today*, the *National Health Guide* and *Health* magazine,' Martha proposed.

'OK, then all we have to do is concoct a good text for the advert,' said Christina. 'First of all, the name of the lottery itself, and then a text about how it works.'

'Yes, that's it!' they murmured in unison. They leaned back in their chairs, closed their eyes and tried to think – all except Rake, who immediately dozed off. Anna-Greta got up and turned on the computer, and when the others each made their own suggestions she typed them into the document. When they had finished she printed the document and gave each of them a copy. Here were, to put it mildly, lots and lots of ideas, she noted. 'Down with bonuses, Up with bonuses, Bonus roundabout, Bonus twist, Bonus bingo and Winged bonus,' she read out loud.

'We're voting for Bonus bingo,' said Christina and Anna-Greta, while Brains and Martha thought that the lottery should be named Bonus wage to those who were left without. That was two against two; they needed a casting vote so Rake was woken with a poke in the ribs.

'Bonus bingo, you what?' Rake muttered as he came to his senses and rubbed his eyes. 'Er, what the hell, name it Cow bingo!' he announced, then puffed up the cushion on his armchair and closed his eyes again.

In the end they all agreed on Bonus bingo, and after a discussion about the bingo lottery on TV and whether Cow bingo was an insult to animals (or not), they finally got their pens out.

'I know,' said Martha. 'We'll advertise with a picture of our target group, all those people who are badly paid at hospitals, health clinics and in home care. Then we write "Bonus lottery just for you" right under the picture.'

Now there was a general murmur of approval and Anna-Greta immediately looked for a suitable photo on the Internet. After a few minutes of scrolling she selected a group photo with nurses, auxiliary personnel and janitors who had lined up smiling in front of some hospital steps. Then she added some text in a smallish font saying that the lottery participants should give their name and address so that the donors could see who would get the money.

'But, dear friends. All of this is very well, but our money won't stretch far. It is like pissing in the Mississippi!' Martha sighed. 'We must get some more.'

'What did you say?' Anna-Greta shouted with her hand behind her ear. 'Singing about Missy Pippy?'

'Like I said before,' Martha went on, 'the bank robbery money won't go very far. We must *think big*, we must think outside the box. I've been thinking about Bielke and—'

'Well, can't we start a political party and get a state subsidy? Then we'd get pots of money,' Brains broke in.

'Not a bad idea. Then we'd get paid for nothing,' said Anna-Greta.

'Not a bad idea – no, it's a rotten idea! No, now we're getting totally sidetracked,' sighed Rake. 'I'm hungry. Can't we just adjourn this meeting and eat our dinner?'

Martha glanced around the room, got up and put her arm in Anna-Greta's.

'You're right, Rake. For big decisions you always need food in your tummy and time to think about it. And now we do actually need hundreds of millions.'

23

The pea soup was coming to the boil on the stove and big bubbles surfaced in the large pan. A pleasant aroma spread. Anna-Greta put in some diced carrots and bits of ham, adding thyme to make it a bit spicy. And even a little *Cederlunds Punsch* followed before she realized what she was doing. Martha leaned over the pan and tasted.

'Um, smells good, but a little more salt and pepper perhaps,' she said and smacked her lips. She put the teaspoon down and pushed the pan away. Anna-Greta nodded, added some more spices and shook a bit of marjoram over it all. She tasted.

'Yes, this will be good. And we'll have crispbread to go with it, and cheese, of course. Now all that remains is to lay the table for the others.' She put the pan back on the hotplate. Martha opened the cupboard and started to take out the crockery. Anna-Greta watched her with a wide smile. They had been together in the kitchen for more than an hour and it felt as if something new and great was in the offing. When she had put out all the plates and cutlery, she sat down to catch her breath.

'We've got some great challenges ahead of us, and without

you, Anna-Greta, we can't deal with them,' said Martha. 'We must get at the *big money*, and it's a case of make or break.'

She rested her head in her hands and asked Anna-Greta to give her an update on their money transfers and everything about Bielke's business dealings. Then she let Anna-Greta talk away without being interrupted. What was so wonderful about Martha was that she didn't care about prestige, but was happy to listen to others. In the end, they had sat down together in front of the computer and studied motor yachts for sale to find out what boats like that cost. They had googled cabins, interiors and swimming pools, and seeing all the enormous luxury had been something of an eye-opener. The motor yachts moored in Cannes, Antibes and Saint-Tropez were literally floating palaces. But when they tried to trace the owners, they met with difficulties. Almost all the valuable boats were owned by companies. The same applied to their neighbour's most expensive boat in Saint-Tropez, a six hundred million-kronor yacht with several decks and a helicopter pad. If Anna-Greta hadn't been so clever at navigating through cyberspace, they would never have traced Bielke's company, but after a few searches they had discovered that it was called Aurora Yacht Inc and was registered in Georgetown on the Cayman Islands.

'No wonder he's never at home in Stockholm. He's fully occupied,' said Martha pointing at the picture of the luxury yacht. 'Heavens above, what a life!'

'If only we could get hold of that boat, then we'd have some proper start-up capital for our Vintage Village or, at any rate, for the restaurant,' Anna-Greta said. 'The only question is how. This is going to be our toughest challenge yet.'

'We can get Nils to drive the boat, Rake's son is a seaman, remember.'

'Yes, what a good idea.'

'Then we must train with yoga and gymnastics so that we'll have the strength to hold on if the sea is rough,' Martha went on.

Anna-Greta nodded, although not quite as enthusiastically.

'If we steal from a tax evader, then we aren't hurting anybody, but we can make a lot of people happy,' Martha continued. 'Bielke has three luxury motor yachts so one more or less doesn't make any difference, does it? And since he hasn't paid tax on them, he won't find it easy to report the boat as being stolen.'

'The perfect crime again! You're a genius, Martha,' exclaimed Anna-Greta and then they laughed loud and long together. Martha saw herself sneaking around in Saint-Tropez and stealing boats while the sun shone and the wind stroked her face. The League of Pensioners would go BIG TIME, very, very BIG TIME!

'Life is a precious gift and every day a glimmering possibility,' she said and she threw her arms out wide in a generous gesture.

'Yes, sure, but we have a little problem,' Anna-Greta cut in. 'We must sell the boat otherwise we won't get the money.'

Martha fetched the bread and put out the last items of cutlery on the table.

'But you know what? I'm sure we'll think of something that'll work. There is always a buyer. Let's eat now. One thing at a time. No crime without good food and planning.'

'Exactly, and with a glass of *punsch* with the soup we'll

probably get Brains and Rake to go along with the idea too,' said Anna-Greta, going to fetch the *punsch* glasses.

'Mind you, it'll be difficult with Brains,' Martha sighed. 'He's always on about us getting married.'

'Um yes, tricky that,' said Anna-Greta coming to a halt with the glasses in her hands.

'Yes, the thing is that men always want to have control over you. Like herding cattle into a pen and locking the gate.'

'Why not suggest to Brains that you can get married beside the Mediterranean. Then he's bound to follow along to Saint-Tropez. Just think what a romantic marriage that would be.'

'But then I must do it for real. No, I can't deceive him.'

'You can't have everything, you must make small sacrifices—' said Anna-Greta, before breaking off abruptly and rushing across to the stove. The pea soup was about to boil over and she quickly took the pan off the hotplate. Then she put in a little extra thyme and stirred the peas. 'You know what? Bielke doesn't pay any tax at all and yet he has three boats worth more than one and a half billion kronor. The jewel is moored in Saint-Tropez. That one is just waiting to be stolen. That can be worth a nice wedding? Please Martha . . .'

Now there was silence, a very penetrating silence, and Martha started to walk round the kitchen table time and time again. She didn't seem at all at ease and Anna-Greta suddenly had a bad conscience for having put pressure on her. When Martha was rounding the table for about the tenth time, Anna-Greta stood in her way and held her arms out to stop her.

'Martha, dear, it was just an idea.'

'Yes, yes I know. Stealing a motor yacht on the Riviera is of course a good idea, but I'd never get married for the sake of it. Besides, we ought to get our activities up and running here in Sweden first. We can't just go from robbery to robbery without sharing the proceeds. Our robbery money must benefit others, otherwise we are just simple crooks. So if we start by renting premises instead of buying, then we can give money away immediately. And if we fetch the drainpipe money from the Grand Hotel too, then that will suffice to pay the rent, the fittings for the restaurant and wages for the staff. When all of that is up and running, then we can start on bigger robberies – like stealing motor yachts and the like.'

'Hello there, won't that food be ready soon? I'm starving to death!' Rake's voice could be heard from the other side of the door.

'Yes. Come in, do,' said Martha opening the door for the others. 'We were just doing a little planning.'

'Hear that, Rake? It sounds ominous,' said Brains with a glance at his mate.

'Nothing fancy, just a few new crimes,' said Martha, who had happened to have heard, and she winked in Brains's direction. Anna-Greta took off her 1950s spectacles, breathed on the glass and polished them carefully with her handkerchief.

'You know what, now you sound like those criminals who think they will never get caught.'

'That's right. Believe me, we are *never* going to get caught,' said Martha.

'Hmm,' said Brains.

24

The street was deserted in the heavy drizzle, but behind the magnificent brick facade the lights were on. At Kungsholmen's police station, the major crime team were working overtime. Chief Inspector Jöback and his men were having a meeting.

'Now we're bloody well back to square one,' sighed Jöback poking his ear with a cotton bud. 'Who the hell brought the Old Blokes Gang into this? They usually use weapons during their robberies, and these jokers at the Nordea bank didn't.'

'The Old Blokes Gang? I'm afraid it was you yourself who—' said his colleague Jungstedt but he was silenced when he saw the look on Jöback's face.

'Can't they install better alarm systems at the banks, so we won't have to deal with this sort of thing?' Muttering, Jöback threw the cotton bud into the waste-paper bin. 'More than ten million kronor missing and we don't have anything to go on.'

'That lady who phoned directly after the robbery, what about her? She had been out with her dog and caught sight of Elton John and Margaret Thatcher outside Nordea bank. She could be an important witness,' Jungstedt suggested.

'An old woman, seventy plus? Are you mad? Grumpy old hags – no, no bloody way.'

'But she said something about Pavarotti too.'

'He's dead!'

'But the robbers could have been wearing masks. Remember that gang who always wore masks years ago, you know—'

'No, they disguised themselves as police officers, that's a hell of a difference.' Jöback clasped his hands over his stomach and couldn't smother a yawn.

'The Gorbachev robbery, then? Those guys who stayed on at the SE-bank after closing time and then looted the vaults. They came out in the morning with drawn weapons dressed up as Gorbachev.'

'Gorbachev, ah yes, the old hag must have remembered that well-known robbery and then her imagination did the rest. No, women should stick to baking and cooking. Not involve themselves in police investigations.'

'And talking of baking. When Blomberg was here with his cakes he talked about the League of Pensioners who stole those paintings from the National Museum . . .' Jungstedt began.

'Usch,' Jöback cut him off. 'Taking a few small paintings off the wall at the National Museum is one thing, but breaking into a bank vault is quite another. Not a cat in hell's chance that a bunch of oldies could use explosives.'

'Don't be so sure . . .'

The discussion was interrupted by a knock on the door and laboratory technician Knutson came in. In his hand he held a numbered transparent plastic bag containing a little chip of dark wood.

'The tests on the samples from the bank are finished, and they show what we suspected.'

'Oh yes?' Jöback twisted round on his chair and picked up a new cotton bud.

'The chip is from a wooden object, and the wood is hazel.'

'Oh, right. Splinter from a wooden object.' Jöback poked deep into his ear.

'We believe it comes from the handle of a walking stick.'

'A walking stick? So the bank was robbed by Pavarotti with a walking stick? Except he's dead.' The irony in Jöback's voice was not to be missed.

'Well, you see, it's from one of those sticks made from hardwood with a decorative handle that elderly ladies use.'

'Like Margaret Thatcher perhaps? And she is dead too.' Jöback threw the cotton bud away and put his hands behind his neck.

Jungstedt gave a resigned glance at the unfortunate laboratory technician and cleared his throat.

'A walking stick could indicate that some elderly people are involved in the robbery. It could be the League of Pensioners. I think we should contact Blomberg again and hear what he has to say. He knows a great deal about that gang of oldies.'

'Usch, the walking stick must have come from a bank customer . . .'

'But there is something mysterious about this chip of wood. It has been subject to considerable force.'

'If you say it came flying into the room as a torpedo, then I'm giving in my notice and resigning!'

The laboratory technician pretended not to hear. He put on some white gloves and took the chip of wood out of the bag, holding it up for all to see.

'The chip of wood has crashed with something with full

force. There are traces of concrete in the wood. There are scratches too and in those we found microscopic remains of rubbish. I don't understand it at all. We found the chip on the floor inside the bank vault.'

Jöback pressed his fingertips against each other and hummed for a long time.

'That sounds complicated. How on earth could that have come about? No, this is nothing for us.'

'But we have a budget for external services. Why not let Blomberg look into this? A splinter of wood from the handle of an old walking stick, that ought to keep him busy for quite a while,' Jungstedt proposed, as he too didn't feel like working on this particular clue.

'But what if he comes every day with his cakes again?'

'No risk. This way we can keep him at a distance. We simply say that we don't want him to come back until he has solved the case. And until then he won't get any more assignments.'

'Wow, Jungstedt, you're a genius. Why didn't we think of that before? That way we'll be rid of him. Hurrah!'

Jöback laughed, got up and signalled to the technician to leave. When he had gone, he turned towards Jungstedt.

'I don't think either the Old Blokes Gang or the Gorbachev robbers are behind this Nordea robbery. But you know what, there could be something in what the old hag said about those masks. The guys behind the Gorbachev robbery might have turned to Pavarotti and Thatcher masks this time.'

'Yes, and Buttericks is the obvious place to buy a mask. They must know which masks they have sold over the last six months. And to whom they have been sold.'

'I know. We can send Blomberg to Buttericks,' Jöback exclaimed with a satisfied grin. 'There he can potter around among all the robbers' masks and whoopee cushions as much he wants.'

'Um, Blomberg is smarter than people think. Don't underestimate him.'

'Blomberg smart? First time I've heard that! No, we'll let him do the boring slog and we can concentrate on what's important.'

'But what if he catches the robbers?'

'Blomberg? Ha, ha.' Jöback roared with laughter and dropped the whole packet of cotton buds on the floor.

Jungstedt got down on his knees and helped him to pick them up. He could make neither head nor tail of him. The new boss didn't seem to take anything seriously. Not, at any rate, tips from elderly ladies. From that moment on, Jungstedt decided to keep track of everything himself. If Jöback made a fool of himself, that was one thing, but he didn't want to get tarred with the same brush. He had a career to think about and he wanted to catch those Nordea bank robbers, and that was that. Whatever it cost. He picked up the last of the cotton buds, got up and went to his room. For a long time he sat behind his desk and stared at the telephone. Then he lifted the receiver and dialled Blomberg's number. Like he'd said, Blomberg was much more cunning than Jöback realized. In actual fact, a great deal smarter than his own boss.

25

'So what about the drainpipe?' Anna-Greta put down her teacup and looked at Martha. The friends had just finished dinner and now were sitting with a cup of tea up in the tower room. It was still light outside. There was a bit of a wind and a roof tile sounded as if it was about to fall down.

'Yes, now listen, it's time we fished out that money from the drainpipe.' Martha sighed and put her knitting down. 'Nobody knows how long Anna-Greta's tights will last.'

'Well, we've heard that before,' Brains pointed out.

'I know, but unfortunately we had some bad luck on our earlier attempt. But just because we failed that time, we can't just give up. There are so many people who need help with their economy today. You know what, women who have worked all their life don't get a big enough pension to live on – indeed, they can't even afford to keep living in the same flat because their pension is so low. They only receive a few hundred kronor more than those who haven't worked at all,' Martha said.

A murmur of reflection went round the room and they all realized the gravity of what Martha had said. And this time Brains understood that he had to succeed. How else would he gain Martha's respect? Rake, too, understood that this was serious. They couldn't make a fool of themselves in front of the women yet another time. The new attempt must be planned very carefully.

'I trust you,' said Martha and she gave Brains a little kiss on the cheek. But deep inside she felt like a spin drier. What if the men botched it up again?

The next two weeks were spent on preparations and then they went into action.

Martha and her friends bit their nails and paced impatiently back and forth outside the Djursholm villa before Christina's son Anders came to fetch them in the minibus. They all felt that this time it was sink or swim. They were simply obliged to get hold of that money for all the poorly paid health-care staff before they left their jobs and the patients started to suffer. Yes, those champions in the country's old folk's homes, hospitals and home care needed to be encouraged with gilded bonuses – just like the boys in the big companies.

The friends in the League of Pensioners ventured out into the night, yawning, to re-acquire the millions in the drainpipe and if it hadn't been for their passion for social justice, they would much rather have been warm and snug in bed. But after a mini-session of yoga and a solid breakfast, they climbed into the minibus ready for a new adventure. While Anders drove into the city, they yet again mulled over the drainpipe money. There were no scientific investigations to ascertain how long five million in banknotes could survive in two old pairs of tights stuffed down a drainpipe, and this was not exactly something they could ask the experts about. The

League of Pensioners must quite simply hope for the best. And thus it was a case of acting quickly so that they didn't arouse too much consternation. And to be on the safe side, this time they had bribed the night porter and the night-duty security guards outside the entrance to the Grand Hotel.

Martha had talked about the fiftieth anniversary of the City Fire Station and said that the members of the pensioners' club would be given a little surprise. Her husband and his colleagues had been members for forty years and would be so pleased to feel that all those years in the service of society were acknowledged. There might be a little noise out on the street for a short while, but the celebration would only take a few minutes and then she promised that the members of the fire station club would disappear just as quickly as they had arrived. When the staff at the Grand Hotel had been hesitant, she had flopped over her wheeled walker and started to shed tears and had said that she didn't want to live any longer. Were the staff really so ill-natured that they couldn't give an old woman a little joy? The security guards squirmed and looked very embarrassed and then Martha had played her trump card.

'In the final instance this is about fire safety, since we are also going to test a new type of fire-extinguishing system. This won't cost the hotel anything at all, and should you wish to purchase the new extinguishers in the future, we promise you a reduction of twenty per cent. Nothing is as important as fire safety and, of course, it would feel good if we test our most modern equipment right outside the Grand Hotel,' she finished off and then she flirted a little with her eyes.

'You'll have to take that up with the management!' said the

oldest guard with his hands behind his back. His uniform was so elegant and it looked as if it had come straight from the posh NK department store.

'But please, I promised my husband. Just a short while. Please! We'll try to be as quiet as we can!' Martha angled her head to one side and let her voice break in that tear-filled way that only an elderly frail woman can manage.

'Hmm,' said the guards and they didn't look especially convinced. But when Martha started snivelling, pulled out her handkerchief (drenched in onion juice) and let the tears pour out, even the man with the elegant uniform from NK melted. Martha blew her nose (on another handkerchief), thanked them for their confidence and promised to be as quick and silent as she could.

Stockholm slept and almost nobody except night workers, late-night revellers and furtive criminals was out on the streets when Anders parked close to the Grand Hotel and the League of Pensioners got out of the minibus. They were wearing the fire brigade's thick, black uniforms and had become much livelier during the drive in from Djursholm. Brains and Rake quickly unrolled the police cordon tape between two cones they had set up at the entrance to the Blasieholm quayside. Then they hung up a printed sign in yellow and black which said: WARNING. They had discussed whether they should put up a sign saying: 'Warning: criminal investigation under way' or 'Warning: explosives' but had concluded that neither idea was suitable. Then they had agreed to just have a sign saying 'Warning' so that people could be afraid of whatever they wanted.

To improve the effect, Brains had suggested that they

should construct one of those robots that looked like the ones that searched for bombs and they all thought that was a good idea. Brains had been given a free hand and they could all hear him hum and sing in his workshop. In the end, he had emerged with a false robot that he had made from an old radio-controlled car that he had hidden inside a black Siemens vacuum cleaner. It all looked very convincing, as did the sign that Christina made with the help of her computer: WARNING: EXPLOSIVES. This was a reserve sign that would only be used if people became too curious and the robot, in turn, would only be sent out in the event of the police – or a taxi driver or a ferry-boat skipper for that matter – becoming too inquisitive. Brains had promised and crossed his heart that he wouldn't bring out his Siemens Special unless absolutely necessary.

'Here it is, we only have to open that,' said Anders when they had cordoned off the area and the League of Pensioners had found the old classic fire hydrant close to the ferry-boat quay.

'Are you sure the water pressure won't damage the money?' Martha wondered and looked on worriedly as Brains, Rake and Anders started to roll out the fire hose.

'But we can't get the tights out of the drainpipe with compressed air, Martha dear. We must use water. And see how fortunate we are with this solid old fire hydrant. We only need to screw and connect,' said Brains.

'Yes, you couldn't have a better hydrant than this,' Anders agreed and patted the dark green construction lightly on the top. 'Now we only need to check the interlocks and that everything is in working order.'

Anders, who was standing right behind Brains, leaned forward and checked the hose very carefully.

'This is going to have a fantastic reach,' he said, very pleased.

'You what?' Christina wondered.

'Reach, the water will shoot out with a hell of a force,' Anders answered.

'What about the threaded hose-couplings?' Brains looked at the hose sections and counted to three units.

'What?' muttered Rake.

'The threaded hose-couplings. We must join the hoses together,' Brains explained.

'Oh yes, right, of course we must,' mumbled Rake.

They had purchased the hosepipe in separate sections because they feared a single long section would be too heavy for them to carry. None of them had the same condition as a real fireman, but they planned to connect several short lengths of hose together so that they would end with a long hose. The men rolled up their sleeves and joined the hoses as best they could and then tried to screw the synthetic hosepipe to the hydrant.

Martha, who had taken a step back, watched all this from a distance. She paced back and forth on the pavement outside the National Museum and tried to keep away while the men worked. It was their turn now. Otherwise she was always the one who ensured that the project was carried out, as with the case of the theft of the Renoir and Monet paintings up at the museum.

She glanced up at the facade and the National Museum's steep steps and smiled a little. A lot of exciting things had taken place here. But this time – this time it was Brains and

181

Rake who would be in charge of everything and if she didn't keep her distance, she would get too involved and start giving them advice. Something that not everybody appreciated. She would just go a little closer and see how they were getting on. She heard the men huffing and puffing but nothing happened. No, they weren't getting anywhere with this. And then she couldn't resist going right up to them.

'Now listen, it would surely be best to turn the water on soon so that we don't get all tangled up in that mess of hoses,' she said pointing at the snakes' nest of hoses filling out the street.

Rake and Brains grunted while they continued in their sweaty efforts to get everything together and working.

'Yes, and then we hose out my tights from the drainpipe at great speed,' Anna-Greta added, together with a loud neigh.

'Sssh,' the others hushed her. 'We mustn't attract attention!'

'No, quite right!' said Anna-Greta with her thunderous voice and then there came an extremely weird noise from her stomach as she tried to restrain her voluminous horsey laugh. She was more sensitive than usual when she was so excited.

When Anders, Brains and Rake finally succeeded in connecting the sections of hosepipe and fastening the end to the hydrant with a spanner wrench, they went to the drainpipe and pushed the nozzle up into the opening. Now that the first light of dawn was reaching Stockholm you could see quite well, but there were still very few people out on the streets. Outside the Grand Hotel it was silent, and the driver of a Stockholm taxi who was on his way to the hotel turned back when he saw the cordon.

Now they were ready to turn on the water, but all the work

they had put in so far had made the members of the League of Pensioners so tired that they had to get their breath back before they continued. The old crooks looked up at the Grand Hotel where the dark drainpipe stood out against the light facade.

'What if the drainpipe leaks?' Christina suddenly asked.

'It won't. Pipes like that don't leak,' said Anders authoritatively, though he had no idea.

'Well, then. Shall we start up?' Martha wondered, and her voice sounded slightly more unsteady than usual.

Brains nodded, took up position by the hydrant and Anders and Rake took a firm hold of the hose sticking up into the drainpipe, and gave a thumbs-up sign.

'Now you will be careful, won't you?' Christina breathed and put her hands over the bridge of her nose as she sometimes did when she was nervous. But the men didn't answer and the next moment a strange hissing noise could be heard, like the sound you hear when the water rushes through a garden hose just before it splits. The fire hose filled out and straightened up and when it was completely round, Anders and Rake pushed the nozzle even further up the drainpipe. Suddenly there was an enormous whoosh inside the drainpipe and the men lost control. The nozzle and hosepipe shot up in the drainpipe at an incredible speed, making an enormous rattling noise. The doorman at the Grand Hotel took a few steps forward and looked very perplexed.

'This shouldn't be physically possible,' Brains gasped as he wrestled with the hosepipe. Now you could hear so many strange sounds inside the drainpipe that it was really confusing and the length of hose still on the pavement started to squirm and turn wildly. A ferry-boat skipper who had been asleep in his cabin came out on deck in wrinkled pyjamas and rubbed his eyes.

'What the hell is going on?' he shouted and took a step towards the quay to lecture the people who were disturbing the peace. 'Oh but, my spectacles,' he realized, tripped on one of the deck planks and fell heavily. 'Aah, bloooody hell!' He swore loud and long and then, groaning, felt his knee while the seagulls flew up from the water in fright.

'Turn it off, turn it off!' Martha shouted, but then Brains became so nervous that he turned the handle of the hydrant the wrong way. Immediately the water pressure became so great that the men could hardly hold on to the hose. The pillar of water got higher and higher until it came to a sudden stop. Inside the drainpipe it shrieked and rattled and the hosepipe bulged so round that it looked as if it would burst.

'Now listen, what's happening?' Martha shouted, rushing up to the hydrant. 'Have we got the wrong drainpipe?'

'Wrong drainpipe? Are you mad, woman!' sputtered Rake while he struggled with the hosepipe.

'What if all the banknotes are ruined? For God's sake, turn off the water!' Anna-Greta appealed.

'You can't bloody well stop a deluge,' Rake hissed and he threw himself down on the hosepipe to stop it from knocking everyone over, while Christina tried to sit on it without losing her elegance.

'This is the day of reckoning!' she exclaimed and clasped her hands together, but she got no further as something suddenly shot up into the sky from the top of the drainpipe at one hell of a speed while a fountain of water sprayed up over the roof ridge and then fell back together with a collection of empty bottles that rolled down the roof. Even higher up, you could see large and dark shape on its way down. It banged into the flagpole next to the Princess Lilian suite, bounced on the copper roof and then slid down towards the gutter where it ended up hanging over the edge.

'Oh no, don't say it's got stuck!' Martha groaned and she peered up towards the roof with her hand over her eyebrows.

'Pah, we'll give it another little squirt.' Playfulness showed all over Brains's face. 'Come on, Anders!'

The two men pulled the hose out of the drainpipe and aimed the nozzle at the roof gutter where what looked like a sausage-shaped bin bag was hanging over the side. The bag started to move from the pressure of the stream of water.

'Will that really work? Oh dear, I shall say another prayer,' mumbled Christina clasping her hands together.

'Christina, the pressure from a fire hose can move a car,' answered Brains at the same moment that the black bag finally sailed over the edge and fell down to the street.

'The bin bag! Hurrah, now we're richer by five million kronor,' Anna-Greta exclaimed when she saw the black bag crash down.

'Shush!' came from the others.

'That's if there is anything left of the banknotes, of course,' Anna-Greta added.

The men turned off the water and had barely had time to disconnect the coupling before Anna-Greta rushed up to the bag to have a look . . .

26

The others managed to stop their friend, but not until she had been promised that she would be the first to count the money did she give way and climb into the minibus. While the others got ready to leave, Martha went in to see the night porter and the night guard and thanked them for their cooperation, assuring them that her husband had been so pleased and that she would always remember their wonderful hotel service. She wished them a good morning and that they would both soon be promoted. Then she gave a small bow and took her leave. But just as she was on her way with her wheeled walker, they stopped her.

'What were those strange noises?'

'Oh yes, goodness me, dear oh dear.' Martha sounded apologetic. 'It was the new pump, the Argo three two one nine. It most certainly didn't live up to expectations. We shall complain to the manufacturers straight away. But at least it is good that we found out now. Yes, wasn't it a dreadful racket?'

'That's putting it mildly,' said the night guard and he pointed to the facade where newly awakened and angry guests on nearly every floor had opened windows and were gesticulating, shouting or giving the international sign for 'Fuck you!'

'Yes, well, things don't always work out as one expects, but if everybody was as friendly and helpful as you there would be peace in this world, I am convinced as to that,' said Martha, and she bowed again and rolled off with her wheeled walker.

The night staff remained standing there and watched her go off. Then they looked up at the facade again and shook their heads. In a way the old lady was wonderful, but this had definitely gone too far. It would be best to report it to the management as well as to the police. Those oldies might decide to celebrate something again.

When Martha reached the minibus, she wrenched the door open.

'Is everyone here? We'd better get out of here pretty damned quick!'

'We were waiting for you.' Anders opened the back door for her and Martha pushed the walker inside. When she, too, had got in and sat down, he drove off as fast as he could without arousing suspicion – after all, they were in a vehicle normally used to ferry the old and infirm. He drove past the Östra Station, took the road past the Royal Institute of Technology and when they reached the Lill-Jan woods, he stopped. He quickly got out and changed the registration plates, then they continued their journey towards Djursholm.

'Weird odour in here,' said Anders.

It did, in fact, smell a bit strange from the back seat. They all looked anxiously at each other. The weird odour was not a good omen, and Martha had to make quite an effort to prevent Anna-Greta and the others from ripping open the bin bag.

'We must be careful. It's better to open it in a safe place where we can take care of the money,' said Brains and Anna-Greta, who had covertly opened the outer bin bag, and was just about to open the innermost one, stopped herself at the last moment.

'Yes, of course, yes,' she said and looked just as guilty as a little boy who has been caught in the act of doing mischief.

'The tights did indeed have reinforced heels and toes but the bags must be opened in an orderly manner,' Martha made clear.

Anna-Greta cast her eyes downwards.

Anders speeded up and when they drove across the Stocksund bridge and were just about to turn in towards Danderyd, Martha saw in the rear-view mirror how Anna-Greta was trying to sneak a hand inside the bag anyway.

'Tut, tut, Anna-Greta, naughty! Didn't we just decide to wait?'

'Yes, but they are my tights,' Anna-Greta retorted stubbornly, but in a voice which grew weaker and even sounded a little guilty at the end.

When they reached their villa in Djursholm they passed Bielke's garden and saw through the lilac hedge that the autumn leaves had fallen upon the lawn on top of the former swimming pool.

'If that pool hadn't been filled with concrete we could have hidden the money there,' said Brains.

'We are not going to hide anything anywhere, we're going to have that money now,' said Anna-Greta, unusually decisive.

'To those in need!' Christina was more precise.

'Yes, whatever happens, we must never be greedy, however much we steal. Promise, all of you!' Martha held her index finger up in a strict gesture.

'Amen!' said Rake.

When they had parked, opened the back door and dragged the bin bag into the sauna in the cellar they could relax and Martha went to fetch the champagne.

'To think that we finally got hold of the drainpipe money,' she said handing out the champagne glasses with a smile of satisfaction on her face. 'We'd better celebrate straight away. And then if the banknotes have been destroyed by insects or gone all mouldy we will at least have had our little celebration.'

Rake looked at the label, held up the bottle so that all could see, and nodded.

'Um. Your philosophy of life isn't so bad at all. A Henriot Champagne *Brut Millésimé*, indeed, you're improving.'

'I agree with Martha. You should enjoy things in anticipation. If it all goes to pot, then you've worried unnecessarily, and if it goes well, then you can celebrate once again,' Brains said.

They all applauded, took their glasses and watched as Brains elegantly opened the bottle. After which he served each of them with a slight bow.

'Cheers, then!' they all called out in unison and quickly took a mouthful before putting the glasses down. None of them was really interested in the champagne; rather, they were like children on Christmas evening. They wanted to know what was in the bin bag.

'Righto everybody, shall we take a look?' said Christina and she had barely uttered those long-awaited words before Anna-Greta was there with the kitchen scissors. When she made a hole in the plastic there was a puff of shut-in odour, of rot, which reminded them of a mixture of compost, old eggs and a privy that hadn't been emptied for a long time. But this didn't bother Anna-Greta. With a few quick snips of the scissors she had also opened the innermost bin bag and before the others had even come close she had pulled out the tights. They all tried to touch the somewhat shabby-looking leg-warmers – all, that is, except for Rake who was more interested to see if his seaman's knots had survived a whole year down the drainpipe. He eagerly picked up the remains of the bin bags and looked for his knots. He cautiously poked the tarred marline and discovered that his double knots and bowlines were still intact but had acquired a greenish grey tinge. What if the bags had leaked? He was now beginning to feel apprehensive and was just about to grumble about the problem when the air was filled with a piercing scream.

'My tights are intact!' Anna-Greta shouted out, ripping one of them open and throwing banknotes up into the air as if she had been Scrooge McDuck in a bathtub full of coins. Banknote after banknote fluttered down and landed on the benches and the sauna floor.

'But usch, it doesn't half stink!' Christina coughed and held her nose.

'And what has happened to this?' Brains wondered as he held up the second pair of tights which was dirty grey and very, very long. It seemed to never come to an end. It was the longest pair of tights any of them had ever seen and it had evidently become extremely stretched when it had been hanging inside the drainpipe for so long.

'Aren't we going to open that one too?' gasped a semi-groggy Anna-Greta who could hardly contain herself after having seen so many banknotes. 'There ought to be two and a half million kronor inside. That pair of tights was almost new, so the banknotes ought to have fared even better than the others. At least they won't smell so bad.'

'Less foot sweat perhaps?' said Rake and he took a mint pastille.

'Empty out the banknotes so we can see how well they've survived. At any rate the tights seem to be dry,' said Martha feeling the nylon.

'Naturally. I know my knots,' said Rake, and he got hold of the foot end of the tights and swung them teasingly above his head until a pile of banknotes fell out. They sailed down and landed on the benches and the sauna stove and Martha gasped in horror. Not until she realized that the sauna stove wasn't turned on did she calm down.

The whole floor of the sauna was now covered with banknotes, five hundred kronor notes, and they were just as excited as if they had just been out on a new bank robbery. Rake felt his blood pressure rising and had to sneak off to get his medicine. He had been given it at the hospital but hadn't told anybody, not even Christina. He didn't like those pills. A seaman was never in poor shape, and an old salt like him didn't need any medicine. No, it didn't fit with his self-image. Nobody noticed when he opened the bottle and took out his three white pills. He swallowed, coughed slightly and then joined the others again.

All day long the members of the League of Pensioners crawled around in the sauna and checked the banknotes on the floor. Some of them had turned dark and some were frayed in the corners, others felt damp and stank, but most of them had indeed fared well in Anna-Greta's tights with their reinforced toes. Martha and her friends couldn't get their fill of staring at over ten thousand banknotes on the floor; they just kept looking at them, touching them and examining every single one very carefully. Brains sang a popular Swedish ballad about seeing Sundbyberg – his old home – before you die, while the others were content to hum 'Money, money, money'. When they had gone through all the banknotes and sorted them in piles, they got out the champagne again, sat down on the sauna benches and toasted one another.

'You know what, when I see a successful mission like this it makes me think we ought to become robbers for real,' said Martha and she raised her glass.

'But aren't we already?' Brains wondered.

Nobody said anything but just looked at the piles of notes until Martha opened her mouth again.

'Now listen, for the time being this is a rather uninteresting and more of a philosophical problem. We have more serious things to think about. How do we distribute several thousand mouldy-smelling five hundred-kronor banknotes to those in need?'

27

'Home care and the health services shall not be given mouldy money,' said Christina decisively and they all mumbled in agreement. Their mood had indeed become slightly dampened when the League of Pensioners realized that ten thousand nasty-smelling five hundred-kronor banknotes would be hard to deal with. The people who received these stink bombs would start wondering, so something must be done.

'Now listen, let's turn on the sauna so that the banknotes will dry. Do we have some vinegar? It's simply a question of pouring vinegar into some bowls and leaving them to stand there a while among the banknotes, that'll take away the smell,' Christina explained, being knowledgeable about household tricks.

'But we must hide the money,' said Anna-Greta.

'Nobody's going to bloody well look for money in a sauna that smells of vinegar,' said Rake.

'Exactly,' said Martha and she disappeared. She was gone a while and then returned in triumph with two large laundry bags. 'When we have got rid of the worst of the smell, we can put the banknotes in these and then store the bags in the laundry room. That'll be a good hiding place.'

'Where did you get hold of those bags? They are the sort that commercial laundries use,' said Anna-Greta.

'Precisely. I found them in Bielke's shed. We can borrow them for the time being.'

'Poor old Bielke. Can't he have anything left in peace?' wondered Brains.

'Pah, we're only going to borrow them a few days,' Martha decided. 'Now we can turn on the sauna and go and have a bit of a rest. We need some sleep after all this hullabaloo.'

The others nodded and yawned widely, happy to now be able to sleep for a while. Brains turned on the sauna at sixty degrees Celsius and Christina and Anna-Greta covered the banknotes with two large light-blue duvet covers with a rabbit pattern from IKEA. Then they went off to their respective rooms, satisfied with the night's achievements. They had got hold of their five million and could start up their Robin Hood activity as soon as the money had dried. For Martha and her friends, there was nothing they liked better than handing out money to those in need, so, even though they were exhausted, they were all in the best of spirits. Five satisfied pensioners went to bed and soon the old Djursholm villa was filled with loud snoring (they didn't all have a special dental brace). The oldies, who had been so excited earlier, now slept soundly with a big smile on their lips and dreamed of bank robberies and good food. Totally ignorant of the fact that the sauna thermostat was faulty.

'What the hell!' The retired chief inspector, Blomberg, swore as he read the text message on his mobile phone. Jöback and his cronies at the station had commissioned him to do some additional investigation in connection with the Nordea bank robbery. And now they had asked him to go to the Buttericks joke shop of all places! His mission was to find out who had bought masks representing Margaret Thatcher, Elton John, Pavarotti and Brad Pitt in recent times. Blomberg stared at the display while his face grew redder and redder. What a task! That was a simple job for a trainee! Were they teasing him? He was so insulted that he could hardly swallow and his cat, Einstein, who realized that his master was angry, jumped up onto his knee, pawed him and put his head in Blomberg's lap. With shaking hands, Blomberg stroked the purring pussy and calmed down a little. His dear Einstein had an unusual ability to sense when something was not quite right, and just now Blomberg was so furious that even a china cat would have reacted. No way was he going to do that shit job. No, he would spend a bit of time in front of the computer one evening and simply collect some information about masks and prices and suchlike. That would have to do. And he was going to send them a bill too, if nothing else because they had insulted him! Besides, he needed to bring in some money to his detective agency firm, otherwise sooner or later the tax authorities would start questioning his accounts. You had to earn some money too, not just make deductions.

Blomberg returned to the daily reports. Since he had started his detective agency he had made a habit of always reading the daily reports from all the police districts in Stockholm and every morning he scanned the various events that had taken place during the night. He was just about to have his second cup of coffee when he noticed a weird report that had been logged by the Norrmalm police district. According to a night guard at the Grand Hotel, a pensioners' club from the City Fire Station had tested a fire hose on the quay at five in the morning. But the thing was that that sort of test was always carried out in the daytime and there was no fire station with that name. Blomberg googled and soon found:

It's a peaceful day in the three-storey LEGO® City Fire Station. The fire chief sips his coffee in his office while a firefighter repairs the truck and another takes a well-earned nap. Spring into action when the alarm bell rings! Slide the firefighters down the pole, load them into the fire truck, van and helicopter to save the day in LEGO® City! There's tons of fun to be had in this massive building set with three vehicles, big, transparent windows and two retracting garage doors. Includes five mini-figures: a fire chief, pilot and three firefighters with assorted accessories.

The City Fire Station was a LEGO set for children! Good God, somebody who was interested in fire stations must have played a practical joke on the staff at the Grand Hotel or there was something fishy going on. Blomberg put his cup down so hard that it almost broke. The Grand Hotel was right next to the National Museum where there had been several serious robberies. Indeed, a single valuable painting in the museum was worth the equivalent of a lifetime's income for an ordinary worker, so criminals were more than ready to target paintings and antiques. Perhaps the Fire Brigade Gang were actually preparing to rob the museum? Blomberg was now very keen. The CCTV cameras outside the hotel might show something; he ought to check those pictures. Then he remembered his old mate Eklund, who was a skipper on the Waxholm ferry boats that served the archipelago. Weren't they moored close to the Grand Hotel, and the skippers sometimes slept on board? He might have seen or heard something. Blomberg pushed Einstein onto the floor, fished out his mobile and punched in the number. Eklund answered almost immediately and after some idle chatter about weather and water conditions, Blomberg came to the point.

'Had something happened outside the Grand Hotel last night? Yes, it fucking well had!' Eklund shouted into the phone. 'Some raving lunatics woke me at five in the morning. And guess what? It was a gang of oldies who were playing with a fire hydrant! They must have had a screw loose, every one of them. I tried to stop them, but fell over and hurt my knee.'

'Oh, nasty, that can be painful.'

'Yes, it bloody well can. But what on earth were those nutters up to?'

'What did they look like?'

'There were five of them. Four had their backs to me, unfortunately, so I couldn't see their faces. But they had those black firemen uniforms. And there was an old woman who paced back and forth in front of the National Museum with a wheeled walker.'

'A wheeled walker?'

'Yeah, one of those Zimmer frames but with wheels. It was as if she was in charge of the rest of the gang. Then they connected a hose to the fire hydrant and that's when all hell broke loose! You should have seen it! Those oldies stuck the nozzle up a drainpipe, right next to the Cadier bar, and turned on the hydrant. Then there was a hell of a noise. I couldn't see any more because I was lying on deck with my knee. But I did see them drive off afterwards in a sort of minibus with a ramp on the back.'

'Like the taxi minibuses, for oldies and people with a handicap?' Blomberg felt his pulse increase. 'So they were really old, then, those people in the City Fire Station?'

'You can say that again! The old woman had her Zimmer frame and the others walked slowly and carefully and with bent backs. Together, they must have been several hundred years old.'

This rang yet another bell for Blomberg. The oldies had been close to the National Museum in the middle of the night. They were, of course, planning a robbery. That was crystal clear. They were going to use the fire hose to break in with. It would probably be really easy to break a window with the jet of water. The pressure of water from a fire hydrant and a large dimension hose with a proper nozzle could be extremely powerful. Blomberg got up and walked around the room with his mobile in his hand while he tried to think. He recalled the theft of two paintings, a Monet and a Renoir worth thirty million. That coup at the National Museum was still something of a mystery and his colleagues had spent a long time on the case. The crooks had never been caught, nor had the criminal league that robbed Handelsbanken sometime later, and on both occasions some elderly people had been seen on the CCTV images. They included an older woman who featured on several, a woman that he himself had believed to be involved. But the lack of evidence had meant that they couldn't pin her to the crime, but now, what if it was her again! Blomberg looked up at the ceiling with his mobile against his ear and got thinking. All the members of the Old Blokes Gang were locked up, and besides, there hadn't been any women members. The same applied to the Gorbachev robbers. But nevertheless, the police still had three unsolved robberies that had been carried out by elderly people: the theft of the paintings at the National Museum, the robberies at Handelsbanken and Nordea. What if it was the work of one and the same group? A new gang with elderly members, including women? Yes, where one of the members was an old woman. A League of Pensioners.

'Were they wearing masks?' Blomberg asked, now quite sweaty with excitement.

'No, not that I could see. But like I said, they moved slowly. I bet you they were over seventy at the least.'

'Eklund, I'm coming to see you so we can talk a bit more,' Blomberg exclaimed, then added a few polite phrases and ended the call. He immediately felt decidedly exhilarated. Oldies on the rampage at five o'clock in the morning. It sounded almost too good to be true. He would soon have them behind bars.

Early next morning everyone in the League of Pensioners woke up in an unusually good mood. After endless troubles and worries about what they should do, they had finally succeeded with their Operation Drainpipe. It was such a great achievement that Rake thought they should celebrate with coffee and something strong to go with it, but then Christina protested and maintained that they must limit all this drinking. This morning she planned a yoga session and then it was a great deal better that they drank a nourishing fruit smoothie instead, one of her specials with lime, orange, apple and banana.

'Or we can do an ordinary good old gymnastics session. Then you can have tea with cloudberry liqueur afterwards,' Martha tempted them, thinking that Christina's health interest went a bit too far sometimes. Her friend threw an irritated look at her.

'Martha, it is only yoga that makes your body supple,' she snapped back.

'But gymnastics makes you supple and improves your general condition,' Martha claimed.

'Now listen, girls, calm down! Before we start swinging our legs this way and that, we must sort out the sauna, mustn't we? That is the most important thing. After all, there's five million down there,' Brains reminded them.

'Yes, you are right,' said Martha. 'First, we'll put all the notes in the laundry bags. Then we can do some gymnastics.'

'Or yoga,' said Christina.

'You go down to the sauna and I'll clear the breakfast table,' Anna-Greta offered, and without waiting for an answer she started to gather up the cups. 'I'll come down later.'

The others nodded and got up and headed for the cellar. But as soon as they opened the door to the stairs they sensed something was wrong. A hot, pungent vinegar smell hit them and made them hesitate.

'Oops, this doesn't bode well,' Martha mumbled and she hurried down the stairs. When she reached the sauna door she saw that the little square window up near the ceiling had acquired a light red covering and when she opened the door she was met by a sour, sticky vinegar mist. She coughed and backed out again.

'What's the matter?' Brains wondered and he opened the cellar window to be on the safe side before opening the sauna door again.

'Oh goodness, uff!' was all he managed to utter before he too withdrew.

Not until they had opened the window and cellar door as wide as possible and got a cross draught did they venture to open the sauna door again, and then they waited some time before actually daring to go in. But despite the door having been open for more than fifteen minutes the temperature was still over seventy degrees and the air unpleasantly pungent. They all realized that something unexpected must have happened. Something *very* unexpected.

'The thermostat,' said Brains. 'Something must have broken. It hasn't worked like it should have.'

The vinegar in the bowls had turned into steam and the moist hot vinegar-filled air had settled on the light-blue duvet covers like brown, unsymmetrical drops. And now the bedclothes with the little rabbits on them looked rather weird, to put it mildly. Martha went up to the covers to pull them aside but hesitated.

'Something tells me that we are about to have an unpleasant surprise,' she said. 'The duvet covers were from IKEA and were *very* cheap.' Her voice sounded thin and sort of eery.

'Yes, right. Buying cheap can be expensive in the long run,' said Rake and he pulled the covers aside so that banknotes flew in all directions.

'Uhuh, what have we got here? Banknotes that stink of vinegar, and they look bloody awful too,' Rake noted and he kicked some brownish five hundred-kronor notes.

'Help, the notes are discoloured and seem to have acquired the pattern from the duvet covers too,' said Brains.

'Yes, exactly. Look, lots of tiny bunny rabbits!' Christina sniffled and held up two of the banknotes against the light. 'Five million full of rabbits!'

Martha, Brains and Rake started to stir the pile of banknotes while Christina, sobbing, tried to stop her tears.

'If we put the banknotes behind glass and frame them, then perhaps we can exhibit them at the Museum of Modern Art,' said Martha, in an attempt to brighten their mood.

'Then we can even frame Anna-Greta's tights too,' Rake said.

'That wasn't the slightest bit funny,' Christina retorted between sobs.

'Hello, down there, how's it going?' Anna-Greta called out from the kitchen, but she didn't get any answer. Then she suspected that something was wrong and when she went down to the others, to be on the safe side she took a bottle of Akvavit flavoured with elderberry and five schnapps glasses on a tray.

'What about a little something to perk us up this morning. We more than deserve it,' she said.

'Deserve? I'm not sure what we deserve, to be honest,' said Martha and she showed her some banknotes.

'Oh my God, what has happened?' exclaimed Anna-Greta almost dropping everything on the floor.

'This,' said Martha, holding up one of the banknotes close

to her spectacles. Anna-Greta put the tray down on the stairs and stared at the five hundred-kronor note a long while. She was completely silent, so silent that the others became worried. Then came that strange sound from her stomach, a sound that grew in strength and turned into a veritable thunder bomb.

'I BEG YOUR PARDON, A RABBIT?!'

'IKEA,' Christina sighed.

'The duvet covers were a special offer,' Brains explained.

Anna-Greta went down on her knees (a manoeuvre she now could do fairly well after Christina's yoga sessions) and poked around in the pile of banknotes.

'Hmm. It is the top layer that is somewhat the worse for wear, but it isn't too bad.'

'What do you mean?' Rake asked. 'We've just destroyed five million!'

'No we haven't! In fact, this has solved a big problem.'

'And I thought we had now been landed with a big problem.'

'On the contrary. I've just realized that this is a wonderful way to launder money.'

'Don't say you're going to put thousands of five hundred-kronor notes in the washing machine. Or did you just want to put them in the spin drier, perhaps?' said Rake.

'Not at all. Listen to me. We'll contact the Bank of Sweden. According to the 2014 regulations about the redemption of banknotes and coins, the bank is obliged to redeem notes that are damaged.'

'Is that true?' Martha exclaimed in delight.

'Even banknotes with rabbits?' Christina wondered and she blew her nose.

'Well, we could perhaps wash them first,' Anna-Greta suggested.

'I know, in the cleaning programme on TV they demonstrate how you remove stains,' Christina informed them. 'There must be some good tips there.'

'I know, we'll scrub off a number or two and then we'll put the damaged banknotes in a carefully sealed envelope and send it to the Bank of Sweden in Broby. If we stick to an amount under ten thousand, we can get them exchanged for new ones. It'll take a bit of time, but that doesn't matter.'

'Will they exchange the banknotes?' Christina looked as if she was about to faint.

'Absolutely,' said Anna-Greta. 'They will even put the money in a bank account that we stipulate. The Bank of Sweden is legally obliged to do this – unless the money comes from a crime or from criminal activity – but we don't need to tell them that.'

Then Anna-Greta held a little lecture about how you remove stains with acetone and water in the right combination. And they all agreed that they ought to wash the banknotes in slightly different ways so that nobody would suspect that they came from the same source. For the same reason, they ought to post their envelopes to the Bank of Sweden spread out over time so that nobody in the bank got suspicious. The two bags in the laundry room in the cellar could quite simply be their own little home bank – without any hidden fees and such nonsense – from which they could take out money when needed.

'Just like a monthly salary,' Anna-Greta summed up.

'Better than a pension,' said Martha. 'With this money we can at least manage well even though we are old ladies. I mean, just think about all the poorly paid women who won't be able to live on their pensions.'

They all agreed about this and joyfully expressed how delightful it was to be a crook and not a poverty-stricken pensioner with the lowest pension. Especially now that the League of Pensioners had so much money that they could share with others. And that meant it was high time to rent some premises so that they could open a restaurant for the elderly.

'We'll start with the restaurant, get experience from that and then we can go on with our Vintage Village,' said Martha.

'Yes, a modern village for seniors which will be a model for the rest of Sweden,' said Anna-Greta.

'No, a model for the whole world,' Martha said. 'We shall show the way for all the others.'

'Oh heavens above, Martha is getting going again!' Rake muttered.

'Yes, indeed,' said Martha.

28

Not all the banknotes had been discoloured, only those that had been closest to the duvet covers. But still there was quite a lot to do. In the days that followed, the sauna room was transformed into a strange arena where Martha and her friends hung up newly washed five hundred-kronor bank-notes with clothes pegs on long washing lines. They had all scrubbed a little bit extra on the numbers and sometimes even ripped off a little bit of the edge, all in accordance with the instructions from Anna-Greta. As long as the banknotes were at least in the most part intact, the Bank of Sweden would replace the damaged ones – but, even though Anna-Greta knew about this, she still found it very hard to actually rip a genuine banknote.

The room was dominated by a strange smell of vinegar and acetone, but gradually the five hundred-kronor bank-notes began to look really good. Of course, some of the banknotes were a bit pink on the edges – just like after an ordinary robbery of a security vehicle – and others had mys-terious patterns after sticking against IKEA's rabbits. But thankfully they had at least managed to get rid of all the ani-mals with long ears, and that felt good.

After working hard in the sauna, the League of Pensioners could now sort the money according to pattern, colour tone and wear. Admittedly, some notes still had a faint odour of vinegar, but that ought to disappear after a while. Pleased with their work, Martha and her friends now put the sorted millions in bundles into the laundry bags, put some dirty laundry on top and put everything in the laundry room. They would stay there while the League of Pensioners now and then sent a few notes to the Bank of Sweden for replacement.

When all this had been done, Martha relaxed a little and together with Anna-Greta talked about future plans.

Lawyer Hovberg had informed them that the Visa card and the company were ready and that the monthly transfers to the City Mission were working fine. It felt good to be supporting the City Mission which had schools as well as giving assistance to those in need, but of course it was even more fun to hand out the money themselves. When the first payments started to arrive at their account in Handelsbanken from the Bank of Sweden, the League of Pensioners started to look around for a place to rent. It was high time to start that Penshy Restaurant.

One chilly autumn day, the entire League of Pensioners set off to the new district at Hornsberg on Kungsholmen close to the centre of Stockholm to look for a good place for a restaurant. They started their walk at Ekedal Bridge, wandered all the way beside the lake, passed a bathing place, several restaurants and then got almost as far as Kristineberg. But everywhere the premises were already rented out or were far too small.

'It seems that we are a bit late,' Brains sighed, who, like the others, was now very tired. 'Perhaps we must wait until something is for sale.'

'Wait? Usch, we haven't got time for that!' exclaimed Martha. 'There must be something available. Why not ask at that cafe over there? The staff at places like that are usually well informed about what is going on in the area and, anyway, we need to reinforce ourselves with a cup of coffee.'

'Yes, we ought to build up a circle of customers in the same area where we are planning our Pleasure Village,' Anna-Greta suggested.

'Righto, next stop the cafe,' said Rake, combing his hair and following the others.

It wasn't a big cafe and when they entered, the smell of freshly brewed coffee hit them. The tables had small white cloths and the birch wood chairs reminded them of 1950s Sweden. They sat down but were so tired that they hadn't the energy to talk. They needed to recuperate for a while, each with a double espresso and a chocolate ball before they got their strength back. Then Martha got up and went across to the cafe owner.

'We're looking for restaurant premises to rent. You don't possibly know of anywhere available around here, do you?'

'Oh, I've no idea. You need to talk to Johan. He fixes everything.'

'Johan? Which Johan?'

The cafe owner didn't answer immediately and the espresso machine hissed quite a while before he turned back to Martha.

'Johan Tanto. He and his family have several restaurants in this area. Good guy. He helped a mate to start a pizzeria.'

Martha got his number, phoned and arranged a meeting. They agreed to meet outside the cafe and the following day the entire League of Pensioners travelled in to Hornsberg again. It was drizzling, grey and chilly, but here and there quite a lot people were moving around.

'Johan, is he in his thirties?' Anna-Greta wondered when she caught sight of a young man lighting a cigarette outside the entrance. He was wearing a black pullover, grey winter coat and was bare-headed. Around his neck a necklace could be seen.

'Well, we only have to ask. Costs nothing,' Rake said. He took a step forward and stretched out his hand. 'Johan?'

The man nodded, extinguished his cigarette and introduced himself as Johan Tanto. He had blond, straggly hair, a ring in his ear and a tattoo visible above his collar. In the old days, a tattoo meant criminality or that you had been a seaman, Martha thought, but nowadays everybody had a tattoo. So how could you tell what people were like?

'I understand you are looking for restaurant premises. We've got a place over there!' he said, and without waiting for an answer he led them down towards the quay. The League of Pensioners found it hard to keep up because Johan walked rather fast. His movements were rapid, almost like a weasel.

'Here it is,' he said after a while and he stopped beside a large barge. 'There was a restaurant here called Vinci and then it became an art gallery. But now that has moved to Södertälje. We thought that this could become a restaurant again. The premises are really nice and could be used for lots of things!'

'A barge,' said Christina, disappointed. She had imagined a

cosy restaurant with a bowing head waiter who received you in a glittering bar. On the other hand, the boat seemed to be in good condition. The hull was painted a dark green colour, while the stern had a lighter shade of green and the gunwale and stays were grey. The old barge was moored with the long side against the quay and after the man had unlocked a gate they could walk on board. Christina noted that the gangplank was wide with proper railings and that there wasn't much of a difference in height between the quay and the hull.

'Nowadays you must have everything accessible for the disabled,' said Johan when he saw Christina's face. 'But that's how it should be, of course.'

He unlocked the door, took a step back and gave them room to pass.

'The barge is firmly secured and there is plenty of room for a good restaurant in there. But it needs quite a lot of work on the fittings, of course.'

'No problem at all, this is just what we want,' said Christina looking at the bare walls. Dreamily, she saw before her how at last they would have the space to hang up her watercolours. Martha, for her part, hummed to herself. The inside of the barge had large, empty spaces, but on the other hand, they could put up walls and fit it with tables and benches. There was even room for a sitting area and a bar.

'Where did this barge sail?' wondered Rake.

'It transported coal in the Mediterranean once upon a time,' answered the weasel-like man. 'Then it was bought by a man from Finland who converted it into a restaurant and it ended up here.'

Martha took a deep breath and sniffed around. She, who

was usually sensitive to damp, wasn't troubled at all but actually found it warm and cosy. This would be suitable for elderly people with chest problems, she thought. Besides, the barge had railings and wheelchair ramps. This could be an Eldorado for oldies! The perfect place!

They went into the kitchen area and Christina noted that there were two cookers, a big workspace island in the middle, lots of cupboards, plenty of worktops and two dishwashing machines. Besides that, there was a very spacious kitchen sink stretching all down one long side of the room.

'This seems really quite fantastic,' she said and Anna-Greta nodded in agreement too. Even Brains seemed to be satisfied.

'Hmm. This doesn't look at all bad. I can have a little corner workshop over there with a carpentry bench and tools for if something breaks. Besides, there is room for engines that I can work with when the restaurant isn't open.'

'I'm sure it will be fine,' said Martha and she went further into the premises. In the bows it was a little dark, but they could fix that with suitable lighting. And there was no harm in having it a little romantic, since they were going to have some speed dating. After going through all the space once more, the League of Pensioners made up their mind. The rent was low and the barge seemed to be in good condition. This is where they would open their Penshy Restaurant.

The next day, when they signed the contract, Martha noticed that Johan Tanto seemed stressed. He was fidgeting with the ring in his ear the whole time.

'You seem to have a lot going on,' she said.

'In this business things are always going at full speed,' he replied evasively, handing over the contract. His eyes were sharp and his movements fast. 'Well, good luck, then!'

He had hardly had time to shake Martha's hand before he showed her out through the door. Brains, who had been waiting for her outside, put his arm on her shoulders.

'You know, my dearest, we forgot something. We forgot to ask what happens if the barge sinks.'

29

'A permit for this and a permit for that! Unbelievable! If I'd known about all this bureaucracy, I wonder if I'd have suggested that we open a restaurant,' said Martha, red in the face with a fat bundle of papers in her hand. Her hair stood out in all directions and she breathed with short, panting breaths.

'Take your medicine, Martha dear,' Brains urged her in a worried voice and he didn't give in until she had found her bronchial sprays and inhaled her daily dose. Then she quickly wiped her mouth, licked her lips and popped the inhaler into her handbag. She picked up the bundle of papers again.

'All these permits! We simply want to open a restaurant, not build a whole town!' she muttered.

The members of the League of Pensioners sat on the benches in front of a fold-out table in the stern of the barge, all except Rake, who had sat down on an old seaman's chest. In front of them lay the application forms, blueprints, sketches and colour samples.

'Now listen. The premises must be approved for the preparation and serving of food. And also we need a permit to serve alcohol, of course,' said Martha.

'Pah, don't bother about the permits. We've never been particularly law-abiding,' Anna-Greta put in.

'It says quite a lot about spirits too. To serve alcoholic beverages we must take a little exam about the alcohol laws,' Martha went on.

'I volunteer for that,' said Rake.

'But it isn't about trying out spirits, it's about knowing the laws, Rake,' Christina enlightened him.

'Oh, well, then I won't bother,' Rake said.

'The restaurant premises must be registered with the building and environmental department as a unit where foodstuffs are handled,' Martha read in a loud voice, 'and when alcoholic beverages are served there must be an authorized person on the premises who is suitable for the responsibility and has good knowledge about the alcohol laws.'

'Oh heavens above, the five of us are almost five hundred years old together and we have drunk spirits for, well, at least more than four hundred years. What we don't know about alcohol isn't worth knowing. So, in that case, we can say that we have knowledgeable people on the premises,' Brains said, and immediately the others agreed with him.

'But listen to this too,' Martha went on as she pulled yet another piece of paper out of the bundle. 'The department issuing permits shall examine the personal and economic background and suitability of the owners of the restaurant.'

'Examine us!' said Anna-Greta with a joyful cry, pushing up her 1950s spectacles onto her forehead. 'If only they knew that our income goes to the Cayman Islands.'

'You mean we do our tax planning so that we can give

away even more money, if I've understood this properly?' Christina stated, to be on the safe side.

'Yes indeed, that's just how it is. Shady deals are not our style,' Martha confirmed.

'Oh really, then I must have misunderstood,' muttered Rake sarcastically.

'I heard that, Rake. But the League of Pensioners only gets involved where the government and parliament fail in their duties. Not otherwise,' Martha clarified.

'Government and parliament? Yes, right, Martha. You haven't thought about becoming the boss of NATO too?' he answered, but only loud enough for Brains to hear. His comrade grinned.

'Usch, all these regulations for every tiny thing. Now I know what we shall do, we'll put up a list of them in the entrance so that the authorities will think that we follow them,' said Martha.

They all agreed that the logic of this was brilliant and Anna-Greta immediately pulled out her laptop. She composed a fancy-looking list of all the regulations and they agreed that Brains would frame this later and that they would hang it up in the entrance. That decided, they all thought they had finished the day's discussion, but no:

'Now listen, it's high time we decided on the fittings,' Martha went on and she arranged a tea break. They all sat down on the red sofa on the afterdeck, and while Martha served tea with ginger and cloudberry liqueur, the five of them sank deep among the cushions. They had purchased the luxurious armchairs and the magnificent plush sofa for their future VIP guests. Eight comfortable velvet armchairs on a little raised stage framed with plants.

'Well?' Martha wondered, letting her gaze wander over the premises.

'I vote for model ships hanging from the ceiling,' said Rake. 'They must be magnificent specimens, everything from clippers to paddle steamers. And it should smell of tarred rope.'

'That sounds lovely,' said Martha.

'Has anybody thought about banknotes?' Anna-Greta wondered. 'Wouldn't it be really fancy to frame them and hang them up on the walls? All sorts of different banknotes and denominations.'

'But Anna-Greta, that reminds us of work; I mean, bank robberies and such. No, forget it,' said Rake.

'Christina, you are the artist among us. How would you like to decorate the restaurant?' Martha wondered, turning to her friend. Martha had worried a long time that she decided too much herself and she was now going to let the others decide too – even if it was so, oh dear, so terribly difficult to lose control. And yes, why not delegate the responsibility to Christina, who was their own artist? She pushed the blueprints across to her friend.

'Christina, can you deal with this?'

And as she suspected, Christina immediately looked so extremely pleased that Martha felt really warm inside. Christina didn't need any more encouragement but let her artistic soul take over.

'First and foremost I shall hang up my watercolours, but I've got another idea too. Do you remember the sauna at the

Grand Hotel with that green light and the jungle music? Why not turn this into an exciting jungle landscape? Not a real jungle, of course, but a bit romantic with tables among the trees and some stuffed animals.'

'A sort of local version of the National Museum of Nature?' asked Rake, pulling out his tobacco.

'I'm talking about a human environment where we say yes to nature.'

'Bla, bla,' said Rake.

Then Martha kicked him in the hollow of his knee so that he turned quiet. Sometimes you must be diplomatic, and now was not the right occasion to tease Christina.

For the whole afternoon the League of Pensioners continued their discussions and Martha, who had persuaded the others to agree to Christina being allowed to decide, now started to regret her own decision. Because whatever arguments the others put forward, Christina seemed impossible to stop. She insisted on the jungle theme and stuffed animals. The others said that this was a restaurant for people and not a zoo, but Christina was insistent. To start with, she had suggested twelve exotic animals, like lions and tigers, plus a bear, but now, after two hours' tiring negotiations, they had got her to choose a smaller number of beasts and those with more of a Scandinavian connection.

'OK. A badger, a bear, a monkey, a wild pig, a fox and a squirrel, I can go along with that,' Christina said forcefully. 'But then we must have birds too.'

'You forgot the guinea pigs,' said Rake. 'They are better and don't take up so much space.'

Martha kicked him in the hollow of his knee again.

'On condition that I can have a forest aroma and a greenish light in the premises. I mean organic lighting,' said Christina.

'You can't bloody well have lighting that makes everyone look nauseous,' protested Rake.

Then Martha suggested that they could have different themes every month, for example seafaring the second month, perhaps flowers the third month, and so on. This calmed Rake and the discussion continued.

'So to sum up,' said Martha, when they had talked this through a while. 'This restaurant is to be nicely furnished and fitted and will always be undergoing renewal. An Eldorado for the elderly.'

'Unless it ends up like a playground, of course,' Rake sighed.

'No, I've had enough of your mean comments, Rake. Pull your socks up, or I'll abandon this project straight away!' said Christina glaring at him.

'Oops, I didn't mean it like that, I was just joking,' Rake ventured.

'I understand exactly what you think. Come up with something better yourself, then! But you can't, can you? You just criticize others.'

'Dear friends, now I think we ought to calm down a little. What about a nice cup of tea with ginger in,' Martha intervened.

'Ginger? Not that too,' sighed Rake.

And with that, Martha realized that they wouldn't get any further that day, so she suggested that they should go home to Djursholm. Christina could go directly to the National Museum of Nature and reconnoitre, if she wanted, find out what was available, and then they could use that as a starting point for further discussion.

'I'll go to the museum tomorrow and see what they have in their warehouse and that will be that,' said Christina, sounding unusually decisive. They all looked at each other in surprise but thought that it would be best to let Christina have her way. If she was going to be responsible for the restaurant, then it was logical that she should decide about the fittings and decoration too.

The next day, Martha (albeit with a certain degree of hesitation) let Christina go off with her children Emma and Anders to the museum to see if the director would be prepared to lend them some of the stuffed animals from the warehouse.

'But if you bring something with you, then for God's sake make sure it isn't infested,' she said as a final bit of advice before she waved them off. She wasn't entirely satisfied with Christina's jungle ideas and had her forebodings. But having once delegated the responsibility, she must now keep her word.

Late that afternoon, when Christina and her children drove up on the quayside, Martha saw that they had rented a large trailer. Curious, she went up to the trailer, lifted the corner of the tarpaulin and gasped. Under the green plastic there was a whole collection of stuffed animals, everything from a badger and fox to a little elk calf and a roe deer – but, thank God, no bear. There was, however, a stuffed wolf.

'They hadn't got a decent bear. They offered us one that was so moth-eaten that I didn't dare take the wretched thing,' said Christina.

'Perhaps it hadn't had any bilberries for a while,' said Rake.

'So you took the wolf instead? Well, of course, that animal is always in the news,' said Martha in an attempt to be positive, staring at the grey-white wolf. Christina had wanted a giant of a bear in the entrance, and this did at least demand less space. But . . .

Martha turned to Christina. 'Do you really that think we should have this in the entrance?'

'Yes, we must welcome our customers,' said Christina.

'With a wolf?' wondered Brains.

'We can have a sign saying "WELCOME!" next to it.'

Then the others tried to propose furnishing the restaurant with books instead and decorating the walls with lovely quotes from the foremost authors, but Christina was not susceptible to the argument. So they shook their heads and gave up. Without knowing it, they had let loose a force of nature.

30

Oh my! What a woman Christina had employed! Like a whirlwind, red-haired Betty, the new waitress, came to the barge with her jolly laughter and her decidedly curvy forms. She wasn't exactly young, but she was oh so feminine! Brains sank down in the armchair and closed his eyes to conjure up the picture of her again. And lo and behold, there she was, dancing in front of him while her trickling laughter whirled around the deck. He found himself smiling and not until a lock of hair fell down inside his collar did he come to his senses. Ah yes, of course, he was at the barber's. And he must behave himself here.

The members of the League of Pensioners regularly dyed their hair so that they would look younger, since they didn't want to be recognized. When you are wanted by the police for bank robberies, you must look after number one and think about everything, and none of them wanted to end up in prison. It was admittedly better there than at a special home for the elderly, but they had got used to their free life. They ate good, nourishing food, did gymnastics regularly and led a life full of content which kept them in good condition. They had a comfortable home in their Djursholm villa and it was only this freedom that allowed them to share out the bank robbery money and help others. It was important not to get caught.

'Is it OK like this?' the hairdresser asked, combing out Brains's brown hair into a smart fringe. Brains had decided on a youthful style, very short on both sides and plenty of hair up on the top.

'Yep, that looks fine,' said Brains, nodding.

'And your beard?'

'My beard?'

'Yes, it doesn't look so smart on elderly gentlemen. Looks rather untrimmed and streaked with grey.'

'All right, then dye it, but I want to keep it,' said Brains firmly and remarkably quickly. He was proud to keep up with the times and his thoughts were on the redhead. Younger women often liked men with beards and he was not going to be old fashioned, certainly not.

'Well, if you want to keep it, I suggest we give it a trim.'

'No, nothing. I want it natural,' answered Brains, who didn't like being corrected. It was enough that Martha was always going on at him telling him what he should do. No, today he felt really rebellious. He had always thought that he and Martha went so well together, but now? She had indeed said yes when he had proposed, but she kept putting off the wedding. First they would have to share out the bank robbery money and now it was the restaurant project that delayed things. Not until that was all up and running – but the restaurant was Christina's baby, wasn't it? Why couldn't his Martha just relax for once? He stroked his engagement ring with his finger. That day when she had said yes had been the happiest day in his life, but now? Perhaps she wasn't suited to be married, perhaps he ought to forget about her and break off the engagement? In fact, he was beginning to tire. One month ago, when the redhead had been employed and had smiled in that friendly way at him, he had found himself feeling joy and from his heart he had given her a warm and sincere smile back. He had felt appreciated, and he hadn't felt like that for a long time. Love is not something that just carries on, it must be cared for, he thought. You could never take it for granted, like Martha did. And if you didn't work for your love, then it will wither away, yes, just like a muscle that you don't use. He had long thought of speaking his mind, but now it didn't seem so important. Something new had come into his life.

Brains's thoughts returned to Betty. For every day that passed, she had come to mean all the more to him. And elderly gentlemen did actually pair up with younger women, he had seen that himself in town and at the cinema. Of course, those men were usually very rich, but the redhead didn't know anything about his finances and, besides, didn't seem to care about such things. She liked him just as he was and had even talked about joining him on his motorbike which he had parked on the afterdeck. Then he had felt the butterflies in his tummy start to flutter, and he hadn't dared say that he was probably a bit too old to drive it.

'Right. That will be seven hundred kronor,' said the barber, taking off the cutting cape and brushing away some hairs from Brains's collar. He flashed a quick smile and went across to the cash register. Brains stroked his cheek a few times, got up in an unusually nimble manner for his age and followed him. Oh yes, his wallet. He had left it at home.

'I can pay by Internet,' he said as nonchalantly as he could. He nodded, put on his overcoat and hat and went out.

'But wait, wait, your card, we must swipe your card,' the barber shouted, but by then Brains had already vanished. He didn't have a card either.

'That doesn't look good,' said Martha when he got back to the barge a little later. 'Why didn't you shave off that beard while you were at the barber's?'

'Martha, that's my business,' answered Brains. He felt his chin with his hand and rushed past her. With firm steps he walked towards the kitchen in an aromatic mist of shampoo and hair spray. He looked around, expectant. Had Betty already arrived? On his way down the stairs he bumped into her and was so surprised that he almost lost his footing. He lowered his eyes.

'You're looking smart,' she said and gave him a wink. 'You look so youthful with that beard.'

'You think so?' he mumbled and blushed deeply.

She quickly brushed her hand over his newly dyed beard and laughed so that he completely lost the ability to talk. Amazing, he thought, that when you least expect it you can feel so warm and lovely deep inside you.

31

The weeks passed and the opening day came all the closer. Everybody expected that Christina would listen to the opinions of the others, but, no. Opening a new restaurant was a major undertaking, she explained, and then it was best that *one* person was in charge and had full control.

As time went by, the others became worried and even a little nervous, but Martha reminded them that the restaurant was Christina's project and that they shouldn't interfere too much. People who were given responsibility grew, and besides, Christina had experience of serving food. During her time as a housewife with responsibility for posh dinners to entertain her husband's business colleagues, she had learned all the dishes that were appreciated in such circles. Of course she had had cooks and waitresses to help in her Östermalm flat, but she still knew the most popular menus by heart.

'We shall serve our guests the very best and be organic without being fanatical,' she had said at their first meeting about menus, well aware that she must tread carefully.

'Not fanatical. Well, that's a relief,' said Rake, getting out his tobacco.

Then Christina had opened a plastic folder with recipes and

225

presented the various dishes. Green health dishes. Extremely green. It transpired that she had almost exclusively chosen vegetarian menus, slimming diets and the stone-age diet. Most of the dishes consisted of various salads.

'Now listen to me, this isn't a bloody greenhouse!' said Rake. 'We can't have a restaurant where people come to eat a starvation diet!'

'Those slimming diets with algae and lentils are probably very good, Christina dear, but people must have something else to eat too!' said Martha, with a forced smile, suddenly aware that she might have given her friend *too* free a hand.

'No, five days a week we shall have vegan and vegetarian,' Christina maintained. 'I feel sorry for the animals. Just remember how badly they are treated.'

'But what about free-range hens?' Martha asked.

'Or why not free-range cattle?' muttered Rake.

'Organic and green, wonderful, Christina, but we must have fish and meat too,' said Anna-Greta sounding very decisive. 'Now let us sit down and go through the menus together.'

But Christina refused and not until they had employed a cook with lots of sensible views could they agree on their Super Food menu. They all praised the cook (all, that is, except for Brains, who was grumpy because he had seen the cook sometimes pinch Betty on her bottom) and finally settled on a menu with twenty dishes with greens, nuts, fruit, berries and vegetarian hamburgers. But that was by no means the end of the problem. Christina had also let her intensive health fads affect her taste when it came to the interior decoration.

One weekend when they had all agreed to take things easy

and rest at home, she had sneaked off to the barge with Anders and Emma, and when the friends had come on the Monday morning, the interior of the barge was unrecognizable.

The fittings and decoration were all in green. It should be clearly evident on the walls as well that the restaurant was organic, Christina had threatened earlier, but now she had turned it into reality. In secret she had painted lots of water-colours in various shades of green, works of art that she had merrily nailed up on the walls, and from the ceiling hung lamps shaped like large gaudy leaves. Christina had certainly proceeded with great enthusiasm and transformed most of the restaurant into a dense jungle. With raised eyebrows and shocked looks, Martha and her friends had walked around in the greenery and examined the creation. There were at least some tables covered with flamboyant sunflower cloths and chairs with seats that resembled green moss, but there were no normal serving corridors, only narrow winding forest paths. And in the midst of it all, from loudspeakers high up, you could hear birdsong.

'Green gives such a feeling of summer,' said Martha bravely.

'Yes, and we're going to have different types of birds too,' Christina chirped enthusiastically. 'On Mondays budgerigars, Tuesdays blue tits, Wednesdays seagulls and Thursdays great tits. Then we can have chaffinches on Fridays and woodpeck-ers on Saturdays and—'

This was simply too much for Anna-Greta. 'We're not going to have a cacophony here! If you don't have two silent days a week I am going to drop out of the project this very minute!'

They all gave a start, because Anna-Greta had always had the ability to take things easy, but now she had raised her voice considerably and had protested sharply. Christina was so shocked that she became completely disoriented and, for the sake of peace, actually agreed that there would be fewer birds at the weekends. (Although she had already prepared an archive of Swedish birdsong, but she kept that information to herself.)

Whatever one might think of birdsong in a restaurant, the sounds did fit in with the interior decoration. That consisted of deciduous and coniferous trees and, in some romantic booths, she had set up mirrors from floor to ceiling so that it looked as if you were in a real forest. Tree trunks were placed between the tables, and here and there were some bushes. A badger, a fox or a roe deer peeped out from behind a trunk when you least expected it, and a squirrel or a woodpecker sat on branches right above the tables. And the wolf? Christina had quite simply moved it into the VIP lounge, and by the entrance she had arranged a shot bar, so you could have a bit of the strong stuff as soon as you came in.

'You mean so that they'll come in a bit quicker?' asked Rake.

'Of course.' Christina smiled and continued her presentation of the barge. 'It is rather exotic, don't you think?' she said and her eyes glowed. And she looked so happy that the others didn't have the heart to say what they really thought.

'We can call the restaurant "Keen Means Green",' said Rake in an attempt to appease.

'No, my dear. We must be more modern. I have given that

a great deal of thought. Now listen. What do you think of "Silver Punk"?'

There was a deathly silence. Silver Punk?

'But this is a restaurant for the elderly,' Brains objected.

'Punk? Isn't it hip dop that's popular now?' Anna-Greta wondered.

'No, hip-hop,' Rake corrected her. 'Besides, I think the restaurant should be called Silver Sailors. After all, this was a sea vessel in the past.'

'That might be. But this is going to be a cocktail bar, we're going to have all sorts and combinations. Silver-haired and those with a punk hairstyle. So Silver Punk fits well,' Christina explained. 'In this restaurant, different generations should be able to mix with each other.'

Of course, they had decided to start a Penshy Restaurant – a place for pensioners – but Christina was right, it would indeed be nice with some slightly younger guests too. Then they went on a final inspection tour of the barge and Martha, who test drove her wheeled walker between the trees on the winding paths, found that she could actually get through, although she was a bit concerned about the romantic booths in the corners. Weren't they perhaps a little too romantic and hidden in the dense greenery so that, in the worst case scenario, unbecoming activities could take place there? She was just about to say this, when Christina stopped and pointed at the dating table.

'There are twelve places here and they are going to be able to see each other's faces properly so that they can flirt. And then there is a bit of space around the sides so that you can simply move round the table if you've got your eye on somebody. And we're not going to have lots of distracting music here, but they'll be able to talk with each other. Next to this, we've got a dating corner so you can have a beer and talk a bit more. Do you get it? Things are going to be lively here.'

'I don't doubt that for one second,' said Rake.

'And who is going to serve at these tables, will it be Betty or . . .?' Brains wondered and pretended to be indifferent.

Martha gave him a suspicious look.

'Who's going to serve here? Well, it'll sort itself out,' Christina commented.

At the dating table, the lighting was warm and atmospheric, and Christina waved to the others to come closer. She put out the hand-painted invitations so that all could see, and picked one up and chirped.

'I intend inviting guests from the business world, artists, actors, musicians and authors, not forgetting rap-singers from the suburbs. Only the in-crowd and people with contacts. Then the press will write about us and the restaurant will become popular.'

'Hang on a second,' Brains objected. 'How wise is it to attract so much attention when we are on the police wanted list? And we must surely test the kitchen and make sure that everything works first. The hotplates and the espresso machine can break down and then perhaps the cook puts too much salt in the food. Wouldn't it be best for us to test before we invite a crowd of people?'

'And we must taste every dish on the menu and ensure that the cooks and service cooperate smoothly before we open the doors to the public,' Anna-Greta put in.

'Absolutely,' Brains agreed, immediately seeing the many opportunities to be able to go into the kitchen and discuss food and kitchen equipment with Betty.

Christina looked thoughtful: 'But how will we get people to come here, then?'

'I know, the bonus lottery and health-care staff. After all, we have the addresses,' said Martha and she thought about all the people working in home care and hospitals who had emailed them. 'We'll invite them to some free evenings where they can test the food. And they will get their first bonus in cash on the way out. That way we won't have to distribute the money.'

'What a good idea,' they all said, and thus agreed to send out invitations so that they could fill the restaurant.

The following day, the League of Pensioners sat with the list and emailed invitations to more than one hundred people in a first round. They all felt very excited and nervous because now their talents as entrepreneurs were to be tested. Only if they managed to run a profit-making restaurant, could they expand the activities to an entire Vintage Village.

'You know what? The Silver Punk restaurant will be decisive for our future,' said Martha.

'Mmm,' they mumbled in unison and nodded earnestly.

32

The red carpet was rolled out, the aromatic (forest mist) candles lit, and on both sides of the gangplank stood large urns with a sea of flowers. A neon sign with the name SILVER PUNK RESTAURANT glowed up on the roof and declared that something new and exciting was happening here. Smoke came from the chimney and from inside the windows a mild greenish light spread. Up on the deck, the dressed-up senior gang was preparing to receive the guests. Martha, in a long dress and a fur stole, paced back and forth on the afterdeck while she looked towards the quay. Rake, in a black leather jacket, black trousers, red ruffled shirt and a cravat round his neck, held his hands behind his back and discreetly tried to see if there were any young girls on the quay, while Brains, in a slightly worn 1950s suit, dug in his pockets for his screwdriver. At the last moment something might not work properly, in which case he needed to be prepared. Anna-Greta was wearing a wide hat with a veil and she wobbled around on high heels in an attempt to look elegant but with the result that she was always just about to fall over.

'Be careful of your thigh,' Martha shouted and Anna-Greta immediately grabbed hold of her walking stick which Brains had repaired, and twisted round so quickly that her heels made two deep holes in the red carpet. But then she remembered the yoga exercises.

'Don't worry, Martha, I do yoga with Christina. That gives you good balance, mark my words,' she said, not looking where she was going and falling over one of the flower pots. When she had got back on her feet, the flowers looked rather flattened and it took her a while to brush down her clothes. But then she threw her head back.

'Yes, I forgot the yoga session this morning, and just look what that leads to!'

Christina, in an elegant yellow two-piece, a warm shawl and red-painted nails, was rushing back and forth across the vessel and simply couldn't keep still at all. She was so wound up that she could have been able to screw herself into the ceiling – if it hadn't been for the fact that she was standing out on deck. After a while, they heard the sound of an approaching car engine.

'See that car over there, they will be the first guests,' she said, her voice now a falsetto, and she pointed to the road where a blue Volvo was heading in their direction. She was so 'high' that earlier that day Martha had even contemplated giving her friend something to calm her down, but then she remembered that Christina was adverse to pills, so she had given her a glass of carrot juice instead. Unfortunately, this was one of Christina's 'white weeks' – no alcohol at all – typical, because just now she could really have done with a glass of cloudberry liqueur to soothe her nerves.

'In the future I don't think we shall have so many flowers here in the entrance; instead we can send that money to

Doctors Without Borders,' said Christina pointing at the large pots. 'It will suffice to have flowers on posters or pictures.'

'Now steady on, we'll have to discuss that later,' Rake chipped in, being the flower-lover and garden expert, and he folded his cravat over an extra turn. 'It would look stupid watering posters, you know.'

'And how are things going with the food, Christina?' Martha wondered, having done her best not to interfere. However, she was now a little apprehensive; perhaps she ought to have asked about today's dishes because there were strange odours coming from the kitchen. But before Christina had a chance to answer, there was suddenly a lot of noise on the stairs and Olof, the cook, turned up. He was round, ruddy, thin-haired and very short. He had worked in the restaurant business for forty years and after recently becoming a pensioner he had taken on the job to keep in touch with his old profession. He was absolutely bright red in the face and waved the menu at them.

'What the hell do you mean by this? Lentils and the water that the potatoes have boiled in! I thought we were going to serve people something tasty to eat, not forbid them from enjoying good food.'

'But this is detox you see—' Christina started to explain but was immediately silenced.

'It says here that the guests can't drink coffee or alcohol, can't have sugar, fish, meat, poultry or processed food. Are you all bonkers?' Olof threw the menu onto the deck, stamped on it and pulled off his apron. 'If it's going to be like that, you'll have to find yourself another cook!'

'Now, now, we'll sort this out. We're going to eat delicious, good food here,' said Martha placing herself between them. 'That must be a little mistake.'

'Mistake? Are you calling healthy food a mistake? Oh no!' protested Christina. 'We're going to have close-to-nature products here.'

'We're not going to eat those weird things, I mean like algae and lentil casserole?' Brains feared the worse. 'I want proper food!'

'Calm down, everybody, that menu is for one of our special evenings. For people who want to test something new or start on a diet,' said Christina. 'Today we are having something else.'

'Well, thank God for that,' Martha muttered and her heartbeat went back to its normal rate.

'Now listen, what about this? Why not charge one thousand kronor for a lentil casserole?' said Anna-Greta waving her walking stick enthusiastically. 'The lesser the amount of food we serve, the more we can charge for it. Do you follow me? What a brilliant business idea, and besides, the guests will lose weight.'

'The bone marrow and bean restaurant. Yohoo!' Rake called out.

'Well, the whole lot of you are as nutty as a fruitcake,' shouted the cook, glaring at the League of Pensioners and pointing at his forehead repeatedly with a fat index finger. 'Food is there to be eaten. It must be good and you must feel satisfied afterwards,' he growled. 'And your damned detox evenings – you'll have to arrange those yourselves, just so you know.'

'But Olof, dear me,' said Christina. 'I've said that we shall serve food that suits all tastes.'

'Tastes? Don't you dare maintain that that muck has any taste. It's just horse pee, fucking disgusting. And what are those weird bags you have in the kitchen? Birdseed?'

'Oh, you do exaggerate. Sesame seed is so nourishing—' Christina protested but she was cut off yet again.

'You'll have to prepare the bird food yourselves. For this evening I've made some proper food. The guests will get lasagne pies with a pine-nut crust, grilled perch, beefsteak with onions and meatballs with mashed potato. There's got to be some order here!'

'Meatballs? Thank God for that. Then everything is under control.' Rake sighed with relief and even Martha could breathe a little easier. She had wanted to go down into the kitchen herself to see what they were up to, but had re-strained herself. If you've delegated, then you must not meddle. And besides, Brains – who had offered to discreetly check things – had looked in at the kitchen several times during the day and had seemed really very pleased. He had claimed that everything was under control. Olof put his chef's hat on.

'Right, then. I'd best be getting back to my pots and pans,' he said and hurried off. Martha watched him leave. Opening a restaurant was much more complicated than she had imagined. Permits, staff, deliveries and lots of guests. Dearie me, what have we got ourselves involved in, she thought. But now there was no going back. The guests were already on their way.

One after the other, they trooped in, hung up their coats in the cloakroom and were shown to the tables by Rake. To her delight, Martha discovered that Christina's complicated forest decoration seemed to work. The guests managed to make their way along the narrow, winding forest paths without bumping into bushes and tree trunks. Some guests looked inquisitively at the dating table above which hung a large sign: SPEED DATING, while others were curious about the raised VIP lounge and the stage with the handwritten sign announcing: KARAOKE WITH A TWIST. But they all looked happy and expectant, because they had never seen the like before. When they were all seated, Martha addressed them.

'I would like to give you a heartfelt welcome to our newly opened restaurant Silver Punk. It is for us elderly who don't have so many dating places, but is also open to others. As you will hear from the name, we welcome young people too. Different generations must have a place where they can meet and mix with one another.'

A happy murmur went round the tables, followed by some humming and hawing and scraping by a walking stick or two, after which Martha went on to describe the dating table. She encouraged those who were widows, widowers or just single in general to sit there, before she informed everybody about the bonus lottery. She leaned forward and picked up a green paper bag with a red heart on it. Those who had received a personal invitation via email would be given one of these goody bags to take home with them, she said, and patted the bag a bit more. Then she asked Brains, Rake, Christina and Anna-Greta to come up onto the stage, stood them in a row, and raised her hands like a conductor. After which they all started to sing 'The Merry Month of May' and a pleasant atmosphere spread through the restaurant. (It was admittedly the wrong season, but the song sounded so good sung in parts with their different voices and it included the word 'Welcome' several times.)

Finally, Martha called upon head waiter Christina to speak, and she described the menu, ending up by cutting a green ribbon of intertwined flower leaves which had been symbolically hung up between two chairs beside the kitchen. Then the cook and the service staff came into the dining area, introduced themselves and were applauded. When the red-headed Betty made her entrance, Brains gave a broad smile and Martha noticed. She looked from one to the other and raised her eyebrows.

After this introduction, the inaugural evening was under way. Rake and the others handed out the menus, the guests ordered their dishes and soon the noise level became higher. Martha went around the tables and made sure that everybody was satisfied and thought that this was exactly like how it was at a real restaurant, except that it was their own. She immediately felt extremely proud that she wasn't one of those people who just talked, but she actually turned her dreams into reality. And if only this worked out well, they would be able to continue with their Vintage Village. But that meant that the restaurant must make a profit because the bank robbery money wouldn't go far. Christina's interior decoration had cost a fortune and having staff was expensive too. But the League of Pensioners were not going to pay 'shadow economy' cash wages, and the tax and benefits were expensive.

And as if that wasn't enough, Johan Tanto, the Weasel, had suddenly raised the rent. When they had decided on the barge, they had been so keen that they hadn't read the small print in the contract. With the kitchen equipment, water and electricity, the rent had become thirty per cent higher than agreed, and at the end of the year he was doubling the rent.

Martha realized that the Weasel was unreliable and could raise the rent whenever he wanted, so it would be better to buy the barge. Together with Anna-Greta she went through the city's register of boats to see what a barge like theirs could be worth so that they could put in a bid. That was when they discovered something strange. Barge A39T was not owned by the Weasel at all, but by Stockholm City. So he had rented out the city's property and taken the money himself and, of course, that meant that the tenants could be evicted at any time! That decided the issue.

With a firm grip of her wheeled walker, Martha had gone to the relevant department at the City Hall and put in a bid for the barge. She explained that she wanted to invest her savings in a healthfood restaurant and she also promised that she would ensure that the barge would be removed at her own cost if – God forbid – it were to sink. The officials in the City Hall had long had problems with old boats that had sunk by the quays so they did all they could to support the old lady, and shortly afterwards Martha had become the owner of the barge.

But the Weasel and his mates had started threatening them. In veiled terms they had described what would happen to people who didn't pay protection money. Martha tried to repress the unpleasant feelings this gave rise to. No, she wasn't going to let those thoughts disturb her now. This evening she was going to have fun.

33

During the evening Christina's mood improved. Admittedly, Olof, the cook, was a bit difficult to handle and he pinched Betty's bottom rather too often, but he cooked wonderful food and the guests seemed to be enjoying themselves. Christina, in her yellow outfit, ploughed between the tables, smiled and asked the guests if the food tasted good. As the hours passed, she became all the jollier and forgot she was having a white week with no alcohol. When Olof got out a bottle of champagne and poured drinks for the staff, she quickly took a glass and toasted. She loved the light bubbly drink from France and on an evening like this one couldn't help but celebrate. After one glass she realized that she should give all the guests free champagne, and after two glasses she realized it was good form to go around and toast all the guests.

Champagne bottles were put in buckets of ice and it wasn't long before Christina turned up with her glass, toasted the guests and entertained one and all with appropriate literary quotes. Indeed, she was in a brilliant mood and she rounded off the quotes with various words of wisdom, one after the other.

'If you want something you've never had, you must do

something you've never done', or 'Doing nothing also means doing something,' she recited and smiled sweetly before moving on to the next table. She worked her way systematically from the bow to the stern, and when she had got halfway she started muddling up all her literary quotes, confusing children's classics with patriotic poetry. Then she started singing too; a song about walking in the forest was just right in these surroundings, she thought. She became all the jollier and more exhilarated for each toast.

When she had got halfway through the dining area she realized she had forgotten the sound in the loudspeakers. So she discreetly took Brains to one side, dragged him across to the sound system over behind the bar, and gave him the list of bird songs that she had compiled. They were sound files and were streamed and that was a bit new for him, but after a few attempts the beautiful song of a blue tit filled the dining room and the illusion of forest and nature made Christina shut her eyes in delight. It all went well until Brains accidentally used the sound file with mating calls for birds. When that started, a horde of noisy seagulls gathered up on deck and it took a while before he realized what had caused that. (Luckily, most birds were in South Africa or even further south at this time of year, otherwise the restaurant might have ended up as a paradise for randy birds.)

'Oh Brains, you are wonderful,' said Christina when he had got the sound files properly sorted, and she raised her champagne glass yet again. 'A toooast to you!'

Martha, too, went among the guests – but with a glass of non-alcoholic bubbly in her hand – and did what she could to keep the joyful atmosphere at its high level. A stylish lady with a white hat and a flowery dress had sat down in one of the stalls together with a younger woman. The lady in the dress was in her nineties and her hands shook. The younger woman helped to cut up the food on her plate.

'Welcome to our restaurant,' said Martha.

'Thank you,' said the lady. 'It is so exciting here!'

She pointed at a fox which could be glimpsed just to her left. The animal – in Martha's opinion rather moth-eaten – had been given a red rosette in honour of the day and looked really rather peculiar sticking its nose out behind a tree trunk. Martha took a deep breath. Oh goodness, if she had seen that in time, she would at least have removed the rosette.

'Yes, the head waiter, our Christina, is clever at decorating and has had a free hand. She wanted to do something different,' Martha explained. 'And the animals teach us a lot about nature. But the plan is to change the interior now and then.'

'How bold,' said the lady. 'But I don't know if I can come here so often. The council home-care service won't let us go out any more.'

'What did you say?'

'The council and the firms they contract are cutting down on everything and if my daughter didn't help me sometimes, I would never be able to leave my flat. But Anne-Marie here is so kind. Besides, she works in nursing too and she understands what it is like for us elderly.'

The daughter nodded, smiled at Martha and cut up the lasagne into small portions for her mother. The old lady's hands still shook and she probably had Parkinson's. When she had finished eating, she wiped her mouth with the green serviette and went on:

'Yes, it really has gone too far. Those council officials, the ones who decide how much help we need, have made a standard list detailing how long it should take to look after somebody. And, you know, the home carers don't have many minutes to do their job with each person who has been assigned help.'

'A standard list?'

'Yes. The home-care personnel now have a list of what they should do and how long it should take.'

'But won't it take different amounts of time depending on the circumstances?' Martha asked.

'Yes, of course, but now they have decided how many minutes it takes to go on an errand, to make a bed, to shower somebody, to dress them, to clean, to help at mealtimes and so on. And now . . .' The old lady held up her fist in front of her. 'And now those idiots have reduced those times even more. Anything to save money. I only get five minutes a week to put my nightdress on.'

Martha felt a rotten feeling inside her. Five minutes? So they were trying to save money on old people who needed support and care? Could that really be legal? Was the council trying to apply business methods like many of those private entrepreneurs that they contracted nowadays?

'They must have lost their minds in the council!'

'Yes, isn't it crazy! Now I can only shower for a quarter of an hour every week. Who are the dirty old men who decide this? And eating – well, that can't take more than ten minutes. But you must have time to chew the food too!'

Martha had to hold on to the edge of the table to support herself. She knew, of course, that things were bad, but she got just as upset every time she heard someone describe what was going on. What sort of people were they who could think up such a system? The venture capitalists who cut corners and lowered standards and then transferred the profits to the West Indies, she had heard about them. But were councils now doing the same? The old lady had more to say:

'You know what? Those bureaucrats who decide, they don't have a clue as to what it is like to be old. They have worked out that we only need five minutes to go to the lavatory. But by then we wouldn't even have got our clothes off. Do they think we have flies that can be opened and closed with a remote control?' The old lady sighed and wiped her brow with a little white handkerchief. 'You know what? I feel so sorry for all the employees who would so like to help us but are not allowed to. If they stay longer than the designated time, then they are told off.'

'So they get told off for being kind and friendly?' Martha went pale and was now finding it hard to breathe.

'Are you all right?' wondered the old lady.

'Just a drop in my blood pressure,' answered Martha and she sank down onto a chair. She was close to tears. What was happening in society? Those in charge seemed to have completely lost contact with reality. A bank robbery now and then wouldn't help much. No, it was a question of basic values – ways of thinking in modern society must be radically changed. Attitudes towards people had become so weird nowadays. Yes, the municipal councils that played at being business enterprises and managers who only cared about profit . . . had they forgotten that real live people were actually affected by their office-desk decisions? Martha opened her waist bag and felt for her asthma spray. Not until she had used the inhaler a few times did she have enough energy to get up again.

'You know, care assistants who work in home care have a monthly wage which is the equivalent to what managing directors have per hour,' she said. 'Per hour!'

'Yes, I know,' sighed the old lady.

'It seems that many company directors and politicians have lost contact with reality. Nowadays it pays better to take care of *things* than of people. It can't go on like that. I want to try to change that!'

'Ah, now you are going to change society again,' said Rake, who happened to pass by just then. 'Good luck to you!'

Martha ignored Rake and turned again to the lady and her daughter.

'The restaurant is treating you to dinner this evening,' she said. 'And when you leave, don't forget the goody bag by the exit, a present that you can open when you get home.' She reached out for the champagne bottle and filled their glasses. 'Cheers, and a warm welcome to our restaurant!'

She went on to the other tables, greeted the guests and made sure that they were having a good time. As all those she spoke to praised the food and seemed very satisfied, Martha regained her good mood and didn't even become angry when she heard the strange birdsong. Christina had her ideas, but the food and the interior decoration seemed to have worked well, so they would have to put up with singing storks or whatever they were. When Martha finally steered her steps in the direction of the cloakroom, she was tired, hot and rather sweaty. She needed a breath of fresh air to cope with the rest of the evening. But when she reached the cloakroom she stopped abruptly. There stood a beefy, muscular man she had never seen before. He was wearing a leather jacket, his hair was cropped very short and his black eyes were frightening. She was just about to ask him to leave when she felt a hand on her shoulder. It was Johan Tanto, the Weasel.

'You must meet Kenta, my mate,' Tanto said. 'He's the one who looks after the cloakroom. The cloakroom fees, that is.'

Martha stared. The mafia and motorbike gangs were known for confiscating restaurants' incomes from cloakrooms. But here? Among a gang of pensioners on a barge? In a fury she took a step forward.

'Now listen to me, you turnip, pack your bags and get the hell out of here!'

Then she unbuckled her waist bag, swung it round her head and, with a hard centrifugal swing, slammed it directly into Kenta's crotch.

34

The guests had gone home and the League of Pensioners had got into their minibus to travel back to Djursholm. Martha turned the ignition key and was about to drive off when Christina prodded her from the back seat.

'Mafia? Is that what you think?' she wondered with an anxious glance towards the rear window to check that nobody was about to follow them. She was utterly exhausted and the make-up from her eyelashes had ended up far below her eyes. The evening had exceeded their expectations, the food had tasted good and the service had worked just like it ought to. She would have been madly happy if it hadn't been for that uncouth type who wanted to lay his hands on the cloakroom fees. That had ruined the entire evening.

'Mafia folk? Yes, I'm afraid I do think they're mafia,' said Martha. 'They are cunning types, that lot. First they rent out the city's barge to us without owning it, and now they want the money from the cloakroom fees. I didn't think the mafia would be interested in us pensioners. To think that they are trying to squeeze money from oldies!'

'But everybody does that!' Christina's voice was shrill. 'Just look at the banks and those special mortgages they try to get us poor innocent elderly to sign up for.'

'What's that?' Brains wondered, not having kept up with what happened in the world of banking.

'The banks encourage the elderly to remortgage their homes. "To provide that bit extra in your life", as it says in the adverts. But after ten years when the mortgages must be paid back they charge such high interest that the people who have taken out the mortgage can't afford it. They must then sell their home. That's how things can go, it's another way of becoming homeless,' said Martha.

'That's a swindle!' exclaimed Brains.

'Yes, and in some ways the mafia is more honest about it. At least there is a clear message and you know what happens,' Rake said.

'True.' Christina nodded, 'But, Martha dear, why did you call the mafia thug a turnip?'

'Well, why not, with all the greens on this barge it is natural to think in terms of vegetables.'

'But your waist bag? Was it really necessary to whack the guy right in the crotch?' wondered Brains.

'But I was absolutely furious! They stole from the money we are going to give to the poor. If they were going to share it out, OK, but they don't care about anybody else.'

'But they didn't want to hit an old lady at least . . .' mumbled Brains.

And hearing those words they all started to giggle, because on more than one occasion the League of Pensioners had got away with things just because of their age.

'But I'm worried that he's going to come back,' said Christina.

'We've sorted out the mafia before and we ought to be able to manage it again too. Just as long as we are flexible,' said Martha.

'Like you, then. Heads down, guys, here comes the waist bag!' Rake said and grinned.

Again a degree of jollity spread among them and there was silence for a while before the next comment.

'I think we should continue with the restaurant as planned and see how we've done after a month or two. Other restaurant owners have survived despite mafia interference,' said Martha.

Her words sank in, and nobody in the vehicle commented. Then she engaged first gear, released the handbrake and drove off in the direction of Ekedal Bridge and then on to Solna. A quarter of an hour later she slowed down outside their Djursholm villa. It was beginning to get light and the decay in their neighbour's garden was easy to see. The flower pots were full of rubbish and the bushes were untrimmed and looked very scraggly. There was still nobody who looked after the garden. And there was no sign of Bielke.

'Have you thought about something? A refuse-collection lorry buried under concrete in the neighbour's garden and mafia visits at our restaurant! At least we don't get bored,' said Anna-Greta and she burst into such laughter that all the others ended up joining in. They laughed long and loud even though they were tired, and they immediately decided to have something tasty to drink before they went to bed. But since they had drunk so much champagne, they settled on chilled fizzy water with crispbread and caviar as a night snack. Because at that point, just then, they were actually so exhausted that they could have eaten and drunk just about anything. Even if it was non-alcoholic.

In the end, the Silver Punk restaurant was open every day in the week except Mondays and besides a few complaints that they didn't serve large juicy steaks, and that the odd guest got drunk and that the cook pinched Betty on her bottom, everything went off surprisingly well. The idea of letting the bonus lottery winners come on board and eat without paying one evening had worked fantastically well, since the guests, in their turn, recommended the restaurant to relatives and friends. The bonus hand-out of one thousand kronor they had been given in their goody bags on their way home, had made them very enthusiastic about the restaurant. The Silver Punk was now always full and during the weekends there was even a queue on the quay.

But there was something that worried Martha. The Weasel had returned. A few days after his mate had felt the full force of Martha's waist bag in his crotch, he suddenly appeared in the cloakroom again. This time he asked for a lot of protection money.

'Surely you don't want anything to happen to your restaurant?' he sneered and looked meaningfully at her. Martha felt something in her heart. It beat irregularly and she was a little out of breath. But she acted as if nothing had happened and everything was as usual. She didn't even tell Brains. She had got her friends involved in this, and now she would deal with it. So she kept up appearances.

But the Weasel kept on at her. He and his mates had also demanded that they should deliver supplies to the restaurant – including meat that hadn't been checked by the relevant authorities – and Martha had, of course, refused. And they even wanted to collect a higher rent. But there too she blankly refused.

'Mister, you should never have raised the monthly rental payments,' said Martha, putting her hands by her sides. 'That put us in a bad mood, so now we've bought the barge.'

'Oh yeah, sure. That's not funny. The rent must be paid by Monday next week at the latest, or else—'

'The barge was owned by Stockholm City, not by you. And we pay rent as agreed until we take over the barge, but not a krona more. If that doesn't suit you, I'll contact the police! Here, you can see a copy of the contract for the sale of the barge.'

Martha showed him the signed contract with Stockholm City, amazed at her own toughness. The Weasel read it, and glared at her with his mouth open; in fact, it was so wide open that the tobacco under his lip fell down inside his shirt. Martha gave him a friendly smile and said in a mild voice:

'Well, thank you for everything up to now, but before we go our separate ways, perhaps I can offer you a glass of cloudberry liqueur?'

'Old-lady booze, no way!' said the Weasel with his eyes now dangerously dark, and he turned his back to her and left. And at just that moment she found him threatening and very unpleasant.

'What about another barge so that we can double our profits?' said Anna-Greta a few evenings later when they had been obliged to turn down several guests from the full restaurant. 'I have noticed that the city has several barges for sale, including one that was owned by the Asphalt Company,' she said and she held up some photos that she had printed out from the city's homepage.

'Don't say we're going to fit out yet another bleeding barge,' sighed Brains.

'All in gree-een,' Rake added mischievously.

'We? No, we delegate the work,' said Martha. 'And if we put the new barge next to ours, and turn it into a cafe and cinema, then it wouldn't be so much work. That would be yet another step towards our Vintage Village. We shall show everybody who wants to scare us away from here that we are not going to give in, and that we will become firmly established here.'

'Two barges that we must look after? Aren't you a bit too optimistic now, Martha?' said Rake.

'But Anders still has no job, so it'd mean an opportunity for him to get regular work,' said Martha. 'Perhaps Anders and Emma can run it together?'

Brains too felt little enthusiasm for the idea, but at a meeting up in the tower room the next day the proposal was voted on and the result was three votes for and two against. Brains and Rake looked unhappy. Once more, the old-lady mafia had floored them!

In the evening when they were on their way to bed, Brains spent an extra-long time in the process. He combed his hair and brushed his teeth for so long, indeed, stayed for such a long time in the bathroom, that Martha got really worried.

'Aren't you feeling well, my friend?' she asked when he

came into the bedroom in his creased flannel pyjamas with the toothbrush in his hand.

'Martha, I've been thinking about something,' he said and he started to walk around in the room while waving his toothbrush. 'Do you have any limits?'

'Your toothbrush, my friend,' Martha pointed out.

'To hell with that. DO YOU HAVE ANY LIMITS, any limits at all?'

'Limits?'

'Yes, you are never satisfied with what you have but always want to start with something new. Can't you just sit down and enjoy life?'

'Sit down? How much fun is that?'

'Now listen. There is something called meditation. It's for folk who can't stop stressing.'

'I'm not stressing.'

'Yes, you are! Betty said that meditation is good, because then you learn to live in the now. To live in the here and now. Perhaps that would be something for you?'

'Oh, I see, Betty said that? Goodness, she is clever, isn't she, that little doll! You know what? Now is now and I am living just now, do you understand? I don't intend being either here or there or future or yesterday or anywhere else!'

'But meditation, Martha dear, then you would be here and now.'

'I know perfectly well where I am! Look at yourself. I'm sitting here on the edge of the bed.'

'But Martha, this is about calming down. Being at peace.'

'You don't say? Well, goodness me! You who are running

around waving a toothbrush while I sit here calm and quiet on the bed. With my hands peacefully resting on my lap.'

Brains grunted and went back into the bathroom with his toothbrush.

He was in there a while and when he came back he was completely quiet except for a humming now and then. He got into bed, struggled with the bedclothes and lay on his side. He smelt of Colgate and shower cream.

'Brains dear, I've been thinking about the new barge. What name shall we call it?'

'You what?! Have you already gone through with that deal?' A groan could be heard from the pillow.

'Just wait, we'll soon have it there. With a larger turnover we'll have more money to give away.'

'Martha! I proposed to you several months ago, but instead of marrying me you have robbed a bank, filled a refuse-collection lorry with cement and opened a restaurant. And now you want to buy another barge. A BARGE instead of a wedding!' With a deep sigh he took her hand and shook his head. 'Martha dear, I think it's quite simply time to break the engagement.'

'Oh, but Brains!' Martha felt a wave of anxiety rush through her body. 'If that's how you feel, then of course I must reconsider.' She stretched across and stroked him on the cheek. 'Perhaps we could have a teeny weeny barge instead?' she said in an attempt at a joke.

Again a groan could be heard and this was followed by a deep sigh as he buried his head in the pillow. Martha looked at him in surprise. He hadn't laughed, he hadn't even shown a shadow of a smile. No, he seemed seriously dissatisfied.

Perhaps he wasn't feeling so well? He had, in fact, looked a bit grey and tired recently. Perhaps it was because he hadn't had time to mess around with his inventions. And she hadn't managed to talk much with him either. But of course that wasn't so easy when you had such a lot going on . . . but she ought, of course, to see that he felt comfortable and perhaps let him do some repairs and maintenance on deck. Then he would feel better. But, on the other hand, he really ought to deal with things himself, not just wait to have everything arranged for him.

'Now listen, Brains, now you really must cheer up. When we rob banks you don't like it, and when we're honest citizens and run a restaurant you don't like it either. Perhaps you ought to do more gymnastics so that you will feel a little better?'

'Gymnastics? No, that's the last straw!' said Brains and he took the pillow and whammed it into the wall.

That night they slept in separate beds with their backs to each other and at midnight neither of them had fallen asleep. Martha cautiously stretched out her hand and took his hand in hers.

'I'm sorry, my friend,' she whispered in the dark.

But Brains didn't answer, he pulled his hand back and pretended to be asleep.

Two days later, the Weasel yet again sought out Martha on board the restaurant barge and demanded protection money 'so that nothing would happen to the restaurant'.

Then Martha felt that discomfort in her heart. Fibrillation.

It was beating irregularly and she got a little out of breath. But she pretended nothing had happened and that everything was as usual.

35

'I'm fed up with that damned old hag. Her and her gang of oldies, they'll have to go.' Kenta took a deep drag on his cigarette and blew out the smoke. 'I'd finally got my pizzeria going and then that riff-raff turn up. It's wiped out my place.' He waved his cigarette in the direction of the empty pizzeria.

He sat talking with the Weasel in a corner of the pizzeria in Hornsberg, Bella Capri. He had been able to take over the place when the former owner had become too old, and he had renovated the premises with money he had borrowed from his mother. At first, it all went well and he had had many customers, both young and old, but since the oldies had opened Silver Punk he had lost customers. Not only did they have good food there on the barge, but it was also cheap too. It had become popular for younger people to hang around there. He sighed.

'They're on some blasted health trend over there. What the fuck. I've tested vegetarian pizza but it doesn't work.'

'They're earning money with that restaurant but refuse to fork out for protection money. Fucking riff-raff!' The Weasel drummed with his fingers on the beer bottle. It would soon be opening time, but that didn't make much difference. The pizzeria had almost no customers before six in the evening and only a few young people and down-and-outs later in the evening. The old women had said they were going to open a restaurant for pensioners and neither of them had seen the place as a threat. But now everybody seemed to have found their way there. The Silver Punk restaurant, what a fuck of a name anyway.

'Isn't there a way to get someone committed to an old folk's home?' Kenta went on. 'Let's send an SOS. That old lady fucking attacked us. And bloody hard too.'

The Weasel couldn't help smiling but he turned his head away so that his mate wouldn't see. Kenta could hardly walk after the whacking from Martha, and had been obliged to abstain from women for a whole week.

'Fucking unlucky. Wonder what she had in that waist bag?'

'A fucking great spanner I'd say, or one of those boules cannon balls, it was third-degree,' said Kenta with a wry face. He remembered the quick hand movement and the hard blow that had made him back away so fast that he almost fell over. A fucking old hag had battered him! He had been so astonished that he'd almost lost it, and, with his hand raised to thump her, he had at the last second realized that he couldn't beat up an old woman. Just one blow and she would have dropped down dead. No, luckily he had been able to restrain himself.

'Like I said, that gang of oldies must be stopped! It's bad enough that the old hag has twigged that we don't own the barge. She refuses to use our cash-in-hand cleaners, she doesn't get her food deliveries via us, she refuses to pay pro-

258

tection money and she's thrown us out of the cloakroom. Every bloody thing has gone wrong!' Kenta flicked the ash from his cigarette onto the floor. His hands shook.

'And now they want to buy another barge, I've heard,' sighed the Weasel. 'Fucking arseholes!'

'Zimmer arseholes!'

'It's time to put a stop to them once and for all. I've had enough.'

'Yep. How shall we do it? The usual?'

'Yeah, the same again.'

Former Chief Inspector Blomberg lifted up Einstein from the keyboard and put him down on the floor with a thud. Thank God the computer was turned off, otherwise it could have ended in disaster. The number of times the creature had laid on X and Z and had had his tail on ENTER meant that it could take at least half a day to clean the computer. The last time the damned cat had also managed to press the DELETE key too, so some of the files had disappeared. And however hard Blomberg had tried, he hadn't been able to restore them. In his anger he had banged the hard drive on the table and in a flash had lost even more files. After that, it had taken him several weeks to collect the reports, CCTV images and important PMs from the police department again. Luckily, he still had access to their system. Now he had learned that he must have a backup on two hard drives – because he didn't want to do without the cat. No, he loved Einstein. Cats were honest. They did what they wanted and not what somebody else wanted. They certainly didn't wag their tails for just anybody, but chose their master with considerable care.

Blomberg switched the computer on, and stretched out his hand for some chocolate. His fingers fumbled in the box of Aladdin chocolates until he noticed that it only contained sticky remains. Einstein was sitting on the floor licking his lips. Damn it! For a moment Blomberg considered throwing the creature out, but then he realized that it was his own fault for having left the box open on the table. And besides, perhaps it was just as well that the cat had gobbled up the chocolates. Since he had become a pensioner, he had put on several kilos in weight. Perhaps it was his new sedentary life and the fact that he had started baking. He ought to stop baking those tasty pastries for a while.

Blomberg put on his spectacles and peered at the computer screen, and while the cat washed his whiskers, he went through what had happened during the night. Nothing much, evidently. What about the Nordea bank robbery investigation? He scrolled down and peered. Nothing new there either. He had long since ruled out the Old Blokes Gang and the Gorbachev robbers, and Jöback and those amateurs at the Kungsholmen station could think what they wanted. No, he was looking for a completely new constellation, but hadn't got anywhere yet. He was stuck. The talk with Eklund, the skipper of one of the Waxholm ferry boats, hadn't led to anything and the mysterious league had not yet carried out any new robberies that could give them away.

And what about the CCTV images? Unfortunately, he had lost all the comparative material from earlier bank robberies in Stockholm in a virus attack, but a few sequences had for some reason survived in his iPad. He fetched the tablet and clicked his way to the valuable sequence. Yet again he watched how the old lady made several calls from her mobile outside the Handelsbanken branch office the same day the bank was robbed. Something stirred in his memory. He had noticed an elderly lady with the same posture on the CCTV images from Drottninggatan right next to the Buttericks joke shop. He went across to his computer again and found the file. Yes, it was her, slightly hunchbacked, but still quite sprightly and wasn't she wearing Ecco shoes? Buttericks was the only shop in Stockholm where you could buy masks of Margaret Thatcher and Pavarotti, and those were the masks used in the Nordea robbery. Blomberg's hand dipped eagerly down into the box of Aladdin chocolates and he picked up some remains. He licked his fingers while he stared at the screen. Hmm . . . that Ecco old lady had actually visited the shop the week before the Nordea robbery and when she came out she was carrying a package.

Blomberg looked at the images in slow motion this time, leaned back and whistled. Skipper Eklund had mentioned an old lady outside the Grand Hotel. What if that was the same person? Perhaps it was rather a long shot, but nevertheless . . . He ought to take his iPad and show Eklund. Besides, now when he looked at her in slow motion it was as if the woman was somehow familiar, as if he had seen her before. Or was it simply that all old ladies looked the same? Pah, he didn't really know; to be honest, he mainly noticed younger blondes. Blomberg yawned and scratched his neck.

The police still hadn't arrested anybody for the bank robberies, or for that notorious theft of the paintings at the National Museum. But the crooks were out there somewhere. What if he could solve this? What a triumph it would be! It would be really great to put Jöback and his cronies in place. But if he was to succeed, he would have to get out and do some under-cover work so that he could make some progress. Why not have a closer look at pensioners' clubs, restaurants, bingo halls and old folk's homes? That league with the oldies must, after all, be somewhere out there, because they wouldn't be at discotheques or punk places. Or was it hip flop nowadays? Blomberg yawned yet again, got up and went across to the fridge to get a cold beer. Or was it hip bop? He found a Carlsberg and with a noisy click followed by a slow hissing, he sank down into his favourite armchair. He would catch that League of Pensioners; he wasn't going to give up. He had a short break, drank the beer and then rolled up his shirt sleeves. With determined steps, he returned to the computer. It there was to be any result, he must get to work.

36

Christina sat with her feet on the table in the VIP lounge with a large notepad in front of her. Her nails were newly painted and she had just been to the hairdresser's and had had her hair done. And in addition she had allowed herself the luxury of buying a lovely trouser suit in red with a matching blouse, an outfit that she thought would fit in well in the Jungle – which is what Rake had named the interior of the barge. Now her friends had spread themselves out on the soft plush sofas with notepads in their hands. The last few weeks' local newspapers lay on the table. They were all poring over the personal ads in deep concentration. The League of Pensioners wanted to get a picture of single people who wished to enrich their lives with a partner, anything to help them to create a speed-dating system of the highest class. Rake opened the *Östermalm News,* the local paper in the poshest district of central Stockholm, and read out aloud in his Gothenburg dialect:

'"Here is a solid, super guy looking for a plump woman, though not obligatory, aged fifty-five to eighty".' He nodded towards Martha. 'There, you see! No need for gymnastics! "Solid, super guy", how about that!'

'But that's what he's written about himself, isn't that obvious?' protested Martha.

Brains grinned, scratched his beard (which was terribly itchy) and looked at Rake with approval.

'Then listen to this,' Brains said in a rebellious tone, and he thumbed his way to the personal ads in the local paper from the southern part of the city. He held up the paper and read in a loud and affected voice:

'"Hello, out there in Stockholm. Is there a plump woman aged fifty-five to eighty who wants a solid, super guy for intimacy, tenderness, cosiness etc . . .".' Brains turned towards Martha with a triumphant look on his face. '"Plump woman". Ha ha. No more gymnastics. What did I say? Take it easy. Meditate!'

'Solid, super guy, but for heaven's sake that must be the same person, can't you see!' sighed Anna-Greta.

'"Here is a cosy, huggable and very large guy in his mid-forties who—",' Rake went on.

'Pah, women don't want fat men who don't care about their appearance,' Christina broke in.

'Or ones with weird beards,' Martha added with a sharp glance at Brains's unshaven cheeks. It must be Betty who was the reason for that; he was trying to be modern, she thought. 'Rake at least had a *trimmed* chinstrap beard,' she added to be on the safe side.

'Now listen, everybody, don't bicker. We must work,' Anna-Greta called out. 'How are we getting on with the dating?'

Things went quiet because they all realized they were losing focus. Martha had given each of them a free hand to create a suitable 'dating card' so that the right people would find each other at the dating table. By answering a list of questions, you would reveal your personality and thus it would allow singles to find one another. The League of Pensioners were searching among the dating sites on the Internet to find inspiration for suitable questions. The idea was to create the best dating questionnaire and not to make fun of personal ads.

'"Fat and poor guy, aged fifty-five, alcohol problems, looking for a cute and nice girl of suitable age, preferably twenty-five to thirty. Should also be youthful and slim",' Rake went on. 'What do you think, Christina?'

'Order in the ranks!' Anna-Greta roared. 'It's important to have the right questions. What we want to do is to bring together widows and widowers and even people who have never been married before.'

'The unmarried ones often remain unmarried,' Brains muttered with a glance at Martha.

'I think appearance is important,' said Rake. 'Height, weight, hair colour and so on. Why not simply ask: Are you attractive, or do you look like something the cat brought in?'

'You can't write that!' protested Christina.

'But you know how things are. At our age one isn't exactly good-looking,' said Rake and suddenly he looked rather sullen.

'Don't forget inner beauty. That is more important than anything else,' Martha informed them. Rake gave her an appreciative look, while also understanding why she thought like that. His friend did admittedly try to be chic, but she didn't always succeed. That waist bag, for example.

'I think we ought to ask about religion,' said Christina. 'That is an important part of many people's lives.'

'Religion? No. That would only lead to argument,' Brains objected.

'Or war,' said Rake.

'I think we should concentrate on people's qualities,' was Martha's contribution. 'I mean like if you love animals, do things you've planned, are considerate or mostly think about number one – you get the idea.'

'Hmm,' said Brains and he put his hands on his stomach. 'Personality, your character, and all that. It would be good if we could formulate suitable questions,' he said. 'And don't forget about the fact that women shouldn't be hopeless when it comes to DIY.'

'Then we really must include a question about whether you are thrifty or wasteful,' Anna-Greta pointed out.

'Can't they just tick a box somewhere if they have debts registered with the national enforcement agency, or not? That ought to suffice,' Rake suggested.

There was a rasping sound from their pens as they all made notes.

'Can we ask if you are satisfied or dissatisfied, like challenges or prefer things to remain as they are?' Christina wondered and she waved her pen.

'Absolutely,' Martha agreed.

'Yes, or if you want peace and quiet or adventure. That says a lot about a person,' Brains chipped in.

A murmur of approval went round the room and there was a little pause while everybody reflected.

'But talking about personal qualities,' said Christina looking up from her notepad, 'temperament is important. I mean, whether you are grumpy and irascible, sad or happy. Some people can easily get depressed, and others don't bother. We should include that too.'

Again a murmur of approval could be heard while they continued to make notes.

'And if the person is happy or is – well, you know what I mean, that sort of anxious type?' Anna-Greta added. 'Some people can have a crisis but be optimists and ready to move on in life. Others just sort of collapse.'

'Hell, this is like being on a therapist's couch,' Rake broke in. 'I know, let's just keep it simple. Why not just fill in whether you are attractive or not, and of course whether you are sexy.'

'Now listen, what we must do is have rather more lofty goals than that,' said Martha in such an acid tone that it would have corroded any frying pan.

'No, you know what? We can make it even simpler,' Rake stubbornly went on. 'The women can tick whether they want you to be loving or if it's just a question of getting down to it straight away!'

'Watch your tongue!' said Martha.

'But for goodness' sake, behave yourselves. ORDER IN THE RANKS!' Anna-Greta shouted this out so loud that Rake sat bolt upright on the sofa, replied 'Aye, aye, captain', and then kept his mouth shut.

The meeting lasted all day long and it was not until the following night, after they had slept on it, that they could agree on the contents of a questionnaire which filled an entire A4 page – or the equivalent of a page on an iPad. When Anna-Greta realized this, she let out a cry of delight.

'Now what about this? I've got an idea. We've got Internet in the restaurant, right? So why don't we give each place at the dating table an iPad and every iPad an email address? We let the participants answer the questions in the questionnaire directly on the iPad and then they only have to send it off. So if, for example, you want a man who is intelligent and kind, then you'll get an answer directly from the man at the table who fits the bill.'

'But how?' wondered Christina.

There was silence for a while and they all stared at Brains.

'Why not install lamps at each place on the table. Then a little lamp would light up beside that particular iPad,' he reckoned. 'The fastest dating in the world.'

'Brilliant, you're a genius, Brains,' Anna-Greta said. 'But then we must chain the iPad to the place at the table or else there would be chaos.'

'Another thing. What if lots of people are "kind"? Then many lamps would start flashing,' Rake objected.

'How delightful! Then you'd have even more men to choose from,' Anna-Greta exclaimed. 'Oh I do love iPads!'

'If you kiss your iPad, then you're sure to get your prince,' Rake said, grinning.

'I know, we can create an app for princes, what about that, Rake?' Brains smiled and immediately suffered a prod to his ribs from Martha.

'OK, then. The lamps are a first point of contact, but then you ought to take the flirtation up to the next level,' Brains said.

'Mating!' declared Rake.

'Mind your manners!' roared Martha.

Brains scratched his beard and frowned. 'Listen. If one person at the table writes that he wants a happy, medium-height woman who likes to bake, and a woman writes that she is of medium height, a happy type who likes pastries, then they can continue to chat on the iPad. She can write what sort of cakes she likes to bake, and he can write what sort of cakes he likes to eat,' he went on.

'Women bake and men eat?' Christina snorted. 'Usch! That's the 1950s. Nowadays men bake too, just so you know. When did you last bake a cake for Martha?'

Brains just sat there with his mouth open and forgot what he was going to say. After prodding his beard with his finger for a while he started up again.

'Yes, well, the iPads and the places around the table have the same number and when the lamp has started to flash at place eleven, for example, then you can start chatting with that person on the iPad directly. If it seems like a decent date, then you press OK—'

'No, you suggest a beer. Come, darling, let's have a beer,' Rake chipped in. 'Are there apps for that?'

'What I mean is, when you strike lucky, then you go with your newly found friend to the dating corner and have a beer. And if you still like the woman—'

'The guy,' Anna-Greta cut in.

'Yes, then you continue with a nice dinner together here on the barge.'

'And we charge scandalous prices for the food. Fantastic, Brains!' Anna-Greta exclaimed.

They all looked at him with such admiration that he blushed and Martha couldn't help but slip her hand into his.

'You know what?' she said, then took a deep breath. 'Now you have created the world's first dating table.'

'Yes, crikey, this is going to be where it all happens!' declared Rake.

37

Only one day to go. It was now time for the long-awaited evening with speed dating and Anna-Greta rushed around on the barge with a confused look. For the first time in her life she had actually constructed her very own computer program and the iPads now had a special app.

She and Brains had trimmed the system so that it worked roughly like a Facebook group. The dating traffic would only take place on board the boat among those who participated there and the questionnaire would not disappear into cyberspace so that everybody could see it and take part.

Those who had paid the admission fee for the barge got the code to the iPads and could go up to them and click their way in. Then all you had to do was press discreetly on the app and the questionnaire appeared. The participants must answer the twenty-five questions that the League of Pensioners had concocted, and describe themselves and what they looked for in a prospective partner. Then the computer program quickly found the person who best matched the criteria, the lamp lit up in front of just that person, and the flirtation could get going.

'This is going to work a treat,' said Anna-Greta. 'Press a button and find your beloved!'

'Couldn't be better,' said Brains, pleased with himself after having set up eight different-coloured lamps at each place. Anna-Greta had insisted that it would be lovely with colours that could show various personal qualities. And if a person had more than five positive qualities, a lamp would light up with a glittering glow: the gold lamp.

'And then you'll understand that you've found the ultimate date,' said Anna-Greta, throwing out her arms. For a moment she had a really dreamy look in her eyes.

'But if everybody wants to date that particular person, what then?' Rake wondered.

'No problem. Then you can wait until the person is available or move on to the next one,' said Christina. 'We have a silver lamp too.'

'Yes, and I even put in one which lights up with a bronze glow,' said Brains now rather proud of having installed all the wiring under the dating table. All they needed now was for an electrician to check it all.

'A bronze glow? Um, then you just comb your hair and flirt as usual,' Rake muttered. 'We can call the dating corner "To the point".' And it was rather clear what he thought the point was.

'Goodness me, no! You can keep your point to yourself. Haven't you realized yet that we are looking out for *inner* qualities?' sighed Christina.

'How on earth can you look *out* for something *inner*?' mumbled Rake.

At that same moment Betty happened to come past with

her shiny, red hair like a drum-roll behind her ears. She was nicely made up and smelled of perfume and walked with sexy, slightly jerky, movements. Brains swallowed and watched as she moved away.

'It is important to find out about somebody's inner qualities. Beauty can be misleading,' Martha informed them with a voice like a laser. 'A beautiful appearance can lead anyone down the wrong path.'

'Well, we're only human,' sighed Brains.

Later in the afternoon when the electrician had checked the wiring and approved the connections to the twelve dating places, the League of Pensioners decided to try it out. Amidst laughing and chatter, Martha and her friends filled in all the questions and sent off their dating cards. For every hit, a lamp lit up, and when Rake had got so many hits that the gold lamp lit up, he was so proud that you couldn't talk to him for a long while. When Martha had filled in what she wished for in a partner and the lamp suddenly lit up next to Brains, she got a little embarrassed. Almost simultaneously, the lamp next to her lit up, and when she looked up, she met Brains's gaze. They both looked down at the table rather awkwardly. They had fallen out and hadn't really got over that, but deep inside they were actually extremely fond of each other.

The League of Pensioners also wrote small messages and sent them off just to make sure that everything worked. Afterwards, they fetched rugs, drew a curtain on which was printed: SLEEPING, and lay down on the VIP lounge's plush sofas for a nice afternoon snooze. It wasn't long before they were all deeply asleep.

A little while later, when Betty came on board with the day's flower arrangement – Rake had managed to get them to agree to having fresh flowers every day – she heard snoring coming from the VIP lounge. She smiled to herself because the oldies had greater ambitions than they could cope with and she often found them asleep in there. Excellent, now she would have a calm period before Martha gave her orders, Christina rushed around and Brains wanted to talk about everything between heaven and earth. She was just about to walk past when she noticed the dating table. It was evidently complete now and everything was ready for the evening. She put down her flower buckets, took a few steps forward and looked at the result. Twelve numbered iPads with lamps around them lay chained to each place at the table. She had to smile to herself. Those pensioners were just so sweet! Arranging dates at their age!

She got curious and went up to place number three, her lucky number. Now what was the password for the iPad? She tried to remember. Brains had told her, but she hadn't really been listening properly. The name of the boat perhaps? She tested. No, that didn't work. What about A39T, the number on the barge? Yep, now she could start up the iPad. To think that the oldies had managed to fix all this. That stern lady with the walking stick was evidently very clever. Admirable! Betty caught sight of the dating app and opened it. Aha, twenty-five questions had to be answered. She held back a little laugh. You had to fill in whether you were nice, kind-hearted, generous and lots of other things. And a bit further down on the questionnaire you could tick if you often got angry or were calm and sensible. Quite a good idea, she thought, because she had once fallen in love with a handsome guy who had such moods that she had had to break it off after four months. With this app she would have discovered his personality straight away.

For fun, Betty started to answer the questions and soon she had filled in the entire questionnaire. As she completed it, a red lamp lit up on the other side of the table which made her take a step back in fright. What was this all about? Could she delete all the answers and go back to the start? She tried to fill in the questionnaire again and this time ticked other qualities. But the red lamp didn't go out; instead another lamp started to flash, this time a green one. If she went on like this, the whole room would soon look like a discotheque before she was finished. She wasn't sure what to do. How did you turn the bloody thing off? She pressed a few buttons but the lamps were still lit up. In the end, she gave up and assumed that they would probably turn off by themselves, just like a computer screen did, if you didn't use it for a while. But before she left, she couldn't resist having a bit of a joke and she wrote: *Hello, darling, I love you!* under the category 'Other'. She smiled to herself and pressed 'Send' without really knowing where it would end up. But what the hell, it would cheer somebody up. Satisfied, she picked up the flower buckets and went towards the kitchen. It was high time to put the flowers in vases and start decorating the boat.

38

'But seriously, Christina. Is it really time to start with the Christmas decorations now in the middle of November?' Martha wondered the next day, gesturing towards the deck. Christina had put up a Christmas tree with colourful angels on it, there were lights on the restaurant roof and glitter around every stay. Here and there hung glass balls and red lanterns, and instead of the usual old car tyres between the barge and the quay she had now hung up fenders in white and blue. Together with the flashing lamps she had put on either side of the entrance down to the VIP lounge, the Silver Punk restaurant now looked almost more like a nightclub than a restaurant.

'Christmas decorations? There is nothing wrong with them, surely?'

'Sorry, Christina, but we do have flowers as well. And those coloured fenders, isn't that just going too far?'

'But colours are so nice, don't you think? A guy in a Mercedes stopped on the quay yesterday, pointed at our ugly old tyres and wondered if we would like some attractive fenders instead. Well, yes, so I thought we should take that chance. He said that he had bought too many for his own boat and didn't need them. It was cheap, too, and he had them in his car boot. He got out some rope and helped to put them in place. You must admit it looks much nicer now.'

'Yes, of course,' mumbled Martha, but deep inside she thought that Christina decided far too much on her own; she did lots of things without asking the others. Martha herself always took up her ideas with the rest of the gang, but Christina just charged ahead. It is a good idea to delegate, Martha thought, but then you risked some people exceeding their ability. She just hoped that wasn't going to apply to her friend. Martha didn't say any more, but to be on the safe side, she decided to keep an eye on her. She was relieved that Christina had decided that the cook should be in charge of the kitchen this important evening, because Anna-Greta had asked her to help look after the dating table. And that was something that Christina was certainly passionate about. The idea of bringing lonely people together so that they could have a more pleasant life had inspired her to such a degree that she had contacted the media. Radio Stockholm and the Kungsholmen district local paper had reported about this new way to meet people, and the restaurant was fully booked for the rest of the week. However, the massive interest was driving Christina nuts. She had been nervous earlier, but now she was close to being a nervous wreck. So Martha had secretly added a bit of rum to their morning coffee and had said that it was a special Colombian blend. After two cups of this special coffee (because it was so tasty, she thought), Christina had – thank God – relaxed and become much happier. And that was lucky for everybody because the restaurant was already full at 6 o'clock and it was high time to open the day's speed dating.

Former Chief Inspector Blomberg had dressed smartly and stood preening himself in front of the hall mirror. In his grey tweed suit, blue lamb's-wool jumper, light-blue shirt and matching tie with cats on, he felt he was really stylish. His shoes were polished to a shine, his hair newly barbered and he didn't have a beard – nor did he have any hair lotion. No, certainly not. He had heard that many women liked men to smell like men, not of perfume, so he made a point of being clean and tidy and that was all there was to it. He ran his fingers through his hair a few times before selecting a scarf that matched his antique grey overcoat. Then he brushed some dandruff off his collar and put on his newly purchased Russian fur hat with earflaps. The new restaurant Silver Punk was actually very close to the police station on Kungsholmen, and since it had been rated with four stars in the local paper there was a great risk that his old colleagues might go there. Preferably, as a private sleuth with his own detective agency, he didn't want to be recognized, but wished to be able to work in peace. Then there was another aspect: the article had mentioned that the restaurant was introducing Stockholm's first speed dating which used a professional computer program to help you quickly find the love of your heart. A tasty meal, dating, and, to top it all, a bit of private detective work – it all suited him perfectly. Besides, he could deduct the cost as expenses for his firm as long as he remembered to keep the receipts.

Humming to himself he went out into the street and

walked a few extra blocks before he reached the bus stop (the health experts had preached that if you got on a bus, you should not go to the nearest bus stop but go to one a bit further away so that you had some exercise). One bus had just left, and with an irritated snort he pulled up his collar and pulled down his earflaps. The lights of the city were reflected by the sky high above the rooftops and the sound of traffic could be heard in the distance. Everything was like it always had been, but he himself had changed his life. Admittedly, it was nice to be able to do your own thing, but in former days he had been married and now that he was a pensioner he felt a little lonely. He got on well with Einstein, but something was missing. A woman, yes, that was what he needed. He found it far too easy to stay sitting in front of the telly or computer and then, of course, nothing happened. Now, at last, the Silver Punk restaurant had got him to act. Because the target group for the restaurant was pensioners, i.e., people his age, but even younger guests frequented the place too, the papers said. And if there were lots of elderly people there, he might come across something that would lead him to the oldies who had robbed the bank. Now he could look out for crooks and women at the same time. Talk about killing two birds with one stone!

He changed buses outside the Central Station and finally got off at a bus stop in Hornsberg (he didn't bother to get off one or two stops early; there was no need to go to extremes). He walked along the quay and didn't need to look long before he saw an illuminated barge with glitter in the stays and a showily decorated Christmas tree up on the roof: the Silver Punk restaurant. Outside, there was a long queue of people dressed for an evening out and when he came closer, he noticed the aroma of spices, cheese and grilled vegetables. Hungry, he fished out his warrant card so that he wouldn't have to queue, but then he remembered that it was out of date. Anyway, he was, of course, meant to be incognito. He glanced at the long queue and with a sigh put the card back in his pocket.

Finally, half an hour later, he had got on board. He left his overcoat in the cloakroom and combed his hair; now he ordered a beer in the bar and started to look at the ladies. He felt the butterflies in his stomach. Many of the women looked really rather nice and they were so well groomed! They must have read many weeklies and seen many make-over programmes on TV, he thought. Nowadays a lot of older ladies also went to the gym. Indeed, many of the fifty-plus ladies here looked very fit, in every respect, and you would probably feel muscles instead of fat if you got your hand on their thighs.

He fumbled with the entrance ticket which included a round at the dating table, and felt rather exhilarated. Trying to look nonchalant, he went up to the Piet Hein-inspired table full of expectation and gave a start when he saw the iPads chained to the table top. What on earth? He circled the table once more and looked closer at the iPads. Aha, they were for the dating. But surely his requests wouldn't be stored there? And what were those weird lamps? Holes had been drilled into the table top and small differently coloured lamps stuck up out of them, framing the iPads. Ah yes, the newspaper had written something about how the lamps would light up in front of the person or persons who had the qualities you looked for. And in the same way, the lamps in front of your own iPad would light up if you yourself met the requirements that somebody else was looking for. He fumbled after his beer glass and drank to the last drop. Good heavens! This could actually be the real thing!

When Christina saw that the dating table was full, she went up to the expectant guests, held out her arms and said in a shrill voice:

'Ladies and gentlemen, a heartfelt welcome to our little welcome dating!' Her cheeks were red, and she was forever brushing away her long, wavy hair which fell down over her face – because she hadn't learned how to fasten the false hair in the correct way. (On one occasion, the entire hairpiece had followed along with her hand.) She looked around and smiled as heartily and warmly as she could, but all who knew her noticed how nervous she was. She had scratched away the nail polish from the thumb nail on her right hand without realizing it, and her hairpiece was a little crooked. Anna-Greta had seen it, but didn't want to make Christina even more nervous, so she didn't say anything. They had their work cut out as it was. There was so much pressure around the dating table that they had been obliged to provide numbered queue tickets and to fix a time limit of fifteen minutes for each iPad. The eager participants longing for a romantic date would have to settle for that, after which they would be shepherded into the dating corner at the bar. But there, on the other hand, they could have a beer in peace and quiet and chat with each other before hopefully continuing into the restaurant for a tasty dish.

The first dating round started somewhat cautiously, but after the lamps started to light up, things got going. A gentleman in a tweed suit, blue lamb's-wool jumper and tie with cats on it, had got several 'hits' and the lamps next to him were flashing all the time. His mood was improving all the time, and the slightly cautious, suspicious look he had shown at first had now been transformed into happy, glistening eyes. After a while, he went off with a lady to the dating corner where they continued to chat, but then he came back and started again.

That man didn't seem to settle for the first opportunity, Anna-Greta thought, and she took an extra look at him. What sort of man was he? Men weren't usually so fussy. Or was it because he wanted to eye Betty, who was always walking past the table on her way to the bar? Anna-Greta had seen him look up every time the full-figured waitress passed by and she and Christina looked at each other and shook their heads. Whatever did that woman have that all the guys seemed to go for?

Blomberg hadn't felt like asking either of the two ladies that he had iPad-chatted with so far, and then tentatively conversed with in the dating corner, to dinner. No, to be honest, he found the waitress more interesting. When she swept past with her tray and her rear end swinging like a ship in a storm, well, he found it hard to concentrate. He was only human, after all. But of course she probably wasn't his type. He would like to be able to talk and discuss with his partner-to-be, exchange ideas and have fun with her. That was why this speed-dating thing was so exciting, as it also considered people's inner qualities. In fact, it was really fun, and he loved it when the lamps flashed. He was particularly curious about the unknown person who had got all the lamps to flash. On Blomberg's iPad, the questionnaire from place number three had turned up and that person had the weirdest of qualities. Well, to be truthful, it was the message under 'Other' that had caught Blomberg's attention. It said: *Hello darling, I love you!* So somebody had discovered him, somebody had understood his not entirely uncomplicated personality. Somebody, but who? Blomberg hardly dared look, but summoned up courage, raised his head and sought out place number three. There, in front of iPad number three, sat a fat bloke with checked trousers and a grey jacket and he stank of male perfume. Blomberg looked around in confusion. There must have been a faulty connection somewhere. Disappointment washed over him and he went to the bar to console himself with a beer. With the glass of beer in his hand he looked around to find the IT manager at the restaurant. Now and then, a tall lady with a stick went up to the iPads and checked them. Could it be her? No, she looked more like Kungsholmen's answer to Mary Poppins – but with a walking stick instead of an umbrella. But when she walked past, he addressed her.

'That iPad over there, you know,' he started, and fidgeted with his beer glass. 'Nice system you've got there, but I think there's something wrong with my iPad. It worked all right to start with, but then – well, I didn't exactly get a Marilyn Monroe, but him over there.' Blomberg nodded towards the fat man.

'Oh my God!' exclaimed Anna-Greta and she gave such a horsey neigh that Blomberg dropped his glass which landed on the floor and broke.

'And besides, he smells of perfume!' Blomberg complained, bending down to pick up the broken glass.

'Usch, so horrid. A real man should smell like a man!'

'Ah, you think so?' said Blomberg, and he looked up with newly awakened interest. Of course, I don't have any perfume, he was on the brink of saying, but he stopped himself at the last moment. Instead, he got up and held out two large bits of broken glass.

'I'm so sorry, I've broken a glass, I shall, of course, immediately pay for it.'

'A beer glass? Pah, that's nothing. A miss in the Pississippi!'

'I beg your pardon?'

'You can have another beer!' With large elk-size strides Anna-Greta made her way to the bar and filled a new beer glass which she gave to him. And before Blomberg had time to react she had ordered the bartender to sweep and mop the floor. Meanwhile she cleared the memory of his iPad.

'So you are looking at the talent?' she wondered when everything was ready and she nodded in the direction of the dating table.

'Talent? Well, I don't know about that. How do you mean?' Blomberg immediately became uncertain.

'Have you found a date?' Anna-Greta wondered and she gave him a flirty wink.

'Err, hmm,' mumbled Blomberg. 'Well, there was that faulty connection . . .'

'Pah, don't worry about that, it's already fixed. No, I'm proud of that dating program. You know, I want every single person around that table to get a hit. A real love hit. With the iPad you find out the inner qualities and in the bar you can check out appearance and chemistry. Not bad, eh? All in one. And besides, you save time.'

'Yes, indeed, it is modern.'

'It took a while to write the program but in the end I put it together.'

'Ah, so it's you, I mean, you know all about computers?'

Anna-Greta picked at the bun at her neck and looked very pleased with herself.

'Oh yes, I do know a little, even though I missed your iPad. I didn't want to give you a fat old bloke who smells of perfume – no, that was not the idea!' she giggled with her hand on his shoulder and a four-footed neigh of such a calibre that he almost dropped his glass again. Then he started laughing too and they carried on a long while until Anna-Great pushed her spectacles up onto her forehead, dried her tears of laughter and said that it was time to get back to work.

'Well, I wonder what went wrong with the iPad?' Blomberg pondered.

'Somebody might have messed around with the system when I had my back turned,' she said.

'Messed around?'

'Yes, you must cleanse the memory between each user. Somebody might have locked the system by mistake. An old message might have remained in the memory.'

'What a pity, it said: "I love you!".'

Anna-Greta angled her head to one side rather coquettishly.

'Yes, we do need love, don't we? But seeing how the lamps have lit up and flashed at your place, you are bound to receive more messages, just wait and see.'

'Even the gold lamp lit up,' said Blomberg proudly and noticed to his chagrin that he was blushing. 'But of course there aren't so many available men in my age group, who are looking for mature ladies, I mean,' he smoothed over while realizing that he was rather stretching the truth.

'You don't say? That's nice. Most elderly gentlemen are only looking for young girls, those pin-ups, you know! But heaven knows how that will make them happier. And once they've got what they are after, they have no idea what they can talk about with the young lady. But our solution is better. Outer as well as inner qualities, all in one.' She threw a quick glance at the dating table where the lamps were flashing away.

Oh goodness, what a language this lady had, Blomberg thought. But *I love you!* Well, of course a younger woman must have written that. And it had been meant for him. No doubt. A girl who was going all out. And she was certainly a real beauty. No, a younger woman wasn't bad at all. But then again, the most important thing was what the woman was like as a person, of course. Blomberg looked down at his hands.

'There are happy marriages where there is a great age difference,' he felt compelled to say.

'Yes, indeed, if the man is rich, that's true.'

Blomberg was lost for words. He took a gulp of his beer and looked musingly at the stern lady. She knew what she was doing. But if old data could be left behind in the iPad, what would happen with his own questionnaire? He cleared his throat.

'You do delete all the information as soon as somebody has left their place by the iPad? I mean, what happened with my iPad, that was a mistake, right?' he wondered.

'Of course. People can be anonymous here. That will never happen again. Integrity is everything. Incidentally, what a nice tie you're wearing. I love cats.' Anna-Greta leaned forward and stroked one of the portrayed cats with her index finger.

'You do?'

'Oh yes, I adore them! Cats are such delightful creatures! Cute and faithful but at the same time with a strong will of their own. Grrr!' said Anna-Greta and she made a playful clawing movement in the air.

Blomberg couldn't help but smile. She wasn't the most beautiful creation on Mother Earth, that Mary Poppins. No, she was tall and straggly and with her hair in a bun, but in some way she was still attractive. She seemed to be full of joie de vivre and optimism and reminded him a little of his mother, one of those people who were secure in themselves and could take care of others. And her hair was well cared for and her eyes glowingly alert. She didn't stink of creams and perfume either. He fidgeted with his beer glass and rocked slightly on the chair.

'I have noticed that you have had a lot to do this evening. But perhaps you have time for a beer? By the way, I'm Ernst, Ernst Blomberg,' he said and he held out his hand.

'Anna-Greta,' she replied and shook his hand so resolutely that it felt as if she was shaking water off a dishwashing brush.

'And when it comes to computers, I might add, I'm good

at that,' Blomberg went on. 'If anything goes wrong, I'd be happy to help out.'

Anna-Greta took a deep breath and looked as if she had been swept off her feet.

39

A white motorboat with blue speed lines came tearing along Riddarfjärden firth, hardly slowed down at all along the Karlberg canal and then increased speed further when it reached Ulvsunda Lake. There weren't many boats out at this time of the year and with the Evinrude 250 H.O. they could zoom along. Scarves fluttered and Kenta and the Weasel seemed for once to be very pleased with themselves.

'Hang on!' shouted the Weasel as he took a wide swing out on the lake before slowing down and berthing at the newly built quay below Hornsberg. The Weasel threw out the anchor and Kenta climbed onto the quay with the rope, which he quickly tied to one of the bollards. Dusk was approaching and that suited them nicely. Without lanterns nobody would see them when they departed later in the evening. The Weasel climbed up onto the quay too and lit a cigarette. In silence they started to walk in the direction of the Silver Punk restaurant.

'Do you want one?' The Weasel held out the cigarette packet, twisted it round and pointed at the text: 'Look at this! Smoking kills. What the fuck do they think we'll do now? Give up? Not bloody likely.'

'Don't smoke them all, we need them.'

'Pah, it'll be enough with one or two for the fenders.'

'All right, then,' said Kenta, and he too took a Marlboro. He lit it from the Weasel's cigarette and looked around. 'But listen,' he said, pointing at the barge, 'do we really have to go down into that spinach again? There's a whole fucking jungle down there. And it's fucking daft, they can recognize us!'

'But don't you get it? We go there, get really sweet with the oldies and then everybody will think we're all the best of mates. Then when the barge meets with an accident nobody will suspect us.'

'But what if somebody is still on board? Fucking dangerous, like; could be arson.'

'That's why we must go round the whole boat. And then they've got good nosh and speed dating. Shit, that's popular! Check it out. Might be something for your pizzeria.'

'Yeah, wow!' said Kenta and he brightened up. 'Speed dating, we'll snatch that.'

'Uhh, look at that queue!' said the Weasel when they had come closer. He threw away his cigarette butt and coughed. 'We're not bleeding well standing there.'

A long queue with elderly gentlemen and dressed-up ladies with fancy coiffures was in the way. Kenta ditched his cigarette too, gave the Weasel a meaningful look and then they pushed past.

'We are standing in a queue here, can't you see?' complained a gentleman with a cap.

'Yeah, I hope you enjoy it,' replied the Weasel and with Kenta at his heel he pushed his way in through the entrance and went towards the bar.

'Two strong beers!' he said. He kept his leather jacket on.

'Fancy place!' Kenta remarked, and he looked around.

They observed the speed dating and smiled at the couple who sat in the dating corner.

'Ah, isn't that cute!' said Kenta.

'I wonder if they've got what it takes – the blokes, I mean,' said the Weasel with a grin. 'And the old dears.' He shut up when he caught sight of Martha. 'Well, now, what have we got there? It's that old hag with the waist bag. Time for some straight talking,' he said and he nodded in Martha's direction. 'That ancient bitch will have a final chance.'

'Watch your bollocks man, danger ahoi!'

The Weasel put down his beer and slid off the bar stool just as Martha was going past. He stood in her way.

'We must have a talk!'

'Oh, how nice. Would you like a beer?'

'No, no, I fucking wouldn't.' The Weasel sighed. Even though she fought, she was always so friendly.

'A man without a beer is like a bank without money.' She held up two fingers in front of the bartender and waited until he had filled two beer glasses. Then she put them together with a bowl of nuts in front of the two men. The Weasel and Kenta exchanged a quick look.

'Back to business. You wanted to talk about something?' she said and she smiled again.

'Yeah, the barge, like. We want to buy it.'

'The barge? Well, you don't say! Regrettably, it is not for sale.'

'Yeah, but we'll pay good.'

'Money isn't everything, boys. Here at Silver Punk we

want to make people nice and happy. Quality of life, you understand? That is much more important than money.'

Quality of life? The Weasel and Kenta looked blankly at each other.

'But you and your gang can take over a restaurant in the south of the city. Just as long as we get the barge,' the Weasel tempted her. He wanted to rid the area of these rebellious pensioners, and had more than once regretted ever letting the Zimmer gang in. He hadn't in his wildest fantasy been able to imagine that they would gang up against him and he had seen the rent and the protection money as a guaranteed income. But had they paid? No! Time to be rid of them, no question about that.

'South? But my good man, what is the point of that?' Martha shook her head.

'A restaurant on firm land doesn't sink, but, um, this barge isn't safe. The hull is fucking ancient.'

'But still you want to buy it?'

Martha tried to be tough, but the underlying threat was very clear. The mafia gang wanted to be rid of them, perhaps even sink the barge? But this was where they were going to have their Vintage Village. Martha weighed things up. Brains had installed automatic pumps so they ought to be safe, but even so, if there was a power cut, things could go wrong. But she certainly wasn't at all keen on obeying these petty gangsters. Somebody had to stand up to the mafia. Crooks, greedy companies and oppressors who didn't pay tax, the whole pack of them must meet with opposition.

'Sorry, but we are not selling. You can try to rent out that restaurant in the south of the city to somebody else. I'm sure it will work out,' she said mildly and she pretended to be completely unaware of the set-up.

'Lady, a lot of things can happen to a barge,' the Weasel said again, in an irritated tone.

'To a restaurant in the south of the city too,' Martha countered.

'Ah, come on, this is fucking ridiculous!' The Weasel gave a scornful grin. 'Right, there isn't much of a choice.' He jabbed her beer glass so that it fell to the floor. 'Now, my old dear, let's do this nice and—'

'Old dear! Nice! Aaaaghh!'

The Weasel saw Martha's notorious waist bag come flying, but didn't have time to cover himself. His crotch felt on fire, and he keeled over. He dropped his glass, the beer splashed onto his flies and the glass rolled off under the bar stool. Kenta rushed forward to intervene, but then Martha stuck her foot out. Her left Ecco Saunter shoe, which had been rated with five stars on the Internet, stood firmly on the floor and he tripped, swirled round half a lap and collapsed.

'You should be kind to old ladies!' Martha hissed and then turned on her heel (of soft rubber) with her waist bag in her hand, before walking off.

'Fuck! Fuck!' groaned the Weasel.

'*Tweet, tweet,*' could be heard from the loudspeakers in the ceiling because Brains, that same second, had turned on the background noises for the restaurant in an attempt to create a romantic mood. Betty particularly liked this little dicky bird, a blue tit at mating time – but the Weasel did not.

'Shut the fuck up! Turn that fucking bird colony off!'

'But look at them stains, wet your pants, like?' said Kenta pointing at the Weasel's flies.

'Pah, just spilt some beer. That old bitch! That whole damned gang has got to go, now, straight away!'

The Weasel seethed and hissed as he limped off to the gents, supporting himself on Kenta.

'Are you quite sure?' Kenta wondered a while later after the Weasel had tidied himself up and they were on their way into the bar again. 'I mean, perhaps we can *talk* some sense into them?'

'If they'd sold us the barge, OK, but now . . . Time to do a recce. We'll go over the barge now and then make a final check in the restaurant after they've closed. No bastard must still be on board.'

There was a lovely smell of wok-fried vegetables and oriental spices and there was a great atmosphere inside the restaurant. Quite a few people from the dating corner had gone on to the dining room and were now flirting for all they were worth, while the service staff swept through the greenery with food and drink. The sound level was high and nobody seemed to notice the guys who moved slowly between the tables looking all about them.

Kenta saw that many guests were in the sixty-five to eighty-five age range, but there were some younger ones there too. How on earth had the oldies managed that? He sighed and thought about his empty pizzeria and thought it was unfair. On the other hand, he couldn't help but admit that this restaurant was nicely decorated. There were no straight lines, everything was softly rounded off and romantic and the forest path was bordered by cosy booths. It had that special quality, the right feeling and atmosphere.

'Look out!' Kenta called just as his mate was about to walk right into a wild boar. The Weasel swerved away at the last second, but wobbled and lost his balance. Swearing, he fumbled for something to hold on to and managed to break his fall on a tree trunk. He braced himself with both hands but his left hand landed right on top of one of the museum's stuffed woodpeckers. Without a sound it imploded and fell down in a squashed lump in the greenery – except for the bird's beak, which had pierced the Weasel's palm.

'Out of this loony bin, this fucking second!' he screamed.

'What about the dating? Aren't we going to try that?' Kenta wondered. 'If I'm going to learn about it, I ought to try it out. Lots of time before midnight . . .'

'But this could be fucking blood poisoning!' roared the Weasel, lifting his hand up to his mouth to try to extract the remains of the beak with his teeth.

'OK, next stop the hospital,' said Kenta with a worried look at his mate.

'But when we come back, then all hell will break loose!' swore the Weasel.

Then he coughed heavily and turned bright red in the face. A bit of the beak had stuck in his throat.

40

Winter had come to Djursholm. A soft white covering of snow now lay on the ground in the gardens and parks, hiding lawns and asphalt. The snow glistened in the light of the street lamps. Martha looked out through the tower room window and followed the white snowflakes that slowly fluttered down to the ground. The oak trees were covered with a thin pearl-white layer and the high grass had been bent and lay buried beneath a white lid.

How many days had it snowed, and how many days had she sat here and looked out through the window? Martha had lost track, she only knew that she wasn't feeling right. After the Christmas holidays she had been struck down with a heavy bout of influenza that had been difficult to shake off, and it had been followed by a very troublesome asthma attack. And on top of it all, her heart was playing up. She ought, of course, to have gone to the doctor's, but she couldn't stand the idea of sitting there at the drop-in surgery waiting for hours; no way was she going to do that. She didn't have the patience. Besides, you could catch something nasty in the waiting room! She had heard all about people who had acquired nosocomial infections, which was the fancy word for catching something nasty in a hospital. You might be admitted for something trivial but you could then die from the acquired infection! Perhaps simply because the hospital management had cut down on cleaning staff to save money. No, she wasn't going to take unnecessary risks; she would treat her influenza and her fibrillation all by herself. Besides, it was modern to take responsibility for your own health and not take too many pills. She had read about that in a book called *The Self-Healing Human*. And that suited her just fine, sitting there on the sofa with her knitting and lacking the energy to go anywhere. She had hardly set her foot in the restaurant since that evening when she had sent the Weasel and Kenta packing. She had deliberately tried to let the others take responsibility and she thought that she had got better and better at delegating. Besides, it was to her advantage. While the others worked, she had time to ponder future plans and work out new crimes, but at the same time she could secretly try to cure herself.

So, just sort of in passing, she had asked Christina about various health tips, advice that she had tried out bit by bit. Sooner or later she would stumble across something that worked. And having heart fibrillation was perhaps only logical considering how much pressure she had been under. Above all, there was the problem with Brains. They behaved in a nice and friendly manner towards each other, but he was brooding on something, she could sense that very strongly. She looked at her engagement ring. They hadn't broken off the engagement, even though he had grunted about that on one occasion, but since that evening when he had thrown the pillow at the wall they no longer talked about a wedding.

Now all he talked about, day in and day out, was that Betty woman. Betty this and Betty that, and he didn't seem to notice it himself. But most serious of all was that he looked so happy when he came up from the restaurant kitchen but his bright eyes faded as soon as he left the barge. That damned pin-up pudding had completely turned his head. Couldn't he see how pathetic his behaviour was? He was an old man and would win any competition for the person with the most wrinkles! But if this was how he wanted things, well, so be it. Martha snorted – but so forcefully that her heart did a double beat. She calmed down. That fibrillation was slightly worrying. But she also had a past as a gymnastics teacher, so it was embarrassing to worry about such troubles. No, she wasn't sickly. She remembered that Christina had said something about magnesium helping . . . yes, she had claimed that it prevented fibrillation and problems with your legs too.

Martha fetched her computer, dragged the chaise longue out onto the terrace and started to google the word 'magnesium'. She scrolled down the list of sites and nodded. Christina had evidently been right, that metal was good for lots of things. Martha decided to ask her friend for some powders and say it was for a cramp in her legs. Then she wouldn't need to let on about her heart condition. Pleased with herself, she put her computer to one side, filled a small jug with cloudberry liqueur and put that on a tray together with some eucalyptus pills. Then she went to fetch Christina's health bible, *The Self-Healing Human*, and two soft cushions. She made herself comfortable on her Bruno Mathsson armchair. Now she could relax with a good book and at the same time look out across Bielke's garden.

She noticed that somebody had moved the garden furniture and she wondered whether Bielke had returned. Unless, of course, it was somebody from the council or a new gardener. But why would Bielke suddenly come home now when he hadn't even been home at Christmas? Now, when it was nice and warm on the Cayman Islands and, later, he could sail his yacht around the Mediterranean. His luxury motor yachts, yes. Martha tried to recall what Christina had said. That's right, his luxury monstrosities were worth far more than five hundred million kronor each and were registered on the Cayman Islands – where you didn't need to pay tax. Martha's brain started to process the information: five hundred to six hundred million, that was a lot of money. In fact, that would be a very nice amount to have! The City Mission hadn't received many millions and the bonus that the League of Pensioners had given to health staff didn't add up to much more than a pathetic thousand-kronor note for each one. Business super bosses and the other bonus sharks would laugh themselves to death. No, the League of Pensioners ought to donate a great deal more. And one of those yachts – well, if they could steal just one, then they wouldn't need to commit any more crimes for a long time. They would be able to share out more money as well as getting a bit of peace and quiet for quite a while. And that would be good for her heart too, no doubt. Wouldn't it be a delightful crime to plan now that she had delegated most of the work to the others? She was bored and had become restless. And that couldn't be good for your heart either.

The Silver Punk project had been fun to carry out, but the restaurant didn't make much of a profit and the new cafe and cinema barge she'd thought about had not yet become a reality since the barge was in poor condition and would have to go into a dry dock for repairs. Such a project would not generate much money either. Martha took a lemon wafer biscuit and poured a thimbleful of cloudberry liqueur into her tea. Why not ask Anders and Emma to take over the restaurant activities, then the friends could go off to Saint-Tropez (far away from Betty) and start the next project? A major project. And it would be really something to steal a huge motorboat that only royalty, oil sheikhs and billionaires could afford; one with a helicopter platform, a swimming bath, luxury rooms and expensive art on the walls. Yes, she had read that people were prepared to pay ten thousand euros a week just to rent one of those seagoing palaces. The very idea cheered her up and she took another lemon wafer biscuit.

It was good to stop and think sometimes, not just rush on in life. Perhaps there was a meaning when you became ill? Your body's own way of telling you that you must take it easy, she thought. She got up, fetched her notepad and pen and immediately felt much perkier. Anna-Greta had also thought along the same lines, on that occasion when they had eaten pea soup with a lot of thyme in it. Brains might not be too eager to commit crimes again, but, on the other hand, she wasn't dependent on what he thought. There were three others in the gang and she ought to be able to get them to agree. Anyway, she might even manage to persuade Brains too; he liked having things to do and there wasn't enough work at Silver Punk. Besides, it would be good to go away with him so that he would have something else to think about other than Betty and the ladies at the dating table.

But how do you steal a motor yacht worth more than five hundred million? It would be difficult, but what a delightful challenge!

41

It was now evening and as usual the barge was lit up and welcoming, moored by the quay. Former Chief Inspector Blomberg hurried on his way. He had brought some cakes with him because Anna-Greta had said something about liking cakes. Indeed, during the last few weeks he had been a regular guest on the barge, going there for a beer and to feel that something was happening. It was so exciting when the lamps lit up round the iPad and when he too got the lamps to flash in front of somebody else. He tested speed dating every evening he went there and had actually eaten dinner several times with ladies he had never met before. Besides, he liked just sitting in the bar and watching when Betty and the other waitresses hurried past. A glass of beer and something lovely to look at, not a bad combination. And then, of course, there was Anna-Greta. Now and then she stopped in the bar and one evening he had bought her a beer.

They had found lots to talk about and the discussions never seemed to end. She wondered how things had gone with his dates, she listened to him and seemed to be interested in his thoughts about life. Indeed, they chatted about most things, although they avoided job talk. He sidetracked the subject and said he had recently become a pensioner and that he had worked as a former consultant in educational issues (the Police really did need more training and he had a thing or two to teach them, so it wasn't a direct lie). But he said not a word about him being an ex-policeman with his own detective agency. That was going to remain secret. Then he could, without worry, milk her for information about the restaurant's guests and in the best case scenario find some clues which would lead him to the League of Pensioners. Besides, she wasn't very forthcoming about her life either. All he knew was that she had worked in a bank, lived in Djursholm and that in recent years she had become interested in computers. So they talked a lot about computers, the economy and 1950s music.

'You must hear something from my vinyl collection,' she said one day. 'I shall bring some records with me.'

'Oh how nice. Vinyl sounds so much better than those CD records or music you download from the Internet,' he said with the appearance of an expert, and then she looked so delighted that he felt really warm all over. The next day she had brought along a vinyl-record player and they had sat in one of the booths (the one with the wild boars) where there was an electric socket, turned on the gramophone and played Duke Ellington and Chris Barber. Now he always took along a vinyl record that they could play and the other evening, when he had played Bill Haley's 'Rock around the clock', it got really lively. Then she'd leaned close to him and said:

'You know what? You and me, let's rock!'

And then she had let out that powerful laugh (almost like a horse's neigh) and given him a thumbs-up signal. Yes, she was good fun, this Mary Poppins, and he found himself actually looking forward to the evenings on the barge. In fact, on several occasions he had stayed until closing time and had not got up the next morning until almost lunchtime. He dutifully sent Jöback and his cronies the odd bit of information about latex masks from Buttericks, and informed them about his daily rounds outside the Stockholm banks. And, of course, he kept an extra look-out for elderly people who behaved suspiciously, but so far he had not had anything to report. As a detective he felt he was becoming a bit rusty, but some time or other that League of Pensioners would make a stupid mistake and then he would nail them. And anyway it was only a question of time before they, too, visited the restaurant. It had become a really trendy place, and sooner or later that old lady who had been seen outside the National Museum would turn up. And it was more than likely that she would be able to lead him to the rest of the league. He hadn't seen her facial features, that was true, but her posture and the way she walked was eye-catching. Not a chance that he would miss her!

'Oh, some cakes! That is nice! And you have baked them for me?' Anna-Greta received him in the dating corner with the warmest smile he had ever seen.

'Yes, I have started to bake a little recently. They smell so good,' answered Blomberg and he held out the bag with the cakes. Anna-Greta leaned forward and sniffed the bag with pleasure.

'Um, what a treat! And full of cinnamon and sugar. Yummy! I *love* cakes! Oh, you are really *wonderful!*'

'Now, now, it's nothing much,' said Blomberg not without

pride, and he felt the irritating redness on his cheeks. 'Sometimes I use cardamom instead. Now that I'm a pensioner I
like to make a cake now and then.'

'Oh, we must taste them straight away,' she said, looking
around the room. 'We can sit in the vinyl stall. Have you
brought a record with you?'

'Of course! Why not let Frank Sinatra sing a little for that
stuffed wild boar?'

'Ha, ha,' neighed Anna-Greta. 'Good idea. And we must
have some coffee too, don't you think?' She waved her hand
as Betty walked past, and asked the waitress to cut up the
cakes and ordered coffee.

'We're working in the vinyl stall,' she explained.

'Oh yes, I can see,' insinuated Betty and she disappeared.
Anna-Greta and Blomberg traipsed off to their favourite
place. When they had sat down, she got out her iPad and put
it on the table. 'You know what,' she said, 'I'd like to discuss
something with you. I think we can take this speed dating to
a new level. A new app.'

'Delightful. Do it!'

Blomberg was enjoying himself. It was so nice to discuss
computer programs with Anna-Greta. She knew about all
that, things that Jöback and his colleagues hadn't a clue about.
She logged in to the dating program while Blomberg put on
a record with Sinatra. Soon the stall was filled with a croon-
ing 'Fly me to the moon'.

'Why not spread the dating program on the Internet and
charge for it?' Anna-Greta went on. She pointed at the screen.
'We could have a membership fee and five per cent for every
date. All of Sweden could join in.'

'You are creative, Anna-Greta. So much happens in your company.'

'When it comes to money, yes. The more you earn, the more you can donate to the poor, you see.' She leaned forward and pointed at some dating icons she was experimenting with. 'Now just have a look at this.'

Blomberg studied the screen. There were three apps formed like hearts and in the middle it said: 'Friendship, Love *and* Marriage'.

'Goodness me. Have you done this?'

'Nothing fancy, but it did take a bit of time, of course.' Anna-Greta looked pleased with herself.

'But why have you got different apps for Love and Marriage?

'Surely you can understand that. Not everybody wants to get married. Perhaps they just want a little fling and are satisfied with that.' She winked and prodded him knowingly in his ribs. Blomberg stole a look at Anna-Greta. She suddenly seemed so different. Was she flirting, or had he made a mistake? At that moment, Betty came back with their coffee and a plate of cakes. She winked at Blomberg, smiled and went off again.

'Help yourself, these do look tasty, and home-made by you too,' chirped Anna-Greta, her entire face glowing. She picked up a slice of cake, flashed him a warm look and took a large mouthful. 'Oh yum, yum!' she exclaimed. 'This is just perfect!'

The next moment he felt a knee against his thigh followed by a hearty smile.

'Men who bake are attractive, you do know that?' she

trumpeted and then laughed again, while she pressed her knee against his. Then all the lights went out. Sinatra's voice slowed down, turned into a deep bass and disappeared the same moment the barge was enveloped by darkness.

'Usch, how horrible,' exclaimed Anna-Greta and she put her hand into his. You could hear murmuring and some frightened cries, bangs and scraping sounds as people got up. There was movement up on deck and some candles fluttered far away. But they themselves remained sitting in the darkness. Normally she would have been the first to go out, but now she stayed behind with him.

'The power will soon be back,' Blomberg comforted her and stroked her slightly awkwardly on the back of her hand.

'Do you think so?' she mumbled leaning a little closer to him. Then the lights started to flicker. Sinatra's 'Fly me to the moon' picked up speed and the barge was once again all lit up. Anna-Greta immediately pulled back a little.

'Aha, now the electricity is back again, or Brains's generator has started up. That is our back-up for power cuts' said Anna-Greta, clearing her throat, and going slightly red in the face. 'Anyhow, the main thing is that the lights are back on. Now everything is back to normal again.'

But everything isn't back to normal, Blomberg thought. Something had happened there in the dark. Between them. Then the lights went out again.

42

All of Stockholm City and Kungsholmen lay in darkness. Here and there you could see weak, fluttering glows in windows, but down at the quay it was quiet and deserted. Only the stars lit up the road. Brains lit his head torch and went to the bow together with Christina. It seemed as if the power would be off for quite a while, but what did that matter when he had his generator. The beam from the head torch lit up the deck, catching the wooden box with fireworks and finally the generator cupboard. The generator hadn't been used for a while, but a genuine Bauer shouldn't cause any problems. He opened the door and took out the jerry can. Best to fill up, but was the generator in good condition, would it start? He turned the petrol tap, waited a few moments and then pressed the start switch. The engine came to life at the first attempt.

'A good job I thought about having this in reserve. Now we'll have some lights again,' he said contentedly, wiping his hands on his trousers.

'Thank you, Brains, what would we do without you?' said Christina as she saw how the lamps on the barge lit up again. 'But perhaps it would be best to close for today,' she continued, pointing at the generator with her high heels. 'That apparatus can hardly run a whole restaurant.'

'Oh yes, a Bauer can run everything,' he exclaimed, putting the jerry can back in its place and closing the cupboard door. They started to walk towards the stern and had got halfway when the generator suddenly coughed and stopped. They stood there in the dark. Brains turned on his head torch again.

'There might be some water in the petrol,' he muttered and returned to the bow with Christina trailing after him. He opened the generator cupboard, shone the torch inside and lifted the jerry can out again. Hmm, it was indeed a bit old and rusty. He ought to buy a new one, a plastic one. Those old jerry cans could get a rust hole somewhere and then water could seep in. He was just about to try to start the generator again when the cook came over with a torch.

'Luckily, we've got so much salad, otherwise people would have complained that the food had gone cold,' he said in a voice dripping with irony. 'Damned power cut. Dark everywhere. They said on the radio that it could last a long time.'

'No problem. We can run everything with the generator. I've just got to fix a few things here,' said Brains bending down to check the pipes. No holes, no air bubbles, no water. It must be something else. Aha, it looked as if there was a loose wire. He fixed it and tried to start the generator again. He succeeded straight away. 'The cable. Careless of me, but now it's humming away.'

'But the restaurant is closed now. I'm not going to serve raw chicken,' muttered the cook.

'Raw food is good for you,' Christina cut in. 'A green restaurant—'

'Greens are one thing, yes. We need power. Electricity, do you understand? You see, if everybody down there lights candles, we'll have a forest fire!'

'But the lights are back on now,' Brains concluded. 'We'd better go down to the others.'

Down in the dining room the guests were noisy, and most noisy of all were the flirting singles over at the dating table. Rake was trying to calm down the lovesick gents, but in vain. His hair was standing on end, his face was blotchy with stress and he looked relieved when he caught sight of his friends.

'Good job you fixed the lights, but the dating doesn't work. Something must have gone wrong with the computer system,' he said.

'It doesn't matter. We must close. People can come back tomorrow,' said Christina looking about her. Then she cupped her hands and shouted out in the dating corner: 'Regrettably, we must close down because of the power cut. Our generator can't deliver electricity much longer. Instead, you are welcome back tomorrow and we shall stay open half an hour extra.'

Then she hurried down into the dining room and shouted out the same message. Guests finished their meals, had problems paying when the card system didn't work, but everything went surprisingly well because Christina said they could come back the next day and pay then, if they wished. So the guests fetched their overcoats from the cloakroom without getting rowdy and everything went off smoothly. Except in the dating corner where there was still a lot of gabbling. In the dark some bold gentlemen had taken the opportunity to grope the thighs of the women, so that one lady got a ladder on her stocking, another kicked the offender on his

310

shins, and a third excited lady had grabbed hold of the hairy, fumbling hand and refused to let go.

Meanwhile, one or two of the more forward ladies had knee-flirted wildly there in the dark despite varicose veins and support stockings, something that certain gentlemen – when the lights came on again – experienced as rather intrusive, since they were really there to see Betty. But one of the prettiest ladies had the worst of it; a seventy-three-year-old madame who looked very good for her age. At one corner of the sofa, three pairs of shoes (male sizes) had tried to toe-flirt with her at the same time, which had resulted in a chaotic mess of toes and shoes. With three heavy male feet on her left high-heel shoe, things went wrong. The heel snapped and the black party shoe with a rose on the toe crumpled up with a hissing sound. Most people had been annoyed because the system of lamps around the iPads had been knocked out by the power cut. Now they were flashing frantically everywhere, and nobody knew any longer whom they should flirt with. In what seemed like desperation, they were all courting everyone and there was no end to the disorder.

'I understand that it can be hard to decide when everything lights up and flashes, but, on the other hand, it does make it that bit more exciting,' Brains said, and he tried to calm people down.

'Dreadfully exciting,' a fifty-five-year-old woman snapped at him, as she sat surrounded by three groping eighty-year-olds. And a ninety-year-old man who hadn't been stylish even when he was in his thirties, sighed:

'How infuriating that you turned the lights back on again. Just as I was about to score!'

Brains patted him consolingly on his shoulder. 'You will be welcome back tomorrow. Our guests usually return. Things will sort themselves out, just you see.'

It took some time to evacuate everybody, but eventually all the dinner guests had left the barge. In the kitchen, too, they had finished up and were ready to leave the boat. The cook took the serving staff up on deck with him and when Betty went past, Brains tried to delay her.

'Sit down and keep me company for a while,' he said taking her hand.

'No, work is over, now it's time to go home.'

'But can't I get you a drink?'

'Are you crazy? No, I'm off home now.' She pulled her hand away and hurried off.

Brains was startled. What on earth had got into her? Quite clearly disappointed, he stood there with his arms by his sides. They had been on the same wavelength, a silent belonging-together based on mutual happiness and warmth. She had smiled with her whole face and always said something friendly whenever they had caught sight of one another. But now? He had evidently misinterpreted her. He shrugged his shoulders, pulled himself together and, muttering sadly to himself, did a round on the barge to check that nobody had been left behind. But just as he was about to conclude that everyone had gone home, he caught sight of Anna-Greta. She sat in the vinyl stall together with an elegant gentleman in a blue pull-over.

'We're closing now. Are you coming?' he wondered.

'Oh right, we were just about to leave. But something has gone wrong with the iPads,' said Anna-Greta.

'Yours too? Yes, the entire dating system has crashed. But you can sort that out in the morning.'

'Yes, of course. But first I must close the dating program properly so we don't lose all the data. It won't take long. This is Ernst Blomberg. He is really good when it comes to computers.'

Blomberg, with his mouth full of cake, gave Brains a friendly nod in greeting.

'Will you lock up, then?' Brains wondered.

'No problem,' said Anna-Greta, delighted, and Brains thought that she sounded just a bit too keen.

'And don't forget to turn off the generator. You only have to twist the switch round.'

'I know,' Anna-Greta called out after him. 'We'll just finish up here first.'

'OK, be seeing you. But we're leaving now. So you'll have to take a taxi on your own later.'

'Yes, yes, that's fine,' said Anna-Greta somewhat absently and she didn't even look up. I wonder if she's fallen in love, Brains thought, glancing at Blomberg. As of late, Anna-Greta had spent all the more time with that guy. So what, that was her business, just as long as she was happy.

'But don't delay too long. The petrol in the generator won't last that long.'

'Things will work out,' answered Anna-Greta joyfully with a little pony laugh. Brains sighed, raised his hand in a farewell greeting and left the scene. Out of the corner of his eye he saw how Anna-Greta and Blomberg again leaned over the iPad. That was what was weird about computers, he thought: the way a tiny little apparatus can have such power over people. Those two had been busy with the iPad all evening. And it was amusing, the way Anna-Greta had changed. She had been so shy and withdrawn previously, but since she had started that affair with Gunnar on the ferry to Finland, she had become a bit crazy about men. Oh well, at least she had smothered that horse's neigh.

When Brains had got his overcoat on, gone down the gangplank and joined the others on the quayside, they waved to a passing taxi which immediately turned in and stopped. The League of Pensioners, minus Martha, who was at home, and Anna-Greta, who was still on the barge, opened the doors and got into the taxi.

'Djursholm, Aurora street, please,' said Brains before sinking down on the back seat, tired. As they were just leaving the quay, he noticed that the lights on the barge went out again. Then he remembered that he had indeed thought about filling the generator with the last of the petrol, but had actually forgotten to do so. The jerry can was still on the deck. For a second he wondered whether he should stop the taxi and go and help Anna-Greta, but then he remembered that she had company. Those two would be sure to manage in the dark. Excellent, he concluded, then he shut his eyes and settled comfortably in the back seat.

43

The water lay black, and far away you could hear the buzz of the city like a distant tone. A man was walking along the Hornsberg waterside path with his dog, and a drunk was sleeping it off on the deck of one of the boats down by the water. No one else could be seen. It was silent and there was almost no wind. The Weasel and Kenta tied up their little motorboat and went ashore. The stars lit up the road.

'Fuck, what a mess, like. The power cut came just at the right time,' said Kenta looking around. The dark facades of houses could be made out along the street.

'Yeah, at last we'll get rid of that barge.'

'But, seriously, are you OK with that?' Kenta wondered, pointing at the Weasel's bandaged right hand. The bandage was a bit loose, was frayed and not properly fixed around his wrist.

'I can bloody well strike a match! The wound is almost healed.'

'OK,' mumbled Kenta, although he wasn't really convinced. His mate had got blood poisoning and had been forced to spend a few nights at Saint Göran's hospital. Now he claimed his hand was all right, but even so. They could have waited another week. But the Weasel had been impossible to talk with and had become totally fanatic. They had to get rid of the barge, and that was all there was to it. They passed the jetty and when they came round the corner, they felt the adrenaline rush. There lay the barge. No lights, no sounds. The Silver Punk restaurant was enveloped in the dark.

'Fucking nice!' said Kenta and he prodded the Weasel in his ribs. 'We just need to light the fuse. Not a bloody soul will see us go on board.'

'And then we leave in our boat with no lights on either.'

They were really close now. You could see all the stars and the light from them was enough for them to see where they were going. When they reached the mooring place they stood close to the barge's starboard side. The Weasel held his finger in front of his lips and they stood completely still while they kept watch. But they saw nothing and heard nothing either. Even so, they waited a little while, but as they still saw no sign of life they sneaked along the gangplank and out onto the deck. They made their way cautiously towards the bow and looked in through the dark windows. They could see some tables and chairs but that was all. No sign that anybody had stayed behind. The Weasel gave Kenta a thumbs-up sign and they continued in the same direction. When they reached the bow, Kenta took off his backpack and pulled out a gas lighter.

'We'll use this,' he whispered.

The Weasel didn't answer but instead went up to the blue-and-white fenders. He gave them a squeeze and smiled when he felt the cotton waste inside. Even the small holes they had drilled in the sides were still there. Everything seemed to be under control. The oldies had set up their little present with the tarred ropes and the prepared fenders just as they had hoped. Perfect! A pity about the pensioners, perhaps, but the old bitch and her friends had simply asked for it! He was just about to take the lighter when he caught sight of a cupboard and an old-fashioned jerry can next to a large wooden box. What the hell? He picked up the jerry can and shook it.

'Almost full.' To make sure, he leaned forward, unscrewed the top and sniffed. 'Yep, it's petrol all right!'

'Just what the doctor ordered! The cotton waste could do with a bit extra!'

'Talk about lucky boys! This is going to burn a treat!'

The Weasel smiled nastily, went a few steps forward and spilled petrol onto the nearest ropes and fenders. Exhilarated, he put the jerry can down so that it splashed over. He screwed the top back on, noticed he had got petrol on his hands, and wiped them on the back of his trousers.

'Right, gimme the lighter!' he said.

'Shouldn't we go through the boat and check there's nobody still on board?' Kenta asked.

'But it's bloody obvious. Not a fucking soul here!'

But Kenta shook his head and, to be on the safe side, went up to the entrance and felt the main door. It was locked. Then he went towards the door to the stairs nearer the bow, but that too was locked. Having done that, he gave in and held up the palms of his hands as a sign that everything was quiet.

'OK, off we go!' said the Weasel and he took the lighter. 'Action!'

'Yeah, yeah, but aren't we going to check the box first?'

whispered Kenta, pointing at the large wooden box next to the generator cupboard. 'You never know. Best to check.'

'Is it so bloody important? Bound to be life jackets. But all right then!' Muttering, the Weasel fumbled with the lid but couldn't find the lock. Perhaps it didn't have a padlock, but something else. Irritated, he felt with his hand along the lid but his bandage fastened on a nail and pulled on his wound. Without thinking, he quickly drew his hand back to get loose, which resulted in the bandage unravelling completely. Swearing, he wrapped it round his hand again. They had better be quick; what if somebody saw them? The power could come back any time.

'Forget the fucking box. You don't think the old ladies have dynamite on the barge! Nope, now we'll light it!'

The Weasel took two Marlboro from his cigarette packet and Kenta reluctantly handed over the gas lighter.

'No bastards are going to compete with us. It's going to end now!' he muttered. He lit the cigarettes and put them next to the coiled rope on one of the fenders. Then he took a step back and watched with satisfaction as the rope started to glow. Now they had a few minutes to calmly leave the barge. There was a nice smell of tar and the next second a small flame flared up. Then Kenta couldn't wait any longer, but wanted to have a last try to open the wooden box. There could be something dangerous inside. He got out his sheath knife and managed to loosen the hinges. He quickly got his fingers in, and lifted the lid, but at the same moment the fire went out.

'Oh, what the hell, we'll have to splash a bit more on,' the Weasel announced. He opened the jerry can again.

'No, hang on a second, I'll just—'

'No, stuff that, action time now,' said the Weasel. He squirted and splashed petrol onto the rope and the nearest fenders.

44

The barge was empty and Anna-Greta and Blomberg had stayed on in the dark. The generator had stopped but they had remained sitting in the vinyl stall. Neither of them had got up to go out, and it was obvious that they weren't sitting there to repair the iPad. It was something else. Blomberg felt how Anna-Greta sought out his hand and leaned her head against his shoulder.

'Usch, it's so dark,' she said and took a firm grip of his fist. He pressed her hand in response and thought about how strange life was. At first he had flirted with Betty, but now he was sitting there with Anna-Greta, who was at least fifteen years older than he was, and it was nice and cosy. Indeed, if Betty had this very second called out to him from the dating corner, he would have pretended not to hear her. He was doing very nicely here with Anna-Greta. In her company he could be himself and they were extremely comfortable together; it was a really homely feeling. He glanced furtively at her in the dark. Would he dare give her a kiss? But what if she rejected him? Then he wouldn't be welcome again on the barge ... No, he didn't dare. It was probably best to take things easy, safest if she took the first step.

'A pity the generator failed. Do you think the power will return again this evening?' Anna-Greta wondered as they sat in the dark while she slowly stroked the back of his hand.

'Yes, it ought to. We'd better wait until the lights come on again. Otherwise we might trip over something.'

'Exactly. You are so wise,' cooed Anna-Greta.

Indeed, that was what it almost sounded like, he thought. She seemed like a shy schoolgirl the way she sat close against him in the dark. Blomberg hesitated a moment, but then leaned a bit closer and pressed his knee against hers.

'Ooh,' sighed Anna-Greta and she cooed even more.

All right, she seems to be on the same wavelength, Blomberg thought, exhilarated. And actually she hadn't rushed up when the generator gave up the ghost, no, she hadn't even suggested that one of them should go up and see what had happened. After all, it might be something simple like needing filling up with petrol. So there couldn't be any explanation other than . . . well, that she wanted to stay down here with him! With his self-confidence boosted, he bent forward and tested with a little kiss on her cheek. Then he felt how her knee pressed against his and the next moment she had put her hands on his head and moved his face closer to hers. He put his arms around her and was just about to kiss her when a sound was heard from down on the quay. The barge rocked slightly, and that was followed by stealthy steps up on deck. Then there was silence again. Anna-Greta stopped and squeezed his hand hard. Then they heard a rustling sound which he couldn't interpret and that was followed by a thud, as if somebody had put down something heavy.

'Usch, oh dear! What was that?' Anna-Greta wondered, pressing even closer to him.

'Sshhh, someone is up on deck.' He put his arm around her waist and held her tightly. They kept still and listened. Now it sounded like whispering voices up there.

'What if they are thieves?' Anna-Greta breathed.

'Could be tramps. I'll go up and take a look.'

'No, don't do that. It can be dangerous. Stay here with me,' whispered Anna-Greta.

He had second thoughts, remained sitting where he was and stroked her hand. After all he wasn't twenty any more. What if he rushed up on deck, and the people up there hit him with a hammer? He cursed himself for not having his pistol, but it had been taken from him when he retired. Then he had never got round to applying for a licence for a new one. The two sat there in the dark, all nerves on edge. They listened and waited. After a while, there were no more sounds of anybody moving up there and it had become silent again.

'They seem to have gone again. Perhaps they were just some guests who had forgotten something. And then they realized it was locked and closed,' said Anna-Greta in a whisper. She stroked him on his cheek. Blomberg had just been about to suggest that they went up, but now he was distracted. It was so nice to sit here with her, and hadn't it sounded rather yearning, her voice? As if she was hoping that they were completely on their own again. And, of course, she could be right, a guest might have forgotten something. Yes, why should he always think like a policeman and believe that every sound was a break-in and every person a crook? He smiled in the dark at his own stupidity.

'Oh you're so lovely,' he mumbled and leaned in closer. She shut her eyes and put her arms around him, but then suddenly sat up straight.

'What's that?' she said and she sniffed the air suspiciously. 'It smells of smoke, doesn't it?'

'No, not at all,' he answered a little too quickly and he leaned against her once more. In the dark there in the vinyl stall his alert professional attitude had given way to something else, something so much stronger. 'You are so lovely,' he said again, and kissed her.

It happened just when the Weasel squirted petrol over the fenders. A puff of flame and smoke came right at him and he stumbled backwards. *Fuck, I poured too much*, the insight flashed through his mind before the flames burnt him and set fire to the bandage. He waved and wildly flapped his hand to put it out, but in vain. Water! A rag! Fucking hell, what could he use to put the fire out? He rushed around and caught sight of the wooden box. Kenta had left the lid open. The Weasel reacted as fast as lightning. If he stuck his hand down into the box and closed the lid, then he ought to be able to smother the fire. He dived forward, stuck his hand in, but couldn't close the lid.

He just had time to scream out, 'Fucking lid . . . !' before the fuse of the first firework started to burn.

'*Peeewiiihuuit*,' came the sound from the wooden box when the fireworks got going. He saw the Galant party box and a green-painted Luxury show box stacked in there, before he was dazzled by a loud sparkling light and had to draw back. Two Bengali Flares started to rotate at the same time that a dozen or so colourful comets in the form of a sun fan shot up into the sky followed by palm bombs and sparkling stars. The barge was flooded in light and the sky lit up with white, red and green cascades of colour.

'I said we ought to check what was in . . .' Kenta started.

'Shut it! Bloody help me,' screamed the Weasel and he tried to sit on his hand to smother the flames. Too late did he remember that he had just wiped the petrol off his hands onto the back of his trousers.

'Aaaah, fucking bloody hell! Keeeenta, help!'

But his mate had panicked and had run in terror towards the gangplank and down onto the quay while the flames spread between the fenders. The Weasel waved his hands up and down but the bandage was alight, the back of his trousers was burning and the inside of his hand stung painfully – and especially so just where the woodpecker's beak had been removed.

'Fucking hell, fucking bloody hell!' he roared out and rushed across the deck while trying to rip off the bandage. Then steps could be heard from the stairs, a key was turned and the door opened with a jerk. An elderly man wearing an unbuttoned fluttering shirt and with a mobile phone in his hand came rushing out onto the deck. When he saw the fire he keyed in something on the display and the Weasel realized that he must have phoned the fire brigade. Then he headed for the gangplank, but was stopped by an elderly woman with dishevelled hair and her clothes in disarray. She was as thin as a drainpipe, and held a fire extinguisher in her hand. When she saw the fire she acted resolutely. She quickly took a few steps forward, pulled out the cotter pin and pressed the handle. The very next second he was engulfed in foam and had disappeared under a sea of bubbles. Helpless, he gasped for air only to get another dose of foam right in his mouth. He coughed, spat and wallowed there helplessly a while before he finally managed to get his hand free and could wipe his mouth and face clean.

'Saved!' noted the woman cockily with a glance at his smoking trousers and sooty bandage, and then quickly moved on to deal with the burning fenders. At the same moment, the man with the mobile was ready; he stopped her and took over the extinguisher. He was just about to put the torch away to carry on the fire-fighting work when he caught sight of the Weasel.

'Ahah, so it's you, you scum! At last! Now I'll put you in the grinder!'

The Weasel got up quickly. Shit, a fucking pig? He threw himself down the gangplank and ran after the fleeing Kenta. Feeling the cold sting through the hole that had been burnt in his trousers, and with the bandage fluttering like a pennant, he fled as fast as he could towards their little motorboat at Hornsberg. Panting, he reached it just as Kenta had got the engine going. His comrade untied the mooring ropes and he jumped in almost at the same second that his comrade opened the throttle. Without any lights, they disappeared into the night in the direction of Huvudsta.

'Hell, that was just one big fuck-up,' groaned the Weasel trying to sort out his bandage. 'This stings like hell!'

'Who would bloody well have thought that there'd be oldies snogging down in the dark there in the barge?'

'And a bleeding pig, too. I think he recognized me. The

Silver Punk restaurant! Usch! What a fucking disaster. Life was easier inside!'

'We'd better lie low a while. Otherwise we'll end up there sooner than we think.' Kenta increased their speed. A gust of wind blew over the water and the surface rippled. Soon the motorboat was just a little shadow far out on the lake.

45

Anna-Greta stood alone on the quay in wet, sticky clothes and felt betrayed. The foam had dirtied her fine dress and her hair was a mess. Admittedly, the fire brigade had managed to put the fire out, and she ought to be pleased about that, but then everything had gone wrong. When the police and the fire brigade had left the quay, Blomberg had said that he must regrettably go home immediately – without giving her any further explanation. Then he had kissed her quickly on the cheek and had just rushed off. Since the power had come on again, presumably he meant that she could now manage without him. But the two of them had had such a wonderful evening together and she couldn't understand why he was suddenly in such a hurry. Oh heavens above, it had turned into such a dismal failure and standing there abandoned in her loneliness she felt totally worthless as a woman. The damned man, one ought to keep one's distance from those men. They always made you unhappy, she thought.

Sad and angry at the same time, she pulled the cordoning tape to one side and went down below deck to fetch her coat. Then she discovered that Blomberg had forgotten his overcoat when he'd left in such a great hurry. Oh well, in that case he ought to come back. She could, of course, simply wait for him, but perhaps it was smarter to take the coat back to him herself. If she went to his home now, he might let her in. Yes, why not, and then they could continue as if nothing had happened. He had mentioned where he lived; wasn't it somewhere near Kungsholmen?

Cheered up by the thought, she put on her coat and took his coat under her arm. She could phone him first, of course. That same moment she felt his wallet in the coat pocket and couldn't resist the temptation. There must be an address there. She eagerly opened his old black leather wallet and started to search. There were some banknotes, a Stockholm travel card for the underground and a Visa card. But she couldn't find his address. Strange. She was just about to hang the coat up again when a little card fell out of the other pocket. She quickly bent down and picked it up. Yes, it was his picture on the plastic identity card. She put on her spectacles and read. Her eyes widened in horror, and she read it again. It couldn't be true. A police warrant card! His police warrant card! Her heart started thumping, and she had to look several times before she could take it in. So that scoundrel had been spying on them! She had nourished a serpent in her bosom (even though it had been really lovely just an hour or so ago).

Feeling exhausted, she put the warrant card back in the pocket and hung the coat on a hanger. Then came the tears, and now she did nothing to stop the flow. Sniffling, she turned off the lights, locked everything, went up on deck and then down onto the quay sobbing all the way. And she stood there outside the police cordoning tape for a long time without even buttoning her coat or putting on her shawl, and without the energy to pick up her mobile and phone for a taxi. A long time passed before she had at last pulled herself together, keyed in the number and ordered a taxi. When the taxi arrived she didn't even bother to hide the fact that she had been crying. It was getting quite light now and the morning breeze was coming in, but she didn't notice and didn't think about it either. If she had been her usual old self and not completely exhausted, she would certainly have noticed that the mooring ropes had been damaged by the fire. But all the way to Djursholm she sat in the back seat and sniffled and didn't notice that the wind was picking up.

When the police arrived later in the day to examine the crime scene, they could see the cordoning tape from far away. But the barge? No, that had gone.

46

'We must call timeout. I think the Vintage Village will have to wait,' said Martha, patting Anna-Greta on her cheek. Her friend's eyes were red from crying, she looked tired and her posture was dejected. She had slept most of the morning and had looked quite a wreck when she woke up. Without saying a word, she had eaten breakfast, refused to answer questions and not until she had drunk her coffee and finished eating had she managed to pull herself together to such a degree that she had asked the others to come into the library.

'I'm afraid I have bad news. Very bad news,' she said straight away with a thick voice. Her friends waited nervously. To be on the safe side, Martha had brought along some cloudberry liqueur and a bottle of whisky, should it be needed, but nobody looked at those delights. Anna-Greta searched for the right words and mumbled something about fire and treachery before she finally came out with what was tormenting her.

'We have been fooled, totally fooled!' she sighed ominously and then started to tell them everything. For obvious reasons she bypassed what she and Blomberg had been doing there in the dark and went directly to the power cut and the generator that had stopped. She went into some detail about the collapsed dating system too, before she turned silent and sort of took some deep breaths.

'Yes, Anna-Greta we know all that. Get to the point,' exclaimed Rake. Then she took yet another deep breath before she started a matter-of-fact description of the fire and how the fire brigade had managed to put the fire out and that nothing more than the fenders, a bit of the gunwale and some loose items up on deck had been damaged by the flames. But then it got harder.

'Come on now, out with it!' Rake snorted. 'I can see that there's something that's difficult for you to spell out.'

Then Anna-Greta started snivelling again, loudly and out of control so that her whole body shook.

'But goodness me, whatever is the matter, my dear?' wondered Martha. She picked up the whisky bottle. But Anna-Greta simply pushed it away and folded her hanky. Then she put her hands on her lap, twined her fingers this way and that way before she exclaimed:

'Blomberg is a scoundrel!'

'Not that guy who is so nice, surely?' Christina broke in. Anna-Greta sniffled a bit more and then dried her eyes.

'Yes, that's him! And we listened to records and then he helped me with the iPad. But—'

'But what?' wondered Brains impatiently.

'He's a policeman!'

'A policeman?!' A buzz of dismay went through the room.

'A constable! That's impossible!' exclaimed Christina, dropping both her nail file and her powder compact on the floor.

'Do you think he knows anything?' Brains wondered.

'Perhaps he visited the restaurant for private reasons. I mean the speed dating and all that.'

'I've no idea. He said that he was a pensioner and some sort of consultant, but it seems he was lying. Because when he caught sight of the Weasel he immediately reacted: "So it's you, you scum!" he shouted and then set off after him. Then I found the police warrant card in his overcoat.'

'But Anna-Greta, in that case it isn't us he's chasing,' Martha reassured her.

'But the Weasel was evidently a criminal and Blomberg knew that. Then he must know everything about the Nordea robbery and the other stuff we have been involved in,' Christina said.

Now there was silence while they all reflected upon what Anna-Greta had told them.

'You know what, there is only one thing to do. I suggest we take some time out and flee the field a while,' said Martha.

'If politicians take time out when they've done something stupid, then can't we do the same? Even if we haven't done anything as crazy as they usually do,' Christina put in.

'Oh yes, and we've done a few dodges ourselves,' said Rake.

Martha looked from one to the other. The rest that she had enjoyed over the last few days had meant that she felt better and could think clearly.

'Now listen. I vote that we hand over the responsibility for the restaurant to Anders and Emma for a while. Christina, your children will quite simply have to run everything until further notice and then we can come back when things have calmed down. And meanwhile, my dear friends, I have a plan.'

'Oh that's unusual,' said Rake.

'I am not a banker, of course, but this much I do understand: our bank robbery money and the profit from the restaurant are a drop in the ocean. Soon we won't have anything left to give away in our goody bags. We need large sums of money to be able to continue with our bonus payments to those with very low wages.'

'And we must never forget culture,' Anna-Greta added automatically in a voice that had become a little brighter. 'But listen. We have our Visa card and there is more money we can take from the Cayman Islands.'

'That isn't enough. We must get at really large amounts!'

'Oh sure, *the big money*. Easy as pie,' said Rake.

'Don't say we are going to be criminals again,' sighed Brains.

'That depends on how you look at it,' said Martha, and she took a wafer biscuit and poured out some more coffee. 'Now, we have handed out several million. Then we've got the drainpipe money and some of the Las Vegas diamonds in the aquarium, but then, well . . .'

'What! Have you got diamonds among the frogspawn?' Christina wondered, amazed. 'I had no idea.'

Martha looked down and her cheeks turned completely red. Because she had actually completely forgotten about the diamonds herself, and had only now remembered after she had been able to have a good rest. They had an aquarium down in the cellar, and inspired by earlier experiences she had realized that an aquarium was just perfect as a secret bank vault. So then she had quite simply tipped their Las Vegas diamonds into the tank and had intended discussing it with the others. But that same day, the friends had bought expensive exotic fish and aquarium plants and there had been such a fuss about it all that Martha had decided to wait until later to tell them what she had done. And, well, she had forgotten all about it. They had all had so much to do in connection with the restaurant that they had even forgotten to feed the fish. By mistake, Rake had also bought a piranha, which had quickly eaten up the other fish and when that, in turn, didn't get enough food, it had also given up the ghost. And the aquarium, with the water getting all the cloudier, had been left standing in the cellar.

'The diamonds from the robbery in Las Vegas, yes.' She cleared her throat. 'I found them in a box and thought that they ought to be kept somewhere safer. And an aquarium is really an excellent hiding place.'

'Next time you'll probably hide the diamonds in cat litter and then empty it all into the dustbin,' groaned Rake.

'If only we had a cat,' Anna-Greta cut in. 'It's about time we got one. Blomberg and me, we like cats and . . .' After mentioning his name she soon ran out of words, lowered her head and pulled out her hanky again. Martha noticed, gave her a quick pat on the cheek and returned to her idea.

'Well, anyway, what I've thought is this: when Anders and Emma have taken over the running of the restaurant, we can continue giving away money to health-care staff as long as we still have some left. Our goody bags have worked well too, so they can carry on with that,' said Martha eagerly. 'But as for us – we are aiming a little higher. Nothing less than five hundred million.'

'Five hundred million!' they all exclaimed in horror, but at the same time looked remarkably high-spirited.

'But Martha dear, what do you actually have in mind?' wondered Brains, upset.

'Um, just a little robbery for the sake of a good cause,' said Martha and popped another wafer biscuit into her mouth.

Then Anna-Greta joined in and described what she and Martha had thought about when they had seen Bielke's expensive motor yachts on the Internet. Floating fortunes that were registered in the Cayman Islands and which their neighbour didn't pay any tax for.

'And so you do realize,' Anna-Greta concluded, 'that it would be extremely difficult for him to report any of them as stolen.'

Anders stood with his hands by his sides and stared at the barge which lay and rocked slightly among some old alder trees in Huvudsta. The stern scraped against the jetty, while the bow had got entangled in some branches. On the deck lay the damaged, burnt sign with the words 'SILVER PUNK RESTAURANT' – the barge had broken adrift and ended up on the other side of the lake. It hadn't been difficult to find.

'Here we see the remains of Christina's Vintage Village. This is how her vision ended up. What fantasies!' he said.

Emma didn't answer, stubbed out her cigarette and went out onto the jetty. The gunwale was damaged, some burnt rope and fenders too, and a cupboard and box had burnt up in the bow. Otherwise everything was intact.

'What fantasies? Mother knows what she is talking about. Why not moor the barge here in Huvudsta instead and then open up again like she and the oldies want? Speed dating and the whole rub.'

'You make it sound so simple!'

'Right. And when the guests have done their dating on the boat they can go for a walk in the greenery here.' Emma threw out her hand towards the slope, the trees and the extensive lawns next to them. 'And up there, you know,' she said, pointing at the old manor house, 'that is Huvudsta Gård, which is where they conspired against King Gustav III at the end of the eighteenth century.'

'And what has that got to do with it?'

'Well, just think. Once upon a time the king's murderers gathered together up there and planned the murder. Don't you get it? We can expand the speed dating with historic walks on Sundays. It'll be a success. I promise.'

A grunt could be heard from her brother, as so often when he was thinking, and Emma lay an encouraging hand on his shoulder. She felt sorry for him. He was a man in his prime, but unemployed. That could put a damper on anyone's interest.

'Hell, I'm so tired of Mother and everything she thinks up. Now she and the others want us to take over again when things go wrong. But that restaurant project is dangerous. Just look, the mafia tried to torch the boat!' He pointed at the charred gunwale and fenders.

'But Mother has explained. That happened in Hornsberg. The League of Pensioners were inside their patch there. But here, here we can do what we want.'

'You think so, do you? We always have to step in and clean up after them.'

'But our children can go swimming here, and there are horses over in those stables. It couldn't be better. If you're going to go all grumpy, then I'll get another partner,' said Emma and her green eyes narrowed. Her brother saw the warning signal.

'Oh what the hell, I'm over forty years old and it is still Mum who decides. Don't you understand?'

'We can tidy up the barge, get rid of the smoke smell and throw out that dreadful wild boar. Anders, pull your socks up!'

'Oh, all right, if we take away the beaver and that wolf too, then—'

'Of course we can. I knew it. I can rely on you!'

Emma took a big stride towards him and gave her brother a hug. They had worked together before. It would work out OK this time too.

'Have you thought about something? Martha is bloody good at organizing. While we slave away with her restaurant she and the gang will travel down to Saint-Tropez. How can she manage to arrange it all like that? Next time it ought to be the opposite.'

'Anders, she isn't going there to lie in the sun. I bet you anything that she has something fishy planned.'

Brother and sister looked out across the glittering water and thought about it for a while. Then Emma said: 'Just as long as Mother doesn't get into trouble. As if it wasn't enough that we must worry about her because she is old. On top of that we have to worry about her ending up in prison!'

47

Indeed, perhaps it all went rather quickly, but as soon as they had the chance to lay their hands on the big money, the League of Pensioners had gone off to Saint-Tropez. If you are going to succeed, you must make an effort, Martha had said. And the thought that Bielke would not be able to report his boat as stolen had triggered the League of Pensioners to make their decision. It isn't every day you can steal about five hundred million kronor without the victim going to the police. So why not make an attempt?

It was already lovely summer weather in Saint-Tropez. Men in open shirts and shorts and women in thin, flowery dresses relaxed at the cafes with a glass of wine or an espresso in their hands, while suntanned and freckly tourists strolled along the quay and looked at the shining luxury yachts. The wind felt nice and warm against one's skin and there was a smell of fish and sea. The League of Pensioners, who had still not acclimatized themselves, walked slowly and sweated under the strong Mediterranean sun.

'But Rake, you don't need to pull your hat down over your head and sneak around just because we are reconnoitring,' said Martha as she eyed him. 'We should stroll along calmly and quietly so that nobody suspects anything.'

The League of Pensioners had been in Saint-Tropez just over a week and every day they had gone down to the harbour to hunt for Bielke's motor yacht, the luxury boat they intended stealing. Of course it was awful to be embarking on a new crime, but on the other hand it felt somehow safe and familiar with a scoundrel they already knew. And that man was a real top dog in the criminal world since he didn't pay tax in Sweden. Martha and her friends had grumbled about his unsuitable style of living and they had discussed the issue almost every day – since what he did was, nevertheless, legal. Law and morality are not the same thing, Martha tried to claim, but Brains, from a working-class background in a Stockholm suburb, thought that they weren't much better themselves. He didn't feel comfortable with their having a company in a tax haven and he didn't grasp much of what it was all about. On the other hand, he enjoyed the heat and thought that a change of environment would certainly be good for them both. As so often, when you were off travelling, you came closer to one another, and he and Martha really needed that now. Things had not gone so well between them as of late, and here perhaps they would be able find each other again.

The sun shone and a pleasant afternoon breeze blew in from the sea. A warm glittering light was reflected in the waves and sailing boats and large motor yachts lay at anchor in the bay. Far away you could just make out a green stretch of coast and the only thing that disturbed the beautiful scene was a rusty container ship from Panama. The local press had written about that Panama wreck and Martha and her gang had thought it looked really ugly. The ship was in such bad condition that it might any day be towed out to sea and sunk since it was a danger to shipping. The League of Pensioners thought it would be good to be rid of the eyesore.

'So you don't like my having my hat pulled down over my forehead?' muttered Rake. He pushed it to the back of his head, combed his hair and mumbled something about fussy women. Why couldn't he have a hat instead of a sunshade, if he wanted! It went very well with his beige summer suit and the matching bandanna. Although, he had to admit, Martha was very smartly dressed today, but just because of that she didn't have to criticize him. He glanced at her and gave a start. Yes, in fact, she had dressed so elegantly that you could hardly recognize her. She had a wide-rimmed hat with a veil, an expensive flowery dress from Dior – or whoever – a chic fashionable pink handbag and white high-heeled shoes with a pattern of small red flowers engraved on the heels. She looked like a countess who was rolling in money. The rest of the gang, too, had fitted themselves out with expensive clothes – Martha had said that as a first step in the planned coup they would charter Bielke's luxury yacht. And to do that they must look like real millionaires, not like upstarts who were trying to imitate the rich. But it would cost ten thousand euros a week, that was what Bielke charged.

'Usch, so expensive,' groaned Anna-Greta.

'What does it matter?' Martha remarked. 'We don't intend to pay anyway.'

'Scandalous. One can't do that,' protested Christina.

'Oh yes we can. Bielke is a tax dodger so it serves him

right. But it will be tough. First, we must charter the yacht, then steal it, and, after that, sell everything. Until then we won't have any money to give away.'

'Oh, I see, yes, well, in that case. Then it's all right,' said Christina somewhat calmer. 'Out in the blue, that's what we'll do, a real to-do!' She tried to make poetry but even she didn't think it was that brilliant.

The old friends walked out along a long jetty where the large luxury yachts were moored side by side with their sterns against the jetty. Mediterranean mooring. Most of them were white, a few were in a variety of shades of dark blue, and they all had a name painted on the stern. Almost all the yachts had one or two decks but, except for a man who was busy washing and polishing one of the boats, they seemed strangely abandoned.

'We've walked around here for ages without seeing the slightest sign of Bielke and his boat. Where is the man?' wondered Brains. He looked at Martha with displeasure.

His fiancée had admittedly accepted the blame for the problems in their relationship, and she had asked him to forgive her and had promised – cross my heart and hope to die – that they would devote themselves to each other here in France. Take things a little easy. So when they had been sitting on the edge of the bed and had had a heart-to-heart talk, he, in turn, had said he was sorry that his head had been turned by Betty and he thought that he and Martha should try to find their way back to each other again. Perhaps even get married, if that felt right. They had hugged each other a long time and he had felt secure and harmonious again. But the plane had hardly landed before Martha became her old self. Almost immediately she set them all to work. Above all they had walked around in the harbour looking for luxury yachts, and they had also tried to find out how they were hired out and how they were manned. He grunted and thought that Martha had forgotten all about him and that her words were empty. Then he felt her hand in his.

'As soon as we've laid our hands on Bielke's boat we can relax and really devote ourselves to looking after each other,' she whispered.

'Um, you think so?' he mumbled. 'But what if he has sailed to Australia?'

'Pah, no way; it isn't a sailing boat anyway,' Martha reassured him.

'Bielke runs a charter business, so the boat will be out at sea. It will come back any day, I promise,' said Anna-Greta.

'Yes, do you hear that, Brains?' Martha squeezed his hand. 'And remember that we are planning for our Vintage Village and in order to give more help to health-care staff in Sweden.'

'Oh yes, the Pleasure Village. Yes, what would Sweden do without you?' Rake grumbled.

Martha pretended not to hear. Instead she steered her wheeled walker past a carelessly coiled mooring rope and a black cat that lay stretched out in the sun. (She didn't really need the wheeled walker, but since she was wearing newly purchased high-heeled shoes, she had taken it along to be on the safe side.)

'Oh, it's so beautiful here,' exclaimed Anna-Greta as she looked out across the harbour. 'And the sea is so invitingly blue that soon I'll jump in with my clothes on.'

'Wow, some action!' exclaimed Rake.

'Don't forget that we are here to reconnoitre,' Martha exhorted. 'Work first, play later!'

'Stop bossing us. We can think for ourselves,' muttered Brains. 'We know we're going to steal Bielke's boat. You are an expert at "first this, first that", but when are you and me going to have time to be together?'

'Quiet, damn it!' said Rake and he held up his index finger. 'Somebody might hear us. There are Swedes down here. And don't despair,' he added, lowering his voice. 'Martha loves you, I promise.'

'If she hadn't needed help from somebody to hotwire boat engines, then I wouldn't even have been asked to follow along,' Brains moaned. 'Go off to the Mediterranean to steal motor yachts. Not a tiny bank robbery any more, no, now she's going to fix hundreds of millions! She has got greedier and greedier just like all the other capitalist idiots.'

Rake put his hand on Brains's shoulder. 'But Brains, you ought to be proud. Who else thinks about how the poor people back home can have a decent life and be able to live on their pensions? Not the politicians, at any rate.'

'No, but—'

'And not the capitalists either. They just hand out bonuses to themselves. Martha, however, has introduced Sweden's first low-wage bonus. She ought to be given a medal!'

'Without capitalists, there would be no jobs. Talk about that they are necessary!' muttered Brains, stuck his hands in his trouser pockets and turned completely silent. But he had to admit to himself that Rake was right about Martha thinking of those that others forgot. She only wanted to support those who were in a difficult situation. He squirmed a little.

'Only I wish she could think a little about us too.'

'You, you mean!'

'Er, yes,' Brains had to concede. 'What I mean is that I would like to sit at a cafe by the water and look out across the sea, enjoying a chocolate cake with a cup of cappuccino. Like everybody else.'

Brains and Rake were lagging behind a bit, and Martha stopped to wait for them to catch up.

'Brains,' Martha started to speak and turned a happy face towards him. 'Wouldn't it be nice to have some cappuccino?' He felt a warm hand in his. 'I've booked a table at Club Fifty-five where they have your favourite cake with chocolate and whipped cream. What about that? We can't just eat healthy biscuits every day.'

'Umph,' answered Brains, blushing. Martha had worked out what he longed for so she had booked a table at the fanciest place in all of Saint-Tropez. Good God, she knew him so well. 'Club Fifty-five at the Plage de Pampelonne?' he stuttered.

'Yes, right, I registered us as members. We are meant to be stinking rich millionaires, aren't we? And how otherwise will we find people who are rich enough to buy a stolen motor yacht?'

Then she smiled, looking pleased and happy, and the next moment he felt a wave of warmth spread through his body. What plans she made! And she could always guess what he was thinking. Of course he got irritated sometimes, but there was no denying what an exciting, unpredictable woman she was! He would have liked to have gone there with her, just the two of them, to sit cosily under a parasol, but all the others had heard her suggestion.

344

'What if we get to see a fantastic old jazz legend or Sylvester Stallone?' Anna-Greta contributed and rolled her eyes. 'Club Fifty-five is where all the celebrities hang out.'

'Or why not Elton John?' said Christina. 'I've heard that he goes there.'

'You know what, I can be Elton John. I have the experience,' Rake cut in.

Christina giggled. 'No, you are fine as you are. Now let's go for a coffee!'

The gang of pensioners moved off towards the beach walk and hailed a taxi. Tired but satisfied, they sank down into the seats and asked to be driven to the Plage de Pampelonne. Their expectations were great, but when they arrived they discovered to their surprise that Club 55 wasn't so special; it looked like one of many luxury cafes by the Mediterranean. A waiter dressed in white showed them to their table and laid out some menus. They had only just ordered their coffee and cakes and were already in high spirits and eagerly looking around for famous film stars. Martha discreetly pulled out her theatre binoculars, but however hard she tried, she couldn't see any celebrities. No, the paparazzi on the beach stalked young, unknown girls.

'Have you seen that? Scantily clad women with breasts that stick right out and Donald Duck lips,' Christina pointed out. It is true that she had had a facelift herself, but there were limits.

'My, my, and look at those tattooed men with their unkempt beards. No, I prefer the cleanly shaven menfolk from former days!' exclaimed Anna-Greta.

'No celebrities – evidently this isn't our day,' said Martha, putting her binoculars away.

'Um, don't say that,' said Rake who only looked around at breast height.

Brains wasn't interested in celebrities but he'd become interested in some boats out at anchor. Fascinated, he watched the large luxury yachts bobbing out there in the waves. Motor-boats, sailing boats and yachts as big as ocean-going ferries. In comparison with them, the boats in Djursholm were like small dinghies.

'Have you seen that motor yacht over there? It must be worth several hundred million at least,' he said, indicating a large dark-blue luxury boat with a helicopter platform.

'Yes, it certainly will be, and just have a look at that!' said Martha pointing at a man in a black wetsuit who came flying by, ten metres above the water surface. He looked like he had come straight out of a James Bond film. When he got closer to the beach, he swept round in wide circles right in front of a horde of girls.

'What a show-off,' snorted Anna-Greta, putting her hands over her ears. 'Dead dangerous!'

'A jet ski like that can go at forty kilometres an hour, at least. People are crazy. Rushing around on jets of water when there are sails,' Rake announced.

'It looks like he's flying on jets of water,' said Christina. 'The billionaires are playing.'

'Yes, he controls the jets with a throttle in each hand,' Rake noted.

'What if cars could use water jets instead of petrol. That would be more friendly to the environment,' Brains reflected.

'You are such a good man. You always think about how you could improve society,' said Martha, looking at him with appreciation.

'But you do too, Martha, with your bonuses to health care and all that,' said Brains.

Then she leaned forward and gave him a hug followed by a warm, wet kiss on his mouth.

'What, goodness . . .' muttered Brains and once again he felt that warmth inside him. He mustn't forget it. And sooner or later that wedding would take place. This encouraged him and he stroked Martha on her cheek. She smiled and opened her flowery handbag. He didn't know what he expected, but she didn't take out a flower, or a notepad, just another pair of theatre binoculars.

'Now you can see the jet ski a little better,' she said. 'How it is constructed and all that. And incidentally, when you are looking, you can keep an eye out for Bielke's boat too.'

'Crime instead of a wedding!' muttered Brains and suddenly he looked very tired.

After they had drunk their afternoon coffee, they ordered a taxi and returned to the harbour where they had a pier and some jetties left to search. Bielke's yacht must be somewhere, and perhaps it had come in today – unless, of course, forbid the thought, he had rented it out for a whole month. While they strolled along the quay they were unusually quiet. The sweet cakes had made them tired and at the same time they were thinking about how serious things were. The new crime was so much bigger and more difficult than the coups they had carried off so far, and it demanded that they must all be on top form. But if they were successful, they would be able to hand out even more bonus payments to those with low wages. And just think how many pensioners there were who lived below the poverty line and had to save on food bills to survive – while the water scooters alone on a luxury yacht like that were worth millions.

Martha fumbled around in her handbag and pulled out a packet of Jungle Pastilles. They were always calming when she was angry. And now she must really keep her nerves under control to manage the coup they were about to undertake. It was more complicated than their previous ones, because they would have to sell the booty too, otherwise they wouldn't get any money. But you couldn't just put an advert on eBay. How could they find a buyer? It was true that they had chosen the most luxurious hotel in all of Saint-Tropez so that they could look for customers, but even so. They didn't exactly have a network of potential buyers. Luckily, the rooms and the beds were comfortable. In contrast to modern offices and other rotten workplaces, they did at least have a nice setting in which to plan their crime. Martha was slightly ashamed, but she had begun to be really fond of five-star luxury hotels.

Kube Hotel on Pearl Beach was just such a hotel with two pools, designer suites, sauna, spa, satellite TV and your own jacuzzi. Here too was a fitness area with exercise bikes, dumbbells, running treadmills and a pool, so that they could keep in good trim. Meanwhile, they continued their reconnoitring because the financiers hung out here too – those indoor-men with shares, fat wallets and muscles. The most important consideration of all, when they had been choosing a hotel, had been the conferences. Martha had sussed that the International Yacht Boating Club were to hold their AGM here and the hotel would be crawling with billionaires. So she had really thought of everything – but the most important of all eluded them. They hadn't seen a trace of Bielke's boat and without that they wouldn't have anything to sell.

48

Martha was in the hotel's fitness centre when it happened. As with so many other important meetings in life, it occurred suddenly and was totally unexpected. Martha had just finished with the dumbbells and looked as if she was about to expire on the hotel's exercise bicycle when she caught sight of him. A nice-looking man, aged about forty-five, wandered into the fitness centre with a towel nonchalantly thrown over his shoulders. He had straight, blond hair, long eyelashes, sky-blue eyes and a very masculine way of moving. When he saw her, he gave her a friendly nod, pulled out a mat and started with push-ups. After doing fifty or so, he took a little breather and got onto one of the exercise bicycles over by the window. He was wearing red Nike Performance shoes and when he pedalled, his thigh muscles tensed up like enormous steel cables. Martha stared. His powerful biceps and well-trained torso without an ounce of fat reminded her of a sculpture by Michelangelo, and the sight of him in all his glory caused her to stop cycling. Confused, she gasped for air, fumbled to find the handlebars and almost fell off.

'Are you OK, my dear?' the man asked in accented English, hurrying across to her. Shaken, she looked up and found herself staring at the shining washboard stomach. Not until he laid his broad, strong hand on her shoulder did she succeed in mumbling something, and, in her confusion, she patted his biceps. Then she realized what she had done and was so mortally embarrassed that she couldn't manage a single word.

'Shall I call a doctor?' asked the man, with a worried look, speaking with what sounded like a Russian accent.

But Martha shook her head, because now she had caught sight of the thick gold bracelet, the gold chain with a cross around his neck, and his gold watch with a compass and diamond inlays. Her brain went on turbo charge. The man had a fortune on him and had a Russian accent, perhaps he was a Russian oligarch? You hardly got richer than that – well, perhaps some Malaysian businessmen and, of course, the eighty or so people in the world who, together, were richer than half of the world's population put together. Whatever, this man was a possible prey for the League of Pensioners. Many of the Russian oligarchs were in their forties and had made their fortunes during the fall of the Soviet Union in the 1990s. They were men who liked to display their riches, and perhaps he even owned one of the Ferraris outside the hotel. If she had been forty years younger, she would have behaved like the 1970s dames in a James Bond film, she would have swayed her hips, fluttered her eyelashes and taken him up to her room. But she didn't have much choice. She pretended to faint, fell forwards across the handlebars and waited for him to be chivalrous and save her. And she had not been wrong. The next second she felt his arms around her body and when he lifted her up off the bicycle and stood with his arm around her shoulders and again asked if she was all right, she nodded in relief. Now she had established contact. And she had also acquired a bit of practical information: he stank of vodka. A rich oligarch who boozed. It couldn't be better.

'I'm Martha,' she said and held out her hand.

'Oleg, Oleg Pankin,' said Oleg and he squeezed her hand so that it was almost crushed. Martha beamed. She had insisted that they should live among rich millionaires and now this had led to something. Pleased with the result, she went up to tell the others.

'What are you dreaming about, sweetheart?' Brains wondered a few days later when he and Martha were recuperating at a little cafe in the harbour together with the others. 'You've been quiet for so long that I'm starting to become really worried.'

The palm trees bent in the wind and the afternoon breeze caused the parasols to flutter. All of them had each had a coffee and now they sat gazing out across the water. Martha looked up and felt as if she had been caught. Her thoughts couldn't leave the Russian. She had told the others about her joy at meeting a Russian oligarch in the hotel gym, but if she had been really honest with herself, that wasn't *all* she was thinking about. Business, that is. Even elderly women like the sight of a handsome man, she had realized, and she had never spent so much time in a gym as she had done over the last few days. As nonchalantly as she could manage, she put down her coffee cup and looked out across the water, careful not to look anybody in the eye.

'Oh, what am I dreaming about? Five hundred million

kronor, of course –' and this was not a direct lie – 'and I'm thinking about Oleg as well, that muscular Russian, you know,' she said.

'Not as a he-man, surely?' Brains wondered suspiciously. 'I've heard you mumbling about biceps and washboards at night.'

Martha shook her head and tried to hide the fact that she had started to blush. She looked even more intently out across the water.

'Usch, this is about how we can lay our hands on his fortune, you understand. Five hundred million, you know; not everybody has that sort of money,' she answered, rather stretching the truth. 'But, of course, a man who takes care of his body is always nice, no, I mean interesting. That is, it makes you wonder how much he trains and what his diet is.'

'Thought as much,' muttered Brains and he looked down at the rotundity that reflected his comfortable lifestyle. 'But my belly is a much better pillow, whatever you say!'

'I know, I know, and don't think that I fall for appearances,' Martha assured him, but now she had bright red patches on her cheeks. She leaned back in her chair. What heavenly blue eyes the Russian had, and how nice it had felt when he'd helped her up onto the exercise bicycle. It was pleasurable, yes, but it was all about business, except – well, perhaps she did simulate dizziness rather too often, but she wanted him to think that she had problems with her balance. Because she had her plan.

★

'Is it really true that you don't fall for appearances?' she heard Brains ask. But thankfully she didn't have time to answer before Rake cut in.

'Have you seen that?' he said pointing. A large boat with a wooden deck was making its way to the pier. The yacht didn't have one helicopter platform but two and an enormous slide down from the upper deck all the way to the sea. On board you could see men in white who were preparing to berth the boat, and some women in their twenties who were waving to friends on land. That was a much finer boat than Bielke's; indeed, it was one of the finest she had seen since they had arrived in Saint-Tropez. They all stood up at the same time and Anna-Greta waved to the waiter.

'Time to pay,' she said, pulling out her spectacles and looking at the receipt. 'It's an expensive view here too,' she grumbled and put the exact amount on the plate. He had been so slow and impolite that he wasn't getting a tip.

'Come on, let's go over there,' said Rake.

'Absolutely,' Martha said and got the others to agree. They had only just reached the pier when they heard a car behind them.

'A Rolls-Royce,' Brains noted and he smiled with his whole face, just as if it had been a real Harley Davidson. A large black limousine was driving in the direction of the boat. It slowed down and stopped close to the gangplank. A uniformed chauffeur hurried to open the door for a man in his fifties. He had a chin-strap beard, a white suit, light-blue shirt with a tie and a yachtsman's cap. But that wasn't what caught Martha's interest, it was something else. The man who had got out of the car walked with long, bouncy steps and with his arms swinging by his sides. And she only knew one person who walked like that.

49

Martha and her friends quickly withdrew against the wall a few metres away where a lorry was parked. Behind it they were well hidden, but they could still lean out and see what was happening on the yacht. Yep, it WAS him. Their neighbour, business tycoon Carl Bielke. The crew stood there lined up on the main deck against the rail, and on the deck above a little girl of around five years old was waving.

'Daddy, Daddy,' she called out in Swedish and jumped up and down in excitement like children tend to do. But Carl Bielke pretended not to see her. Instead he stopped and turned to the crew. Smiling, he walked around the deck and talked to them and snapped at the girl when she called out again. Not until he had done a complete round of the deck and had been inside the bridge did he take the stairs up to the uppermost deck where the girl was waiting. Martha watched the scene, all eyes.

'Good God!' she mumbled and thought about the son she had lost when he had been about the same age, a child she had grieved over ever since. Here her rich neighbour had a very-much-alive daughter but he didn't care about her. A man for whom belongings and prestige seemed to be more important than his family. She shook her head and immediately felt very sad. Christina must have seen her because the next moment her friend was next to her, putting her arm over her shoulder.

'He who doesn't realize how rich he is, is poor, and can never be really happy,' she said with a glance at the boat. 'We might be doing him a good turn when we steal his yacht.'

'Yes, a man who has several luxury cruisers can probably never be satisfied,' Martha responded.

'Unless they are tax-deductible of course,' Anna-Greta pointed out.

'Ah yes, perhaps that is why he has bought a new one, if that is indeed his,' said Martha.

'But look, it says *Aurora Four*, the same name as his home address in Djursholm – Auroravägen, that is. So it must be his. Perhaps he has sold one of the other boats because this big one must be worth much more than five hundred million. There you are, the rich are always striving for something bigger and more expensive,' Christina commented.

'Exactly,' Martha agreed.

'But we aren't one bit better. Every crime we plan has to bring in more money than the previous one,' said Brains.

'Er – um . . .' said Martha. 'But you know why. Even more money for those in poverty; you haven't forgotten that surely?'

'Sssh, somebody might hear us,' Rake warned them, but, like the others, he couldn't tear his eyes away from the enormous luxury boat. They saw how Bielke gesticulated up there on deck, disappeared and then came out again with a whisky glass in his hand. Then he was joined by three young women half his age. They sat down on the deckchairs beside a pool with glasses in their hands.

Anna-Greta stared. 'This boat is certainly extremely expensive. Let me see . . .' She tried to remember all the boats she had googled and did some rapid calculations in her head. 'Two helicopter platforms, three decks, a water slide down to the sea, two swimming pools and water scooters, yes, that would be worth six to seven hundred million at the very least.'

'Excellent! Then we can raise the bonuses to all the home-care staff,' said Martha.

'But a palace like that is hard to steal. We will need help,' Rake commented.

'And such an expensive boat must be much harder to sell,' Christina added.

'But it will bring in more money!' said Anna-Greta, her eyes glistening.

Not until Bielke had vanished with the women to his cabin did the friends dare be on their way. Despite itching wigs and careful disguise they had realized that they could be recognized. Better to be on the safe side. But before they left, Martha got out her mobile and photographed the yacht. She zoomed in on every detail of the boat and even went out on one of the other jetties to take pictures of the bow and the starboard side. She worked away and did everything to portray the luxury yacht in as attractive a light as possible. And in the end she even asked Brains to take some pictures of her and the boat. She quietly sneaked up to the jetty railing and stood there with a smile like someone showing off their property.

That evening, the League of Pensioners sat up until late and concocted plans. And before they went to bed, Rake had phoned his son Nils, the first mate. Since he was a seaman who had spent many years at sea and had experience of different types of vessels, he would fit perfectly. It was just such a skilled seaman they needed.

'You see,' Rake had said to the others, looking important, 'a theft like this can only be carried out by real seamen. So you need both Nils and me.'

The next day, Martha cautiously opened the door to the conference room where the International Yacht Boating Club was holding its meeting. She pretended that she had walked into the wrong room, but she had time to see that many of the middle-aged men that she had earlier seen by the pool were there, including Oleg, who was looking at a pile of brochures and documents. She silently backed out of the room, closed the door and looked for the sign next to it that showed how long the conference was booked for. Oleg and his colleagues would be busy all morning. So she had time to prepare herself.

A few hours later, Martha went down to the gym as usual and started her afternoon session, and this time she had her large flowery handbag with her. She carefully put it down next to the bike before mounting it and starting to pedal away. Just as she was beginning to get a little sweaty, Oleg came in with his naked torso and his white towel over his shoulder. It was time to put her plan into action. The two smiled at each other and the Russian started his customary push-ups. When he had finished and was just getting onto an exercise bike, Martha made a few slight groaning sounds. Then she slowly started to climb down from the bike. When she didn't get any help straight away she groaned a bit more so that Oleg looked up. Then she pretended to fall down roughly like Anna-Greta used to do when she slipped with her walking stick. Now Oleg was there in a flash and he picked her up and she waited – a rather surprisingly long time – in his arms until her body slowly came to life again.

'Oh dear me, I think I must have lost my balance,' she explained.

He helped her onto her feet and she felt his strong arms around her and closed her eyes with a sigh.

'Is everything all right?'

'Yes – yes, I'm fine,' she mumbled and she pretended to be a bit groggy, as though she hardly knew where she was. He took her hand and put it on the handlebar of the exercise bike.

'Hold on to this!'

'Oh, your hands are so . . .' she mumbled but managed to restrain herself at the last moment. Even if it had been quite a while since forty-five-year-old men had held her in their arms, she must retain her authority and sharpness. 'Dearie me, I've got so old,' she complained apologetically, then she wobbled a little, clutched at the handlebars and tried to look very unhappy. 'My balance, you know, not so easy when you get old!' she pointed out. 'But I do my exercises. Because I don't want to sell my new motor yacht. Absolutely not.'

'Yacht?'

'Yes, my super yacht. Looks like Spielberg's famous one, you know, but with two helicopter platforms.' She saw how his eyes started to glisten.

'But a rough sea and poor balance can be a dangerous combination,' Oleg pointed out.

'But the boat is my precious jewel, so beautiful and very new. And if I sell, I would lose too much money. No, I'll manage to keep my sea legs somehow.' Martha gripped the handlebars hard to keep her balance, tried to get back up on the bike but wobbled again. He was immediately there to support her and help her straighten up again. She shook her head, was silent for a moment and then hid her face in her hands.

'No, this is not going to work any more!' She started to sniffle. 'I have tried everything to train my muscles and balance, but I can't manage it. I will have to sell the yacht. But I don't want to. Whatever should I do?'

'Let me help you. Sit down here on the bench and I'll fetch a glass of water.'

Oleg disappeared and returned with a bottle of Vichy water and a glass. He poured the water into the glass for Martha.

'You know what, it would probably be better to sell before you hurt yourself,' he said, and made sure she drank properly. 'Out at sea anything can happen. A new motor yacht, you said?'

'Yes, one of the biggest and finest in the Mediterranean. My husband had it built two years ago but he died shortly after it was launched. That was last year and now—'

'A newly built motor yacht, luxury class?'

'Yes, a fantastic ship, several storeys high and with two pools and helicopter platforms. Here, have a look!' She bent down with surprising agility – considering that she had just lain helpless in his arms – and picked up her mobile from her bag. She scrolled through some pictures. 'It is a dream, a sailor's dream!' She sighed and let Oleg get a glimpse of Bielke's motor yacht. He leaned forward to get a better look.

'Can I see?' he asked, and when she handed him the phone he scrolled through the photos. He became all the more keen. 'A real beauty, absolutely fantastic!'

'But it is probably too expensive for you. My husband paid ninety-five million dollars to have that built, and we have hardly used it. So I would want at least ninety million for it. But who has so much money? Perhaps one of your friends at the conference?' she said and pointed in the direction of the conference room.

'So you can think of selling it, after all?'

'I don't know. Perhaps.' (She didn't want to sound too eager.)

'Would you accept diamonds? I mean, a quick deal with about half in cash and the rest in diamonds?'

'All women love diamonds,' she said and pretended to wobble again.

When Oleg went back to the conference room, he bumped into his colleague Boris Sorokin who had been born in Moscow but had lived in London since he was ten years old. They usually spoke English as Boris's Russian was a bit rusty. There was a break between two presentations and time for coffee. They went into the lobby and each took a cup and some cakes and sat on a sofa. All around were tables and chairs, and hotel guests passed behind them on the way to their rooms or reception. It was hot and the air conditioning hummed away.

'Interesting seminar, pity you missed it,' Boris started up, but was immediately interrupted by Oleg.

'You remember that old lady in the gym I told you about?'

'The one who was a bit unsteady on her legs?'

'Yeah, that's her. She owns a fantastic super-yacht with two helicopter platforms. Newly built.'

'Wow! Just what we've been looking for.'

'Her husband died and now she wants to sell. It's a real beauty, has three decks and two pools and the fittings are really top notch. She gets dizzy and that's why she can't keep it any longer. She's probably a bit senile too. She wants ninety million dollars. A quick sale and we can bargain.'

His comrade ran his fingers through his hair and grinned.

'Fleece a poor old lady?'

'She's a rich old widow and she's too old to look after a yacht like that. A pile of dollars and diamonds and the boat is ours. I promise you.' Oleg laughed. 'We don't need to commission a shipyard and wait two years for it to be ready. I'll just charm her and it will all work out. It isn't often you get a chance like this.'

'I've seen her. She has such a friendly smile, seems nice, I thought. Shall we really . . .?'

'Opportunities in life come along slowly, but disappear quick as a flash. Hell, let's go for it!'

The men slurped their coffee and were so engrossed in their discussion that they didn't notice when Martha walked into the lobby. She was on her way to her room, but when she heard what they were talking about she stopped close to the back of the sofa and eavesdropped. Boris took another cake and turned to Oleg again.

'OK. Say that the boat is as fantastic as you claim. Then we'll bid sixty-five million and we can raise that to seventy, if necessary. Then we'll take the boat to Cyprus and sell it again for eighty-five to ninety million. That would give us a nice little profit.'

'Yes, but first we must have some fun with it and cruise around a bit. Vodka and girls, you know. I saw some tasty goodies on La Place that we could take with us. No ghosts like that Martha. No, senile old hags are not much good for anything. And you should see her double chin and dachshund ears.'

'Dachshund ears?'

'Yeah, sagging breasts that almost reach the floor. Oh no, women shouldn't get to be more than thirty. And after thirty-five it's time to get out the wheelbarrow.'

'But didn't you say she was nice?'

'Yeah, sure, a sweet old lady right enough. Kind and means well, but what the fuck. I'm talking about something pretty to have in bed. And she must cook decent food too. What else would you need women for?'

'Yes, what else would you need women for,' Boris agreed. 'But, yeah, arrange a meeting with her so that we can have a look at the boat.'

'OK, I'll do that. Just have to charm her a bit extra in the gym. And you make sure we can get the diamonds and cash ready, right?'

'I'm an old hand at this. Best to go for a quick sale before anybody else finds out about it.'

'Then we're agreed!' Oleg gave him a thumbs-up sign and grinned.

But he might not have done if he had seen who was standing behind the sofa listening: an old lady who was muttering to herself in Swedish. Lots and lots of swearwords.

50

It had started to get dark and the lamps in Café Tropez were lit. The boats rocked slightly at their moorings and groups of tourists could be seen strolling down in the harbour area. Gradually the restaurants had started to fill up and the cafes were already more or less full. The gang of pensioners had each ordered a caffè latte and indulged in cakes and gateaux to fortify themselves. Now they were prepared for action.

'Righto, are you ready?'

Martha tried to make her voice sound steady although she was just as nervous as the others. She was still dreadfully angry about what she had overheard outside the conference room, but she kept that rage to herself. Personal failings should not get in the way of what was of the essence. They were now going to steal Bielke's yacht and everything else she would have to deal with later. Earlier during the day she had talked with Oleg about the sale and he had seemed decidedly keen to buy. But since she was worried that somebody might be able to expose their shady deals here in Saint-Tropez they had agreed that she would show him and his Russian friends the boat in Cannes. There they would be able to strike a deal and, if they could agree, the Russians could take over the boat directly. But this required a considerable effort from the League of Pensioners. They not only had to steal the yacht but they also had to get it to Cannes. Why did she always think up such complicated crimes? Couldn't she be satisfied with a bit of simple embezzlement, as Brains used to say? At this particular moment she was prepared to admit that he was right. Martha put her arms around her flowery handbag and looked out across the water. Pah, it would probably be all right.

With two skilled seamen like Nils and Rake aboard, everything should work out. And she had insisted that Oleg and his companion should bring cash with them, otherwise she wasn't going to sell. Her husband had taught her that that was how things were done. No cheques or credit cards, absolutely not, only cash! Only then would Oleg be able to take over the boat directly.

This time Martha had been careful to make sure that she kept Brains in a good mood, and she and Anna-Greta had planned the coup together with him. Besides, they had practised climbing ladders and getting in and out of motorboats. Rake's son, Nils, who had arrived from Gothenburg, had also been there at the briefings and they had even used stopwatches. But there was, of course, a great deal that could not be foreseen. For example, nobody knew how long it would take to find the yacht's registration papers and to con the crew. They must reckon with having to improvise. And seeing as those Russians were so rich, the risk of being tricked was not so great. One luxury yacht more or less. Pah, a Russian oligarch was good for several billion!

'You make it all sound so simple,' Brains sighed.

'In this business you must be an optimist!' answered Martha – with a lump in her throat.

She looked across towards the yacht. Thank God the weather was good and a slight onshore wind made the boats in the harbour bob gently at their moorings. No gusts of wind or other unexpected factors. No, the weather wouldn't be causing them any problems. She took some deep breaths and studied *Aurora 4* which had been moored right out at the end of the pier. She had seen Bielke leave the boat by helicopter earlier that day and when she had walked along the pier and spoken to a member of the crew she'd been told that he was going to London on business.

'He'll be away over the weekend so we are going to take some leave now,' the crewman had said with a smile. 'But then it will be charters. Ten thousand euro for a week. What about that, lady, something to think about?'

'Terribly expensive,' Martha had replied.

'Market price, you can't charter a boat like this any more cheaply.'

'Well, then. In that case I want to charter it for one week. I shall just go and fetch my friends,' Martha had said, and she'd put her handbag over her shoulder and walked away humming to herself. On the esplanade she'd waved to a taxi and on the way back to the hotel she'd thought it over. Since it was Friday, Bielke would certainly be amusing himself in London on Saturday and Sunday and then have his meetings and bank transactions on Monday. It would be tight, but this was a golden opportunity that they simply couldn't miss. When the taxi had stopped outside the hotel she'd almost forgotten to pay, she'd been so eager. From the lobby she'd then gone straight to Anna-Greta's room and, as expected, she'd found the others there too, each with a cup of coffee out on the balcony.

'Now listen, everybody! The time has come. We are on stand-by. Only the captain, the first mate and the engineer are still on board,' she'd almost shouted out. 'We must strike now!'

'Are you really sure?' Christina had wondered and she'd picked up her nail file.

'Now or never!' Martha had said and then, almost as if she were telling a fairy story, she'd told them again about how the jet set lived their lives on the Riviera. 'Like I said, the wealthy ones have several yachts with a stand-by crew in various harbours. When the owner wants to go out to sea, he rings the captain of the yacht he wants to use. Then the crew in their turn contact the rest of the staff so that everything is ready for departure when he arrives.'

'By helicopter or speedboat direct from Nice airport,' Rake had filled in.

'Exactly. And since Bielke isn't going to use his yacht this weekend there are only three crew on board,' Anna-Greta had added. 'The captain, the first mate and the engineer.'

'I'm beginning to understand,' Christina had mumbled, putting away her nail file.

'Besides,' Martha had continued, 'Bielke intended to hire out the boat. So I said that we want to charter it for a week. But first we just want to have a closer look and be given a guided tour on board.'

'Now I understand even better,' Christina had said.

'You want us to set off straight away, of course?' Brains had said, realizing that this was for real.

'Indeed,' Martha had answered.

Then they had got their things together, dressed up for a sea outing and had even taken along some extra clothes and equipment which they thought might come in useful. Everything had happened so quickly that Martha had hardly had time to be nervous.

But now they were all sitting here and it was action stations. Everybody was tense but ready. By now it had got dark and the light from the pier lit up the motor yacht. It was time to get going. Martha took out her mobile and punched in the number to the captain.

'Yes!' she said afterwards and put the mobile away again. 'That commander sounded really friendly. We can go on board now.'

The gang of pensioners looked at each other in silence, paid an excessive amount for the coffee and got up. They fidgeted with crumbs and serviettes. None of them said anything, they didn't even sing a jolly song; they just stared at the yacht. But in the end Anna-Greta couldn't keep her mouth shut.

'Just because you are sitting in a cafe in the harbour which happens to have a nice view, you have to pay twice as much for coffee. But it's the same damned coffee. Scandalous!'

Rake nodded, brushed away some crumbs from his trousers, adjusted his suit and combed his hair. He looked again towards Bielke's boat.

'They are bound to have a fancy espresso machine on board, just you wait and see. And the thought of getting a closer look at a motor yacht in that class. Wow, this is quite something!'

'Rake, we're not here simply to look at it. Just so you know,' mumbled Martha.

Christina delved into her handbag, took out her lipstick and improved her lips. She powdered herself and puffed up her hair. She had actually wanted to have a hat that matched her dress, but Martha had said that it was not practical because her hat sat on her head so loosely that she could lose it. And whatever sort of robbery you carried out, it was dangerous to leave tracks.

'But you've got a hat!' she protested.

'Indeed, but for good reason – you are so elegant and pretty anyway, you look so chic and young. No, you don't need a hat,' Martha had decided.

'Don't try that with me! I say like Mark Twain: when your friends start to flatter you, commenting on how young you look, it is a sure sign that you have grown old,' said Christina and she jerked her head back. 'And just so as you know, I'm taking my handbag with me!'

'Yes, of course, Christina. You need that!' said Martha nodding. Then she went up to Brains, took his hand, squeezed it lightly and gave him a quick kiss on the cheek.

'This is going to work out all right, you'll see. A robbery like this is not a challenge for us.'

'No, much easier than a bank robbery. Isn't that what you said, my dear?' sighed Brains. And he felt nauseous. And completely green in the face.

The five pensioners in their newly purchased clothes and expensive jewellery walked at a leisurely pace towards the pier in dark clothes. Because Martha had insisted on black. It made them look elegant and she, also in a black outfit, wanted to look rich, old and dignified. This time they had left their Ecco shoes at home, and instead had equipped themselves with hideously expensive boat shoes which were all the fashion among boat people. When they reached the yacht, Martha fished out her mobile. A few minutes later a well-dressed elegant man with a suntanned face and impeccable white suit came down the ladder. He looked slightly confounded when he discovered the five oldies, but when he discovered that they were customers, he welcomed them with a bow.

They were then given a tour around the boat which Martha would not soon forget. If there hadn't been a slight bobbing now and then when a motorboat drove past, she would have thought they were in the Princess Lilian suite at Grand Hotel in Stockholm. The captain took them from the luxuriously fitted dining room in light grey with blue velvet curtains and matching lilac cushions, to the over-furnished salon in brown with a Chagall on the walls. Then he showed them the room for afternoon tea with comfy flowery armchairs, glass tables and crystal vases, and the library which had classic literature such as Dickens and Cervantes on the shelves. (Christina let out a few enthusiastic cries.) After that the tour reached the spacious bedrooms with large TV screens that could be let down from the ceiling and bathrooms with built-in multi-coloured lighting above the washbasins and bathtubs. Martha was so overwhelmed that she completely forgot why she was there, and if Brains hadn't pinched her and whispered: 'Don't forget what you have to do!' she might have spoiled everything.

The captain took them up to the command bridge and,

thankfully, there was a lift so that they didn't have to worry about stairs and banister rails. Rake and Brains both became more lively when they set eyes on the navigation equipment with GPS, echo-sounding sonar and compass and Rake stood there with his legs apart at the control panel and adopted a knowledgeable expression although a lot of what he saw looked extremely new and modern. Thank God he had asked Nils for help, and his son would soon come on board. Nils was on stand-by on the pier not far away and as soon as he received the signal he would come up the ladder. They had timed everything precisely and knew that it would work. But before they did anything else or signed a charter contract they must get hold of the owner-registration certificate. Without that proof that they owned the boat – at any rate for a while – they wouldn't be able to sell it.

'Christina, are you ready?'

She was, although she looked very pale, despite all the powder, rouge and lipstick. She felt an enormous responsibility and knew that they were all a bit anxious about how she would carry out her task. During the last planning meeting they had agreed that if anybody should discover her she should flirt madly or play confused or stupid. Men always fell for that immediately and usually became very pleased with themselves. So you only had to distract them straight away. Martha had heard that the papers were normally kept up on the bridge somewhere and Christina had been tasked with finding them. Now it was simply a matter of finding the box where the original documents were kept.

Christina dropped back, discreetly distancing herself from the others and while Martha and her friends kept the crew occupied she started to search. She quietly stayed on in the map room and started to go through the wide, solid pedestals of stacked drawers. Slowly she pulled out drawer after drawer, opened envelopes, browsed through sketches, maps and bundles of papers without finding anything. She bit one thumbnail, leaving a mark, and that gave her a start. No, goodness, she was getting silly, she mustn't be nervous now. She must pull herself together! Further inside the room she caught sight of a desk and hurried across to it. Now she was more eager and resolutely pulled out every drawer as quietly and carefully as she could. Now and then she threw an anxious glance towards the others.

'So we can depart tomorrow?' she heard Rake ask.

'Of course, I will call my crew and the boat is all yours.'

'Yes, you have no idea how right you are,' Christina mumbled to herself while sweat formed large stains of dampness under her arms. Where in heaven's name did the captain keep his papers? Not in his cabin, surely? Could they be in a private safe? She threw a glance around the room to see if she had missed anything, a security box, a cupboard or a shelf. She saw some map books and crime novels, otherwise the book shelves were empty. Then she heard steps and realized that she must leave the room. She carefully crept out onto the bridge again and smiled in a forced manner when she walked right into the arms of the captain.

'The toilet, please?' she stuttered.

The suntanned man beamed with a wide smile and indicated with his hand down towards the port side. Just as she walked past him she discovered a brown A4 envelope with an empty coffee cup and some receipts on top of it. The envelope lay next to the safe in the map room and it looked as if somebody had put it down, realized that he didn't have the key with him and then gone off to fetch it. She stopped and noted that the captain had returned to the others. She quickly picked up the envelope and swept it into her handbag. Her heart was pounding inside the dress material and a drop of sweat appeared on her upper lip.

While Martha and the gang were still out on deck Christina remained inside, opened the envelope and peeped at the papers down inside her bag. Some were filled with text she couldn't read, and there were receipts and notes torn out from a notebook, but there were also two A4-sheets that were thicker than the others. And they had stamps on them too. Could they be . . . yep, this was it! Here they were, the papers for the boat and the certificate of ownership for *Aurora 4*. How could the captain be so careless as to leave such important documents lying around? She hurried to catch up with the others and gave the pre-agreed thumbs-up to Martha who in turn nudged Rake, after which he nodded, picked up his mobile and punched in the number to Nils. Now! Now there was no going back.

It took a few minutes but then Martha saw how Nils came out from the shadows and walked towards the boat. When they had established eye contact, he took up position down on the pier, looked around him and lit a cigarette. That was the agreed signal number two. Martha breathed deeply again, fidgeted with her old-fashioned blouse with its lace trimmings, pulled down her hat with the veil and turned towards the captain.

'What a wonderful boat. We want to charter it, of course.

But what about a little outing with it first? Yes, just a short trip. And of course we'll pay the charter fee, we'll pay that in advance.' Martha dug down into her large, flowery handbag and fished out her iPad.

'We can deal with that later.' The captain smiled.

'Oh no. What if you charter it out to somebody else? No, give me a charter agreement and you'll get the money. The account number please?'

The captain scratched his chin but there was not much he could do when Martha got going with her persuasive tactics. He turned on his heels and returned to the bridge. That very same moment, Christina came up with the papers. Martha threw a quick glance at them and saw that it was the certificate of ownership with Bielke's name on it. She folded the papers and put them in with her money and keys in her waterproof 'All-weather wallet' inside her blouse. For a brief, scary second she was afraid that the captain would discover that the certificate was missing, but why would he look for it now? The polite gentleman dressed in white was only away a short time, but when he came back he had a folder under his arm.

'If you only want to charter the boat for one week, then I am authorized to arrange that,' he said and put a charter contract down on the table. Martha signed – the illegible handwriting that she had become so clever at using in situations like this – after which she pushed the papers over to the captain. When he too had signed, she picked up her iPad and asked for details of the bank and account number. He wrote it all down on a piece of paper and handed that over to her. Martha nodded to Anna-Greta, who sat down next to them and helped to find the bank on the Internet. She clicked her way to Transfers and filled in the number.

'Right, then,' said Anna-Greta but she stopped and looked up before she had pressed the enter key: 'But what about going on our little trip first. I love boats!'

'Oh yes, that little test outing, captain, we must do that now,' said Martha and pushed the iPad to one side.

'I know that you and your crew will be with us so we will feel we are in the best hands, but we would so much like to see what it feels like to sail in this boat. Ten thousand euro for a week is, as you will appreciate, a great deal of money, so everything must feel right.'

'Of course,' answered the captain obligingly and he gave a sign to his colleagues to make things ready. Martha got up. The yacht was one of the fastest and most modern in the Mediterranean and, besides, it was brand new. The crew would presumably need to become better acquainted with the boat and would probably be only too happy to agree to the little trip, she had worked out. And she hadn't been wrong. The first mate and the engineer lit up.

'It isn't much fun being moored here in the harbour, and we've time for a little trip,' said the first mate, and the engineer nodded eagerly, almost giving a salute, before taking the lift down to the engine room. The first mate took up his position on the command bridge.

'Great!' exclaimed Rake when the engines started up and he could again breathe in that familiar smell of diesel.

'Oh how wonderful!' Brains lied, not really wanting to go out to sea at all, as he would have preferred to have watched

TV or enjoyed a good dinner. Or why not simply a nice little walk among the workshops in Saint-Tropez.

'Why don't we drink some champagne and celebrate our little trip here in the Mediterranean?' Martha suggested, and she fumbled in her handbag to pull out the bottles of champagne she had brought with her.

'The best champagne in the world!' Martha enthused and she waved one of the most expensive champagne bottles she had ever bought. The captain, who had already asked the first mate to cast off the mooring ropes, was distracted by Martha's bottle waving, and it didn't get any better when she took a firm hold of the lapels of his uniform jacket and pulled him out onto the deck.

'*Arret, arret!*' he called out to the first mate and then turned towards Martha.

'But madame, I must . . .' he began, but Martha just leaned her head to one side and prodded him with the champagne bottle.

'This is a really superb champagne!' she gabbled on. 'Come on, why don't we?' She smiled and strode across to the nearest deckchair where she plonked herself down. The chairs were placed around an oval table together with some cane furniture not far from the inflatable water slide down into the sea. There was a large bubble-pool close by. She pushed the captain into the chair next to her and then pulled out some champagne glasses from the big handbag. The captain, who realized that the charter fee had not yet been paid, understood that he must humour his customers and so he gave in. With a smile he accepted a glass and signalled to the first mate to take over the bridge. But he had hardly got the glass in his hand before Martha grabbed hold of the first mate too as he walked past them.

'*Pour vous!*' She beamed and gave him a glass too. Now Anna-Greta, Rake and Christina came and sat down as well, and then Rake opened the bottle with his customary elegance and filled their glasses. Martha put out some crisps and salted peanuts and opened a can of olives which she put on the table. Then she raised her glass, gave a toast and made sure everybody drank their champagne. When the engineer came up on deck, Brains opened the second bottle.

'Aren't we going to leave now?' the engineer wondered, but he was soon silenced with a glass.

'Well, cheers to you too!' Martha called out, and again she made sure that all the crew emptied their glasses which she quickly filled again. Then she started humming a drinking song, after which the League of Pensioners sang some Swedish songs in parts before ending their mini-concert with 'What shall we do with a drunken sailor?'.

By now, a warm and merry mood had spread to all on board and Martha triumphantly held up the empty bottles above her head in a wild gesture of victory. She pointed to herself and the captain and threw out her arms.

'Now it is time to dance, is it not? A cheek-to-cheek!'

'A cheek – oh no, no, I don't think, I must—' he began, but was stopped by Martha who put her hand on his chest.

'Captain, you love to dance, I can see that in your eyes!'

Somewhat irritated, the captain lifted her hand away and tried to push past, and as he did so he caused Martha to lose her balance. Taking a few wobbling steps backwards, she stumbled and fell straight into the water slide. She tried to grab the edge but the water slide was wet and the next second she had landed on the soft, inflatable plastic and was sliding down at great speed towards the sea.

'Help, help, my God, she can't swim!' Brains shouted shrilly, and he waved his arms and began to take off his shirt.

'No, no don't!' the captain objected, as he felt he was responsible for what had happened. Without even bothering to take off his jacket, he threw himself into the sea. The first mate and the engineer – now both a little tipsy too – also rushed to the railing and threw themselves in. Martha herself, who had actually fallen onto the water slide on purpose, was the only one to take things calmly. She heard the three splashes when the crew jumped into the sea, and smiled to herself. Getting them to leave the boat had worked better than she had dreamed, and now the yacht was in the hands of the League of Pensioners! She now squawked like a seagull three times which was the pre-agreed signal that everything had gone well, and then she swam away from the bottom of the water slide and into the shadows under the pier. There she stayed completely still while she looked to see where the captain and the others were. When she caught sight of them, she moved behind a big pillar and hid there while the three frantically searched for her. Christina, who was watching from up on deck, got rather worried.

'Must try to help, what if something happens to the crew,' she mumbled, rather tipsy, and she looked around for a life-buoy. She blustered around up on deck but couldn't find anything, so she tried to find life jackets instead. But she couldn't find any life-saving equipment at all. All she could see were some colourful swimming toys by the pool. There was a beach ball and two smiling inflatable sea horses. Those will float nicely and are easy to hold on to, she thought. She leaned over the railing and threw them down.

'What the hell? Bath toys? I think I'm going to faint,' groaned Rake and he put his hands on his forehead.

Down in the water, Martha stayed hidden while the crew continued their desperate search, and when the captain and the others started to search closer to the harbour, she swam off in the opposite direction. When she felt she was safe, she quickly raised her hand above the water and waved so that Nils would see her. But she had been too careless. The men in the water managed to catch a glimpse of her too.

Nils, in dark clothes and with a blue marine sports bag over his shoulder, realized that they had seen her. He had been standing ready with a lifebuoy and binoculars up on the pier and had seen Martha's dark silhouette swish down the water slide. As soon as he saw her land in a fountain of water, he threw out the lifebuoy. Then he opened the bag and pulled out the wire cutters hidden among various women's clothes, gloves, a shawl, a hat and some heavyweight belts. He checked that there was no one watching, rushed up to the electricity distribution board cupboard, and cut off the main cable. The lights on the pier all went out and the motor yacht and everything round about also fell into darkness. It was a good thing that they had a reserve plan, he thought, and he noted with satisfaction that the men now seemed to be swimming in the wrong direction. All he could hear was their splashing and their calls to Martha.

'Madame, madame!' they shouted, but nobody answered.

'Elle est là, elle est là! Nils called out, and he threw the sports bag in a wide arch towards the place where Martha had first plopped into the sea. The bag fell in with a big splash and slowly started to sink. On the surface floated a scarf, ladies' stockings and a hat – of exactly the same type that Martha had worn. Then he ran quickly to the little platform out on the pier where he had promised to wait for her.

'Well, I did pass my swimming test in school with full honours!' she panted with a blocked nose and her mouth full of water when Nils had got hold of her arm and, with considerable effort, had pulled her up onto the pier. When she was on the quay, water dripped from her clothes and her hair was completely sodden. Nils lifted up his jumper and pulled out her waist bag with money, a plastic bag with a little towel and Martha's light summer dress with the flowers on it. She quickly dried herself, stepped out of the wet black dress and pulled the dry one over her head. But she kept her boat shoes on. Because whatever else happened, she must not fall down. Using the water slide had been risky enough, and when you are old you really should keep two feet on the ground. Then she dried her hair as best she could and pushed the wet dress and towel into the plastic bag.

'Lovely, Nils. Now the boat is all yours. Good luck!' she said and she patted him on the back. The evening breeze blew towards the quay and the port side was rubbing against the fenders.

'I'll deal with the mooring ropes from the bow,' he said and he loosened the heavy rope with some difficulty. Martha watched and followed him to the bollard near the stern where she helped too. Now it was a question of moving off quickly. At any moment the crew might return and try to get back on board the yacht again. She anxiously looked out over the water but couldn't see them in the dark. Nils followed her gaze.

'It's all right, Martha, the crew are busy diving to find you. By now your hat, scarf and stockings will be floating around down there in the inner harbour.'

'Pity about the hat, but it was a good idea,' Martha said.

'Righto, all hands on deck!' said Nils and he managed to catch hold of the ladder before the boat slipped away. He checked a final time to see if the captain and his men were visible, but there was no sign of them. He hurried up the ladder and then took the stairs two at a time up to the bridge. At last he would be able to manoeuvre a ship again!

'I knew you would manage it,' said Rake, proudly, when he saw his son in the doorway. 'Everything is under control. So I'll go down to the engine room.'

'Fine. The engine is going, and the ropes have been released. That's it, then. Now we only have to get up speed.'

But Rake didn't hear him, as he was already on his way down to the engine room in the lift. Nils pulled the joystick towards him with a heavenly smile and was delighted. Everything had gone according to plan and now they were on their way! And he just loved being out at sea again!

Feeling most satisfied despite her wet hair, Martha stood on the quay and watched as Nils over-excitedly boarded Bielke's boat and made his way up to the bridge. It had taken more than a week to plan the coup, but they had also succeeded in carrying everything out, right down to the smallest detail. She was so pleased that she waved as the yacht slowly made its way out of the harbour, and, full of enthusiasm, she fumbled for her flowery handbag to get the champagne out. This most certainly called for another toast! She fumbled a long time but only felt her waist bag. It was then that she remembered that both the handbag and the champagne with the accompanying glasses were still there up on deck. And that wasn't the worst of it. She, too, should have been on board.

51

Some distance away from the big motor yacht one could hear a violent splashing and a great deal of swearing in French. And even though the lights on the pier were not working, there was enough light for both the stranded Martha and the restaurant guests in the harbour to see when three men with a scarf, a hat with a veil and two smiling inflated seahorses splashed back to the quay. The white newly ironed uniforms were wet, the shoes were full of seaweed and the captain's new uniform cap had floated away.

'MERDE!' echoed out over the water when the crew realized that the boat had left the pier and was on its way out of the harbour.

'Merde!' swore the captain when he realized he had been conned and, besides, had also been photographed when he had clung on to one of the sea horses.

'Merde,' hissed the engineer when he heard the engines get up into high rev and saw the yacht head out to sea. Swearing, he tried to free himself of the scarf around one trouser leg and the old-fashioned ladies' stocking in nylon that had fastened around his neck. Together with the others, and soaking wet and furious, he climbed up onto land just below one of the restaurants.

When the men stood there with a hat with a veil and stockings on their uniforms, Martha came walking in from the pier. In the light of the restaurant she caught sight of them, stopped and nipped in among the shadows. She waited until they had turned away and then she slipped along the wall and managed to get past them. She reached the street and quickly waved down a taxi.

'Cannes!' she said and then settled comfortably in the back seat. Admittedly, she wasn't on board the boat, but this would work just as well. Even better, when she thought about it. Now she could travel by road to Cannes where Oleg and his friends awaited them at the restaurant. But first she would stop off at one of those department stores which were open in the evenings. She must make a photocopy of the certificate of ownership and buy a new handbag and a bit of this and that necessary for the negotiations.

Out on the water, the luxury motor yacht *Aurora 4* was leisurely making its way out of the harbour with a very happy Nils at the helm. He, Anna-Greta and Christina stood up on the bridge and looked out through the windows in fascination while the lighthouse at the end of the pier slowly passed them. And Brains was totally absorbed with all the technical apparatuses on board. He went from one to the other, between the GPS, computers and weird joysticks, his entire face one big smile, and thought that life was exciting. Of course, his beloved Martha could be a bit trying at times, but nobody could deny that things happened when she got going. And most of the time they were fun things.

'Martha, come and have a look at this,' he called out, with his gaze on the modern GPS. When he didn't hear any answer, he went out on deck to fetch her, but his dear fiancée was nowhere to be seen. Somewhat confounded, he scratched his neck. When had he last seen her? Yes, that was it. She had just whooshed off down the water slide at one hell of a pace and landed in the water where she had made those seagull noises. But then what? She was meant to quickly get back on board again. He felt his panic growing, and he rushed to the railings to see if she was still down there in the dock. But the sea was like a black mirror and apart from seaweed and a glove floating on the surface, nothing could be seen. He wet his lips and felt a sinking feeling in his tummy. Martha hadn't got back on board. Whatever could have happened? He rushed in to the bridge.

'Stop the engines, we've forgotten Martha!' he shouted out.

'What did you say?' asked Nils, who had his hands full trying to manoeuvre the beast he was now in command of. The motor yacht *Aurora 4* was by no means as simple to steer as he had first thought, and on the bridge they had installed a new computer system that he was not familiar with. Besides, he was not used to a joystick and all the other controls.

'Martha, we must fetch Martha,' Brains shouted.

Nils fumbled with the joystick and looked anxiously out through the bridge windows. A hell of a lot of boats lay at anchor ahead, and they were in the way. At that moment, the door burst open and a breathless Rake came in. He was sweating and his hair stuck out at all angles.

'Er, Nils, this boat, it's . . .' said Rake, twisting his bandanna with his fingers. 'I mean – in the engine room, like – damned complicated. Only buttons and electronics. The entire machine room looks like a disco palace.'

Nils, who had just managed to avoid a collision with a little sailing yacht, stared at Rake.

'But Dad, what the hell?! You told me that you can manage any boat at all and that you had kept up with developments, oh yes.'

'Well, yes. I have. But this boat, you know . . .' answered Rake, sounding unusually pathetic. 'This is a newly built motor yacht. And engines perhaps aren't my best subject. I was better as a waiter.'

'But you have boasted that you know your way around any engine room whatsoever!'

'You'd better learn quick. We must go back and pick up Martha!' Brains butted in.

At that moment, Nils made a very quick decision. They were out in the roadstead and would soon be in the middle of the seaway among lots of big boats. There was only one thing to do.

'Drop the anchor! NOW!'

'But, no, I don't think—' said Rake.

'But we can't lose Martha, you must see that,' yelled Brains, almost hysterical.

'Now listen, she is not a person who allows herself to be lost,' Rake countered. 'And besides, this anchor winch is a bit different to what I am used to. It would probably be best if we kept going.'

'Oh, bloody hell!' hissed Nils and suddenly he looked rather exhausted.

While Martha sat in the taxi on the way to Cannes, the captain, the first mate and the engineer remained on the quay and tried to smarten themselves up as best they could. Tired and furious, they wrung out their clothes before putting them back on again.

'We swam in the wrong direction!' the captain groaned, pulling out his mobile to phone the police. 'Those oldies stole the boat; I can't believe this has happened. Damn them!' He punched in the number on his mobile but it was totally dead, had a wet sweet paper in the casing and was very damp.

'How the hell can we explain this?' the first mate moaned. 'We've been conned by a gang of pensioners.'

'Is this yours?' a woman came up and asked. She held out a merrily smiling sea horse and inclined her head respectfully to the captain.

'*Merde!*' could be heard yet again, possibly even louder than before. He grabbed the smiling inflatable sea horse and threw it out into the water with all his force. At least that was what he tried to do. But unfortunately it didn't reach all the way, but caught on a rusty steel wire and was punctured. Accompanied by a hissing sound, the smile slowly turned into a grimace while the sea horse deflated and ended up in a heap on the quay. The captain groaned, and signalled to the others that it was best to leave quickly. But they were too late; people were standing in the way. One of the restaurant's owners rushed forward with towels and tried to dry them off as best he could while several guests took out their mobiles and started to take photos. The captain wanted to phone the police, and he asked if he could borrow a mobile to phone them, but everyone had only seen a bunch of oldies go on board. Besides, both the captain and the other two were definitely a bit tipsy, so the guests just smiled, laughed and took some more photos while *Aurora 4* sailed out of the harbour.

'Is this yours?' a young blonde asked, holding up a sodden captain's cap.

'Of course it's mine,' said the captain and he put it on, only to snatch it off again even quicker. A little shrimp and an old condom had fastened in the lining. The captain swore again, cleaned the rubbish out of his cap and then put it back on.

'They stole the yacht, phone the police!' he shouted out, pointing out to sea.

'I know,' said the restaurant owner and laughed, while the guests waved, smiled and took photographs. And every time the captain got angry and flapped his arms frantically, they all waved back merrily.

'It's going to collide with other boats,' the captain howled as he almost lost his footing. And he had hardly said those words before a heavy scraping sound could be heard followed by a dreadful crash when the motor yacht met with something in the dark. Then he hid his head in his hands and loudly yelled out again:

'*MERDE, MERDE, MERDE!*'

52

The yacht shuddered and Nils sheered off sharply. They had bumped into something but had not got caught and had become free when Nils got more power from the engines. What a relief! But the anchor? Rake had run around out on deck and looked, and Nils had also looked here and there at the instrument panel to see if he could find a familiar anchor symbol. Dropping anchor had been so obvious that he hadn't even thought about it, but now he was standing there fumbling. No, of course, how stupid he was. The anchor winch was out on deck and would have to be manoeuvred from there. He was just about to rush out and start it up when he bumped into Brains who was now considerably calmer.

'No panic. We don't need to anchor. Martha will take a taxi, of course. I know her,' Brains said. 'If I go down to the engine room and help Rake, then we'll get things working so that we can make it to Cannes.'

'Are you sure?' said Nils, relieved.

'Sure as hell. Engines are basically the same. I know about that. It doesn't matter where they are.'

They were lucky. Or perhaps Nils was a skilful captain. Eventually, he found all the commands he needed for the engines as well as the navigation system and immediately felt so much more confident. Besides, he had sailed in the Mediterranean before and in the sea lanes he didn't need to be afraid of running aground. With his self-confidence boosted, he steered out on the black water and into the sea lane and soon he and the League of Pensioners had left Saint-Tropez far behind them. No other vessels could be seen anywhere near them and things got a bit calmer on board. So calm, in fact, that Nils put on some classical music and enjoyed listening to the strains coming through the loudspeakers. After a while he had forgotten their precarious situation and stood there merrily gesticulating while he hummed along with Verdi's 'Prisoners' Chorus'. He was happy, he was out at sea, and so totally immersed in the music that he gave a start when Brains came rushing in to the bridge.

'Nils, we must turn off the transponder,' he said. 'Every boat and harbour authority can see where we are, remember.'

'Oh yes, damnation, I forgot that,' answered Nils and immediately he turned it off. 'There is so much to think about just now. I hope they haven't traced us.'

'I don't think anyone has bothered about us, thank God. And this is the first bleeding time we've stolen a yacht. It's always difficult when you do something the first time,' Brains consoled him. 'Bank robberies are almost easier.'

What a thing to say, thought Nils. This lot were certainly not your average pensioner types!

The taxi came to a halt outside the little family restaurant Quai des Brunes in Cannes where Martha and the Russians had agreed to meet. Here she had a good view over the harbour – which was strategic – and she had also heard that this restaurant had such incredibly tasty food. While she waited, she enjoyed a small starter and a glass of wine and just as she asked to look at the menu again she caught sight of Oleg and his companion. The two men were elegantly dressed and each carried a briefcase. She put her serviette down and waved to them. Then she got up to say hello, wobbled a bit and had to support herself against the table. Not because the wine was strong, but because she was faking dizziness. When Oleg hurried to help her, she immediately waved him away and tried to sit down again with as much dignity as she could muster. She had become really good at playing the role of a feeble oldie and she even thought it was rather fun. A pity, though, that she sometimes really did feel her age.

'Are you all right?' Oleg asked, concerned.

'Pah, I got up too quickly, that's all,' she said. 'Blood pressure, you understand. But how nice to see you. What about a little something to eat? One should never do business on an empty stomach.'

Oleg and Boris exchanged glances and then nodded. Best to do what the old lady wanted.

'Of course,' mumbled the two Russians and they looked through the menu as best they could. They didn't know French, and English wasn't their best foreign language, but they were familiar with some dishes and drinks. When the waiter came back, they ordered deep-fried octopus and wine, together with a bottle of vodka. While they waited for the food, Martha started to talk about the sale. And she was careful not to mention that she had re-named the yacht, which was now called *Aurora 5*, and made a few changes in the papers. But as Martha always said: You should never say too much. And sooner or later presumably he would find out.

'Gentlemen, *Aurora Five* will soon be here, but before we go on board I would like to have a look at the diamonds.'

'The diamonds? Now?' wondered Oleg, nervously, and Martha could discern a tone of uncertainty in his voice. 'No, not when everybody can see. We'll do that on board.'

'Er, I am not sure about that. My husband always said that one can't be too careful. I just want to quickly check that they are genuine,' Martha went on, pulling out a magnifying glass and placing it on her serviette on the table. 'Put them here, please!'

Once again, the men exchanged glances, and Oleg looked very uncomfortable.

'Let's look at the yacht first.'

'There is one thing you should understand,' said Martha, her voice now sounding suddenly quite sharp. 'You are not the only ones who want to buy. Your colleagues at the hotel with plenty of capital were very interested. My goodness, there are so many of you rich people at that conference. One bid ninety-eight million dollars, I can tell you, but I didn't go along with that. I had already promised you. You see, I keep my word. Well, so –' Martha paused a few moments for effect and then gave them both a penetrating look. 'Either I get to look at the diamonds now, or we can forget about the whole deal.'

She raised her wine glass and took a large gulp.

Oleg squirmed where he sat. The old lady was tougher than he thought. But Boris seemed almost a little amused, and for him it evidently didn't matter. He lifted up his briefcase, opened it and discreetly laid three diamonds on the table.

'What do you think? These are cut in facets and brilliants. The left one is valued at nine million, I bought the one on the right at an auction for twenty-eight million and here is the excellent, pink brilliant-cut stone which is valued at about thirty-six million.'

Martha prodded the glittering stones, picked up her magnifying glass, and looked at the most expensive one. She hummed appreciatively and was just about to examine diamond number two when the waiter approached. She discreetly slipped the diamonds under the tablecloth and smiled heartily.

'Tell me. Before we do business there is one thing I would like to know. What are you going to do with my husband's yacht?'

'We are going to keep it for ourselves. Cruise in the Mediterranean, invite our friends and have a good time. It will be moored in Cyprus. Yes, we Russians don't have to pay tax there.' Oleg broke into a contented laugh.

'No tax. So smart!' said Martha with fake admiration in her voice.

'Yes, a good investment. We have many yachts and properties. Paying tax is not for us.'

'No tax at all, really? So clever! My husband always used to swear about how everything he earned went to the state.'

'Poor guy! No, tax is what amateurs pay. With a good lawyer and a company you can fix most things.'

'Goodness gracious me, you are so clever,' sighed Martha and she was just about to pick up the diamonds again when the waiter came in with their food. 'Yes, perhaps we should eat first.'

While they ate, Martha continued to question them about

their businesses and soon the two of them were boasting wildly about their transactions and investments. The more she praised them, the more the two Russians told her. They dealt with billions of dollars but they didn't pay any tax at all. In the end, she couldn't restrain herself any longer.

'But what about health care, roads and schools – who pays for that?'

Oleg and Boris couldn't grasp what she meant.

'We pay for our own children's schooling, of course, and we have private chauffeurs.'

'But the others who can't afford that?'

'Well, it works out somehow.'

Oleg and Boris looked at each other somewhat perplexed by her questions.

'But there is one thing I wonder about,' Martha went on, and she carefully wiped her mouth for a long time with her serviette. 'You and many other wealthy Russians have your capital in Cyprus. Well, I don't understand the economy, of course, but how does the Russian state get money so that they can pay for schools, health care and roads and so on? I mean, if nobody pays tax?' Martha asked, adopting an innocent face and taking a gulp of wine. Then she wiped her mouth carefully with her serviette and tried to look as uncomprehending and naive as she could.

'Er, what do you mean?' Oleg wondered with a degree of irritation in his voice.

'I thought people paid tax so that a community will function. Yes, that everybody sort of helps. But it was my husband who looked after that side of things, so perhaps I have got it all wrong, of course.' Martha broke into laughter and smiled as merrily as she could. 'But you seem to know all about it and I am happy to sell the boat just to you.' She picked up the diamonds again and held them against the light. 'And such fine diamonds too! When I see these, it makes me so happy!'

The men looked at each other and laughed, relieved, feeling that they were once more in control of the situation. But while they ate, the Russians' words rolled around inside Martha's head. With a good lawyer and a company you can fix most things. And yet they still made use of public services. Just like crooked businessmen all over the world. And not only did they sponge on the system and not contribute themselves, but they boasted about it too! Martha thought about what it was like back at home in Sweden with all the cuts in government expenditure on care for the elderly, home-care services and the low wages for jobs where you looked after people. Oh Jesus, so many things made her angry nowadays. Her heart started to beat faster. Now she was sitting here with two really big fish and she felt challenged. Of course she was going to sell the boat to them. But suddenly she wanted to do something more, something much more. Something that would teach them a lesson.

53

When they approached Cannes, Nils changed into a white uniform and put on a captain's cap he found on board. On their way into the harbour he had completely embraced the role of captain and had even become a bit reckless. If Anna-Greta hadn't shouted out, he would have come close to colliding with the breakwater and the pier. Thankfully, she had managed to warn him in time so that with Rake's help he could finally make fast the boat at the quay.

'Can we moor here, then?' Rake wondered nervously, sweating on his back and with an anxious look at the mooring ropes.

'The harbour authorities won't be so alert at this time of day. They'll be sitting having dinner. We should be on our way again before they wake up,' Nils answered though he was a bit worried himself too. Those harbour officials would want to look at certificates, registration papers and lots of other boat documents and that was perhaps not such a good idea just now. He sincerely hoped that Martha had got hold of the Russians so that the business deal could be carried out quickly. But he had worried unnecessarily. Martha was the first person he saw when he looked over the railings. She was waiting down on the pier together with two elegant men with briefcases, Oleg and his companion. But just as he was about to wave to her, he saw another two men who came up and joined them. They were two large, well-built men who looked like bodyguards. He fumbled for his packet of cigarettes but realized that he had stopped smoking. Bodyguards. Bloody hell!

Brains, also in a white uniform, smiled in relief when he caught sight of Martha; a smile that soon faded when he noticed the two beefy men who followed after the Russians. And that wasn't all he saw; didn't Martha seem unusually pleased when she looked at them? Elderly gentlemen who looked furtively at younger women was one thing, but Martha! Brains took a lot of quick breaths before he had pulled himself together to such an extent that he could wave to them down below and invite them on board.

When they had come up on deck and then settled in the saloon, Rake brought out the champagne and bowed a few extra times for the Russians. But Martha gave him a stern look. No alcohol until the business was concluded, they had agreed on that! But now she was obliged to toast them and wish them welcome to her boat, while at the same time sincerely hoping that the Russians wouldn't become angry with too much alcohol in them. To be on the safe side, she decided to hurry things along.

'Perhaps we should go on a tour of the boat straight away,' she said and she got up. 'I want you to be satisfied with what you're buying.'

'I can show you the engine room,' said Rake.

'I'll show you the bridge,' said Nils.

'And we ladies can show the rest,' said Anna-Greta.

'But what about the crew?' wondered Oleg. 'It would be nice to meet them,'

'Naturally,' said Martha. 'But I said they could go ashore this evening, because we can manage this tour ourselves. But they are on stand-by so I can phone them any time, of course.'

The men were satisfied with this explanation and for the next hour the League of Pensioners took care of them. Rake let the group have a quick look in the engine room, but he didn't go into much detail about horse-power and engines because he was afraid that a single wrong word might give him away. Nils showed them the bridge and had the air of a real expert and said beautiful and wonderful about everything and patted the radar and the compass as if they were old friends. Christina, for her part, was in charge of the guided tour inside the boat and she took this most seriously. She accompanied them from room to room and spouted on using design and artists' terms as if it was an exam on art history. But the Russians listened, interested, as they were taken from the luxuriously fitted dining room to the elegant saloon with black leather armchairs, an oak table and a Chagall on the wall (at this point, Oleg gave a whistle and went up to the painting, studying it closely. He even looked at the back before he hung it up again in its original position, humming as he did so).

The party continued to the afternoon-tea room with its luxurious cream-coloured armchairs, glass table and crystal vases filled with roses. In the library they all stopped for quite a while as Christina went on at length about how fond she was of Chekhov, Pushkin and Pasternak. But when she tried to quote from them in Russian, nobody understood her at all so she had to settle for a short, shy 'Kalinka'. By now, Oleg and his companions were rather tired and they didn't brighten up until they were shown the big wide beds and the bedrooms. When they got to see the elegant rooms with giant TV screens that could be folded out from the ceiling with a remote control and the bathrooms in blue mosaic with red lighting in the basins and bathtub, they cheered up and after that it felt as if the yacht was as good as sold. The little red motorboat with a cabin, the water scooters and the jet ski on the lower deck, these they passed strangely enough rather quickly and Martha hoped it was because they had already decided. After the tour of Bielke's newly stolen boat was complete, the party sat down in the saloon again. Martha brushed the table with her hand, wiping away dust that wasn't there.

'That's it,' said Martha. 'You buy?'

Oleg and Boris had a lively discussion in Russian and Martha didn't understand a word of it, but then Oleg cleared his throat and switched to English.

'Nice boat, yes. We'll pay 65 million dollars.'

'That's an insult to my husband's memory!' exclaimed Martha with a rhinoceros-like snort. She got up abruptly and gesticulated so wildly that the fruit bowl fell onto the floor. 'He built this with love and with the help of the best French architects' bureau, and it cost him all his savings and now you don't want to pay what it is worth!' She sat down again, closed the zip on her waist bag and looked around angrily. 'No, there is not going to be a sale, that's obvious.'

Oleg and Boris exchanged a quick glance and didn't comment on Martha's outburst. Instead, with an elegant movement of his hand, Boris lifted up his briefcase and put it on the table. He opened it wide. On a green velvet cloth lay a row of glimmering diamonds, even more beautiful than those she had seen at the restaurant. One of them reminded her of the famous African diamond, a 59.6 carat Pink Dream diamond that had been sold at Sotheby's for 83.2 million dollars. This one wasn't as big, of course, but was just about as beautiful.

'Goodness gracious me!' said Martha and, somewhat overwhelmed, pressed her hand on her chest.

'Smelling salts!' Anna-Greta squeaked, and stretched out her hand to get hold of the stones.

'No, no, keep your fingers off,' muttered Boris and he pulled the briefcase towards him. The bodyguards moved a little closer to Anna-Greta, but Martha tried to look more distanced and to stay calm.

'Don't think that a few diamonds can distract me. I can of course lower the price a little, but I won't go below eighty-five million.'

Oleg discreetly prodded Boris in his ribs and picked up one of the brilliant cut stones from the briefcase. A light-blue, gleaming jewel in a casing of gold.

'Seventy-five million, then?' He coughed slightly into his clenched fist. 'Plus this beautiful rare stone from South Africa.'

Martha shook her head.

'No way. But I don't want to be impossible. You can have the yacht for eighty-two million.'

'Including the painting by Chagall?'

Martha hesitated, she hadn't thought about that. The paint-ing was worth a lot of money.

'Perhaps,' she answered.

The Russians discussed together for quite a while and every-one in the League of Pensioners felt uncertain and very uncomfortable since they didn't understand what the men were saying. It was nerve-wracking enough to steal a boat, but it was darned well even worse trying to sell it. And the men were talking this Cossack gobbledy-gook!

The negotiations went on for many long minutes which became an hour at least before Martha noticed that they were now very close to each other. They finally settled on a price of eighty million dollars including the Chagall painting.

'I'm selling at a loss!' said Martha finally with a broken voice and she tried to look sad. 'A good job my husband isn't still alive. He would never have forgiven me.'

'Oh yes, you have struck a really good deal,' Oleg pointed out. 'Not many people can pay cash in dollars and diamonds. You'll have no problem with the banks and you know too you won't be conned. The world is full of swindlers.'

'Swindlers? Oh how dreadful!' said Martha.

'Right then, and here are the dollar banknotes!' said Oleg, lifting up his briefcase and opening the lid.

'Heavenly!' exclaimed Anna-Greta when she saw the dollar bundles and she was there in a jiffy, grabbing a pile. With practised fingers she started to flick through the bundles, stop-ping now and then to examine a banknote or a watermark a bit more. All the time humming contentedly to herself, while flicking through them so quickly that the Russians were really impressed.

'You seem to be a real professional, madame,' said Oleg politely.

'I was Stockholm's sharpest bank official,' she hollered, looking pleased. She laughed in delight. 'And we women always try to be cleverer than you men.'

Anna-Greta had soon checked the banknotes and when she looked up from the pile of money, she pointed at the diamonds.

'And now we would like to see all the diamonds too,' she said resolutely.

'Of course,' said Boris patiently, and he laid a red velvet cloth on the table. Then he pulled out one diamond at a time which he placed on the cloth with an elegant gesture. Old veined hands turned and twisted the stones and now one could hear ums and ahs, sighs and sudden deep intakes of breath as the valuables passed from one member of the League of Pensioners to the other. Martha, however, controlled her enthusiasm and critically examined diamond after diamond under her magnifying glass.

'Goodness, this is indeed wonderful,' she said after each new stone and, if nothing else, she understood that these were the real thing. Of all the diamonds she had handled since they left the old folk's home, these were the most beautiful precious stones she had ever set eyes on.

'Formidable, great, wonderful,' said Oleg of every stone, but now slurring his words a little since Rake (without Martha's permission) had given him and his friends vodka. 'Nice, nice, yes! In a business deal all must be satisfied.'

'That's what my husband said too. But what if one or two

404

of these diamonds are worth more than you think?' Martha went on. 'That would be terribly unfortunate.'

'They could also be worth less,' Boris broke in.

'Hardly, your diamonds are superb! Think of the four Cs: Colour, Clarity, Cut and Carat – the four qualities that decide what a diamond is worth. One or even two of your diamonds seem to have a higher carat than you think,' Martha went on and she put the magnifying glass to her eye again. She looked and hummed and hawed and twisted them this way and that. 'Yes, I really don't wish to fleece you, you see, but in that case I would pay you back. I want things to be correct.'

'So nice of you, but—'

Martha whistled and handed a pink diamond to Oleg. 'This diamond, for example. I think you have undervalued it. It would be best to hand it in for an independent valuation. If it is just a few hundred dollars, then that doesn't matter, but if it is more, then I really must do what is right, and pay back the extra to you. Sometimes diamonds can be wrongly valued by as much as five or ten million, and I certainly don't want to swindle you. My husband was always very fussy about everything being done the correct way.

'Ten million, wow, that is a lot,' mumbled Oleg.

'Yes, it is indeed. Just tell me which account number I should pay the money to, and I shall arrange the rest.' Martha pulled out her notebook, adjusted her spectacles and leaned her head to one side. 'You do have a company, I assume. So give me the name, and your bank and account number, please.'

Give her his account number? Oleg hesitated. But if the old lady was so keen to do things the right way, then it would feel wrong not to do as she said. And, after all, it was better that the money ended up in his account and didn't just vanish into the wrong one. He dug out his wallet, took out a business card, turned it over and wrote down the information on the back.

'Yes, I have heard that diamonds can be very hard to value sometimes. So thoughtful of you,' he said politely and handed her the card.

'Thank you! Well, all you have to do is take over the boat.'

'But the papers?' said Anna-Greta and pointed at Martha's flowery handbag.

'Oh yes, of course,' said Martha.

The Russians nodded understandingly while Martha fumbled with her handbag to find the certificate of ownership and the contract which Christina had so skilfully managed to copy. She pulled out the papers, signed them (with her usual illegible handwriting) and handed them over to the Russians.

'Here is the documentation,' she said with a bountiful smile.

When the Russians had quickly browsed through them, she discreetly added an extra page without anyone noticing and then stapled that paper together with the others. Then she asked Oleg to sign each and every sheet just like she had heard that one should do with contracts.

'Now the motor yacht is yours,' she said, pulling the briefcases towards her. 'Is it all right if you take over the boat tomorrow, early morning?'

'Early tomorrow? Yes, fine.'

'Because we would like to sleep here tonight as it has been a long day and we are terribly tired.'

'Yes, we are old, after all,' Anna-Greta filled in.

Oleg and Boris exchanged glances. This wasn't exactly how business was usually conducted, but one night more or less didn't make any difference. Besides, they were in a decidedly good mood after having bought the boat at such a cheap price.

'Naturally,' said Oleg.

'No problems,' Boris added.

'You could sleep on board too, of course,' said Martha with her warmest and most accommodating smile, and she noticed how the others in the League of Pensioners gave a start. Because this was not part of the plan. But Martha looked so determined – as she always did when she had made her own, absolutely inflexible decision. Brains gave her a prod in the ribs.

'My dear, what are you up to?'

'Just wait and you'll see!' she whispered and winked. Then she winked at Rake, who obediently filled the champagne glasses.

'Cheers, then!' exclaimed Martha and she raised her glass. 'Nothing beats a good business deal. We are all happy, aren't we?'

The Russians nodded and clinked glasses, while Brains and the others wanted to leave as quickly as possible. They couldn't understand why Martha stayed on at the crime scene and even wanted to spend the night there. At any moment, the boat could be reported missing and then people would start looking for it. But she seemed unusually calm.

'Martha, whatever are you up to?' Brains asked again.

'Trust me. We had an extremely good plan, but the new one is darned well better! Come with me, and I'll tell you more.'

54

The League of Pensioners had retired to Anna-Greta's cabin on the middle deck, while the Russians stayed on in the saloon and played cards. By this time, Oleg and his companions had become so noisy that it was hard to have a conversation. Besides, Martha was anxious to make sure that none of them would hear a single word of what she was going to say. Not even in Swedish. So the cosy cabin – or bedroom, as she called it – with its duvets, curtains and cushions was absolutely perfect. Martha looked round at the friends and said with a very quiet but clear voice:

'Oleg and Boris don't pay any tax. No tax at all, even though they are so rich. And besides, they called me an old hag. Gaga and senile, they said, the nerve! They are slimy scoundrels of the very worst sort! How dare they! You don't insult an elderly lady and go unpunished.'

Anna-Greta and Christina nodded in agreement and looked really angry.

'So horribly inconsiderate. Idiots! One simply can't behave like that,' said Christina.

'Without us old ladies, the world would come to an end.

Culture and social life would collapse and there would only be football and computer games left,' Anna-Greta said.

'Usch, don't exaggerate! Without us men, the world would come to an end, just so you know. All this talk of old ladies. No, young, pretty dames – now that is something!' Rake said, and the very next moment he got a hard kick on the shin.

'That's quite enough!' hissed Christina, and Martha screwed up her face like a raisin. She gave him a look that could have cut a diamond. But it had no effect on Rake.

'But get to the point, then, Martha. You had something important to tell us.'

'Oleg and Boris behaved so disgracefully, you can't imagine. Talked about me as if I was just worth so little,' Martha went on and she showed a minimal gap between her thumb and index finger.

'You worth so little? No, the bastards!' said Rake.

'It is dreadful to grow old and hear all this shit. No, I won't stand it! So I thought we would deal with Oleg and co and their ageist attitude towards elderly ladies. They made me so angry that I got lots of energy, so now I've thought up a plan. A devilish plan, I can tell you. A new robbery, one might say.'

'Oh no, no, not another crime! You are much nicer when you aren't so energetic,' Brains groaned.

'Around five hundred million kronor, that's how much we could get,' said Martha, looking rather proud.

'You what! Another five hundred million!' Anna-Greta yelled so that her hearing aid fell onto the floor.

'Now listen to me. I'm thinking about that transponder up there on the roof. That shows where we are, doesn't it? I mean where Bielke's yacht is.'

'Yes, right, but I turned it off so that nobody can see where we are,' said Nils.

'Exactly. But sometimes it can be a good idea if somebody *can* trace the vessel too. So, Brains, can you go and fetch it please?'

'Now you must jolly well explain what you're on about,' exclaimed Rake.

'Well, it's like this. We'll need the transponder for our new coup and the Russians must not be allowed to see anything.'

The members of the League of Pensioners stared uncomprehendingly at Martha and shook their heads. What had happened? Was Martha going completely crazy? An embarrassing silence followed. None of them did anything, nobody reacted. But in their heads, there were lots of thoughts. Then Martha leaned forward and whispered something into Brains's ear. The others saw that she was telling him something, but couldn't hear much more than: 'Please, Brains, can you just do what I'm asking you? You'll see . . .'

Martha and Brains continued to talk for a while and then suddenly he looked remarkably alert and grabbed hold of Nils.

'Right, now I get what she means. But we must hurry! We must go up onto the roof straight away. It's important, of really colossal importance!'

Nils tried to protest but when he saw that Brains was going to go up himself anyway, he had no choice but to follow along. He didn't want Rake's good friend to trip over and hurt himself out there in the dark.

'All right, then,' he mumbled, but on the way he went into the storeroom and fetched two head torches and a toolbox.

Then the two men took the lift up to the upper deck. Once there, they stopped for a few seconds so that they could hear the Russians, but the only sound was a distant bawling. They nodded to each other, put on the head torches and opened the door out towards the roof.

'It ought to be somewhere here,' mumbled Nils, turning on the head torch and looking around. The lights from the Cannes seafront glimmered on the water, and above the sea, stars were clearly visible. There was a new moon too. The two men crouched under the radar and carefully made their way towards the bridge.

'What a bit of luck, look over there!' said Brains after a minute or so when the beam from his torch fell on something rectangular in metal just above the bridge. Nils nodded, sought out a big screwdriver and spanner and set to work. It was a bit awkward to get at everything and the screws and bolts had been pulled very tight, but soon he had succeeded in loosening the yacht's transponder from its base. The men wrapped it in a pullover which they then put inside Brains's sports bag before they returned to the others.

'Here it is, the transponder, an AIS Match Mate!' said Brains, pleased with himself, and he pointed at his bag. 'Mission accomplished!'

'You are fantastic, but now I'm sure we would all like to see that thingamajig too, wouldn't we?' said Martha. Upon which the men lifted it out of the bag and put it at the end of Anna-Greta's bed. The thingamajig, painted grey and with dials and buttons, looked rather boring and insignificant. But it was evidently very important.

'Um, that's a great box.' Rake hummed and studied the

mysterious contraption which hadn't existed back in the days when he went to sea.

'It looks like a vinyl-record player,' Anna-Greta pointed out and carefully poked the apparatus with her index finger. 'Does it play music?'

'No.' Brains smiled and patted the box. 'This is the smartest thing on the seas since radar arrived. The apparatus sends and receives radio signals automatically and then other ships and port authorities can see where you are. They can keep track of the ships' speed, course and position.'

'Crikey. If they are looking at us now, they will be very surprised,' mumbled Rake and he pointed at the bed.

'They'll think the ship has run aground and collided with a bed,' giggled Christina.

'Crikey,' sighed Rake, *'But what are we doing with a transponder on the bed?'*

'Well, this is what I have in mind,' Martha began and she looked really pleased with herself. 'When the Russians turn on their AIS, nothing will happen because we have taken it. OK? Neither the authorities nor ships in the area will have a clue as to where Bielke's yacht *Aurora Four* has gone, and it will take a bit of time before they react.'

Anna-Greta's eyes lit up and she gave a shrill whistle.

'A stroke of genius!' she cried out.

'We have a plan and if we can pull this off we can give health care at least another five hundred million,' said Brains looking important.

'Exactly. Me and Brains, we have talked this over,' Martha went on, and she squeezed his hand as a sign of mutual understanding. (Coming up with solutions together with this

413

man was the best thing she knew, and now Brains had that ingenious and satisfied look about him that he normally only had when he had thought up a new invention.)

'As I've said before, bank robberies only give us pocket money,' Anna-Greta cut in, now beginning to accustom herself to larger sums.

'Yes, but if this plan is going to work, we must sneak away from the Russians. And it would be best to do that right away,' said Martha.

'But my God! Oleg and Boris are Russian oligarchs. We must be careful. It isn't dangerous, is it?' Christina took a deep breath and wrung her hands so much that they almost hurt.

'Not if we behave just like normal, then they won't suspect anything,' said Martha. 'But now they will get their just deserts! They only have themselves to blame. Tax dodgers and bullies of women. No, mark my words, nobody insults an old lady and gets away with it!'

'Amen!' exclaimed Rake.

'Now you won't let your emotions gain the upper hand, I trust, Martha? Then it is so easy to lose focus,' Anna-Greta warned.

'Oh no, they are just going to get a little punch on the nose, that's all,' answered Martha. And then she asked for silence, leaned forward and presented her plan.

55

The League of Pensioners had talked things over and were now only too well aware that they had a very arduous task before them if Martha's plan was going to be successful. And the worst of it all was that they mustn't be off their guard or fall asleep during the coming hours because that would jeopardize everything. Now it was one o'clock in the morning and they must stay awake until dawn. This was rather a contrast to life in old people's homes where you were tucked up in bed at seven in the evening. Or as Rake had said: 'Not only are we going to commit crimes, but now we must also do them in the middle of the night too!'

'We are developing and becoming all the more polished,' Martha considered.

'First and foremost, we must stay awake until the Russians have fallen asleep because the briefcases are still there in the saloon,' said Anna-Greta.

'Oh yes, of course,' muttered Martha. 'I almost forgot that detail. On the other hand, the contents of the briefcases is ours and we have earned it honourably.'

'But won't it look a bit suspicious if we just fetch them and then disappear?'

'Agreed,' said Brains. 'There ought really to be a retiring age for robbers. So much can get screwed up just because you forget. Mind you, we would have avoided all this if people could afford to live on their pension.'

'True. And robbers are in the same situation as women. None of us can afford to retire. So criminals, stick to your last!' said Martha.

The members of the League of Pensioners kept themselves awake by playing bridge even though their eyelids wanted to flop down all the time, and Rake was so tired that he didn't even have the energy to cheat. But in the end, things became quiet down in the saloon and Christina was sent down on a scouting mission. When she came back, her cheeks were bright red.

'Oleg and the others are asleep!'

'Excellent. Gather your things together and I'll follow with the briefcases,' said Martha. And while the others collected their belongings, Martha went as quietly as she could down to the saloon to fetch their booty.

When she reached the room, she saw the Russians lying sprawled over the table with their heads resting on their arms – all except Oleg, who lay stretched out on the sofa. His mouth was wide open and he snored loudly. There were empty bottles everywhere and sticky playing cards next to the table together with piles of betting chips that had fallen onto the floor. Martha shook her head. Evidently they had been playing for money too. What decadence! She straightened her back and walked in as ordinary and nonchalant a manner as she could (in case one of them was spying on her behind half-closed eyes) up to the briefcases. Then she stood still a while and listened before she carefully lifted them up and went towards the door. She tiptoed out and had just reached the deck when she heard a call from down on the quay.

'*Attention! Vos papiers s'il vous plaît!*'

A young man in a T-shirt and shorts and with a clipboard in his hand was staring up at the boat looking very important. Yes, of course, the harbour authorities had staff who went round on the quays checking. Nils had said that you could only be moored by the quay for one hour, maximum, then you must move off or anchor further out. Or, of course, you could go into the harbour office and pay the harbour fee and some other stuff. But then they would check your certificate of ownership and lots of other papers at the same time. Martha hesitated for a moment or two, then she walked up to the railing.

'*Excusez-nous!* Us, that is,' she said, putting down the briefcases and pointing at herself. '*Nous avons eu des problems, mais maintenant, voilà* (that sounded very French) our captain will sail any minute.'

'*Il faut aller maintenant!*' said the pompous young man.

'*Naturellement!* Right away, *tout de suite, immédiatement, direct,* swisch, swisch!' said Martha, ever ready to oblige. She heard the Russians begin to wake up in the saloon. Now they must make their getaway as quickly as possible. She bumped into Nils on the stairs.

'Nils, we must leave the quay and anchor out there straight away. They want our papers.'

'Damn and blast, now that,' he said, and turned back up the stairs. 'Rake, can you man the engine room?' he called out and hurried up to the bridge.

417

'Aye, aye, captain,' answered his father, feeling the adrenaline boost straight away. Action stations. Now they must get the engines going immediately and gently manoeuvre the boat out to where they could anchor. And they must do that without turning any of the other boats by the quay into matchwood! Brains stood there at a loss until he realized what he had to do. Cast off the ropes of course! He took the lift down but got off on the wrong floor, and when finally he got it right, he heard how the ropes landed in the water with a heavy splash. Martha had asked the young man on the quay to help. Another boat was evidently on the way in.

The engines started up, Nils inched the throttle forward and Bielke's boat slowly headed out into the darkness. When they reached the roadstead, Nils let the boat lie at anchor. This time Nils managed it well but just as they dropped the anchor the door to the bridge was suddenly opened.

'What are you doing with my boat?' shouted Oleg, angry as hell. Nils quickly rolled up his sleeves so that his anchor tattoo became visible on his wrist.

'Harbour authorities,' he explained, and threw out his hands. 'Sorry. But don't worry. The crew is on its way.'

Then Oleg looked a bit calmer, but Nils could see that he had been drinking and needed to hold on to the compass to stand steadily. Then Martha came rushing in with her mobile in her hand.

'Our captain,' she said, and pointed to the mobile. 'The crew, you know, will be here any minute. So we shall go and fetch them. Pick them up, you know,' she said as naturally as she could and just as if the entire crew was included in the sale. 'Don't you worry. We will organize this. My husband always said that you should take things easy and enjoy life. So don't you worry, go back to sleep.'

Oleg was intelligent and had a sharp mind, but it was the middle of the night and he had drunk too much to allow his brain to function properly. In such situations, he took orders from others and didn't think so much himself.

'Ah, yes, captain, good!' he said simply. He shrugged his shoulders and returned to the saloon. He had lost his Ferrari in the last round of poker and was very keen to win it back again. Martha glanced at Nils.

'You had better open the ramp. We need the motorboat NOW, the red one, you know. And don't forget any important papers or other stuff. We must leave within five minutes.'

With those words, Martha went off and fetched Brains and the others who were groggy with tiredness and were simply longing to be able to go to sleep.

'To the motorboat, hurry now. And don't forget your things!'

Tired and somewhat unfocussed, they picked up not only their own things but also a bit of this and that they happened to think might come in useful. Above all, blankets and cushions so that they could have a nap on the way back to Saint-Tropez. And Anna-Greta took the Chagall painting too because she had always had a soft spot for the artist. But since she was ashamed of her art coup she didn't say anything to the others but simply slipped the painting into her backpack.

'I had been madly trying to think up a good excuse to take the motorboat and leave the yacht without arousing suspicion,' said Martha when she caught up with Brains. 'And then

419

we were helped by the French port authorities. *Voilà*. Now everything will work like we wanted!'

'Let's hope so!' answered Brains and he sneaked his hand into hers. Together they hurried hand-in-hand all the way down to the ramp where the motorboat was waiting. But just as they were about to climb aboard, Martha stopped and turned red in the face.

'Oh, forgive me, Brains. The briefcases!' She had forgotten them in Anna-Greta's cabin.

'I've already carried them down,' said Brains smiling.

The water lay dark and black in the bay and the motorboat could steer right out through the open stern. If we had only been a little younger, we could have taken the jet ski and had a bit of fun too, Martha thought, strangely enough actually realizing her limitations. Nils, who had had the presence of mind to check that the petrol tank was full, started the engine. At the second attempt it started up with a low humming, and he nodded to Rake, who cast off. They were on their way.

'OK, now let's get out of here!'

'No, wait a moment,' said Martha. 'We mustn't forget the most important thing.' And then she pulled out two cans of paint spray. The white was the same shade as the colour of the boat, the black of the same make as the lettering of *Aurora 4*. Christina nodded and, as they went out, Nils manoeuvred the motorboat towards the stern so that Christina could reach. He brought the little boat up close so that it prevented anyone from seeing what they were up to, from both the sea and from up on deck, and Christina was quick.

Like the pro she was, she rapidly painted over the number '4' in the boat's name and replaced it with a '5'. With her head torch and a little paintbrush, she also improved the lettering of the number so that it exactly matched in size and angle with the lettering of *Aurora*. She pulled back a little and checked the result. With the quick-drying paint she had changed the boat's name to *Aurora 5*, just like it said in the Russians' certificate of ownership.

'Finished! Sometimes things actually go better if you are in a hurry,' she said, pleased. She signalled to the others that they could leave. They slowly slipped away from the motor yacht. For the sake of appearances, Nils steered in towards quay number five where the hypothetical crew would soon come aboard. But when they were almost there, he pretended that the engine had stalled and the boat started to drift. The League of Pensioners waved their arms and pretended to be desperate, while the boat drifted further and further away from the quay. The harbour disappeared in the background and when they were sufficiently far away from both the piers and the eyes, Nils started the engine again. Then he opened the throttle to max. The gang of pensioners still had one extremely important task to finish off. And to do that, they must return to Saint-Tropez.

56

While Nils drove the motorboat at full speed towards Saint-Tropez, Martha gathered the gang of pensioners together to further explain to the sleepy members what awaited them.

'Sorry to have to rush you like this. But the transponder can be our fortune.' She pointed at the little apparatus which Brains had on his lap.

'Yes, you have said that,' said Rake. 'So fortune in life is a transponder, you mean? Indeed! You go from clarity to clarity!'

Martha pretended not to have heard, but went through the plans in detail.

'Do you remember that derelict ship just near the entrance to the harbour in Saint-Tropez, the Panama boat, you know?' Martha went on, ignoring Rake. 'The dreadful vessel that we thought was an appalling eyesore.'

Everyone nodded.

'It will be sunk on Monday.'

'Don't say we are going to steal that wreck too,' sighed Rake.

'No, quite the opposite. We are going to rejoice when the old tub is sunk. With Bielke's transponder on the roof.'

Anna-Greta whistled shrilly and then burst out in such a loud horsey laugh that they all put their hands over their ears.

'Aha, now I understand,' she said, and she looked decidedly content. 'So we put the transponder on the Panama tub and when the boat sinks, the authorities will think that Bielke's boat has disappeared, right?'

'Exactly. When the Panama boat sinks with the transponder and all, the authorities can suddenly no longer see "Bielke's boat" on their screens. It disappears and will never turn up again. And then we report the boat as stolen . . .' Martha went on.

'. . . and get the insurance money,' Anna-Greta filled in, her eyes glistening with pleasure. She had already understood the plan and smiled widely. 'You did fix the papers, didn't you, Martha?'

'Yes, and the Russians didn't notice anything. Hopefully it will be a while before they realize they have been conned.'

'Tell us again, how will that work?' Rake asked, not really remembering.

'The Russians bought the yacht *Aurora Five*, while we have the papers for *Aurora Four*, which is insured. It is the tiny details that make the difference,' said Martha, looking really satisfied with herself.

'You know what, we ought to get out some wafer biscuits and the cloudberry liqueur right away,' said Christina.

'Hang on, we mustn't celebrate until everything is tied up,' Rake said. 'Lots of things can happen.'

'Absolutely,' Anna-Greta agreed, realizing that they didn't have the money yet.

'The problem will be to try to fix the transponder on the Panama wreck without anyone seeing. I suppose that will be my job,' said Nils with a sigh, without taking his eyes off the seaway. At any moment at all, motorboats could turn up out there and be dangerously intrusive. A murmur of agreement could be heard from the others.

'Yes, that should be done as soon as it gets light,' Brains said. 'And on Monday we will activate the transponder with my remote control and then we drive to the airport. It should work.'

Martha nodded and the others went along with it too. And Anna-Greta couldn't refrain from contentedly stating that she had the certificate of ownership, the contract and all the boat papers. Everything they would need to get the insurance money.

'Take care of those papers. They are the original documents; the Russians only got nice copies, Christina. And Oleg was unusually careless when he signed. He didn't notice that it said *Aurora Five* and not *Aurora Four*,' said Martha.

'So we own *Aurora Four*,' Rake summarized, and he had to admit that Martha really had thought this through.

'Exactly, and soon the Panama wreck will disappear with Bielke's transponder and Lloyds will lose five hundred million kronor at least. Tiddlypom!' Martha sounded very satisfied.

'You are very sharp, Martha dear,' Brains said, and there was a tone of admiration in his voice.

'Oh no, not like you,' said Martha, diplomatically as women do, taking his hand in hers. 'And then I added that extra page in the contract. Oleg and Boris will get a shock. You should never call elderly ladies "old hags" and "senile". That can cause you a lot of trouble.'

'That's enough, you make me nervous!' said Rake.

When Oleg woke up the next day, he discovered that it was unusually silent. He had a throbbing headache and it took a while before he realized where he was. Martha, and the boat purchase, yes that was it. Yes, his skilful bargaining had been too much for her! He had bought the super yacht for a give-away price! He smiled contentedly. Now he would fix some coffee and something tasty for breakfast. He looked around. There ought to be something edible on the boat. Perhaps Martha could knock up a good omelette for them. He got up and stretched his arms above his head. Boris and the other two were still asleep. He thought about waking them, but decided it would be nice to be on his own for a while. Apart from the sound of the sea, it was completely silent and you couldn't hear Martha's bossy voice anywhere. Presumably, she and the others were still in bed asleep in some of the cabins on the upper deck. He wandered around for a few minutes and felt the delightful thrill of having become the owner of such a fantastic boat. Then he remembered the jet ski and that little motorboat. He hadn't had a proper look at them. Whistling, he took the lift down to the lower deck and discovered that the motorboat had gone. Oh yes. Martha had said that they would go and fetch the crew. And that was the last he had seen of the gang of old pensioners, when they'd been heading towards the quay. But they hadn't come back . . . it seemed to be taking an awful long time; had something delayed them? Whatever, they would come back sooner or later and then he would have a long talk with the captain and the members of the crew. He wanted to make sure they were capable of taking the boat to Cyprus.

He went and woke up the others and while they waited he made breakfast for everybody. Thankfully, the fridge was packed full with delicacies and he succeeded in producing a delicious morning feast with omelette, croissants, fruit, juice and lots of coffee. Oleg had found beer and headache pills too, which rounded off the breakfast, and then they each took a sun lounger and went up on deck. They had spent several intensive days at the conference and it was nice to relax a little. For a brief moment he was worried that something might have happened to the old lady, but even though she sometimes got a bit dizzy, she was in fairly good trim. No, he was worrying unnecessarily. Any time now, they would come back. Quite simply, something must have delayed the crew. He found some sun lotion next to the pool, rubbed it on and put his hand up to his head. He had drunk a lot of vodka last night. Perhaps he ought to take another beer, or why not a pick-me-up from the bar counter. But no, it was probably best to have a calm talk with the crew first. If only his headache would go. You felt so slow-witted and listless the day after some heavy drinking. The next time, he would be more careful and drink a bit less. Oleg closed his eyes and stretched out on the sun lounger. Life wasn't bad at all. He and Boris had managed to bargain and reduced the price by twenty million dollars! Good God! Old ladies shouldn't do business! But other people's misfortune was his own good fortune!

*

The League of Pensioners had now reached Saint-Tropez and Rake kept the motorboat in position so that Nils could climb up onto the abandoned Panama old tub. His legs felt like jelly and when he was on his way up he was afraid he might slip and fall. Some marine organisms had established themselves on deck and in some places there were large patches of oil. The stairs were perforated with rust and there was no railing. Even though he was only wearing a T-shirt, he was sweating. At this time of the morning, it wasn't so hot, but the climb up from the motorboat and having to carry tools and the transponder, that was hard work. Now he was almost there, but he must still fasten the transponder properly so that it would work. Martha, of course, had said that it was a simple job to do, but running up and down on bridges and roofs, manoeuvring large motor yachts and even being expected to be a fitter and take part in an insurance fraud – all that made considerable demands on a man.

He wiped some drops of sweat off his upper lip and pressed the transponder closer to his chest. Just one careless step and Bielke's AIS would end up in the water. And with it five hundred million kronor – well, at any rate, if you could believe Anna-Greta. She had worked out that figure as being the amount they would get from the insurance, and they might even get more. But first the signal must be sent so that the harbour authorities would know that *Aurora 4* was out at sea and then could also register that the motor yacht had disappeared suddenly. But then, of course, God forbid that he should drop the transponder. This should have been a job for two men up here, somebody who could help a bit, but now he must do it all himself. What would happen if he slipped? On the other hand, Rake or one of the others in the League of Pensioners would not exactly be of much help if he did slip.

Two more sets of stairs to go. If only he could find a suitable place above the bridge wing where he could fasten the apparatus with screws, then all would be OK. Perhaps by the railing next to the radar? Here, the transponder wouldn't be visible from the water, but the signals could reach every point of the compass. Excellent! Bielke's AIS was not impossibly heavy. In fact, it wasn't much bigger than an old-fashioned video or a vinyl-record player. It ought to work. But just this very minute it felt as if it weighed several tons. Had his dad and the others realized that they had actually given him the responsibility for five hundred million or so? Why ever had he agreed to do it?

Rake and his friends were always thinking up all sorts of mischief, but it was often Nils himself who had to carry out the tasks. And as soon as he had finished one job, the gang came up with something new. Those pensioners were far too energetic and really rather troublesome. On the other hand, he had to admit that now he had a new life, his days were filled with activity and it was actually more fun than his old job. Going to sea had felt like a challenge when he was young, but now being a seaman often meant monotonous and repetitive work, and you hardly ever could go ashore. So really, he didn't have anything against all these new and weird tasks he must carry out, it was just that the responsibility for the transponder felt almost overpowering. They could have refrained from telling him that so much money was at stake. It wasn't until he had agreed to do the job that they had informed him that the transponder would show where Bielke's boat was before the radio signals vanished and the Panama old tub sunk. An insurance fraud, five hundred million kronor. He almost dropped the apparatus just thinking about it.

He turned round with a sigh. The sun was about to rise and the sea was calm. The old fishing village Saint-Tropez was still asleep and no other boats were in sight. There was only Rake in the motorboat down below, waiting for everything to be ready. Nils took a deep breath and hurried up the stairs. He skilfully avoided a plastic bucket, a rusty pipe, an open chest with old life jackets and some old boxes on the intermediate deck and finally reached the stairs up to the uppermost deck. Quickly he took the last steps and was at last out on the deck above the bridge. Carefully he walked along the rusty and slippery roof. Where the hell could he fasten the apparatus? There was rust and steel everywhere. Luckily, Christina had camouflaged the transponder with some old paint, rust and a bit of dirt so that it would look like a part of the Panama shipwreck. But the AIS must be screwed down; yes, it must be firmly attached so that it would sink with the ship.

On the starboard side, some boats were now approaching in the distance. He felt a growing panic. No, he must decide where the wretched thing should be fastened; he couldn't dither any longer. The bag with his tools rubbed against his legs, and the transponder now felt even heavier. He looked around and right next to the railing he discovered a wooden beam which looked stable. He went up to it, put the transponder down and the bag of tools too. He ought to be able to nail the blasted thing to that beam. He checked in his bag.

Yes, there were some long nails and a hammer. He quickly grabbed them and was just about to start when Rake shouted out:

'The police!'

Nils stood up quickly and saw that one of the boats he had noticed earlier was now on its way towards them. And yes, it was indeed a police launch, it said *GENDARME* on the side. Damn! Oh well, he might just manage it. Quick as he could, he picked up the hammer, put some ten-inch nails in his mouth and pushed the bag to one side so that he could get at the wooden beam. But that was when it happened. The bag bumped into the transponder which then slowly slid towards the edge and tipped over it. Without a sound, Bielke's AIS fell down onto the deck below. There was no thud, no crash – there was just silence.

'What the hell!' Nils roared when he discovered the faux pas. Horrified, he got up, looked over the edge and stared down. The apparatus wasn't on the deck below but must have ended up in the water. Er, five hundred million gone? No, that doesn't happen in real life, only in films. And there was no way he could tell anybody what had happened, he couldn't even tell God almighty himself!

'Hurry, the police can see us,' Rake called out from down in the motorboat.

Nils was sweating profusely, and didn't know what he should do. But a quick glance at the approaching police launch made him decide.

'I'm coming,' he shouted out. He hung the bag over his shoulder and managed to make his way down the stairs and then down the rope ladder. But when he reached the motorboat he didn't say a word. What was there to say when you had just lost five hundred million?

When Rake and Nils returned to the hotel, the rest of the League of Pensioners had checked out and were standing there waiting. They had booked rooms at a smaller and less fancy hotel outside Saint-Tropez where they would stay until the Panama tub was towed out to sea. But first Brains must get the transponder turned on with the remote control so that they really would be certain that everything was working before they went on board the plane to Stockholm.

For the next twenty-four hours all of the members of the League of Pensioners found it extremely difficult to sleep and they ate almost nothing. Christina went around handing out fruit and fresh organic salad but nobody felt like eating anything. And Nils suffered the most dreadful anguish. He knew that he ought to tell them what had happened, but he didn't dare. And deep inside, he nourished a wafer-thin hope that he might not have to tell them the truth. Because when Brains used the remote control he would of course think that there was something wrong with it, yes, that there was a technical problem that stopped the signal from reaching the transponder. And then nobody would ever discover what had really happened. But Nils was ashamed of his own thoughts. You shouldn't behave like that. But the alternative? Well, that was ten times worse!

57

The harbour master in Saint-Tropez was making a last round on board the Panama-registered ship *M/S Maria Bianca*. The notorious old tub would at last be sunk. For almost a year, they had been trying to get rid of the rusty monstrosity from the harbour, but without success. If the mayor hadn't personally got involved, it probably wouldn't have been possible at all. But the Philippine crew had long since abandoned the boat and the harbour authorities had not found a responsible owner. Nobody had been prepared to pay to break up the vessel, let alone to sink it. But now it had gone so far that the boat had become a sanitary problem and, besides, everyone was afraid that the damned hulk would sink in the middle of the harbour. Now at last the old derelict vessel would be towed out to deeper water. But first he would have to check that all the oil tanks were empty and that there was nothing left on board that could harm the environment. He sighed over having to do this dirty work, but the tugs were ready and waiting so it was best that he did it as quickly as possible.

Harbour master Hardy started at the very top and then systematically worked his way down through the vessel. He had reached the middle deck when it suddenly struck him that they ought to salvage the fire extinguishers and life jackets that were still there. They would always come in useful. He went out on the deck and almost tripped over a plastic bucket and a rusty pipe before reaching the chest with life jackets. But, *mon Dieu!* Those, too, looked in very bad condition. He got hold of the one on top. The cloth was faded, almost rotten, and when he gave it a little pull it immediately tore. He dug down a little deeper in the chest and pulled out another jacket. This had a wide neck, was made of old-fashioned cork and the orange cloth had become faded and was very delicate. He tried pulling that and again the result was that it ripped. No, there was nothing to salvage here and one could just as well forget the fire extinguishers. They wouldn't be any use either. He was just about to throw the jacket back into the chest when he caught sight of something that gleamed. It looked like a transponder of some sort. Had the Philippine crew been smuggling technical equipment? He lifted up the apparatus but then saw that it was an ordinary AIS Match Mate that must have been used on board the vessel. It looked rusty and damaged and when he poked it he got rust on his hands. No, damn it, that was worthless, it wouldn't work anyway. He put it down on the deck and hurried on. Half an hour later, he had gone through the whole vessel and checked everything. Not a single screw on this old tub was worth keeping. He brushed the dirt off his uniform, pulled out his mobile and gave the tugboat captain the go-ahead. Then he asked to be picked up.

While the Panama boat was being towed out by the tugs, Hardy drank coffee with the crew on board and played a hand of poker. And a few hours later, when the coast was only visible as a light grey haze on the horizon, he gave the order to sink the *Maria Bianca*. Two seamen went on board and opened the sea valves, while other crew members detached the towing cables. Then they picked up the two men and steered away from the sinking vessel. Harbour master Hardy and the others went up on deck and stood by the railings for a long time watching as the old tub slowly sank.

'What a wreck, not worth a cent,' he said with a snort. But he was quite wrong about that.

The League of Pensioners had had a restless night. The cheap hotel they had chosen had been filled with noisy guests who had partied during the night and none of the oldies had got much sleep. Anyway, the members of the gang of pensioners found it hard to relax. When they had heard that the Panama ship would be sunk in the morning, they had packed all their things and were ready to leave for the airport. But first they must activate the transponder. With dry eyes and after an extra cup of coffee, they took a taxi down to the harbour to check out the vessel.

When the taxi had stopped and they had gone out along the quay, they saw two tugs by the derelict ship and realized that they wouldn't have to wait much longer. Then they walked out to the end of one of the jetties to get a better view of what was happening. To be on the safe side, none of them was using a wheeled walker or anything else that might help people to recognize them, and Anna-Greta and Martha were wearing wigs. Red hair this time. Brains and Rake had

434

dressed in sailing clothes and wore fashionable boat shoes. They blended in well.

'Righto. All we have to do is activate Bielke's motor yacht, *Aurora Four*, come!' said Brains with a grin. He held up the remote control and pointed it at the Panama ship. He pressed a few times, checked the batteries and pressed again. But Bielke's transponder didn't react.

'Damn and blast, that's weird!' he exclaimed in surprise, and he didn't usually swear. 'I haven't got any contact. It's just dead. Oh, God, I can't get the transponder to start up!'

'Of course you can. It worked earlier,' said Christina.

'Yes, come on now, Brains, try again!' Martha urged. 'A lot is at stake.'

'Five hundred million kronor is not exactly peanuts,' Anna-Greta pointed out.

Brains checked the batteries, raised and lowered the remote and tried going to the very end of the jetty to get contact. But he looked angry when he came back.

'Nothing works! I don't understand the reason for that.'

'Perhaps the reception is poor today,' said Nils trying to look as normal as possible. As if he was innocent and as if five hundred million didn't mean anything at all.

'But it worked before when I tested it,' Brains insisted.

'Of course, but a lot could have happened since then,' said Nils, cautiously, and when he said this he wasn't actually lying.

'What if it was the rust paint,' exclaimed Christina, wringing her hands in despair. 'What if I have painted away five hundred million!'

'No, no, you can't have done that,' Rake tried to console

her, and he gave her a little hug. 'I watched when you painted it, and you were very careful indeed. You didn't splash paint anywhere.'

They all became silent and stood there a long time, confused and numb, which you could hardly avoid being if you had just lost five hundred million. What should they do now? Tired and dejected they looked out towards the vessel. Up on the deck a uniformed man was talking on a telephone. He waved and then climbed down the rope ladder and boarded one of the tugs. The crew attached towing cables and after a while the two tugs turned towards the horizon. Soon the sound of their engines grew louder, the cables tightened and they started moving off.

'Hmm,' said Brains, 'I shall go right to the end of the pier and see if I can get contact there.'

He walked as fast as he could and when he got to the very end and again pointed the remote control at the vessel, something happened. It was as if the transponder had woken up after a long, long sleep, and sort of stretched and come to life. At first the signal was weak, but when the vessel out there turned a little, the apparatus reacted more strongly. Brains cheered. Now the harbour authorities and other vessels could see that Bielke's motor yacht was leaving Saint-Tropez and going out to sea. There was of course a minimal risk that somebody would discover that the transponder was now on the Panama wreck instead of a luxury yacht, but everybody was fully occupied in towing the old tub out of the harbour and making sure that it didn't collide with the boats round about. Before anyone would have had time to digest the information, Bielke's yacht would be far out at sea and then, a moment later, it would suddenly vanish. Sunk and off the screens forever. Brains hurried back to the others, beaming with joy.

'Somebody must have moved the transponder because just now I got in contact with it,' he said. 'Everything is working. Now let's be off!'

'Did you get it started? Goodness, you're a genius,' mumbled Nils, looking frightened. So the transponder had not fallen into the sea but had landed somewhere on the deck where he hadn't seen it.

'Pah, engines and other technical things, they're easy, but don't try me on computers,' answered Brains.

'Right then, next stop the airport,' Martha ordered – but not until she had given Brains a big hug and praised him for the most valuable contribution in the history of the League of Pensioners. And while the Panama boat with Bielke's transponder was en route to its fate at the bottom of the sea, a shocked Nils arranged two taxis. Then they all went off to Nice airport.

58

The entire group boarded the aircraft, made themselves comfortable in their seats and slept all the way to Stockholm. And then they had some luck, because there is no other way to describe their progress through Customs at Stockholm Arlanda airport. To be on the safe side, Christina had bought a little children's roulette kit with lots of pretend banknotes. She had also gone to a souvenir shop and bought some bags of coral, pretty little stones and shells which she mixed with the real diamonds – just in case – but everything went well without any troublesome questions. Christina explained this by telling her friends that she had swayed her hips a bit more, and that had evidently been to good effect.

'Hmm,' said Rake and Brains in unison, and then they mumbled something about that not making much difference nowadays, because the Customs officials were used to it. They added the final bit of the explanation at the very last moment, because what they really thought (and neither of them dared say it out loud) was that hip-swaying ladies in their late seventies didn't have the same effect as younger talent.

And then there was the briefcase with the dollar banknotes. For some reason, a Customs official became interested in it.

'Can I have a look?' he asked, stopping Martha.

'Monopoly!' Martha cried out shrilly, and she pulled out some dollars. 'I know, I shouldn't gamble but what does it matter as long as it's pretend money. Do you want some?' And she smiled so suavely that the official simply couldn't help but smile too.

'What? Er no, no,' he said and waved her on.

When the gang of pensioners had finally tottered out from the airport terminal, they were relieved and shaken, but also confused and in their rush they happened to get into an illegal taxi. So when they reached Djursholm the driver charged them an obscenely high price; it was actually about ten times as much as what it ought to have cost.

'Yes, right,' said Martha, and she started to look for her purse in her handbag. 'I'll pay, I'll deal with this,' she told her friends in a tired voice and asked them to get out and take their luggage. When that was done, she arduously manoeuvred herself out of the front seat and closed the door. Then she rolled up a bundle of banknotes and gave them to the driver through the side window.

'Here you are, and that includes a tip. I might have paid a bit too much, but you are really one of the best taxi drivers I have ever travelled with!' she said in a friendly tone. She raised her hand as a farewell and pulled out her mobile. The driver smiled, lit a cigarette and looked contentedly at the bundle of banknotes. He inhaled a few times, then unravelled the bundle. And stared. There was only just about enough to cover the cost of petrol, lots of small denomination notes. He angrily opened his door to chase the old lady, but stopped almost straight away. She was standing a few metres away with her mobile by her ear and one hand on her hip.

'Now you listen to me, you taxi fraudster! You shouldn't con old ladies. I have phoned the police,' she said briefly, putting the mobile back in her handbag. She looked so threatening and determined that the driver backed off, swore at her, made a rude sign with his finger and then drove off.

'Oh my God, you haven't just phoned the police, have you?' Christina wondered, horrified.

'Are you crazy? I was just frightening him. I am allergic to that sort of bad behaviour.'

'But why did you ask the driver to take us to Bielke's address, then?' Brains wondered and he looked around at the garage entrance. When he had got out of the taxi and taken out his suitcase, he had discovered, to his surprise, that they were outside the neighbour's house, not their own.

'It is best that nobody knows where we live.'

'Poor Bielke, he does seem to get landed with all sorts of problems!' mumbled Brains. 'By the way, why has he got a motorboat outside his garage?'

'Yes, it wasn't there before. And the hedges have been trimmed and the lawn cut. What if he is on his way home?' said Anna-Greta.

'I couldn't care less, because now I just want to go to sleep,' roared Rake, who had had enough of all the nattering, and nobody objected because they too were completely exhausted. They walked slowly across to their own house and when they went in through the front door they were so tired that they all went up to their rooms and went to bed with their clothes on. And they didn't hide the briefcases in the sauna, but slipped them under a bed. They didn't want these banknotes – and perhaps even the diamonds – to smell of vinegar.

59

Financier Carl Bielke sat on the plane from London en route for Nice. He had spent a good weekend in the British capital and his business deals had been brilliantly successful. He had managed to acquire two properties in the city centre from a bankruptcy and had already signed the contracts and transferred the 380 million that the deal cost. He would have the waste pipes replaced and do a bit of renovation on the facade in one property, and a luxury makeover of the panorama flats in the other, and then he could soon increase the rent considerably. That would bring in many millions over the years. Now he could really indulge in a few days' holiday!

He and his two secretaries got off the plane in Nice and when they had gone through Customs he went straight across to the counter for the helicopter service and slammed his briefcase down.

'The same as usual. Full speed to Saint-Tropez, please!'

Very pleased with himself and in an excellent mood, he sat down with the two young ladies and waited for the helicopter to be ready. Meanwhile, he phoned his stand-by crew in Saint-Tropez and asked them to prepare for a little outing.

'What about a week touring the coast, with some visits ashore here and there?'

'Sorry, we can't do it,' said the captain, his voice sounding unusually pitiful. And, yes, then with a broken voice he had said that Bielke's new motor yacht had sunk. His *Aurora 4* must have gone to the bottom and, according to the preliminary reports from the harbour authorities, the vessel had vanished from the screens at lunchtime that same day. The weather had been good and no collision had been registered. But the boat had disappeared and was presumed sunk.

'What the hell!' shouted Bielke.

The captain tried to explain and didn't manage very well. He mumbled something about a new crew having borrowed the boat to train how to handle it, and when the yacht disappeared from the screens he himself had thought that they had turned off the transponder on purpose and anchored at some secret place for some nefarious reason. Yes, the ladies from the Saint-Tropez fashion week were still in town . . .

'Yes, you understand,' said the captain. He said that several hours later, when there were still no signals from the vessel's AIS, he had got suspicious. 'We were conned,' he sighed. 'Those types disappeared with the boat out to sea.'

Carl Bielke was so angry he could hardly breathe. Earlier, the captain had told him of a gang of pensioners who were going to charter the boat. Had they had with them a crew of their own, an incompetent pack who had let the boat founder? But then surely the rescue services would have been involved, an SOS sent out, and the oldies would have been reported missing. But just think – God forbid – what if somebody had hijacked the boat? The captain, whose voice now sounded even more pathetic, did indeed claim – after being pressured by Bielke – that it was the oldies who had stolen the yacht after he himself and the others had ended up in the water. They had later found the little motorboat abandoned in a bay. But Bielke did not believe that, of course. Pensioners with wheeled walkers can't steal a big motor yacht, that much was obvious, so naturally it was the captain and the others who had drunk too much, enjoyed themselves with the young models from Saint-Tropez and then tried to explain away what had happened. Presumably, one of the girls had cooperated with the mafia – probably a boyfriend who had asked his girl-friend to put a sedative in the crew's drinks. Then when the captain and the others snoozed away, they had been dumped somewhere – after which the gangster gang had returned to the yacht and steered it out to sea. And then, of course, they had turned off the transponder. Now all they needed to do was rename his newly bought boat, repaint it and perhaps make a few changes to the fittings, and they would have car-ried off a fantastic coup. Yes, that's what must have taken place. And the fact that *Aurora*'s motorboat had been found was a clear indication that something had happened. What a farce! How could the crew fall for such a simple bluff? And by now the cunning scoundrels would be on their way to Naples or some other mafia port.

While the helicopter approached Saint-Tropez, he looked out over the glittering sea and thought about what he should do. Already, a year before, he had come to the conclusion that it was hard work having three large motor yachts in different ports. So for quite a long time he had been contemplating selling one of them and concentrating on two really large

444

yachts instead. He would have one for himself and the other for chartering. So from that angle, what had happened perhaps wasn't such a bad thing after all, but a freak of fate that had made the decision for him. Yes, good God, it wasn't such a total disaster after all. Now all he had to do was rake in the insurance money and move on in life – even though he would miss that Chagall painting, of course. With these thoughts, he calmed down, put his arm around the ladies and kissed first one and then the other.

'You know what? Let's spend tonight at a hotel and then we'll decide what to do tomorrow. There's a market, if you want to buy something. And we can go to Club Fifty-five and swim. If we tire of that, we can potter around in town. I need a watch and Van Cleef's jewellery shop has lots of beautiful jewels that would suit you. What do you say?'

The young ladies looked admiringly at him, so delighted that he hugged them both. Then he went to a luxury hotel with the two beauties and enjoyed himself royally all night. It wasn't until the next morning that he remembered that the insurance papers were in the map room on board the motor yacht. In his yacht that had sunk! Or been hijacked . . .

60

Oleg was absolutely delighted with his new motor yacht *Aurora 5* and very pleased finally to be on the way to Cyprus. There had been problems with the crew which never turned up, but then he had hired his own. He hadn't time to wait. The conference was over and Martha and her old fogey friends were history. Now he and Boris would have a holiday, pick up some girls on the playa and take things easy before they started working again. He took a drink with ice and went out on the bridge. They were approaching Famagusta. Lovely. Soon they could be seated at a restaurant and eat something tasty. Perhaps a Mediterranean platter with shrimps, mussels and lobster; that would do nicely. He stood for a long time up on the bridge and looked over the bow, until the boat slowed down and moored at the quay. When they had secured the mooring ropes and he was about to go ashore, he saw a group of seniors waiting on the quayside. Thirty or so oldies with wheelchairs and wheeled walkers stood down there waving. Oleg leaned over the railing, confounded.

At the front of the group stood an energetic elderly gentleman in shorts, a white blazer and Bermuda shirt waving a little flag on which it said *Aurora 5*. He called up to the deck and asked to speak to the captain. When Oleg, rather surprised, climbed down the ladder and shook hands with the gentleman, he heard that his *Aurora 5* had been chartered for a cruise in the Mediterranean starting next week. The travel group comprised a gang of pensioners in their seventies and now the oldies wanted to go on board and have a look around.

'You have made a mistake,' Oleg laughed.

'Oh no!' said the man, and he showed Oleg a certificate written in beautiful italics that he had received via email from the Senior Peace pensioners' organization. It was a diploma (which in appearance was similar to some of Christina's very best works) with a border of flowers in watercolour, a long ornamental text and two illegible signatures. At the bottom of the page was a logo with five grey panthers. Oleg shook his head and tried to wave the man away. But he wasn't going to accept that.

'Here is the certificate, and besides, I have a piece of paper that shows that it has all been paid for,' said the man, pulling out yet another document. 'You are the owner of *Aurora Five*, aren't you? This vessel is part of a senior fleet of three modern yachts which have been chartered for cruising in the Mediterranean. We shall depart tomorrow for a fourteen-day cruise.'

'No, completely wrong,' Oleg maintained, but his laugh was a bit more nervous this time. 'That agreement might perhaps have concerned the former owner, but not me. I have just bought the boat. Let me fetch the contract, and I will show you.'

Irritated, Oleg hurried up to the bridge where the safe was, and took out the papers that he and Martha had signed.

Not particularly worried, he quickly thumbed through the documents. But when he looked more closely at them he discovered an extra sheet which he hadn't noticed earlier – with his own signature down in the right-hand corner. Surprised, he picked it up and started to read:

In connection with the purchase of *Aurora 5*, I, the under-signed, Oleg Pankin, the new owner of this motor yacht, hereby commit myself to hosting two free Mediterranean cruises each year for elderly pensioners. The cruises are reserved for those of limited means who otherwise would not be able to afford such luxury. The cruise guests shall be entitled to free food and drink on board and outings arranged in connection with visits to ports. The costs involved are to be paid for by the owner of the cruise vessel.

'What the hell is this!' he yelled out and now he began to be seriously worried. 'Have I signed this?!' He swallowed many times, walked to the edge of the deck and took a firm hold of the railing with both hands. Then, leaning the upper part of his body out, he shouted in Russian something that could roughly be translated thus: 'This is no goddamned old folk's home. This is my motor yacht. Off with you!'

Upon which he gave the captain the order to cast off. A stressed Oleg steered westwards to Capri where, he had heard, the mafia tended to spend their summers. It was said to be calm and quiet for those who occupied themselves with obscure business deals. Perhaps he could acquire a peaceful abode there?

*

And Capri was where Anna-Greta managed to trace the yacht. Via a blog written by a former resident of Djursholm, who was also a Facebook friend and ran the San Michele Foundation – Axel Munthe's house in Capri – she found out that *Aurora 5* had berthed at Capri. At the Foundation they knew everything that happened on the island, and now her friend told her that a mean and angry captain had refused to allow elderly pensioners on board, even though they had booked a cruise. Anna-Greta marched in to Martha, furious.

'Our efforts with Senior Peace have come to nothing. Oleg is not cooperating at all on that charitable activity.'

'What a scoundrel, a real big-time scoundrel!' Martha swore. 'Admittedly, I did play a little trick on him, but now I'll show him! He had a chance to think about other people – and not only himself – but he didn't take it. So now he only has himself to blame!'

'So we are going to activate plan B?'

'Naturally! Do it, my dear!'

And so it came about that the two elderly women sat in front of the computer to try to carry out their wily and well-thought-out plan. Martha pulled out Oleg's business card.

'Here is the name of the bank and the account number. To think that he actually gave me this information.'

'No crooked businessman can imagine that he might be conned by an old lady.'

'No, and especially not by a senile old hag with a double chin and dachshund ears,' Martha said, and she smiled.

Together they tried to gain access to the bank and the account but when that didn't work, Martha went to fetch some coffee, cakes and a bowl of fruit. That usually helped. But not this time. All day long, Anna-Greta sat there trying to hack her way into the account, without success. And for every hour that passed, she got all the more glassy-eyed.

'Perhaps we've got the wrong account number, or could it be extra difficult in Russia?' she said every time Martha looked in and wondered how she was getting on.

'Take your time, my dear. I know it is difficult. Even the police can't manage that sort of task.'

The police! Anna-Greta thought about Blomberg and realized that she could ask him for help. She had missed him, but to meet a real policeman was to challenge fate. And it wasn't just about her, but the entire League of Pensioners. But, a few days later, she was still struggling with her attempts to hack the Russian account, and Irish coffee, cloudberry liqueur and cognac – not to mention organic fruits and Christina's vegetable drinks – hadn't helped. Anna-Greta was getting nowhere.

'I do actually know one person who could help us with this,' she finally let on, coughing drily into her palm and not daring to look her friends in the eye.

'But who, my dear?' wondered Brains.

'Blomberg. He has been an IT consultant and knows lots of stuff.'

'But that man is a police officer, for heaven's sake!' said Martha strictly. 'Have you gone mad?'

'But he has retired now. Yes, I checked up on him with the Pension Authority. And don't forget that it was Blomberg and I who got that speed dating sorted out.'

'It's dangerous, Anna-Greta. He is bound to still have his old contacts,' Christina pointed out anxiously.

'But I think he has fallen for me. Every week while we were away he sent vinyl records to the restaurant barge with sweet little messages and he has also asked about me there. So even if he were to suspect something, he wouldn't tell on us.'

'What are you saying? Is he trying to court you? You haven't let on about that before,' exclaimed Rake, horrified.

'No, I didn't dare. But, God help me, I have really missed him!' Her voice was unsteady and she pulled out a handkerchief to carefully dry her eyes. Then she started to sniffle. Nobody said a word.

'All you others have somebody to be with, but not me,' she went on in a pathetic voice. 'I would so much like to see him again. You can't imagine how I've longed to do so. And then he could give us some valuable tips. And I don't have to tell him what it is about.'

'But can he really help us with this, without getting suspicious?' wondered Brains.

'He—' Anna-Greta sniffled and then blew her nose loudly. 'Yes, I think so. There is a lot at stake. It will take some time before we get the insurance money, so Oleg's money would be a great help in the meanwhile. If he gets about three hundred million dollars in income from his various business activities, and we arrange a discreet transfer from his account to ours on the Cayman Islands, well, then we could get at least a million dollars a month directly into our robbery fund. Then we can give half to the home carers and invest the other half in our Vintage Village. That would be yummy, wouldn't it? It must of course all be done so that nobody can trace us. But just think, what if we can pull it off! My, oh my, what a lot of money!'

'There are a lot of *ifs* there too,' said Rake. 'The whole thing definitely sounds a bit iffy!'

'And what if we end up in prison?' Martha remarked.

'No, help!' exclaimed Christina. 'Putting yourself entirely in a man's hands is always a problem. And a policeman besides! Um, I don't know if—'

Then Anna-Greta got up and left the room, sobbing loudly. The others remained sitting there, looking at the door after her. They all wished her well, but this felt very uncertain.

Anna-Greta kept within bounds for a few days, but when she still failed to make any progress with the Russian accounts, she phoned for a taxi and asked to be taken to the Silver Punk restaurant in Huvudsta. She stepped out of the taxi and threw a glance at the illuminated barge. Anders and Emma had been very successful with the restaurant and the speed dating was so popular that it was full every day and they had to hand out queue numbers at weekends. Anna-Greta smiled when she saw the barge moored there. It looked so cosy and she had so many nice memories. She had, actually, meant to come here earlier, but there had been so much going on with the lawyer and their financial transactions. And she had been a little afraid and uncertain too. But now! What if she should find Blomberg here? Nobody need know about it. Then they could meet again and click their way through various programs and Internet sites on the computer like they had done before. And that had been so nice. There was nothing dangerous about that, was there?

That evening she sat for a long time in the bar and even took part in the speed dating, but no new beau turned up and no Blomberg either. And as the evening grew later, she became all the more despondent and finally decided to go home. She had got as far as the cloakroom and had just put her coat on when she felt a hand on her shoulder.

'Anna-Greta? Oh, at last!' Blomberg smiled with his whole face and gave her a hug. She couldn't say a word, and she hardly dared look at him.

'Oh my goodness, is it you?' she finally managed to reply with the quietest voice she had ever used.

'How nice to see you,' he said and he looked really pleased. Without even asking, he took off her coat and hung it up again. 'Well, did you like the vinyl records?'

'Oh yes, indeed. Bill Haley and Sammy Davis, what a delight! So kind of you to send them. But I have been really angry with you. What happened to you that evening? You just disappeared. I thought you had regretted everything and didn't want to meet me any more.'

'Come along, we can't stand here!' he said, taking her hand and pulling her along to the bar. 'Of course I wanted to meet you. But it was an emergency. Those guys, the Weasel and Kenta, were on the wanted list, you see. I came to see you to explain, but you had gone and you didn't leave any message.'

'Just a little holiday,' mumbled Anna-Greta.

'In the middle of everything? Gosh, but let's have some beer now. Two Carlsbergs,' Blomberg ordered and then turned to her again. And while they drank their beer he described how he had caught the criminals, got them convicted and that it had been quite a feather in the cap for him and his detective agency.

'So you are a detective, then? Why didn't you tell me that earlier?'

'Well, one has to be discreet, it goes with the job.'

'Er, yes, I suppose so,' said Anna-Greta and she felt less confident. 'But it was a pity your job was so much more important than us, I mean—'

'You are right. It shouldn't be like that. But now I have come to realize that life is so much more than just work. One must live too. I have been on courses. Do you want to see?' He pulled a book out of his briefcase that Anna-Greta thought looked very exciting.

'We can go and sit in the vinyl stall, so you can show me,' she suggested, and remembered several things one could do there – especially when the lights went out.

Blomberg beamed, ordered another two beers, and took them with him as they went to sit in the stall. He proudly handed over the book with circles and leaves on the cover. When she started to look through it, she saw that it contained outline drawings that he had coloured himself. There was a lovely big peacock and some drawings with flowers too. They had all been filled with happy, intensive colours.

'Mindfulness, one feels at peace,' he explained and pointed at one of the drawings, the one with the peacock which he was most proud of.

'You take things easy, then?' wondered Anna-Greta slowly turning some more pages.

'Exactly. That business with my detective agency, you know. Not a quiet moment. Morning and evening, there was always work. It wasn't me, it was the scoundrels who decided my working hours. I have scrapped that now.'

'Scrapped? But in that case, if a scoundrel you were hunting should go past here now, would you stay sitting with me?' wondered Anna-Greta.

'Absolutely.'

'You wouldn't even pick up your mobile and phone the police?'

'If one has stopped working, then that's it. Pensioners who try to cling on to their old working identity are pathetic. No, I have started a new life. I have bought up lots of vinyl records and have started a shop on the Internet. Selling old jazz and genuine 1950s music. Not bad, eh? It's fun, I can tell you.'

Anna-Greta sat quietly and looked at him, not knowing whether she should dare to trust what he had said. She ought to test him. But how?

'Yes, fun indeed,' she mumbled, her thoughts elsewhere.

'You don't seem to be on the ball,' said Blomberg. 'Are you worried about something?' He took her hand and stroked it gently.

'I have had some bad business deals. Me and my friends, we sold a boat in France. But we didn't get paid,' she lied.

'Was it a lot of money?' He rather clumsily stroked the palm of her hand and her long, thin fingers.

'An awful lot. Now I wonder if one can hack into his bank account. What do you think?'

'Oh God yes. I was an IT expert with the police after all. I am really good at that sort of thing.' He lifted her hand, kissed it quickly and she started to tremble.

'Do you mean it?' said Anna-Greta, now enthralled, and she realized how hopeful she sounded. If he went along with this, then perhaps they could trust him. People didn't just hack into other people's accounts any old how. It was a risky business. And illegal too. Was he prepared to take such a risk for her sake? Then that would mean he really liked her.

'Come to my place and I can show you,' he suggested.

Anna-Greta felt warm all over and at that particular moment she wanted nothing more. But she controlled herself. 'Or what about meeting here at the same time tomorrow?'

Blomberg nodded. 'I'll bring my computer with me. And Anna-Greta –' he leaned forward and stroked her gently on her cheek – 'forgive me. I promise. No more criminals. Don't forget that I have started a new life.'

That remains to be seen, Anna-Greta thought, but she didn't say it out loud. Instead she smiled and said: 'Yes, right, that would be lovely.'

At breakfast the next day, she hardly said a word and the others wondered whether she was ill. But she just shook her head and went on staring straight ahead. It didn't even help that Martha poured a little whisky into her coffee on the sly. Anna-Greta was alarmingly silent.

'We are losing several million a month just because I can't hack into that account,' she finally said, sighing.

'Well, consult a computer expert, then, because you are keeping clear of Blomberg, aren't you?' said Martha, a severe look in her eyes. 'Better to wait, or even do without the money altogether.'

'Um, yes, of course. But several million a month? I wonder . . .' said Anna-Greta, and she got up, faked a yawn and left the room. She wanted to be alone with her thoughts.

Anna-Greta kept to herself all day, but when evening arrived she again took a taxi to the barge. She had her iPad with her and Oleg Pankin's account number – and a terribly bad conscience for not having dared say anything to the others.

'I must be by myself a while,' she had explained by way of excuse. 'And I might be rather late home. And, yes, perhaps I'll drop in at the barge too, because they have some problems with the iPads there.'

Then Martha raised her eyebrows and looked at her friend suspiciously. That Blomberg man didn't still go there, did he?

'You do take care, I trust, Anna-Greta?'

'Don't worry. I won't get pregnant,' she answered, and she tossed her head and went on her way.

When, half an hour later, Anna-Greta went on board the barge, Anders and Emma greeted her heartily and gave her a knowing look when she ordered a large strong beer.

'Going to the vinyl stall as usual?' Emma wondered. And then Anna-Greta blushed.

'Yes, indeed. Love sitting there. It is rather special,' she answered and sincerely hoped that they wouldn't gossip to Christina.

Blomberg had already arrived and he sat waiting for her. Anna-Greta immediately felt very weak in her knees. He was dressed smartly and had had his hair cut and had taken his computer with him. He held up a computer game and before he closed the lid she could see that he had reached 251.

'Oh gosh, you are clever!'

'Just luck, but good for your brain,' he answered and got up. Just like the previous day, he gave her a hug before they sat down together. The vinyl-record player was broken and had been taken away to be repaired, so it felt a bit different in the stall and they were both a little shy. In the end Blomberg said: 'Well, then, you were having problems hacking into an account, you said?'

Anna-Greta nodded, turned her iPad on and clicked her way onto the net. 'Somewhere in Russia there is this account I have to hack so that I can get my money,' she told him.

She handed him the slip of paper where she had written Oleg's name, the bank and the account number.

'Hmm, that bank is familiar,' he said and smiled at her. 'That's where billionaires usually have their accounts, like those Russian oligarchs, you know. So this Oleg must have lots of money.' He hummed, impressed, and unconsciously licked his lips. He worked with great concentration and soon managed to access the bank. He whistled. 'Do you know this man? Wow, who'd have thought it?'

'So you can see directly from the account number that he has lots of money?'

'I've more than thirty years' experience of scoundrels,' Blomberg answered proudly, and he leaned forward and almost disappeared into the computer. Soon his eyes looked almost feverish and his fingers moved so quickly across the keyboard that they almost hovered. He didn't drink his beer, he didn't even look at her; he was totally sucked into what it said on the screen. And he clicked and hummed while innumerable digits and account numbers came and went. In the end, Anna-Greta thought there were more digits on the screen than there were midges by a stagnant pool on a summer's night up in the north.

458

'Ernst! Can you show me what you are doing?' Anna-Greta wondered and she tried to disguise her impatience.

'Not now. Wow, that is quite something!'

'What did you see?'

'Anna-Greta, this man has about four hundred million dollars coming in every month.'

'Goodness gracious!' mumbled Anna-Greta and she too tried to access the account.

'Can't you show me how you got in?' she asked and stroked him gently on his neck. And then he turned round, leaned over her iPad and instructed her slowly, step by step. Finally, he told her how to get past the firewall.

'Oh, so exciting,' exclaimed Anna-Greta and she clapped her hands. 'That scoundrel didn't pay a krona for the yacht. He owes me –' she breathed in and thought about what would be a suitable amount, 'yes, twenty-nine million dollars is what he should pay me. He ignores all my reminders and has threatened revenge if I go to a lawyer. But if I could take a little directly from his account? Yes, fix a transfer that would pass by unnoticed.'

'So much money, Anna-Greta! Tell me, what secrets are you keeping from me?'

'Well, it was a charitable foundation that owned the yacht and I looked after their financial affairs. It's so embarrassing, you understand.'

'Yes, of course,' mumbled Blomberg and he seemed to swallow the lie and didn't even notice that Anna-Greta had proposed something illegal. He had become so zealous and his eyes shone. 'So shameless, so shameless, no, I don't like big scoundrels!' Now he was full of indignation and so quick that Anna-Greta couldn't keep up. 'So you want twenty-nine million from the bastard?'

'Yes, but an automatic transfer so that it won't be noticed. And a smaller monthly amount over several years. Otherwise he might discover it.'

'No problem,' said Blomberg, now with considerable authority in his voice. And then he showed her how he did it and she got really warm with joy. So many men keep their knowledge to themselves, but he was generous and shared things, no doubt about that. And then he arranged the transfer to the account number she had given him, while she watched as he did it, made notes and memorized what he had just taught her.

'There you are, it isn't harder than that. We, in the police, have checked the accounts of these wealthy types before. Your scoundrel in Russia will hardly notice that we've been inside his account and pinched a little. And if he should notice anything, he can't trace your company anyway. You're a rascal, Anna-Greta, I can see that you have an account on the Cayman Islands.' Blomberg laughed heartily and looked at her with amusement as well as admiration in his eyes.

'What! Can you really discover that?' exclaimed Anna-Greta, horrified as well as impressed.

'On the net you can see everything, darling,' he answered, and he held her under her chin and gave her a quick kiss on the mouth. 'That was that! Back in a jiffy,' he said, pointing with his thumb over his shoulder to the gents, and hurrying out.

'Ah yes, yes,' mumbled Anna-Greta, dazed. What had he

actually done, and how had he gone about it? she pondered, leaning over her iPad. She had also become curious about those account numbers he had hacked, but when she tried to click her way in, it didn't work. Just as she was about to try again, she heard a familiar voice.

'I thought as much. Emma said you were in here,' said Martha, sitting down in the stall. 'You're waiting for him, aren't you?'

Anna-Greta blushed a brighter red than she had ever blushed in all her life. She felt that she had been caught in the act and couldn't utter a word. She ought to have known better; of course Martha would have seen through her.

'My dear friend, I came here to warn you before you do anything stupid. Once a policeman, always a policeman. Please, don't meet him.'

'Once a scoundrel, always a scoundrel,' Anna-Greta answered defiantly and looked furtively towards the gents behind Martha's back.

'Don't you realize that we could all end up in prison for several years? Just because you've fallen in love,' said her friend in a low voice. 'I beg you, please: forget him!'

'Easy for you to say; you have Brains. You don't know what it is like to be on your own. Everyone is more important than yourself. The person you are married to, children or grand-children. All the others always come first. You haven't a chance.' Anna-Greta fumbled for her handkerchief.

'But you have us, your friends!'

Anna-Greta didn't answer, and the next moment Martha saw how she froze. Martha followed her eyes. Oh my God! It was that constable she herself had met when she had been at the police station once. And the policeman seemed to rec-ognize her too. Was this the Blomberg that Anna-Greta had talked about? Martha got up quickly to leave, but then stopped herself. She couldn't dash off now, it would look so strange, indeed even suspicious. So she stayed where she was. Blom-berg was first to collect his wits.

'Ernst. Ernst Blomberg. Nice to meet you.'

'Martha, Martha Andersson,' said Martha and she smiled, although it felt more as if she was chewing on some super glue.

'Nice barge this, isn't it? And good food here at the Silver Punk restaurant.'

'Yes, it is really nice here. And vinyl records and the Inter-net too.'

'Very modern, everything, yes,' said Blomberg and he looked at Martha so intensely that it gave her the shudders.

'Well, then, I was just about to leave,' Martha stuttered and she nodded to Anna-Greta. 'Nice to have met you so unexpectedly. But now I won't disturb you any longer.' She withdrew and hurried off. Blomberg sat down, white in the face, yes, almost nauseous.

'Do you know her?' he wondered.

'We usually say hello,' said Anna-Greta looking away. 'Childhood friend.'

'You know something, I have seen her before,' whispered Blomberg. 'On CCTV images. Close to those banks that were robbed.'

Anna-Greta sat there silently. She didn't dare say anything. Just waited.

'Those unsolved bank robberies in Stockholm, you know,'

Blomberg went on. 'I think she is involved, you see. She is the only person who is on the CCTV images from outside the Nordea bank *and* Buttericks. And she has also been seen outside the National Museum when the paintings were stolen.'

Anna-Greta found it hard to talk and had to gasp for breath and words at the same time. 'But my God! Martha is the kindest, sweetest and most honest person there is. She got a prize in school for good behaviour!'

'The biggest fish swim in the calmest of waters. She ought to be interrogated.'

'Mindfulness!' Anna-Greta shouted out. 'HAVE YOU FORGOTTEN THAT?!'

'What?' Blomberg gave a start. 'Yes, yes, of course.'

Anna-Greta put her hand on his knee and pulled him towards her.

'You know, if only you would relax and stop thinking about your old job, we could have a really nice time,' she said. And then she kissed him so that it quite took his breath away. Yes, because Anna-Greta knew how to kiss.

Later, when she had gone home with him and, without feeling shy, had cuddled and kissed passionately until midnight, she said an emotional goodbye and took a taxi to Djursholm. With her hair a mess and her lips slightly swollen, she sneaked in through the door and sincerely hoped that nobody would see her. As soon as she reached her room, she turned on the computer and started to look for those account numbers he had clicked on. Were there really so many accounts in Russia? She searched and clicked but only got more and more tired, and in the end fell asleep where she was sitting.

61

The next day it was time for a general meeting. The insurance money had arrived, and Martha laid the table with coffee and the usual wafer biscuits and cloudberry liqueur up in the tower room. Brains and Rake walked in from the lift with Samsung mobile telephones sticking out of their pockets. They had played computer games again, but didn't want to admit that to the girls. And Christina, who had just had her hair done, came down the stairs with a new way of swaying her hips which perhaps she thought was suited to ladies in the seventy-plus age range. And she had changed her make-up too, as well as acquiring a new coiffure and a new colour for her nails. Now Rake was sure to notice how stylish she was, wasn't he?

'My dear friends,' said Martha raising her glass with cloudberry liqueur. 'You have done really well. I am very proud of you. How many scoundrels manage to steal more than one thousand million kronor in a year?!'

'Hmm, we know that a bank robbery is only a bit of pocket money. And that the banks themselves steal hundreds of billions from us ordinary mortals,' said Anna-Greta with the look of an expert.

'Yes, yes, but that is just pretend money that they lend out. We've got real money. And now we've just received the insurance money—' She didn't get any further before a car was heard outside. The gang of pensioners exchanged anxious looks, got up quickly and went up to the window. A blue Volvo had driven into Bielke's place and stopped on the garage approach behind the motorboat. Two men in grey got out.

'Oh look! Could they be from the Labour Exchange or the National Statistics Office or something like that?' said Christina, pointing. The two men walked round the house and peered in through the windows, looked into the outhouses and examined Bielke's motorboat. They took out a notebook, took some photos and some measurements. After about half an hour's inspection, they got back into their car and drove off. As they turned into the road, Christina saw that it said 'DANDERYD MUNCIPALITY' on the side.

'What was that about?' she wondered when they had gone.

'Usch, that felt a little uncomfortable. What if they have been tipped off about the missing refuse-collection lorry?' said Martha.

'Martha, dear, most bank robbers don't bury lorries in concrete,' Brains consoled her. 'It must be something else.'

'But I've got a bad conscience about Bielke. We have really put him in quite a pickle.'

'A ruthless tax-dodger who lives in luxury and doesn't share with others? No, it serves him right. Don't forget why we steal, Martha. Today we have sent out twenty thousand payments with a bonus for the low-paid staff in home care. The health clinics and hospitals have benefitted too, and the museums have got a million each. Couldn't be better. And Bielke still has two motor yachts left,' said Anna-Greta and she put a portion of snus under her lip. (Blomberg had advised her to stop smoking cigarillos because he was worried about her health.)

'Yes, yes, I know, but even so . . .' Martha sighed. 'We wrecked his swimming pool.'

'But he's got the whole of the Mediterranean and the Caribbean, if he wants. He doesn't need a little pool here, no way. And just look what a nice garden it turned into.' Brains pointed at the well-tended lawn which lay where the swimming pool had once been. He put his arm round her shoulders and they looked out across the garden that somebody had been looking after over the last few weeks. Talking of that, why had Bielke suddenly started to care about his garden? Had he changed the garden firm, or was he going to sell? Three weeks later, the League of Pensioners had the explanation when a taxi pulled up outside Bielke's house. The five heard the car and immediately went to the balcony to check what it was. Mr Carl Bielke himself stepped out together with a woman who must have been at least twenty years younger. (Always so difficult, that, as Martha used to say. You never knew if it was a daughter or a new mistress.) They stood a long time in the driveway and just stared. Then he went up to his boat and ripped something off which had been taped on the side. Martha and the others watched as he read the piece of paper, then he shook his head and started to gesticulate wildly. Then the five couldn't restrain themselves any longer, but went down the stairs and nipped out into the garden.

'Welcome home!' said Martha leaning over the fence.

'Yes, welcome back. How are you doing?' Brains added in a friendly voice.

'What the hell has happened?' Bielke yelled, waving the piece of paper. 'I don't understand this at all. The swimming pool has gone and this damned paper was stuck on my boat. Have you seen or heard anything?'

'Oh my goodness, what can have happened?! We see and hear badly nowadays,' said Martha. 'But there have been some strange types here now and then. We have seen that.'

Bielke didn't seem to be listening. He was quite simply too angry to be able to absorb any information.

'I come home to have a holiday in the archipelago and then what do I find? I asked a friend to get the boat ready so that I could simply hitch it up behind the car. And just look!' He threw out his arms and groaned. 'Somebody has cleared the garden and stuck a piece of paper on my boat. What the hell is going on?'

'Is it serious?' Christine wondered, all innocence.

'Have a look yourselves. You can't have anything safe here.' He handed the piece of paper to Christina. 'No, I'm never going to set foot in this country again.'

'Wait a moment, I need a magnifying glass,' said Christina and she signalled to Brains to go and fetch one. 'Right, now let's see,' she went on when he had returned. She unfolded the paper and read out loud: '"This boat has been confiscated as we have ascertained that you have not paid any tax for it. If you wish to appeal against this decision, you must do so before the end of June".'

The decision was signed by a certain Anne Forsen at the Tax Authority.

'Oh goodness gracious, what a to-do! You poor thing!'

Christina exclaimed loudly and put her hands over her face in a theatrical gesture.

'So those damned greedy bureaucrats have confiscated my motorboat! You have to pay tax on everything nowadays,' Bielke swore and spluttered so that one almost expected steam to come out of his head. 'A tiny little boat like this, and they want to tax it! Fucking hell! And we don't get anything for all this tax money either.'

'Yes, it is dreadful, isn't it?' said Martha with her most empathetic voice. 'But one must understand the Tax Authority too, don't you think? A lot of people don't pay the tax they ought to, and then how can we afford proper schools and hospitals?'

'What the hell are you saying, you old git? You must be crazy. To think that we have people like you living in Djursholm! A disgrace! I simply can't live here any longer. This damned country is shit! I'm moving abroad!'

'To the Cayman Islands, perhaps? I have heard that you will be left in peace there,' said Anna-Greta, a picture of innocence.

'Well, I'm not going to stay in Sweden at any rate! No way! No, one can't live here any longer, with all this fucking idiocy!' He took his lady under her arm and stormed off towards the house. But then he made a little mistake – just like Rake. He wasn't looking where he was going, stumbled over the garden gnome, fell down onto the lion sculpture and hit his forehead on the lion's paw. Then the League of Pensioners discreetly turned round and went back into their house so that he wouldn't see them giggling.

★

A month later, Bielke went ahead and sold the villa. With the refuse-collection lorry and all. Anna-Greta was curious and started to search the Internet for information about him. And yes, he still had his Facebook account and strangely enough even his blog. There you could see him smiling on a selfie next to an almost submarine-like motor yacht that reminded one of that owned by a Malaysian businessman – one of those boats with a price tag of more than one thousand million kronor. The yacht was anchored off Saint-Tropez and Bielke had written something under the photo:

'Have bought a new boat, what a beauty! Now I am going to stick to just two boats, because it was too much work with more. Madeleine and me are going to get married in the autumn and then we shall sail to the Caribbean. This boat can manage it. I love the sun and the sea. Who wants to be stuck in cold Sweden?!'

62

The League of Pensioners had had time to get their strength back and Martha had smartened up the gym down in the cellar. The walls now had climbing bars and she had bought some new mats, dumbbells and three treadmills for on-the-spot running. And even two exercise bikes. Every day she made sure that they did their exercises, and Brains had actually been very active recently. Perhaps he had finally realized how important regular exercise was? She didn't know, but she was very pleased regardless.

Brains had put down the dumbbells and was looking at his stomach. He had lost several kilos since he had started on Christina's yoga and Martha's gym sessions which the far-too-energetic women had arranged almost every day. But even though he was beginning to look really handsome (in his own opinion), Martha hadn't even mentioned marriage again. They were engaged, and that was that, and since they had returned from Saint-Tropez he had really made an effort to please her. But now he was tired and felt he had come to a crossroads. He would either have to give her up and move on in life, or present her with an ultimatum. But before he did that, they ought to have a proper talk, as the psychologist experts said. He had a shower, using his best shampoo and soap, and when he was finished he asked Martha if they could have a chat under the parasol out in the garden. She looked at him, somewhat surprised.

'Oh my, you do look serious.'

He mumbled a sort of answer and Martha went out via the kitchen and made them each a refreshing bilberry smoothie and added some strawberries. That ought to get him in a good mood. They sat down on two separate garden chairs.

'Martha, you know that I like you, but it seems that you don't want to marry me.' He said it like it was. Martha drank her smoothie so slowly that her teeth began to look an unseemly blue. And she felt very uncomfortable.

'We've been so busy with coups and bank robberies,' she answered, evasively.

'Yes, right. I have waited for our wedding for almost a year. And we have carried out all these robberies and thefts, but there has never been a wedding.'

'No, as I said, there has been rather a lot going on,' Martha mumbled, and she stirred her smoothie so much that it would have been dizzy if only it could.

'Perhaps you are dreaming of somebody else? Somebody with a lot of muscles?' Brains asked, looking furtively at his flabby upper arms which had, however, acquired a few new bulges.

'Oh goodness me, what an idea! No, no, not at all.'

So you don't just dream about motor yachts, bank robberies and goody bags for the poor, then, he was about to say, but managed to stop himself. Instead he said:

'I've been thinking. Getting married perhaps isn't your sort of thing.'

'No, that's right,' said Martha, perhaps a bit too quickly and very relieved – but immediately she became aware of what she had said and now looked, if anything, even more embarrassed. 'Well, marriage doesn't guarantee love, and nor does it guarantee love till death do us part. But if you live with somebody you love because you *want* to, well, that is something else. The real thing, sort of,' said Martha with her cheeks glowing red. Brains was silent for a few moments while he tried to understand what she meant.

'The real thing? So you do like me, is that what you mean?' he wondered.

'Of course I do. I love you,' she said right out. As soon as she had uttered those words, she realized what she had said. She didn't dare look him in the eye because now she was more embarrassed than she ever had been all her life. But Brains could see that. He got up courage, went into the house and came out again with a beautiful little neatly wrapped package. It wasn't a hard box or anything like that, but just a little soft one.

'For you. I have thought about giving this to you for a long time. But there have been so many robberies and crimes and the like.'

'Oh, that is nice of you,' Martha mumbled. She smiled and ripped open the package. 'But it will be six months before I have my birthday.' Inside, wrapped in tissue paper, she could see something black. A shiny black leather strap with tassels. Like the sort of thing that young people have on their wrists.

And that the punks had had on the barge. Brains cleared his throat.

'Yes, well, this doesn't commit anybody to anything, and it doesn't require us to go to the altar. But it does perhaps show that we are a couple,' he said, pulling a similar leather strap from his pocket. 'Besides, this is more modern.'

Then Martha simply had to smile again, and when she looked at him and the leather strap in his hand, she was so moved that tears came to her eyes. She put her strap on and tied the edges, and then put the other one on Brains's hairy, firm wrist. It didn't actually make them look like punks exactly, but it was *cool*.

'Brains, a strap like this around my wrist is better than any marriage in the world. Because it means that you and I belong together.'

'And love each other?'

'Yes, what did you think?' said Martha.

Then Brains got hold of Martha's hand and they went upstairs to their room. And that day the two of them stayed in their room for such a long time that the others got a bit worried. But when they came downstairs again, hand-in-hand, and with a black leather bracelet on their wrists, everyone understood. Christina hurried down into the wine cellar to fetch a bottle of the finest champagne, and Anna-Greta got out glasses, crisps and olives. Then they toasted and celebrated together, even though Anna-Greta wasn't really present – her thoughts were elsewhere. Without the others actually knowing, and despite them all having appealed to her, she had continued to meet Blomberg, but in secret. She couldn't resist him. But she knew that it was dangerous.

63

Several weeks had passed and Anna-Greta had yet again been to see their lawyer, Nils Hovberg, to arrange the business of the League of Pensioners. The sun shone and Anna-Greta played 'My Way' with Frank Sinatra at full volume while she drove home in her Ferrari with a portion of snus under her upper lip. Since they had come home, she had regularly visited Hovberg to keep track of all their transactions. There had, of course, been some complications with getting the insurance money from Lloyds, but they had had the certificate of ownership, the contract and all the other necessary documents, and with the lawyer's help it had gone surprisingly quickly. Money that – as usual – did not go into their own pockets but to their fund which was now registered on the Cayman Islands under the name Fence. By now, they had transferred so much money to the fund that even their scoundrel of a lawyer had been mightily impressed.

'You really are busy bees, even though you are pensioners,' he said and whistled out loud when he saw the latest deposits.

'We have had a whole life to build up energy, you understand,' answered Anna-Greta merrily.

'But one thousand million kronor!'

'Well, it is only the first million that is difficult,' said Anna-Greta nonchalantly and she looked for an ashtray until she remembered that she had given up cigarettes and now only used snus.

'With you as a client I certainly have a lot to do.' The lawyer smiled, and Anna-Greta put on a big smile too. Yes, Mr Hovberg was a good lawyer. With his professional discretion, he had refrained from asking about the source of the money – even though he immediately raised his fees of course. He obediently placed the League of Pensioners' money where it got the best interest and he really knew what he was doing. And that meant they could pay out even more money to those in need. Now, every month, large sums were transferred directly to a bonus fund for the lowly paid working in home care and health care – and all of these transfers went by way of subsidiary companies so that the payments could not be traced. And twenty per cent went to the planned Vintage Village.

'Wonderful, thank you for your help,' said Anna-Greta an hour later, and she got up to leave.

'Yes, a lot of companies and bank accounts to keep track of, but it works well,' Hovberg remarked, and he showed her out.

A lot of bank accounts to keep track of? Suddenly she remembered those account numbers in Russia that Blomberg had hacked. She still had them somewhere and had intended having a closer look at them the same evening but had been so tired that she had simply fallen asleep. Then she had forgotten about it. It was really high time that she checked how things were going with those transfers from Russia. Down on the street, the Ferrari had got a parking ticket but she just snorted and threw it in a wide arch into the closest waste-paper bin and drove off. Then she soon regretted what she'd done, backed the car and picked the ticket up again. It was probably best to pay anyway. You should never, never leave any tracks.

'To think that it is so simple to fool the tax authorities and cheat the state of thousands of millions,' said Martha later that evening when Anna-Greta told them about her latest meeting with Hovberg. The League of Pensioners sat in the library and drank their evening tea while they talked business. 'Those people at the tax office don't seem to understand anything. Isn't it dreadful! Sweden needs the money.'

'Yes, how can it happen? Those money trolls ought to be kept under control. Because who is going to pay for the elderly and the poor when we have to retire?' Christina asked.

'But now *we* are still here, and *we* have money and *we* really do have possibilities to create something good. I've been thinking about that Vintage Village you have mentioned, Martha,' said Anna-Greta.

'Vintage Village . . . what's all this vintage talk! Haven't we got a better name?' Brains cut in.

'Pleasure House Village,' Rake said, grinning.

'I know, we shall create the world's best home for the elderly. A home for senior citizens of the world – or whatever they usually say, those politicians when they don't know what they are talking about,' said Martha, ignoring the comments from the men.

'Then they call it *world class*,' Rake corrected her.

'Yes, right. A world-class retirement home. We can call it The Brilliant!' exclaimed Christina.

'What an excellent idea,' they all said in unison and they looked really pleased.

'But the name?' Martha wondered. 'Why call it The Brilliant?'

'Well, I was thinking of our aquarium, of course, our piggy bank,' Christina answered. And yes, the idea for the name had come when she had been standing looking at the aquarium in the cellar. Nowadays it contained more glimmering diamonds than fish. Their aquarium had actually become the private bank vault of the League of Pensioners. They all thought that since one couldn't trust the banks these days, you had to create something yourself. In an aquarium it was easy to see if somebody tried to steal anything (hands were visible and the water became muddy). And if you put up a big sign proclaiming: WARNING – PIRANHA FISH, then it wouldn't be the first place thieves would look. Admittedly, you didn't get any interest on the 'money' there, but banks didn't pay any interest now either. And you didn't have to show proof of your identity or stand for ever in a queue to withdraw your money – only to find out that you couldn't. Even worse, your bank money could be confiscated without warning in bad times. No, with the aquarium, all they had to do was sweep up their assets with a little net – and dry them on a towel.

Thus it came about that they began to plan a home for the elderly – The Brilliant – and soon they were fully occupied with that. At first it felt rather strange not to be doing anything criminal, but Martha and the others soon got used to it.

They had once run away from an old people's home because the conditions there were intolerable, and now they had the opportunity to create one. They wanted a dream home where each person had their own pleasant room with access to all modern conveniences. Where there were plenty of staff, who got paid decent wages and had decent working hours, a place where everyone was treated with respect, served good food, could be outside when they wanted, and could have a calm and comfortable life. And such a place would suit even them perfectly too, because after all this running about to get hold of money and having to hide from the police, they were actually rather worn out. As with so much else, it was a matter of bringing things to a close, and doing so at the right time – in their case, before any of them got caught and put in prison! Now what mattered was that nobody found out about the crimes they had already committed.

Anna-Greta stood in front of the mirror in the bathroom and wrinkled her forehead. She had borrowed some of Christina's make-up and was powdering her cheeks lightly – just so that her skin would not look shiny and uneven, without it being obvious that she had used powder. However, she didn't stop in time, but kept on going until her skin looked completely dried-up. Her thoughts were elsewhere, on Blomberg. Yes, she had such a dreadfully bad conscience for having gone on seeing him. A policeman. She had definitely tried to keep away from him, but after all their conversations, after their lovely times with music, and after being able to hug him and hear his compliments, she was lost. Yes, and then things had turned out like they did. She met him in secret. Despite the fact that she wasn't 100 per cent certain about him. And even though there had been some warning signs, she didn't want to see them. Because if you are really in love, you don't want to see.

One evening, Blomberg suggested a walk around the Skansen park on Djurgården. He had something important to tell her, and wanted to make sure that nobody could overhear him. (A by-product of his earlier profession, Anna-Greta assumed, but still she felt the first signs of a knot in her tummy.) So they went there and walked hand-in-hand past the old houses and the paddocks for the animals.

'I must tell you, Anna-Greta. I simply can't keep it to myself any longer.'

This sounded so ominous that Anna-Greta immediately leaned her head against his shoulder to be consoled.

'The police are after Martha,' he went on. 'I have talked with Jöback and his colleagues at the Kungsholmen station. They want to get at the CCTV images from the bank robbery that I have. There is damning evidence, images of her.'

'But you don't have to hand them over? A poor old woman, I mean—'

'But it would be the end of me as a policeman and of my detective agency.'

'Good God, man! Didn't you say that you had given up? You and your mindfulness and all that?'

'Yes, sure, but it isn't so easy just to give up your old profession.'

'What about the vinyl records? You had opened a shop on the Internet.'

'It's not doing very well, actually. So, I don't want you to be upset about this, but I really ought to—'

Anna-Greta halted abruptly and her eyes were suddenly as hard as mussel shells.

'Just so you know. If you so much as suggest that Martha might be involved in a bank robbery, then you'll never see me again. Understood?'

'But—'

Anna-Greta tossed her head and strode off looking very determined. She marched out from the Skansen park, waved down the first taxi she saw and went straight home.

Once inside the front door in Djursholm, she briefly said hello to the others and then went directly up to her room and closed the door. She opened her iPad. She had wanted to do this for a long time, because she had felt deep inside that something didn't fit. The possibility. When she had been with Hovberg and checked how much money had come in to their account in the Cayman Islands, it didn't seem to be exactly what she and Blomberg had agreed on. There wasn't so much difference that anybody else might have noticed, but with her capability to do sums in her head and remember figures, she realized that some money must have disappeared. Had Blomberg pressed the wrong key when he was busy dribbling between the Russian accounts?

She laid out her old notes on the table and tried to reconstruct what Blomberg had done. And when she had been busy with her iPad for several hours, she could trace him back in the history right up to Oleg. She drummed with her fingers on the keyboard and studied the screen. Hmm. Yes, there was the transfer from the Russian's account to the League of Pensioners account. Good, that was correct. And there . . . but there? Small amounts of between eighty thousand and ninety thousand Swedish kronor had gone via many subsidiary companies to an anonymous account at the same time that the League of Pensioners got their money. Strange. She tried to trace the name. It was really tiring, but a gnawing feeling inside her made her struggle on and not give up. Then she stopped. Her shoulders sank and she smiled to herself. The trail led to an account holder called the Einstein Limited Company. So it had been right, that weird feeling that something was fishy. Einstein! That was the name of Blomberg's cat of course. Had the experienced policeman fallen into the simple trap of naming his company after someone who was close to him? Yes, it must be her Ernst, and she immediately felt a sense of relief, a liberation so great that she couldn't restrain herself any longer. She rushed down into the library, to the others and joyfully announced:

'Blomberg is a villain! He's a real scoundrel and I have found out about him!'

'Well, goodness, Anna-Greta, what are you saying? Is he seeing other women?' Rake wondered.

'No, go up to the tower room and I'll make some evening tea for us all.'

And since they all realized that Anna-Greta had something important to tell them, they obediently got up and did as she said. And there, up in the tower, when they had all been served a cup of steaming hot tea, she started her tale. With her cheeks glowing red with shame, she confessed that she had continued to see Blomberg in secret, but she had felt that she had been in control all the time. And that's how it was. She had been right.

'So,' she concluded her little presentation, 'he is just as

crooked as we are. Now I shall go to see him and tell him what I know, and say that he must destroy all his evidence and CCTV images. Otherwise I shall go to the police.'

'Absolutely necessary,' Rake said. 'But then perhaps he can become one of us? What do you think?'

'Usch, there is only one League of Pensioners,' said Christina.

'Yes, right, but we do need an assistant,' Anna-Greta chipped in. 'Our international activities are starting to wear us out. Me, at any rate. I have too much to do nowadays.'

'We were going to stop, weren't we?' Christina added. 'Unless we have a relapse and carry out a new bank robbery, I mean.'

'Exactly,' said Anna-Greta. 'But if we do have a relapse, then we must go for the big money. Yes, why not ask Blomberg to help us to empty the accounts of the big tax dodgers, for example?'

They all thought that was such a good idea that, with five votes for and none against, they decided there and then to involve Blomberg in the gang. Then champagne was taken out of the fridge and they toasted one another and their future.

The next day, when Anna-Greta was going to meet Blomberg, she didn't wait for him at the restaurant but went straight off to his flat.

'The Einstein Limited Company, you are clever,' Anna-Greta began.

Blomberg looked absolutely horrified. 'Er, just a bit of extra income,' he answered evasively, uncertain as to whether she had found out about his secret transfers.

'You know what, Ernst, I love people like you. Oh God, how exciting! Because you are both a crook and a policeman. That spices things up a bit!'

'Hmm,' said Blomberg.

'And now, if you will simply destroy all your fishy files about the bank robbery, then I promise not to expose you.'

'Hmm,' said Blomberg.

But this time he was in love, really and truly in love for the first time in his life. And he had learned something from his various experiences in life. So later that evening, when they had talked everything through calmly and quietly, he opened the fridge and took out some delicious herring fillets. Then he turned on his computer, and clicked his way to the folders with the files containing material about the bank robbery, put the fish next to the keyboard and went and sat on the sofa with his arms around Anna-Greta. And it wasn't long before his beloved cat Einstein jumped up onto the desk and walked on the keyboard just as he had expected. Thus file after file was deleted as Einstein enjoyed the herring, after which a smiling Blomberg turned his back to the cat and concentrated on Anna-Greta instead. He didn't even hear when the herring fell onto the floor and the cat jumped down after them, long before all the files had been deleted. Because he was in love, really and truly in love, and then you make mistakes. But what did it matter when finally he was going to retire and start a completely new life?

Epilogue

Anna-Greta was carrying a whole pile of vinyl records and Martha was busy putting up balloons and paper streamers along the walls in their new premises. Brains, for his part, was occupied with connecting the two retro record players, Christina was laying and decorating the tables and Rake was out in the kitchen keeping an eye on the cook. This evening the League of Pensioners would have their Wednesday dance as usual. Or the rave-up of the week, as Martha liked to call it. They were still saving money for their Vintage Village, or Happiness Village, as they now called it. But in the meantime, they had opened their residential home for seniors in rented premises where they could also serve food.

The daily activities in the home were already established. They tested most of what they planned to have in their future Happiness Village. Blomberg had been given a corner in the premises where he experimented with a new form of speed dating, a simple variant with apps in mobile phones. And the people who won the speed dating of the day could get a free ticket to the barge and continue there with a luxury dinner. The League of Pensioners and assistant Ernst Blomberg cooperated closely with Anders and Emma over in Huvudsta.

'Shall we play some Elvis Presley?' Anna-Greta asked when Brains had connected everything. '"*Jailhouse rock*"?'

'Why not? It will keep us awake,' said Brains with a happy grin.

And then Anna-Greta lowered the needle onto the record and turned up the volume to max.

Fifty-five-year-old Sten Falander, the chairman on the Saint Erik Housing Association, pressed the pillows against his ears and groaned. What a hellish noise! Those oldies kept on partying late at night too! He could never have dreamed of elderly people making such a noise. Martha Andersson and her friends who had rented the premises were aged between seventy-seven and eighty-four and he – and the rest of the committee – had thought that they would be easy and quiet tenants. But no. When he complained to the municipal authorities about all the noise being a health hazard, they had laughed at him. Elderly people are nice and quiet, he was told. And he shouldn't come to the municipal officials with all these lies just because he wanted to get at the premises. So he couldn't get them evicted either. No, when he had tried, they had accused him of ageism, and the city had threatened to report him to the Equality Ombudsman.

They had called themselves The Brilliant Retirement Home – but for Falander it was a nightmare! That Martha Andersson, she had called it a modern form of retirement home when she was looking for premises to rent. In the same building there was a fitness centre, a spa and a swimming bath. Martha thought that would be perfect, and she had smiled in such a friendly way and looked so sweet. Yes, he

485

had fallen for it, big time. But then! Oh God, he had let the devil over the drawbridge!

Frank Sinatra's 'My way' vibrated through the walls virtually every day – but at least that was better than the popular Swedish ballads and the hip-hop music that they had played of late. And the dance music on Wednesday evenings made the windows rattle. He complained to the pensioners and put letters in their letterboxes and then they answered with a friendly assurance that they would definitely lower the volume and they apologized profusely. But the next day it was the same miserable story again. They didn't mean to be a problem, they had simply forgotten. So they said.

But it wasn't just the music. They had billiard tables too and played roulette. How was that possible? He hadn't caught them red-handed yet, but he strongly suspected that they had turned the premises into an illegal nightclub with gambling for high stakes. He hoped so, because then he might be able to get them evicted. There was something fishy going on, that much was certain, when the eighty-two-year-old drain-pipe woman on the board of the retirement home could afford a Ferrari! But on the occasions when he had made an unannounced visit, he hadn't discovered anything suspicious. Falander pressed the pillow against his ears and tried to sleep. 'Jailhouse rock' echoed inside his ears, and almost before that had faded away, 'A Gotland summer night' with Arne Lamberth was trumpeted out into the night at full volume. Nooo! That was just too much! The time was half-past eleven.

Falander got out of bed, got dressed and combed his hair. Then he went down and used his master key to get in (to be on the safe side, in case they tried to slam the door in his face). Anyway it would have been pointless ringing the doorbell; they wouldn't have heard it even if they had had their hearing aids turned on.

First he went past the room for chiropody and nail polishing, then the large room where they had their own private hairdresser's. The office was closed for the evening, but in the room where the nurse hung out, there was a light. And there was lots of activity in the kitchen. Two elderly cooks were busy preparing late-night snacks and he was attracted by the aroma. Outside the kitchen hung a menu and he stopped to look.

My, my, what fantastic dishes! Here were nuts, fruit and greens, and, of course, fish and poultry as well as a roast on Sundays. He had to restrain his impulse to ask if he could have a taste, went past the kitchen and came into the big living room. In there, dance music was blaring away, and oldies with and without walking sticks and wheelchairs were taking a turn around the floor. A bit further away, the drainpipe woman was standing in front of two record players, waving her arms above her head – the resident DJ.

'Arne Lamberth is great, isn't he! What shall we have next, something jolly?' she called out in a loud voice.

'No, "Rock around the clock"!' shouted an elderly gentleman with a bandanna around his neck.

'Yes, that one!' shouted a group of oldies in the bar and immediately they moved onto the dance floor. The whole gang must be at least twenty-five years older than he was, but they looked much younger. He had, admittedly, heard that some Japanese up in some mountain region (in Japan, presumably) could often be more than a hundred years old, so it wasn't impossible. But how could eighty-year-olds in Sweden look so young? He was on his way to the record players to ask the lady to turn them off, when he caught sight of a schedule with the daily activities. Once again, he stopped. Good God! This gang of oldies had yoga and gymnastics every day, and lots of courses besides. And the choice! Watercolours, cooking, and an advanced course on Swedish and foreign literature. In addition there were special courses in pottery, woodwork and silver work. So that was why there had been so much hammering in the building recently. And as if that wasn't enough: on Fridays they organized mindfulness and speed dating.

He found himself standing there, scratching his neck. Could it really be true? Yes, they seemed to *work* as well. He was looking at a poster about a Senior Service Pool, where the oldies offered their services as party-organizers, helping with your garden, baking and even assistance with solving crosswords. These old people even organized courses about computers where Einstein IT taught you how to transfer money via the Internet. And made sure you didn't get tricked by hackers.

He shook his head and glanced furtively at the bar. Now he didn't have the energy to care any more about how they had got permission to serve alcohol. He just wanted a beer. A large beer.

'Hello, there! Aren't you going to dance? We are short of men. Come on, now, join in . . .' said an elderly lady, peering at him. Joie de vivre glowed in her eyes. It wasn't the one who looked like a drainpipe, no, it was that Martha woman who had persuaded him to rent out the premises. He was lost for words.

'Dance? I want to sleep, the music is so loud that I can't—'

'But for goodness' sake! Get some earplugs and sound-insulating windows, then. Come on now!'

'But—'

'One should amuse oneself while one can, don't you think so?' she said. And when Falander saw her outstretched arms he couldn't say no. So when the disc jockey played 'Heartbreak Hotel', he followed her out onto the dance floor and they danced. And for the next dance, it was he who asked her. 'Fly me to the moon' was on the record player and Frank Sinatra's smooth voice filled the room.

'Shall we dance?' he asked rather shyly and she nodded so sweetly that he felt completely lost. From her and all the others round about, there radiated such joie de vivre and warmth. One should live life and amuse oneself while one could. Wasn't that just what she had said, that Martha?

Acknowledgements

The League of Pensioners has now struck again and in *The Little Old Lady Behaving Badly* the gang has given the author plenty to do. And in such circumstances, it is great to have help and support en route.

My warm thanks to my Swedish publishers, Bokförlaget Forum, who have worked with this book. Mega thanks to my publisher Teresa Knochenhauer for a thorough and constructive going-over of the manuscript, and to my editor Liselott Wennborg for all the work she has put in, all her tidying up and polishing. My thanks also to Anna Cerps for proofreading, to Agneta Tomasson for production and to Désirée Molinder, who was the production manager. Similarly, thanks to Sara Lindegren and Annelie Eldh in the communications department, who worked to introduce the book to the public and to Göran Wiberg, Bernt Meissner, Torgny Lundin and Bo Bergman, who have visited bookshops throughout the country to market the books. They have had the help of Nils Olsson's delightful covers on all three books in the series with their distinct flavour.

Outside the publishers, many good friends have been of invaluable help. My warm thanks to Lena Sanfridsson for your constructive criticism and professional help and Inger Sjöholm-Larsson for all your wise views. You have made my job much more fun. I would similarly like to thank Ingrid Lindgren for her feedback – quick as a flash – to my writing efforts as the book has gradually grown, and to Gunnar Ingelman, whose constructive criticism and joyful cheers have followed the writing process from the first to the last chapter. A big thank-you also to Mika Larsson, who gave me her direct, honest opinion of the text and content, and to Barbro von Schönberg for her knowledgeable and positive feedback which pleased the author. Thank you too, Agneta Lundström, for your lovely support.

A warm thank-you also to Isabella Ingelman-Sundberg for friendly, quick and lovely support, Fredrik Ingelman-Sundberg for happy inspiration and jolly solutions to problems, and Henrik Ingelman-Sundberg for your always wonderfully candid criticism.

I would also like to thank Magnus Nyberg who, with his direct and unembellished approach, has let me know what is good and what might perhaps be improved and Solbritt Benneth, who went through the first manuscript in detail. A big thank-you also to Kerstin Fägerblad, who has read all my books from the very first to the most recent in the first version, which I have much appreciated over the years.

I would further like to thank my teachers at Manuspiloterna, Kurt Öberg and Fredrik Lindqvist, for brilliant teaching about characterization and film dramaturgy.

Warm thanks go also to Maria Enberg, Lena Stjernström, Peter Stjernström, Lotta Jämtsved Millberg and Umberto Ghidoni at my Swedish literary agent's, Grand Agency.

Thanks to your work, the League of Pensioners has been sold to lots of different countries in the world and *The Little Old Lady Behaving Badly* has already started its journey along the same export track. A big, big thank-you!

Finally, I would like to thank Hans and Sonja Allbäck, who have inspired me and supported my writing over many years, and thanks to Rehné and Kim-Benjamin Falkarp at Fryst for inspiring conversations and the best ice cream in Stockholm.

THE LITTLE OLD LADY
WHO BROKE ALL THE RULES

CATHARINA INGELMAN-SUNDBERG

Seventy-nine-year-old Martha Andersson dreams of escaping her care home and robbing a bank.

She has no intention of spending the rest of her days in an armchair and is determined to fund her way to a much more exciting lifestyle. Along with her four oldest friends – otherwise known as the League of Pensioners – Martha decides to rebel against all of the regulations imposed upon them. Together, they cause uproar: protesting against early bedtimes and plasticky meals.

As the elderly friends become more daring, they hatch a cunning plan to break out of the dreary care home and land themselves in a far more attractive Stockholm establishment. With the aid of their Zimmer frames, they resolve to stand up for old-aged pensioners everywhere. And that's when the adventure really takes off . . .

The Little Old Lady Who Broke All the Rules is an incredibly quirky, humorous and warm-hearted story about growing old disgracefully – and breaking all the rules along the way!

'A good-natured, humorous crime caper'

Independent on Sunday

THE LITTLE OLD LADY WHO STRUCK LUCKY AGAIN!

CATHARINA INGELMAN-SUNDBERG

The little old lady is back! This time, Martha Andersson and her friends – the League of Pensioners – have left behind their dreary care home in Stockholm and are enjoying the bright lights of Las Vegas.

This is their opportunity for a new lease of life and they plan to make the most of it. But before long, they are up to their old tricks. And with ingenious tactics, a pair of false teeth and a wheelchair each, they plot to outwit the security system at one of the casinos. As their antics become more and more daring, Martha and her friends head back to Sweden to continue their money-making schemes. However, they aren't the only ones planning on stealing bucket loads of cash and soon find themselves pitted against a gang of dangerous criminals.

Can the group of elderly friends work together to outsmart the younger robbers and get away with their biggest heist yet? Or will this job be a step too far for the League of Pensioners?

extracts reading groups events

competitions books new

books discounts extracts extracts

competitions extracts discounts

books new events reading groups

events books

extracts reading groups

new titles reading groups

interviews

books events extracts extracts events books

discounts events interviews new books extracts

new books events

events new events new books extracts

discounts extracts discounts

www.panmacmillan.com

extracts events reading groups books

competitions books extracts new